DARK EYES OPEN

By
Luis Monzon Pineda

DARK EYES OPEN

Copyright © 2020 Luis Monzon Pineda
All rights reserved.
ISBN: 979-8-5859-6470-0

Dedication

For Mom, Dad, D, D, M, and all my family and friends, you know who you are, and now hopefully, you will see, what you have meant to me.

DARK EYES OPEN

Prologue

March 31, 2074. The City of Old Los Angeles, 4:15 AM

Beyond the neon lights of downtown OLA, down a network of dark alleyways, stood a series of three-story, red-bricked apartment buildings, cast in shadow, tucked away, forgotten.
In one of the apartments in one of these buildings, at 4:15 am, a Man stood in Anell Schmitt's darkened bedroom, over Anell's bed. His arm extended, the Man gripped a gun pointed at a huddled mass on the mattress before him. Exhaling slowly, the Man squeezed the trigger once, then again.

The gunshot flashes lit up the room, and the silencer at the end of the muzzle did its job.

The Man stood there a moment, inhaling the smell of gun powder, smiling.

A wandering thread of smoke rises from the end of the gun.

The Man waited to hear if the muffled gunshots had awoken anyone on the floors above or below the apartment. He waited for the sound of movement or stifled cries, which he would be plugging with more bullets. The silence persisted. Smirking, the Man drew back the covers.

His eyes opened wide, and his nostrils flared as he glared at a pair of pillows and a mattress punctured by two tightly spaced bullet holes and no dead body.

Across the city, in his girlfriend's cramped apartment, Anell sighed. On a hidden camera feed, he and his girlfriend had been watching events unfold. Now, the Man rummaged through Anell's bedroom belongings consisting of little more than one bed, one dresser, and a desk.

"He's gone, Goddamit!" The Man said into the microphone pinned to his lapel. "No, the room's been stripped bare. It's not here."

"It's here, with me, Asshole. Nice try," The skinny twenty-year-old, Anell, said.

"Good thing that feed only goes one way," Anell said to his girlfriend Daisy.

Daisy stood up.

"What are we going to do, Anell?" She said, standing in the warm glow of the bedside lamp, wearing an oversized white t-shirt.

Anell looked up at her, "I don't know, Daisy," He replied while he lifted the stamp-drive to the light. "Whatever we do, we can't do it from here," Anell said. He looked into her eyes. He reached out, pulling her towards the bed. She sat down beside him.

"The first thing we have to do is pack up your things and get you as far away from here as possible," Anell said.

"What are YOU going to do?" She asked.

Anell looked at her, then at the picture frame sitting on Daisy's dresser. A photo of the two of them taken on Anell's first day as an Old Los Angeles Police officer. His first day on the job. Daisy looked back at the same photo.

"Feels like that was so long ago," She said.

Anell flexed his jaw, "Daisy."

"Anell, don't you dare say you're not coming with me," She said.

"I'm coming with you, of course, I am. There's just something I have to do first."

Daisy placed her hand on her belly, "Anell, I need you. WE need you."

"I know, I know. You don't have to remind me, please. This is important, Daisy. I can't just stand by and watch things fall apart. What kind of world will we be leaving behind? In what kind of world is our baby going to live. If we do nothing?"

"Anell, this little one is going to come into a world with both parents."

"Of course."

"No! Anell, promise me."

"Daisy? Please."

"Anell, PROMISE me."

Anell took a deep breath. "I promise."

"Whatever you do, it can't lead back to us, Anell. Not now, not ever."

"It won't. I have an idea, and the first step is destroying this," Anell said, holding stamp-drive in his palm. "I have a way I can get the message out without it ever leading back to us."

"And then?"

"Then, we head for the Northern Territories. I have a plan, set up new identities for us, a stash of credits. I've planned for everything. We're going to be away from all of this, away and safe."

"All three of us."

"Yes, all three of us. Let's get packed. You head out tonight, and then I catch up with you tomorrow night," Anell said as he peered at the monitor to see the Man leave the room, then the apartment. "We're safe for now, but not for long."

"Wait, why tomorrow night?" She asked.

"Tomorrow night, I've got a meeting, in secret, with someone, well, with the only person left who can turn this thing around," Anell said. He pursed his lips and shook his head.

"What is it?" Daisy asked.

Anell said, "I just realized that if this plan works then, well, no one will ever know who we are or what we did."

Daisy smiled and placed her palm on Anell's cheek. Looking into his eyes, she said, "Who you are? You are the man I love, and what you did? Is keep your family safe."

Anell smiled, and they kissed. Shortly after that, they left the apartment, never to return. Daisy headed for safety. Anell ventured out into hiding, waiting to set up the meeting.

Chapter 1

Old Los Angeles, March 31, 2074

It was a starry night, the 31st of March, 2074. A figure stumbled down Victory Boulevard in Old Los Angeles, on a visionary path just beyond the reach of every streetlight's glow and the gaze of every streetcam along the way.

Detective Beth Lago was keeping her chin nestled below the collar of an oversized hooded sweatshirt. The top of the hood was hanging low enough to obscure her face.

She was finally approaching her destination, a row of brownstones a hundred feet away.

Almost there.

She thought.

A bead of sweat trickled down her spine.

In the distance, she heard a stir of echoes that sounded like muffled screams.

She felt her neck tense up, and she fought every instinct to look up or show she had taken notice. A pressure in her gut made her feel uneasy. Something wasn't right. Just then, the screams faded, replaced by cackles of laughter. She knew it! It was just the kind of trap a pair of uniforms had fallen into about a month prior and not more than three blocks from here.

Stepping up the front porch of the third brownstone, she felt a flurry of vibrations from the phone tucked in the pocket of her sweatpants. Three buzzes meant the city-wide curfew would be starting in fifteen minutes.

At the front door, she reached toward the lock with one hand, holding a set of keys, jigging them in a simulated motion, as she swiped a card in the crease in the frame of the door with the other hand. Unlocking, she pushed the door open—a long creak and then vast darkness inside. Stepping through, she tightly gripped the gun tucked inside her sweatshirt pocket while peering over her shoulder. She held her breath as the door slowly closed behind her, and then it locked. The lights turned on, and she exhaled. Climbing a short set of stairs, she approached a door labelled 3103. She pressed her thumb on an inconspicuous area of the dark red door, the trill of a motor, a dull scraping sound, then it unlocked.

Once inside, she flicked on the light and pulled off the hooded sweatshirt.

Walking down the hallway, she stopped in front of a mirror for a moment. She peered into her dark green, almond-shaped eyes, contoured by long dark eyelashes and a demure visage. Freeing her chestnut brown, shiny locks from her sweatshirt collar, they bustled and unfurled, settling just beyond her shoulders.

Observing the darkened rings under her eyes, she sighed and smiled.

I know, but there's just no time, especially not for sleep, Beth.

Her gun made a loud thud when she placed it on a table in the middle of the room that would be the dining room in a typical apartment.

Turning off all the lights, she sat on the floor by the window. Peering at her flexphone now wrapped around her wrist. The screen on the phone turned a deep blood red, and at that very instant, through the window, she could see all the streetlights below turn the same deep red. The curfew had begun, 8 pm on the dot. She closed the window curtains and prepared for her mission.

-----:-----

The apartment was almost empty, but for a couple of tables, a closet filled with firearms and tactical gear and a fridge containing exactly one item that could qualify as food, an expired jar of pickles.

She had gained access to this location through Cap, her supervisor from when she was in Homicide and whom she had followed to Missing Persons Division last Spring. All investigations were kept local. The days of federal agencies she had read about in history class had long since passed.

When she had first arrived at this location, she had noticed particular features of the apartment, clues to its past. The hardwood floor was filled with tiny holes and scrapes only visible when lit at specific angles. To the untrained eye, the marks seemed of little importance. To Beth, they were the marks of particular kinds of equipment like tripods. The markings were equidistance and at just the right angles.

It was only later that she confirmed the facility had been an operating base for secret missions of some kind for one of those law enforcement agencies from back before the Dark Times.

In the bathroom, she got into character, the first step: putting on the disguise. As she dressed, she carefully made sure her sidearm and backup were adequately placed and accessible.

Maddux had put together the outfit for her on the "down-low," as he called it. There was no way Cap and the rest of the Old Los Angeles Police Department would have sanctioned what she was going to do later on that night. She couldn't even fully tell Maddux all the details. The ones you trust, you call on them only when you need them when you're in dire straits or mortal danger or whatever the term is for being totally in the crapper.

She peered in the mirror, dark brown contacts to cover her hazel green eyes, a red-haired wig to cover her dark hair. The outfit was supposed to be the hip kind of style that those rebelling over the citywide dress code would wear. It consisted of a sort of jumpsuit with a zipper from ankle to the neck, impossible to wear with a Kevlar vest, not that she'd be able to wear one while going undercover anyway. The colour, this godawful thing called Seafog, and Military issue boots, black.

Now, she waited, sitting in a darkened apartment, she gazed out the window at the cityscape, lit up but lifeless, or at least, so it seemed. She saw her reflection in the glass, dark-eyed. She got a curious sense like a different person was peering back at her through those eyes. She waited by the burner phone for the call that would send her back out into the monochromatic jungle to meet with an informant. A man who was, in fact, the only person she knew of who could prove the existence of a mole in the OLAPD.

-----:-----

The message came in at 10:16, just an address and a time. Beth recognized the location immediately. It was an underground bar just outside the Scourge, a few blocks from the safehouse. She wondered if she was wearing the right outfit.

The bar was a familiar spot for the Lustlers, addicts of the so-called "love" drug. A dead-end pseudo medication meant to treat depression, which ultimately became outlawed and now exploited at ultra-high doses to create seemingly endless euphoric feeling and, well, lust.

-----:-----

She exited the safehouse through the back exit into a dark alleyway. Travelling during the curfew meant travelling almost entirely undetected, which meant knowing a specific path out of sight of the twenty-five hundred streetcams all over the city. The streetcams were programmed to point in particular directions at particular times, governed by a secret algorithm. Being an OLAPD detective did, have some perks.

At 10:00 pm, she arrived in the dark alleyway where she knew there would be an entrance to the bar. She waited a few minutes, and eventually, a door opened beside a dumpster, and some Lustlers stumbled out, googly-eyed and sweaty. She squeezed by them and down a dark hallway and finally, through a gap in a dark curtain. She had stepped straight onto a dance club's balcony overlooking a dancefloor where partyers jumped and convulsed to a chunky type of electronic music she recognized as Euphoria. Just the kind of music that would put all the Lustlers over the top, she thought. The atmosphere was intense, and the air itself seemed to sparkle and glitter.

She didn't have any specific instructions, so she stood by a long glass bar filled with neon coloured lights and waited. She was in the prearranged spot and at the exact time. The informant would have to be the one to find her. She had no idea as to the informant's physical appearance. She waited, but after twenty minutes, nothing.

She decided to step outside to take a break from the lights and music inside. She stepped back up the long hallway. She parted the dark curtains, and that's when a figure appeared in front of her wearing a strange faceless mask. It was still pitch-black in the area where she stood, but she felt the figure grab her wrist and place something in the palm of her hand.

"Trust no one," a muffled trembling voice said before turning around and opening up a door. A foul stench filled the air. The figure vacated and stepped out into the street. Just then, before Beth could say a word, a gunshot blast and then, the figure's body flung toward her. Thrown back, she fell down the long hallway. It was dark, and Beth struggled to see. She had the sensation of wetness on her face, and her ears rang something awful. After a minute, Beth wrangled herself to her feet. Somehow, she still had the object in her hand and tucked it into her pocket. Beth then dropped to her knees and tried to check the figure's body for wounds, but the darkness obscured everything. By then, she could tell it was a man. She managed to find his neck and checked for a pulse—nothing. He was dead. Gritting her teeth, she headed after the shooter. Keeping low, pushing the door open, she made her way into the alleyway. Beth scanned up and down the alleyway from behind a dumpster. She peered up at the rooftop ledges overlooking the bar's entrance but still had no idea where the shot had come from or if there was still an active shooter on the scene.

Partygoers must have started catching on to what had happened, the music had stopped, and through the closed doors, Beth could hear a kind of hysteria kicking in, filled with screams of lustlers and a general commotion. Suddenly, a group of lustlers burst through the doors, and the echo of gunshot blasts.

"Get down!" She yelled at lustlers. She was grabbing the arms of those within her reach. "Get down as low as you can. If any of you have a phone – call the police!" She said. Pulling out her gun from inside her boot, she pointed it up at the rooftop of the building opposite the alleyway just as the gunshots had abruptly stopped. Scanning the rooftops, she couldn't see anything. It was far too dark. Taking cover behind a dumpster, she spotted a man wearing a shirt with "security" emblazoned across the chest hiding behind a dumpster opposite her, "You! Are you security staff here!?"

"Yes, Ma'am," The man replied.

"Okay, do you carry? Are you armed?"

He shook his head.

The gunshots started up again. The rapid firing suggested they were being attacked by one shooter using an automatic weapon or a group firing in tandem.

Beth yelled over the sound of the gunshots, "I need you to go back through those doors and make sure no one else comes back out this way! A shooter is firing from an elevated position. He's going to be able to pick off every person that comes through, we're already pinned in, and it's going to be a massacre! When you get back inside, call the OLAPD and tell them there is an active shooter on the premises. There's one vic already. Tell them to send a bus— an ambulance."

The man nodded.

Beth said, "I'm going to draw their fire. Okay!? I'll cover you. Stay as low as possible. On the count of three!"

The man nodded. Beth gestured with her hands, raising one finger in the air, then two, and then three. "Go!" She yelled as she popped up and pointed her gun at the rooftop, and when Beth saw a flash that looked like a gunshot, she fired back multiple shots, emptying her clip before retaking cover and reloading. Gunshots peppered the area around her, and the drumming of bullets smacking concrete and the dense metal of the dumpster. In the corner of her eye, she had seen the security guard make his way back through the doors. After a few seconds, the gunshots stopped, a minute passed, then a few more. Beth stood up and scanned the rooftop, and when she felt it was safe, she ushered away from the remaining lustlers who had been taking cover around her.

She then spotted the flashing red and whites of OLAPD arriving on the scene.

Time to head out.

She could see the lustlers she had helped surrounding the first patrol car on the scene. The last thing she needed right now was to explain why she was in disguise running her rogue operation. She ducked back down the alleyway, sprinting back down the same meticulous path to the safehouse. She made an anonymous call to report all the information she could about the shooting from her burner phone.

---:---

In the bathroom of the safehouse, she peered in the mirror, her face covered in blood.

After showering and changing, she headed down to the basement and out the back exit. She rushed to her car, parked six blocks away.

She had promised to be back home by midnight. She was precisely fourteen minutes late.

When she arrived home, she entered the house as quietly as she could. On the living room couch, she found Debbie, the nanny, fast asleep.

After sending her home, Beth checked in on her adoptive daughter, her niece, Sara. Fast asleep, Beth blew her a kiss.

In her office, Beth looked closely at the object the man at the bar had handed her. From a drawer, she pulled out a repurposed tackle box. Using its contents, she dusted the item for prints. Using her work phone, she took a picture of the prints, a few seconds and then a message appeared, "Beth Lago and Other." When Beth tapped the "Other," a message appeared "No Match Found." That's strange, she thought. The object itself was a virtu-card, a holograph projecting business card. Tapping it with her index finger twice, a bright blue cube of holographic light appeared above it. It rotated slowly, and one side read: DIT, the other side read: CEO Carl Dresdin. Could this be the object?

None of this made sense. Beth heard a beep from her phone, a message from Maddux.

"I get the same thing... no match found," Maddux's message read.

Beth called Maddux from the burner phone.

"That's strange. Where did you find this again?" Maddux asked.

"Shooting at a nightclub," Beth replied.

"When?"

"About an hour and a half ago."

"Ok, yeah, down at a lustler hangout, underground bar. It looks like there was one victim, but it says here he was a known vagrant. Heck of long rap sheet, petty crimes mostly. This guy is an addict, Beth."

"That IS strange." *A vagrant? Just the kind of person you'd pay to deliver a message or, in this case, a virtu-card.*

"Okay, Maddux, thanks for your help. You're a good man. Goodnight."

"Beth?"

"I'm fine, Maddux. Not a mark on me," Beth said. She could hear a sigh on the other end.

There was a long pause, even for Maddux, "Beth?"

"Yes?"

"It's nothing. It's just this stuff is getting messier and messier. I just worry when you're out there, you know, alone."

"I know what you mean. Maddux? Are you suggesting I'm in over my head here? Because I think that conversation is years overdue!"

Beth could hear a chuckle on the other end of the line.

"I'm glad you're okay, Beth. Next time though, I'm riding shotgun."

Beth smiled, "Goodnight, Maddux."

"Goodnight, Beth."

As Beth lay awake in bed that night, the same thoughts circled in her head. She had hoped this night would bring answers but instead, she got nothing but more questions. What did all of this mean? Eventually, she pulled out her phone and searched for any information about Dresdin Industrial Technologies and CEO Carl Dresdin. On the surface, he was wealthy, powerful, and influential. If she wanted to find something, some indication of shadiness, she would have to dig more in-depth because the outer layer of this man's life was squeaky clean. It is going to take some time, she thought, to unravel this mystery and figure out what was going on.

Chapter 2.1 (Part 1 of 3)

Beth Lago

I awoke with a gasp.

The nightmare was over, and still, heart-pounding, in a cold sweat, I couldn't stop from shivering. I took a deep breath, exhaling slowly.

Rolling onto my back, I stretched out my arm, but I felt a cold space in the spot where someone's warmth lay a long time ago.

I peered over at my nightstand past the picture frame—the image of Sam and a more vibrant version of me. A bright banner rolled around my flexphone, indicating the time, 7:02 AM.

I slipped out of bed. As my toes touched the floor, I heard a voice cry out.

"Aunty Beth!!!"

I smiled, hearing the energy in Sara's voice.

I remembered the date and clutched my pendant. *I hope she likes it.*

-----:-----

"What is it, Aunty?" Sara asked while sitting up on her bed, surrounded by a sea of multi-coloured plush dolls.

"Well, open it up, and you'll see," I replied.

Sara's delicate fingers guided auburn tufts behind each ear before attempting to open the little white box. When the lid finally lifted, she smiled and raised the box's contents to her eyes.

"Do you like it?" I asked.

"It's beautiful!" she squeaked, her eyes wide and glowing.

She lifted the thin silver chain above her head before letting it drop down around her neck. I reached in front of her chest, gently gripping the pendant in my hand.

"Do you see, Sara? What does that say?"

"F-F-For…. Oh! Forever!" she shouted.

I pulled my pendant out from under my shirt.

I said, "See, sweetheart … Mine says 'Together.'"

"Together?"

"Right, Sar-Bear."

"Together-Forever."

"Exactly, Together-Forever."

Sara then wrapped her little arms around me, hugging me with all her might.

"Thank you, Aunty!"

"You're welcome, honey. Now make me a promise …."

"Okay."

"I want you to remember that no matter what happens, we will always stick together."

"Okay," she said with a smile.

"And we must always wear our pendants, no matter what ... because these pendants ..." I lifted mine and brought it closer to hers. "Belong ..." I brought my pendant even closer, and I could see hers start to lift slightly... "Together."

Suddenly, the magnets in each pendant came close enough to attract. They collided together with a loud *snap!*

Sara giggled in delight and hugged me again.

Old Los Angeles, Central Precinct 6:20 PM

Like an engine, the precinct hummed with activity. Within the Pit, there were dozens of conversations occurring all at once. Phones were chiming and ringing. Drawers were slamming. Each division had its section, and by the looks of it, someone in Narcotics Division was celebrating a birthday. They'll have a slice of cake now, drinks later, and a hangover tomorrow— beside Narcotics lay Homicide Division. They were the quiet, intensely brooding bunch. Beside them lay Missing Persons, my division. We were just as intense and seemingly always on edge.

The day had gone by fairly quickly. An hour before the end of my shift, I rubbed my temples. A stack of case files sat to the left of me. Upon first arriving, my first task had been researching the feed from last night. I had pulled up our internal log program and was about to enter the query particulars when I realized just how much of a bad idea that would be. Maddux was IT, and he had what we called a 'ghost' profile. He could navigate through all OLAPD databases without leaving a trace. A mole would undoubtedly try to see if someone was trying to pick up his or her breadcrumbs. Then, I realized that I would have to find a way to compare notes with Maddux outside of work.

I looked back at the stack of case files and my current task at hand. We were, in fact, in the midst of an epidemic of sorts. The number of high-profile disappearances had skyrocketed in the last few months. I laid out the images of eight missing girls, from each of the files, in front of me. Each girl has disappeared in the last ten weeks. Each of them has vanished without a trace, and each of them is related to a high-profile figure. Among the group, there was a granddaughter of a judge and the daughter of a politician. And yet, no reports of ransom or demands. These girls were simply here one moment and then gone the next. And then there was the image of the latest missing girl, Brooke Hastings. Her wavy hair, bright eyes, and ear-to-ear smile—I looked at her, and all I could think of was Sara.

Brooke's case didn't seem as high-profile as the others but nonetheless important, nonetheless heartbreaking. I had promised her mother an update on the case tonight and had run the conversation over in my head several times, searching for the right words. Perhaps, there were no "right" words for what I had to say. Taking a deep breath, I lifted my head for a moment's distraction.

In front of me sat Tilly, short for Tillman. Distinct from the other officers in the pit with his slender frame and salt-n-pepper hair, he was staring at his computer screen. Noticing my gaze, Tilly tilted his head, directing his dark eyes my way. He gave me a stiff nod and a broad smile.

As he started packing up his things, he leaned in my direction and asked, "So, should we expect you tonight?"

"Tonight? Oh! That's right. You closed that case -- a cause for celebration, but I can't. I have to make an important call at seven," I said, standing over my desk now, returning each of the images to their respective files.

Tilly walked around my desk, took one look at a picture on my screen, and asked, "Is that your MP?"

"Yeah, Brooke Hastings, thirteen, disappeared three weeks ago."

"Let me guess. Your important phone call is to the girl's mother, and you promised her an update on the case."

I sat back down, "Yeah."

"You're stressed out because you haven't made any progress."

I nodded.

He said, "You feel guilty, and you're dreading calling her parents because you feel like you've let them down."

"Am I that easy to read?" I asked.

Tilly lowered his bag and sat down beside me. He leaned in close.

"I wish it got easier. I remember the first call I had to make," Tilly said with a distant look in his eye. "I think it must have haunted me for... well, for a long time."

"What was the MP's name?"

"I'll never forget, Ashley Burra." He took a deep breath, "Back then, I'd lived and breathed that case. For three months straight, I hardly slept and barely ate." He shook his head as if to shuffle free the memory out of it.

"What happened?" I asked.

Tilly took a deep breath.

"MP cases will seriously mess you up."

He scanned the room, the Pit had been gradually emptying, and the last few day-shifters were sieving to different exits, some lingering. He furrowed his brow, and I imagined he was pausing to choose his next words carefully.

"The advice I can give you is to pace yourself, Beth. Sometimes, you'll think that not knowing is the hardest part. Then, one day, you'll get that horrible call. Then, you'll wish you could go back to the time when you didn't know, but by then, it's too late."

I felt my shoulders drop.

Tilly shrugged and said, "Ok, let me put it this way. This little girl's mother and father have something that we often forget about."

"Which is?"

"Hope … Beth. Parents, no matter how desperate things may seem, will never give up hope. A parent wants to know the truth about their child's case, and where possible, they fill the unknown parts with hope. They're also gauging you and where you stand."

I peered at the image of Brooke on my screen and said, "… That I won't give up hope, either."

Tilly smiled and started walking away. Without looking back, he said, "We'll miss you tonight, Lago. You owe me a rain check on that drink."

I smiled.

I took solace in Tilly's words—as long as we were still looking, there was still hope. I felt terrible not sharing the developments of the night before with Tilly. I couldn't help but think that it was better this way, for now. At least until I could get more definitive information. Besides, the time may come when I'd had to pull Tilly into my rogue operation. For now, it may be better to keep things secret and keep him safe.

Back to the task at hand, I pulled up the phone number for Mara Hastings, Brooke's mother, on my computer. I was about to dial the number on my flexphone when an alert flashed on my computer. I could feel my heart skip a beat. My cellphone display read:

EAM—Emergency Alert Message — sighting of subject: Brooke Hastings.

I peered toward Cap's office and realized he would've received the same alert. I rose to my feet, energized. It was standard procedure to enter images of a missing person into Ocular. This system monitored the over twenty-five hundred CCTV cameras in OLA, but I'd received nothing to date.

-----:-----

Sitting at his desk, holding his phone, Cap rose from his chair like a spritely twenty-year-old as I entered. Few signs of his fifty-years, except for perhaps his brush-cut silver hair.

He greeted me with a smile and added, "Hey, Kiddo," as he walked toward me and then in the direction of the holo-table just to the right of the door.

We stood at opposite sides of the two and a half by six-foot holo-table. Cap dimmed the lights before pressing his thumb against the tabletop.

"Would you like to do the honours?" he asked.

I pulled out my phone and read aloud the sixteen-digit EAM code. A light green 3D holographic map of Old Los Angeles appeared an inch above the table in a bright flash. A small light blue sphere appeared on the map. It repeatedly flashed like a beacon.

Walking around to the holo-table's long side, Cap dipped his arm into the 3D map and opened his palm facedown over the beacon. The holo-table then zoomed in on the area.

He said, "That's the source of your EAM sighting, and it's just outside …."

"The Scourge," I said.

"What else came through with the message?" Cap asked, turning away from the holo-table, toward me, before crossing his arms.

I peered at the details of the EAM on my phone, "There's nothing here, which doesn't make any sense. Oculus must have malfunctioned during the transmission."

Cap said, "Okay, well, if the data isn't in the network, then there's only one other place it could be."

I started inputting the coordinates into my phone.

"Not so fast, Beth. I hope you're not thinking what I think you're thinking." Cap said.

"I'm getting ready to go out there."

"You're not going out there alone." Cap pulled out his phone. He made a call, and a minute later, there was a knock at the door.

"Come in."

The door opened, and in walked Senior Lead Officer/Shift Supervisor Mark Eccles.

I'd only spoken to Eccles a couple of times. Upon entering, he scanned the room, peering in my direction. Clean cut, rigid-jawed, and dark-haired, Eccles stood a few inches taller than Cap. I'd heard he was in his mid-forties, but up close, he looked at least ten years younger.

"Have you two met?" Cap asked, but before we could reply, he continued speaking. "Eccles, I need you to back up Lago here. You're heading to the Red-Zone just outside the Scourge."

-----:-----

In the Equipment Room, Eccles and I strapped on our bulletproof Kevlar vests. I'd already called Mara Hastings, Brooke's mother, advising of a follow-up call tomorrow. I made no mention of the Alert Message for the moment.

As we prepared to head out, I felt both exhilaration and fear. We would be the first uniforms to enter the Red-Zone in at least the last six months. Cap advised us to make this a quick in and out mission. The OLA Tactical Unit was on assignment. Therefore, backup would be limited to zip tonight.

As I prepared, my thoughts kept drifting back to Sara. I worried about what would happen to her if something were to happen to me.

When Sara came into my life, I'd made a clear choice. I'd hung up my badge, determined never to return. Looking back, I could still remember every detail of that night three years ago, the night Jenny, my sister and Sara's mother, died—the night my life changed. I'd suffered through it a thousand times over in my sleep. "Take care of her … She's special." Jenny's final words to me while she clutched my hand before it went cold and before the long beep emanated from the machine at her side. Sam and I became Sara's family. Then three months later, Sam mysteriously collapsed at work. After that, we learned he had a rare heart condition. Suddenly and quietly, he passed one night in his sleep. After that, I did what I had to do. Short on money, and after unsuccessful attempts at other jobs, I returned to the thing I'd done best. I'd intended it as a temporary solution. However, until I could find another, less dangerous, job -- this was it.

Before leaving the equipment room, I kissed my pendant and tucked it under my shirt.

"Are you ready?" Eccles asked.

"Ready to move, Sir," I replied.

-----:-----

As we sped along in the electric-powered patrol car, I managed only intermittent glimpses at SLO Eccles. The sun had already begun to set, and it was quite dark, but every few seconds, we'd pass under a streetlight's glow lighting up the cabin's interior.

Although the patrol car's navigation system did all the driving, Eccles kept his large green eyes focused on the road ahead.

Like many parts of Old Los Angeles, the landscape was a mix of the old and the new. Giant towers of steel overshadowed fractured ruins of stone. I often felt, well, amazed by how much it had changed since the Dark Times. Bonfires and rubble, bodies, and pain filled these streets just fifteen years earlier. As far as we'd progressed, things still weren't perfect. There was always a note of caution in the air. The citywide curfew would begin in thirty minutes, and yet the streets were almost empty along our route.

On Victory Boulevard, I caught a glimpse of a group of girls walking down the sidewalk together.

"I know what you're thinking," Eccles said with a smirk.

"Sir?"

"You're wondering why all girls in Old Los Angeles seemed to dress the same."

"No, I know why, Sir. I just wish things were different."

"It would sure make our jobs easier," Eccles said.

<<ETA ten minutes>> The vehicle's interactive computer system declared in its typical well-mannered female voice.

-----:-----

"Sir, Cap asked that I brief you before we arrived," I said.

Taking the E-sheet from the case file on my lap, I tapped it onto the dashboard. The windshield turned opaque before lighting up. A picture of Brooke Hastings appeared in the top right-hand corner. "Brooke Hastings disappeared on January 3, 2074, presumably, as she walked home from school." A green path appeared on the screen, indicating her route home. "She was supposed to have arrived by five o'clock that afternoon. Her parents worked two jobs at the time, so Brooke usually spent her evenings alone until around eight. Her mother, Mara, arrived home at about a quarter after eight that night. After searching the entire house and then checking with the neighbours, she reported Brooke missing at 9:04 pm."

"And then?"

"Well, Sir, that's where the trail dead-ends. There were no sightings of Brooke in the neighbourhood or on the route home. I've interviewed her friends, teachers, and family. At the house, there was no sign of a break-in or struggle. Apart from a handful of false sightings, nothing's come up. There were a couple of promising hits on the Amber Alert, but they delivered nothing."

-----:-----

I shut off the windshield screen. We were entering the OLA downtown core. On the road immediately ahead of us, I spotted a virtu-billboard. This one was an enormous translucent white cube of light about three stories high with the "DIT" emblem at its center. I recognized it from my research the night before. As we drove through the giant holographic billboard, the voice of a woman surrounded us.

<<Life is precious. Let's preserve it together. Don't forget to see your doctor about your monthly vaccine. DIT: Building and protecting a brighter tomorrow >>

As the woman spoke, outside the patrol car, a hologram of a man appeared holding a test tube. Then the image of a boy appeared receiving an injection from a man dressed as a doctor. At the end of the advertisement, the boy's image reappeared with his mother in the background. They were both waving and smiling.

-----:-----

<<ETA five minutes>>

In the distance, I could see the barricade of the two-dozen toppled cars that marked the exact line where civility ended, and the Scourge began.

"Have you ever been?" Eccles asked.

"Five years ago ... I came back with a souvenir, Sir," I replied as I lifted my sleeve and extended my forearm outward.

"How many stitches? And you don't have to address me by rank while we're on this, well, mission."

"Eleven stitches. And how should I address you, Sir?"

"Eccles, Ecc-lees, is just fine ... How did it happen?" Eccles asked while turning to face me.

"It's a long story," I replied.

"Okay, fair enough, maybe better we save it for another time," Eccles said as he smiled and nodded.

<<ETA 1 minute>>

"All right, this is it, Lago. We're almost there," Eccles said ominously. "Remember what Cap said."

"Expect the unexpected. Stay sharp, stay frosty." I parroted.

<<Arriving at destination>>

-----:-----

I took a deep breath before stepping out of the patrol car. My heart pounded in my ears. The Scourge lay only a few hundred feet away. I felt a rush of adrenaline as I panned the landscape.

The area looked like a ghost town. It was pitch black in some spots and partially lit in others. Hardly any streetlights worked, and the ones that did flicker like lightning flashes in the distance. An eerie silence surrounded us. Gusts of wind kicked up dust and pieces of garbage from toppled over cans. Other than Eccles, there was no other human for miles around. Nonetheless, the hairs on my neck stood on end. I felt certain we weren't alone. We approached the twenty-foot tower with the CCTV camera at its apex.

"Something isn't right. Tell me about the message you received from Ocular," Eccles whispered.

"I received an Emergency Alert Message."

"But what did it contain? Did you actually receive an image or a video feed showing Brooke?" Eccles asked as we continued walking toward the tower.

"No, the alert message came through without any of that information. I was planning on downloading it from the source."

As we drew closer, I noticed that the service box at the tower's base containing the camera's connections was open. I directed my flashlight at the open metallic box.

On a small five-inch screen inside the box, a message read, "Data Empty," and another message indicated the date and time in smaller letters. "It doesn't even look like it's active anymore," I whispered. "There's no way this camera triggered the Ocular system."

Eccles said, "That's not good. I think we're going to have to abort. Come back tomorrow with a tech team. I think, for now, we better get out of here."

I looked back at him. He had put his hand on his holstered gun, and he was peering around in every direction.

"Back away from the box, Beth. Let's get the hell out of here, right now."

His eyes were opened wide, and his tone, unwavering.

As we turned to walk back to the patrol car, I felt a tickle on my neck. Like a reflex, up went my hand to confirm my pendant's position. I gasped. It was gone.

"Eccles," I said in a tone just a notch above a whisper. Eccles turned around, and when I dropped to one knee to see if it had fallen, he did the same.

Suddenly, we heard it, a gunshot blast in the distance followed by the impact of a bullet on the concrete post behind my head. I felt another shot whistle past my left ear. Then it sounded like a violent hailstorm had erupted. I dropped further and began slithering my way back to the car as bullets exploded around me. The ten or so feet to the patrol car now felt like a mile. In the darkness, I snaked my way, shielding my head from shards of splintered glass and chunks of concrete debris. A cloud of dust formed in front of me so big I lost sight of Eccles.

As I hid behind an abandoned car, a tremor ran through me as I wondered if I'd ever make it out of here. I estimated the direction of the gunshots, and I withdrew my gun. The shooter or shooters were riddling wrecked car a few yards in front of me with a barrage of bullets. Eccles must be behind it, I thought. I took a deep breath and waited for a pause in the gunfire, and when I heard it, I rose and sprinted to the next car returning fire as I ran. I found myself swallowed up by another cloud of smoke and debris. I dropped to the ground and crawled with my head down. I felt someone grab my hand. I pulled Eccles up, and we sprinted to the patrol car. I opened the door while Eccles returned fire, then he swung me around his body into the backseat. He dove in after me and slammed the door shut. Crouching down, I heard the sounds of metallic bangs and shattering glass.

Eccles yelled to the E-ssistant, "Get us the hell out of here!"

<<Destination, please?>>

"Central Precinct, escape-speed, now!"

I heard the sound of tires screeching and the hail of bullets gradually dissipating.

"Goddamn it, are you hit?" Eccles shouted as though he still needed to yell over the sound of bullets firing.

I could barely hear him as my ears still rang. I read his lips. "No, I don't think so," I replied as I tried to catch my breath. "You?"

"No."

"What the hell was that?" I asked while shaking off shards of glass from my body.

Eccles shook his head before saying, "An impressively orchestrated ambush."

"But why?"

Eccles peered back at me with an intense stare. There was a film of sweat on his upper lip and redness on his face. He answered, "I don't know. Hate? They hate the police and all we stand for."

"So you think they meant to target the police, in general, and not us specifically?"

"They couldn't have targeted us specifically, Beth. No, no, that's not how these people operate."

"You don't sound so sure, Eccles."

"We'll investigate, of course, but this is probably just a bunch of punks trying to take out some cops. How would they know that you and I would be there?"

The thought ran through my mind. Could it be the attackers targeted me? Was this part of what happened last night? Was my cover blown? I had to be sure before bringing Eccles into this.

I looked down at the pendant and chain in my open palm.

"Is that why you dropped to the ground?" Eccles asked.

"Yeah, it's the strangest thing. It didn't break. It just somehow came undone."

"Well, strange or not, you dropping down for that little piece of silver probably saved your life."

-----:-----

Eccles ordered the ballistics on the bullets embedded in the patrol car's frame back at the precinct.

"Don't expect any results until at least tomorrow morning. Don't worry. We'll find the bastards who shot at us," he said as he walked away.

I filed the E-report into the precinct's reporting database.

Sitting at my desk in the Pit, I wondered who had hacked the Ocular system. How did this person manage to trigger a sighting of Brooke Hastings? I approached Eccles, at his desk, in the pod on the other side of the Pit.

"It's just blind luck. I think you're giving these guys too much thought. They're not that complicated. They found a CCTV camera that wasn't working, and they manipulated it in their favour," he said while turning away in his chair. He started inserting an E-sheet into a drawer at his desk.

"I just get the feeling there's more going on here," I said.

Filing away E-sheets, not lifting his head, he asked, "Like what? Do you still think they deliberately targeted us? I don't know, Beth, I mean, it was just a fluke that I was there."

"And me?"

Eccles glared back at me with his eyebrows raised. He said, "Now you're just paranoid."

"Am I?"

"I'd say! Why do you think that, Beth?" He asked while directing his attention to his computer screen.

"Haven't you ever had a gut instinct before, Eccles?"

Eccles paused. He looked up at me with his round, green eyes. He said, "Let's say you were right. Let's say someone was targeting you. Why would they devise such an elaborate way to take you out?"

"What do you mean?"

"Why not eliminate you while you're on your way home or sitting on the toilet?"

"Eccles."

"I'm serious, Beth. Why would someone go to all that trouble?"

I crossed my arms, and I looked in the direction of my desk. I said, "Maybe this has to do with Brooke Hastings."

"What do you mean?"

"Maybe I wasn't necessarily the target by name. Maybe the target was just the officer who was going to respond to the EAM ultimately. Whoever did this might have done it without knowing who that would be," I said.

"You think their goal was to thwart the investigation into Brooke Hastings' disappearance by eliminating the investigating officer?"

"Well, it's just a theory at this point, but yes."

"Okay. For that to be true, then someone with considerable means and expertise is willing to kill a cop over this little girl's disappearance," Eccles said.

"Not only kill a cop but also make it look like it was a random cop killing," I added.

I resisted telling Eccles about last night. I didn't think Eccles was the mole, but I couldn't accept putting anyone at risk without at least some confirmation. I was more certain than ever that we had a mole with clearances high enough to infiltrate our secured systems and knowledge of how to manipulate data without leaving a trace. To them, faking an EAM might not have been that hard. I realized that my theory needed proof and that I couldn't continue this conversation with Eccles without divulging information about my work searching for the mole.

"I guess we'll have to take this one step at a time," I said.

"Umm ... right. We'll wait for the results on those ballistics, and we'll send a tech team to check out that CCTV camera. We can't do much more than that. It's been a long day. We almost got ourselves killed, for God's sake. For now, try to relax. Maybe go and do something that'll get your mind off of this."

-----:-----

At 9:00 pm, I started packing up to go home. I had started walking away from my desk when a young dispatcher burst through the Dispatch Center doors. After nervously panning in every direction, he eventually centred his gaze on me.

"Lago, Beth Lago?" he asked shakily.

Eccles, who had stepped away from his desk, managed to appear just in time to interject. "Is there a problem?" Eccles asked.

"I'm not sure, sir. I've got a possible 10-57 at 823 Romeo Lane".

I shook my head in disbelief. That was my address. The fact that it was a 10-57 Missing Person was even more devastating.

"Who is ... the 10-57?" Eccles asked.

"Beth, I'm sorry ..." the dispatcher mumbled.

"What?" I asked in confusion.

The look on the young dispatcher's face could only mean one thing. The Missing Person was a child. It was Sara. There was a pause, as I didn't know what to do or how to react. I could feel my face turning flush. I felt dizzy. I was sure that I was about to pass out when at the last moment, a picture on my desk came into view. It was a picture of Sara sitting on the front steps of our house. The sight of her curly brown tresses and crooked smile gave me strength. I felt a resurgence of energy. Sara needed me, and I wasn't about to let her down. I wiped a tear from my eye before heading for the door. Eccles stepped in my path.

"Beth! You shouldn't drive. I'll take you. Try to stay calm. Don't worry. We'll find her." He turned to the dispatcher and said, "Dispatch all available units. Send out an Amber Alert with the description. Who was the caller?"

"Debbie Marks, the girl's babysitter," replied the dispatcher.

In the precinct garage, Eccles and I climbed into a patrol car. With sirens blaring and lights flashing, we rushed in the direction of the house. Eccles disengaged the E-ssistant and took manual control of the patrol car.

"E never drives fast enough," he complained.

In the car, I made repeated calls to the house and Debbie's cell phone. There was no answer on either line. I could feel my hands going cold. Despite the curfew, Eccles still had to weave in and out of traffic as he dodged other slow E-drivers. He kept telling me not to panic and to stay positive. I became increasingly convinced I would be unable to do either. As we drew closer to the house, I could feel a lump building in my throat.

When we arrived at Romeo Lane, we began the long ascent toward the house at the top of the hill. In the distance, I could see the flashes of red and blue lights surrounding the house. With a heavy heart, I braced myself for what lay ahead.

Chapter 2.2 (Part 2 of 3)

Beth Lago

We came to an abrupt stop behind a long row of patrol cars. A cloud of dust kicked up in front of us before disappearing into the night. Eccles was peering at me, brow furrowed. It was clear he was choosing his words carefully.

"Beth, we don't know what's happened yet. Until we know for sure, though, we have to handle this the same way we would any other potential disappearance."

"I understand," I replied as I tried to open the door. Eccles had kept it locked.

"That means no questioning of witnesses, no collecting of evidence. If there's a search, you can coordinate and suggest locations, but you shouldn't participate in the actual search. Anything you could find, even by accident, could become --"

"Tainted ... I know, Eccles, please. We're talking about my Sara here. She's only six-years-old. She's out there, alone and scared." I could feel my hands beginning to tremble. I took a deep breath.

Eccles said, "I know, I know. We're just taking the necessary precautions. I'm sure she'll turn up safe and sound."

I hope so.

As I jumped out, I felt an unfamiliar bite in the air. The smell of burnt rubber filled my nostrils. Running toward the house, I felt struck by a sense of confusion. The sight of so many police officers in front of our tranquil house had caught me off guard. The two-story white house with the light blue window shutters now intermittently glowed red and blue. As we approached, I spotted someone sitting on the front porch. When she spotted us, Debbie, our babysitter, ran towards us. I hugged her tight as I tried to ease her shaking body. I fought away the tears. Wave after wave, questions rolled up in my mind. I found the strength to resist. As I held her up, I glanced over at Eccles. He nodded back.

I placed my hands on Debbie's shoulders, and I gently peeled her away from me. "Debbie, this is Senior Lead Officer Mark Eccles. He's with the OLAPD. He's going to ask you some questions about what happened. Please tell him everything you know."

Debbie looked up at me with tears in her eyes. The vibrant, youthful girl I'd known was gone. She had fallen to pieces, and it took everything in me not to follow.

"I'm sorry, Mrs. Lago," she said as she wiped tears from her eyes.

I didn't know how to respond at first. "I know. Right now, we have to focus on finding Sara. Okay?"

Debbie nodded her head repeatedly as she continued crying. I could feel my emotions building, as well.

I had to keep it together. We all did.

"I need you to be brave, Debbie. We don't have much time."

"Okay. Mrs. Lago, okay," Debbie said.

Eccles put his arm around her as he led her away. Debbie gripped my hand one last time, mouthing the words, "I'm sorry," before turning around. I took a deep breath. I raised my eyes to the sky as I focused all my strength and poise.

Keep it together, Beth.

The officer who had been with Debbie when we'd first arrived was Dalton. He stood by, only a few steps away from us. I'd assumed he was the first to arrive on the scene. I looked over at him, and I nodded in acknowledgement.

"Beth, I'm so sorry about all of this."

"I appreciate it, Dalton. I just ... I just need to find Sara. Could you please brief me?"

"Of course."

-----:-----

"After arriving, I secured the house. I then proceeded to confirm that Sara was not present." He dropped his head before continuing. "The girl, Debbie, was a lot calmer when I questioned her. My gut tells me she's not involved. I think you did the right thing by getting Eccles to question her, by the way."

I simply nodded. I knew he was right. My presence would have only complicated matters.

"What did she say? What happened?"

We walked in the direction of the house. Once inside, I glanced up the staircase in the main foyer leading to the second level and Sara's bedroom. Dalton continued walking past the stairs and down the hall toward the kitchen.

"She said that she had put Sara to bed around 7:00. Between 7:00 and 7:30, she read her a bedtime story. At 7:30, Debbie said she left Sara's bedroom, closing the door behind her. At that point, she returned downstairs, eventually settling in the dining room. She said she spent the next hour and twenty minutes sitting at the dining room table studying."

"Okay ..."

"At ten minutes to nine, she climbed up the stairs and opened Sara's closed bedroom door. It was at that point that she realized that Sara was gone."

I struggled to remain composed. I fought to keep my thoughts organized and logical.

"Please tell me you've sent out search parties, Dalton."

"Of course. I've set up a perimeter a mile wide, and I have three teams of officers branching outward from the house. They've all received electronic Amber Alerts on their phones with Sara's description," Dalton said.

I sighed in relief, and it looked as though Dalton had followed protocol to the letter.

"Any canvassers?" I asked.

"No, not yet, but soon."

"Thank you for filling me in."

"Don't mention it. Heck, you deserve to know what's going on. I just want you to know that we're doing everything we can to find your little girl."

I nodded. "Thank you. So is there anything else?"

"Yes, actually, there is! I should have mentioned this earlier."

"What is it?"

"Debbie reported she had closed Sara's bedroom window on account of the cold. When she checked on Sara later, the bedroom window was wide-open."

My eyes widened.

"Did you seal off her bedroom?" I asked.

"Yes, at least until the Forensics team arrives."

I rushed outside the house and around to the west-facing side and Sara's bedroom window.

I glimpsed in the direction away from our home, down the hill. On Romeo Lane, the houses were all single homes. Only one house, ours, sat at the top of the hill and the next closest lay fifty feet away and at the bottom. The only traffic toward the house came along Romeo Lane.

It was a quiet neighbourhood, the kind that Sam and I had once only dreamed of living and which had only been made possible by Sam's job.

I couldn't believe this was happening.

I wished Sam was here right now. He had a way of telling me something, anything, to calm me. It was like his superpower. Nothing could dampen his spirits, or at least he never let it show.

Looking up at Sara's second-story window, I took a few steps back. In the moonlight, I could still make out some of the window frame's detail. Panning my surroundings, I tried to imagine how anyone could have climbed up there or down. There were no trees in the vicinity. Along that façade of the house, there was only Sara's window and then a one-story drop.

Dalton took up position beside me.

"If I had to guess, I'd say it wasn't possible. Not without a ladder or something," Dalton said as he looked up.

"You guys got anything?" Eccles asked as he walked toward us.

"Working out a possible point of egress or regress," Dalton replied.

Eccles turned to both Dalton and me. He said, "Okay, where are we so far? Dalton?"

"We have the Amber Alert out already, tagging the event as a possible abduction. We've set up a perimeter, and we're set to start door-knock canvassing along the road. We've established initial protocols. Just trying to cover a few different possibilities," Dalton said.

Eccles said, "Thank you, Dalton. I think you brought up a good point, we need to orient our efforts based on the possibilities, and as we get more information, hopefully, we can wind up with one main theory of what's going on here."

I confirmed my agreement with a nod.

Eccles said, "I think we should organize our strategy based on the possible scenarios. I count at least three boxes. We can have Box one assume she wandered off somehow on her own. For this box, we can search for her in the common areas she would go. I don't know if Sara has ever sleepwalked. Whether she has or not, I don't think we should rule that out as a possibility," Eccles said, looking in my direction.

I confirmed my agreement with a slow nod as I searched my memory of any past Sara sleepwalking experience, but none came to mind.

"Beth, are you okay?" Eccles said in a lower tone as he turned to me, "Do you think you can organize that box?" Eccles asked.

"Yes, of course," I responded.

'Thank you, Beth. For Box two," He paused, furrowed his brow, "We should treat as though somebody took her. I don't mind guiding that box. So far, we have forensics on their way to examine this room, the outside window. We also have the Amber Alert, which has gone. Box three, an extension of Box One, considers the possibility she wandered off and is hiding, or she didn't wander off at all and is trying to go somewhere specific. Dalton, Beth, I suggest you guys team up and organize that box."

Dalton and I started heading to the front of the house when my legs started shaking. I dropped to one knee.

"Beth?" Eccles called out.

Grabbing my arm, he helped me up slowly. "Are you okay?" he asked.

I wanted to answer, but I couldn't. My mind was spinning. Sara was in danger, and I felt utterly helpless. I could feel the pressure mounting with each passing minute.

"We should get you out of here," He said.

"No, no, I'm okay. Please. It's just a lot to take in at once. I can help with the search."

Eccles locked eyes with me.

"Are you sure?" He asked.

I took a breath, clasped my hands, "Yes," I replied.

"Okay, if you need anything, you let me know. Oh, and Beth, it's going to be okay, but to be on the safe side, focus only on coordination, right?"

"Of course."

-----:-----

Dalton and I compared notes. He explained that he had sent out search teams to scour three areas—two parks and a nearby schoolyard. Dalton offered to check on each of the teams personally and assign canvassers to go door-to-door within the neighbourhood.

I assigned the next round of search teams.

After collecting a map from a patrol car's trunk, I spread it out on the hood. I glanced down at my watch -- 9:31 pm. Forty minutes had passed since Debbie reported Sara's disappearance.

"Can I get everybody's attention, please?" I yelled in the direction of the dozen officers who stood before me. Startled at first, they approached. I assigned Paulsen, one of the more senior officers in the precinct, with the task of holding up a flashlight and pointing it down at the map.

"Okay, we have three areas of interest. About four hundred yards northwest, there's an abandoned shelter," I said as I pointed to an area. "Six hundred yards north by northwest, there's a collection of caves," I said while pointing to another spot on the map. This time my finger began to tremble slightly. "Finally, directly north, there's a half-finished building foundation. I'm sending you to these spots because Sara knows each of these places well. Please be thorough in your search. Please hurry. It's getting colder out there by the minute. Report back any observations."

"You heard her! Let's move out!" Paulsen said.

"We got this, Beth," another officer said.

Flashlights in hand, each of the teams marched down the hill before disappearing into the darkness.

Alone for a moment, I had a chance to gather my thoughts. I couldn't help thinking that all of this craziness was connected—the shooting last night, the attack earlier tonight and now this. Statistically, the thought these events were not connected was virtually impossible. The message was loud and clear. It read aloud, STOP!

I shook my head at the vile genius of it. If they had killed me then, someone else might follow my work. By taking Sara and keeping her from me, they know I will stop for fear of harm coming to her. I needed to focus my efforts and trust the possibility that Sara could still be saved.

Standing in front of the house, I closed my eyes, and I tried to imagine the way this might have happened. At some point between 7:30 pm and 8:40 pm, one or more assailants entered the house through the bedroom window. I pictured Debbie sitting at the dining room table. The front and back doors were within Debbie's line of sight. The bedroom window seemed the likeliest point of entry. From her bed, they managed to grab Sara without making any noise at all. Quietly enough to avoid Debbie's attention, who sat one level down but at the opposite side of the house.

How did you do this?

I recalled a memory of Sara at age four, wrestling, squirming as a nurse ordered me to hold her still. She was receiving a routine vaccination, but it took two male nurses to hold her down. She's stronger than she seems. Somehow, despite her strength, they'd managed to carry her down a tall ladder.

What did you do then?

In my mind's eye, I imagined an escape vehicle. There would have been tire tracks if they had parked on the lawn. Debbie would have heard the sound of a car speeding off.

How did you get away?

There was only one way to the house – along the gravel road. I tried to envision an alternative. Then, it hit me—a cliff's edge behind the house and a three-story drop, and then, a highway.

You had a car waiting.

No, you had a truck waiting there. You used a vehicle big enough to transport a ladder—perhaps a maintenance or repair van.

I grabbed my radio, "Lago to base."

There was a crackle of static. "Base here."

"Eccles, can you amend the Amber Alert to include the possibility of the use of a maintenance truck or van on Interstate 5."

"Amend the Amber Alert. Why?" Eccles asked.

"I'm behind the house. There's a cliff leading down to the highway. They would have needed a ladder."

"Okay. Copy that. Beth?"

"Yes?"

"Forensics teams are on their way. They should be here any minute."

"Okay, great," I replied.

Instinctively, I started walking toward the back of the house. As I walked, I looked around for signs of footprints or a trail made by a ladder dragging. I saw neither. The darkness prevented me from seeing much of anything on the ground.

After several steps, I arrived at the six-foot-high fence that lined the cliff behind the house. The fence looked intact. It consisted of five-foot vertical wooden planks fastened at the top and bottom by horizontal wooden beams. Between the wooden planks, there were gaps where dim blocks of light shone through. If my suspicions were correct, they had to have found a way past this fence. After carefully panning the entire length, I noticed one gap that seemed uneven. Stepping closer, I reached my hand out at the planks on either side of the uneven gap. Touching them, I realized they were loose at the bottom, and I could swing the planks laterally.

This is how you did it.

I stepped through the gap, and I found myself no more than six feet from the cliff's edge.

Standing at the edge, I peered downward.

This is where you took Sara.

I peered at the area around my feet, but I could see nothing.

"Standby for searchlight activation," Eccles said over the radio.

Suddenly, a massive area lit up around the house. I stepped back through the gap in the fence and away from the cliff. The perimeter lights made it possible to see the tall grass at my feet. I caught a glimpse of something shiny just beside my left foot. My heartbeat's rhythm sped up. I knelt slowly. My eyes locked on the spot where I'd seen it. The wind rolled over the blades of grass, making them undulate like waves in a dark green ocean. Between waves, it sparkled back at me. On my knees, I parted sections of grass around it. I felt tears trickling down my nose as I saw it more clearly. A silver pendant, with an engraving on its face, glittered brightly. I barely managed to read it. "Forever."

I cleared my throat and inhaled deeply.

"Lago to base."

"Base here."

"I found something. I need someone over here to take pictures and collect evidence."

"Copy that. The first forensics team is checking out Sara's bedroom. I'll send the second one your way when they arrive. What's your location?"

"I'm behind the house, ten yards south."

A brilliant flash lit up the sky, followed by a deep rumble.

One drop fell, then two, and then like a dam breaking overhead, it began to pour.

"DAMN!"

Reacting as quickly as I could, I snapped a picture of the pendant with my phone. Using a latex glove from my pocket, I lifted the pendant, holding it within my jacket's vest portion. I could barely see where I was going as rain and wind furiously pounded against me. I hurried back to the front of the house.

As I passed the side of the house, I saw a group of men with "Forensics" written on their jackets, desperately trying to lay down a tarp. Looking at the ground, I wondered if they were already too late. Large puddles had already formed—any chance of finding footprints or trace evidence was washing away with the rain.

I shakily handed the pendant to a tech outside Sara's bedroom and headed straight for the bathroom inside the house. Having my stomach tied in knots all evening and feeling overwhelmed with dizziness, I collapsed in front of the toilet. A minute later, I picked myself up off the floor. I opened the faucet and splashed cold water on my face. It had finally caught up with me. Finding Sara's pendant, seeing the rain wash away potential trace evidence, the thought of Sara in danger, all of it weighed me down. I could feel myself falling apart. A mix of shock, disbelief and adrenaline had kept me from fully absorbing all that had happened. Sara was all I had left. I had barely survived Sam's passing. I couldn't think of what would happen if I lost Sara too.

Peering at my reflection, I begged for Sara's safe return. Looking down, I saw one red drop in the sink, followed by another. My nose was bleeding. I lifted my head to stop the flow. The room started spinning, and then there was only darkness.

-----:-----

I felt somehow distant. Although I couldn't see anything, I could hear sounds. Voices echoed from afar.

"Beth! Beth!"

"Can you hear me?"

"Beth!"

I opened my eyes to see two familiar faces.

"Oh! Thank God. She's awake. Tell the paramedics to stand by," I heard Cap say.

"Cap?" I asked.

"Yeah?"

"I had a terrible dream."

"I know. I know."

With the help of Cap and Eccles under each arm, I coiled up to my feet.

"What happened?"

"You passed out, Beth," Eccles whispered.

"Sara?" I asked as I looked at Eccles and then Cap.

They both shook their heads, and my knees buckled again. The two men helped me down the hall and into the study. They lowered me onto a chair.

"I'm going to check on the search teams," Eccles said. He patted me on the shoulder on his way out.

"How long was I out?" I asked as I massaged my temples. Looking up at Cap, I noticed his clear blue eyes staring back at me. He looked different from when I'd seen him earlier in the day. He put his hand on top of mine.

"Not long, Beth, twenty minutes or so," Cap replied.

"Twenty minutes!" I quickly grabbed onto the chair armrests. I lifted myself, but before my knees could lock, my head began spinning again.

"Easy, Beth. Why don't you sit here for a few minutes?" Cap stated in as soft a tone as I had ever heard him use.

"Any leads yet, Cap?"

"I'm sorry, Beth, we're doing the best we can."

"I shouldn't have left her alone," I said.

"Don't blame yourself. You didn't leave her alone. You left her with someone you trust."

I dropped my head.

"Hey?" Cap asked.

"Yeah?"

"We're not going to give up ... So don't you start."

I lifted my head and looked directly into Cap's eyes. I said, "I won't ever give up, not on her, not ever."

Usually stoic and composed, Cap looked back at me and nodded.

"Cap!" a voice hollered from down the hall.

A young Forensics technician I didn't recognize popped into the room.

"I think you better check this out." The dark-haired technician said.

He got up and began walking toward the door. I got up as well.

Cap looked back at me.

"You didn't think that I was going to sit there forever," I said.

"No ... of course not," He said.

"I'll stand behind you, and I won't touch anything."

In Sara's bedroom, the technician briefed both of us. He started by pointing at the nightstand beside Sara's bed. Within the four-walled room, Sara's bed pointed outward from the center of one wall. The one window in the room lay along the wall to the right of the bed. The bedroom door lay directly opposite the window. It seemed as though the forensics team had logically begun searching in the area between Sara's bed and the window.

The young technician said, "We've uploaded every fingerprint we found to the Territory Fingerprint Identification Database, and each one came back as identified or verified -- like the babysitter, Debbie's prints. We thought we had checked every potential surface until we looked at this picture frame. Officer Lago, is there anything you could tell us about this frame?"

"It's facing the wrong way."

"Then we might have found our first lead."

"Are you going to elaborate?" Cap asked as he stood crossed-armed.

"This isn't a digital picture frame. It looks like one, but it's just a plain glass frame. I haven't seen one of these in years," the tech said.

"I bought it at an auction. I collect old things. It's a hobby of mine," I said when suddenly, I realized his point. "Nowadays, digital picture frames have fingerprint-resistant glass!"

"Exactly!" The young tech exclaimed, "The perp or perps likely made the same mistake we initially made. They must have knocked over this frame and then figured it was print-proof glass. One of them picked it up with their bare hand."

He pointed to the corner of the frame.

"He or she left a juicy palm print, right there," the tech said.

"Good job ..."

"Marv, sir."

"Good job, Marv. Have we had any hits on the print yet?"

"No, not yet at least, not in the Territory Fingerprint Identification Database of Known Prints. We're checking unknown prints right now."

In identifying fingerprints, "unknown" prints referred to prints picked up in an investigation that never matched up to a person. It was a way of linking together separate cases involving the same possible suspect.

I felt a mix of excitement and frustration. I knew from experience just how much of an ordeal it would be to find anything related to past cases. So many records were either lost or destroyed during the Dark Times. Nonetheless, I tried to keep my spirits up.

"Keep us updated, Marv," Cap said as we walked away.

-----:-----

Cap and I made our way downstairs and out the front door. As I stepped outside, I felt overwhelmed by what I saw. A chain of patrol cars extended the entire length of Romeo lane to the bottom of the hill.

"They just started showing up. Tilly, Saints, and even Samson, they're all out there lending a hand. We have officers from four adjacent territories here, helping in whatever way they can," Cap stated as he stood beside me.

Looking outward, I saw that the thunderstorm had subsided to a drizzle, and additional perimeter searchlights had sprung up all over the grounds.

Cap said, "We've already started canvassing the neighbourhood, and we've received a few calls about suspicious trucks and vans. Nothing definitive has come up yet, but it's only a matter of time."

I looked down at my watch and regarded the time ... 10:36 PM.

"We're going to find her," Cap said.

Dalton approached from a distance and gestured to Cap that he would like to speak with him.

A few yards away from me, I could hear them.

"We still haven't found anything," I heard Dalton whisper.

"Keep searching, damn it."

"Yes, sir."

-----:-----

An hour after hour passed, and still no sign of Sara. Eccles, Cap, and I ended up working through the night. We checked in with the canvassers, monitored and reassigned the various search teams, and even scoured over old case files searching for possible similarities. Saints and Tilly volunteered to check in with all registered sex offenders in the area. For all our efforts, we came up empty-handed.

-----:-----

Cap allowed me time away from the precinct in the days that followed, which I used to investigate various potential leads unofficially. Each day, Cap would give me an update on the search. By 11:00 am on the tenth day, however, Cap called me into his office to advise me that although the case would remain open, the official search effort would end that night.

Eventually, the crime scene unit cleared my house. After spending a week and a half at a hotel, I returned to my home, alone and heartbroken. After several tear-filled hours, I eventually picked myself up. There was a part of me that had hope, and I protected it fiercely.

That night, as the sun had set and the majestic searchlights shut down, I felt the battle had only just begun. While standing at the edge of the cliff, I made a promise. I swore with all the passion and rage that I could summon that I would get Sara back. I pledged to never leave this Earth before finding Sara and then bringing her back home.

Chapter 2.3 (Part 3 of 3)

Sara Lago, April 2, 2074. 1:03 AM

It's dark, she can't see much, but there are gaps in the weave of the dark fabric over her head. She can't move her arms or legs.

She is indoors in some building.

How did I get here? She wonders.

She decides to run the events over in her head.

First, she must have been sleeping, and then, there was a hand over her mouth—the smell of cheap aftershave. She tried to scream, but she couldn't. She struggled to regain her breath from the scare she got. She tried to push and punch and kick, but there were two of them, one of them holding her upper body and the other is holding her legs down. The one cupping her mouth replaced his hand with a cloth. It smelled of chemicals, something vile. Then, only black. When she next opens her eyes, one of them is carrying her over his shoulder. Her hands were tied together. The cloth hood slipped off and fell to the ground. She tried to scream, but she realized she had a cloth over her mouth and tied around her head tightly. She looked around and realized where she was, and she was in the field behind the house. She kicked and twisted, she tried to run back toward the house, but this was when she realized her legs were tied together. She felt hands grasping her ankles and pulling her back. They had her again. She needed to leave something, something to show where they were taking her. She clasped the necklace around her head. She felt a thud on her head, then the feeling of cold liquid and then only black again.

Now, she's sitting in a rigid chair with a cloth bag over her head. She hears the sound of several footsteps approaching. They echo with each step. She must be in some kind of a big room with hard floors like the hallways at school or a classroom. The footsteps stop. She hears a voice, and she doesn't recognize them. She then hears the sound of keys in a lock and the creaking of a hinge, and an echoing slam like a metal on metal like the lockers at school when you slam them closed. The sound of more footsteps approaching even closer, or perhaps the same people she can't tell. She can feel her heart pounding in her ears. Then she feels someone touching the cloth hood over her head and stinging pain. She winces.

"What the hell is this?"

"What?"

"Is she bleeding?! Bloody bleeding! You know what our orders were."

"She was going to get away, and the tranquillizer wore off, don't act like you don't know what happened."

"Idiot! The Boss is not going to be happy about this."

"I'll accept full responsibility."

"Damn right, you will."

Suddenly, there was a loud beep and the trill of motor and more footsteps, but these were of just one person. The sound of these footsteps approached very slowly. She counted the paces. As she counted, she could hear shuffling as though the other two men were somehow nervous. Finally, the steps were as close as the other men were, thirty-six footsteps all together.

"Sir, Boss."

"Sir."

Then, she felt it, the feeling on the same part of her head. It felt like being tapped and the same stinging pain.

"Who did this?"

Sara imagined this must be the voice of the third man, and his voice sounded strange, a bit like a robot. It reminded her of some music she'd heard before.

"It was me, Sir. I apologize."

The robotic voice continued, "I said, UN-harmed, didn't I say UN-harmed? Does UN-harmed somehow mean 'bleeding from the head,' where you're from?"

One of the nervous men responded, "No, Sir, you see, she woke up and she was going to escape, and ... well ... No!, NO PLEASE! NO!" The man screamed.

Then Sara heard it, a loud BANG! that echoed loudly and hurt her ears, she couldn't help but scream and then she heard the sound of a series of thuds like a bag of potatoes hitting the ground.

The robotic voice said, "Didn't feel like hearing the excuse at that time. How about you?"

"N-no, Sir."

The robotic-sounding voice said, "Clean up this mess. Give the girl another sedative, and I imagine she'll have a tough time sleeping tonight otherwise. Keep her blindfolded, patch up that wound of hers, close up this cell and let her get some rest. Remember two things from here on in, one, there is an eye in the sky, so I am always watching, and two, if you don't want a bullet in your head, she better not lose a single hair off of HER head. I want her to be utterly and completely unharmed. Understood?"

There was only silence.

"Nod, if you understand, okay! Good. Good. Now, Little-one, I know you're scared, and you want to go home. However, you're going to be here for a little while, and I sincerely apologize for the bump on your head. I sincerely do. From here on in, I want you to know that we won't harm you or keep you any longer than is necessary. Nod, if you understand me."

Sara nodded.

"Good! Good!"

April 9, 2074
One week after Sara's disappearance…
Cameron Maddux

"I'm calling it a day, guys. I'm exhausted," Maddux said as he waved goodbye to the remaining officers in the Pit. Suddenly, his flexphone wrapped around his wrist started flashing, but he managed to cover it with his palm before he believed anyone had noticed.

"Hello?" He said, answering the call from his EarPods, and now in the hallway exiting the precinct.

"You know how a deal works, right?"

Maddux's heart rate jumped, and his throat immediately went dry, the last few steps to fully exit the building before responding. In a lowered voice, he said, "How did you get this number?"

"Not the right response, Maddux. I thought I was clear, we give you the credits, and you deliver the location," The voice said.

Maddux got into his car. He paused for a moment, "I can't do it. I thought I could, but I can't."

"Maddux, you really disappoint us. What do you expect to happen now? Are we supposed to deliver you a refund?" The voice said.

"I'll give the credits back. I don't need them," Maddux said.

The call suddenly disconnected. Maddux was now sweating.

Something didn't seem right.

He started his car and exited the precinct parking lot when his phone flashed, *"New Message,"* Appeared on the screen. Maddux tapped the screen as he drove, and the message read: *"1400 Victory Boulevard."*

Maddux couldn't believe his eyes as he read the message—it was the address to the safehouse Beth used. Maddux felt a shot of adrenaline rise up his body.

Beth was at home, it was her day off, and she had fallen asleep on the couch in the living room.

On the coffee table, her phone flashed, but she was too asleep to hear or see.

Maddux called Beth again frantically as he sped toward Victory Boulevard. His mind raced at the thought of what these people would do to her. He called Beth again, no answer. He didn't know if she was there or not, but he couldn't risk it.

Fuck.

He scolded himself.

He called back the number that had called him minutes earlier. There was an answer on the line but only silence. "Hello? Listen to me, if you hurt her in any way, I swear I'm going to kill you. We made a deal. She would not be harmed."

"You're right. We had a deal, which you broke. You'll never see *her* again," The voice said before the call disconnected.

Maddux told the E-ssistant to release control of the car as he raced frantically to the safehouse.

He called back the number, there was an answer again and then, silence. "If you harm her, I'll…."

"You'll what?! You're a tech geek, Maddux. You don't got the balls to do anything. We have her, call again, and she's dead," The voice said. Suddenly, Maddux heard a terrifying sound, a scream of a woman and then a loud thud. The call then disconnected.

Tears were streaming down Maddux's face as he closed in on Victory Boulevard. His mind was spinning—he knew he couldn't call it in. He'd already broken so many laws.

You can fix this, Maddux. Just think.

<<Victory Boulevard. Arrived.>>

Maddux withdrew a handgun from the glove compartment. He decided he'd gain access to the building by the back entrance, gain some intel on what was happening inside and then. He'd have to call it in. He had no choice. There was no way anyone but Beth or him could gain access to the back entrance, he thought.

Maddux grabbed the handle of the car door with his left hand, which was trembling. He took a breath and thought of Beth and the pain she must be experiencing. He looked in the rearview mirror, wiped his eyes with his sleeve.

"I'm coming, Beth," He said as he climbed out of the car. He approached the row of brownstones and ducked behind the first one and into the alleyway. He approached the entrance from the side, strafing the wall. He was about the enter the building when his flexphone started to ring.

He stepped back to his previous position and answered using his earpods, "Hello?" He said in an ominous voice, terrified of what he would hear.

"Hey, what's up?"

"Beth?"

"Sorry I missed your call. I fell asleep," Beth said.

Maddux sighed. "Are you okay? Are you safe?"

"What? What do you mean?"

"Beth, where are you right now?"

"At home, why?"

Maddux sighed again. "Beth, I messed up."

"What? What do you mean?"

"I got in with the wrong people. I'm sorry," Maddux said as he rushed back toward the alleyway. "Beth, I would never do anything to put you or Sara in danger. You must know this, listen to me; I never gave you up!"

Beth perked up and shook her head in confusion, "Maddux, calm down. Where are you? I'll come and get you."

Maddux turned around as he walked down the alleyway to see three men approaching him, and when he turned back to face forward again, he spotted two more men. One was carrying a gun.

Maddux withdrew his gun from its holster. "Beth, the safehouse is compromised. Stay away. I'm sorry. Beth? I love you. Goodbye."

Suddenly, Beth heard several gunshots ring out. "Maddux!" She screamed. Before the call disconnected, Beth received a message. It was a location tag. Beth realized at that moment that Maddux was at the safehouse.

Beth Lago

I had called in the shooting and had rushed to the scene myself, but all efforts were too late. My dear friend had been riddled with bullets. An investigation into his murder revealed that his sister had been in a hospital dying of a rare blood disease. The kind that was genetic in origin was about as rare as winning the lottery and getting struck by lightning the same day. The detectives later told me that they believed he'd been bribed with credits, enough credits to get his sister the surgery she needed but had been unable to afford. They also told me that Maddux's phone had been replaced with a duplicate, and they had been tracking his movements for some time. Once he had led them to the safehouse one day, they no longer had any use for him, and so they set up this ruse to do away with him like he didn't matter. I had made enemies that I didn't know existed. With the safehouse gone, I put my rogue operations on hold. I felt trapped. I realized that my unseen enemy knew more about me than I knew about them, and until I could gain the upper hand, I'd suffer more losses.

Maddux's sister got her operation in the end. The OLAPD kept Maddux's records, and Maddux's sister never learned her benefactor's identity.

Chapter 3

Dr. Trevor Miles, Wednesday, November 7, 2074

It's been sixteen months, three weeks, and two days since Dr. Trevor Miles' team first started work on The Project.

Each day, they arrived at the lab to spend twelve, often thirteen, hours locked away underground.

All of the fruits of their tireless labours finally culminated at this moment. The anticipation was electric as the team awaited the test results that would reveal whether the last year and a half had been a success or a failure.

Gathered in the central diagnostics lab on the DIT campus, they sat patiently awaiting the results. Trevor was fidgeted in his chair, shifting his weight and rhythmically tapping his pen in rapid staccato on the table. His eyes darted to his hand, and his body tensed as if he had just realized his pen was fluttering as fast as his heart. He ran his fingers through his hair and took a deep breath as he puffed up his chest and flashed his team members a confident smile.

-----:-----

Just under two years ago, Trevor had suffered a failure, which had shaken the foundations of his self-belief. He seldom let himself forget it.

His wife, Tia, also never missed a chance to remind him. Marital betrayal wasn't easily forgivable, and Trevor knew this fact all too well. The consequences of one action can have far-reaching effects. His failure at the Ridge led to his resignation, then an impromptu change of address to the Territory of Francisco Bay. Like a domino effect of causality, each event caused the one to follow, but something unforeseen happened after the move.

A recruiter for Dresdin Industrial Technologies tracked him down. Trevor found himself in a state of disbelief when one of the world's biggest firms contacted him unexpectedly. He had just been reading an article about the company's CEO, Carl Dresdin, only a week before the call.

Trevor had felt butterflies in his stomach upon arrival at the majestic DIT central headquarters that day. It was a late interview at five o'clock. Trevor made sure to arrive early. He waited in his car before marching up the thirteen steps towards the building. The headquarters' main building was trapezoidal. The entrance rose higher than the rest, about three stories. Wrapped in glass, it glittered like a rose-coloured diamond as the sunset glowed behind it.

While sitting outside Dresdin's office, awaiting his hiring interview, Trevor barely managed to keep his nerves in check. As he looked around the Welcome Office, he spotted a stack of magazines on the table in front of him. Naturally, the magazine on top was the one featuring the article he read only days before. The headline read, "Carl Dresdin, Mr. Future?"

When Trevor finally met Dresdin face to face, he remembered thinking the CEO didn't look at all like he had in his picture.

In his sixties, Carl Dresdin had silver-coloured hair and a tall frame. He had light brown eyes and a steely stare. As the two shook hands that first day, Trevor didn't know just how prominently each one would figure in the other's life.

The first few minutes of the interview had gone very well, but for a question that lingered in Trevor's mind. Driven by his great curiosity, he stated his problem with little reservation, "Why did you choose me, sir?"

"I beg your pardon."

"What drove you to seek me out?"

"It isn't often I get asked by someone WHY I'd picked them, but I know your situation is a little different, so I'm going to give you a pass on this one. The reason I sought you out is on account of what happened with you at the Ridge."

"Oh ...," Trevor replied.

"Now, wait, before you get all flustered, listen to me a minute. We all make mistakes, Trevor. Sometimes the way a person carries himself or herself, after the mistake, actually tells you more about them than the mistake ever could have. I don't believe you meant to do what you did. It was a lapse in judgment, but you learned an invaluable lesson there, and I doubt you'll ever make that mistake again, will you?"

"I can, with confidence, say that I will NEVER make that mistake again, sir."

"Good, I know you won't. You understand, of course, that if you did something like that here, then I'd only have one action to take."

"I understand, sir."

"This is your second chance, Dr. Trevor Miles. Don't cock it up!"

On the weight of that first interview, Dresdin had decided to make Trevor a permanent employee at DIT.

By the middle of week two, the rigours of endless psychological and security testing solidified Trevor's grit and self-control. Working for a big corporation wasn't new to him, as he'd worked for several—the Ridge likely being the most notable. He'd garnered a decent understanding of how these companies functioned and learned the nature of the beast. DIT, however, seemed like a different creature altogether. They required police clearances, retina scans, fingerprint analysis, and DNA samples. Trevor found the personality tests particularly concerning. One of the tests, a multiple-choice one, seemed designed to test judgment and ethical tendencies, but Trevor noticed many of the questions only allowed for unethical answers. Trevor figured he'd have to select the lesser of two evils. Trevor hated choosing any evils, so he manipulated his answers. After all, he'd drafted similar tests. Trevor knew he had to answer in the least conspicuous way possible. He needed to minimize the cowboy factor that many of these tests served to identify. The "What would you do?" questions regarding choosing between his loyalties to the company and helping a specific person in danger, if answered truthfully by Trevor, would have shown his affinity toward tragic heroism. Typically, one would see this as a positive trait in a leader. Trevor knew there was a difference between being a hero and thinking of oneself as a hero. They wanted the former and wanted to avoid the latter. It was a tricky thing—an invitation to reveal one's ego. DIT was looking for this type of data told Trevor more about the company than the test would ever reveal about him. Through his answers, he depicted himself the way he suspected they'd wanted him to seem—docile, calm, and trusting that things would work themselves out if only he'd just let it be.

On Thursday of the second week, they presented him with a non-disclosure agreement. The seventy-two-page document tested Trevor's patience and his speedreading abilities. DIT reserved the rights and ownership to any and everything he did at work and reserved the right to take whatever measures necessary to protect itself and its interests. They defined measures necessary to be determined by DIT executive branch and not subject to justification or prior notification. Trevor inadvertently laughed aloud when he'd read that last bit. His laughter stopped at the sight of the serious faces on the DIT legal suit-laden types sitting across from him. After an hour of careful review, he confirmed his tenuous approval with a signature. Minutes later, he found himself in front of Dresdin, receiving a full briefing on the project.

After several minutes filled with shock and confusion, a man named Willy Taylor, director of security at DIT, escorted him to the lower levels. Trevor noticed how different Willy looked from everyone else who worked at the headquarters. Trevor detected no signs of dark rings or puffiness under his eyes, and he had a cool swagger that seemed out of place beneath an impeccably tailored suit.

On that day, the two men walked down the long hallway leading to the elevator, which would bring them down to the Research and Development lower levels.

The DIT Headquarters was a massive complex. It consisted of a network of buildings spread across a half-mile squared campus. Although each of the buildings' upper levels served a purpose, it was within the lower levels that the action took place. Underground tunnels connected the buildings. It was like an underground city complete with an in-house physician, a pharmacy, and a convenience store. There were even small artificial parks with grass and trees fed by UV lighting. The DIT Headquarters' covert operations occupied the underground levels of the main building. Within this structure, the deeper the levels went, the higher the secrecy level and, therefore, security.

Trevor was shocked to find a security checkpoint in the hallway on the way to the elevator.

They'd approached a glass wall with a rectangular doorway, which led to a metal detector and body scanner. Four men flanked the checkpoint. The men were dressed entirely in black with bulletproof vests and automatic weapons slung across their bodies. When they approached, each of the guards nodded at Willy.

After passing through the metal detector and body scanners, the two men walked to the elevator. There was a small console in the wall with a goggle-shaped rubber receptacle. Willy walked up to it and placed his eyes in front of the receptacle. A moment later, there was a beep and trill of gears moving in the wall in front of them. A panel on the wall slid back and to the side, revealing a key slot. Willy withdrew an oddly shaped key from his pocket and inserted it into the slot.

"A new key is given out each day, based on a random rotation. I hope you've been paying attention. Tomorrow you'll be doing all of this on your own. Ensure that you don't lose it upon receiving the key at the first security checkpoint upstairs. If you do, you won't be able to leave the building. If you don't follow all the security protocols during the allotted timeframes, then you could trigger a building-wide lockdown."

The elevators slid open, and the two men stepped through.

"I'm a nice guy, but those brutes back there wouldn't be happy if you were to cause a lockdown."

"Okay."

Willy laughed. He said, "Don't worry. You'll be fine."

"I'm just not used to so much security."

"Is that so? You do know that DIT used to specialize in security?"

"Yeah, I know."

"Good, because your life from now on will be the Project and believe me, you'll be thankful for all of this security when you find out what's down there."

"Dangerous?"

"Valuable."

"How valuable?"

"Some would be willing to kill for it, Dr. Miles."

The elevator doors slid open to a small hall and another retinal scan.

Another door opened in three layers. First, a thin metallic door, a thick geared door of the calibre used in bank safes, and then a glass door. The two men stepped into the lab where Trevor would be spending the better part of his days. Two women and a man stood before them.

"Dr. Trevor Miles, meet your new team."

"Dr. Sylvia Torville, Neurology." A timid woman with short dark hair wearing a plain black dress extended her hand.

"Hello."

"Dr. Pax Sills, Computer Science and Systems Engineering." A short man with dark hair, baggy clothes, and a fidgety disposition shook hands with Trevor.

"... And this is Dr. Marjorie Armande, she specializes in Psychiatry and Neurology just like you." A curvy woman with wavy, honey-brown locks and a slim sleeveless dress shook Trevor's hand vigorously.

"Dr. Miles, I've followed your work for years. I'm a huge fan," she said.

"Thank you."

Dr. Miles tried not to blush over Marjorie's effervescent attitude and her lively appearance. Her light blue eyes sparkled as she looked at him through her long, dark eyelashes.

"Well, now that I've brought your great minds together, it's now time for me to go. Have fun, kids," Willy said as he walked away.

Dr. Miles turned to the three young doctors. He knew he had to say something inspirational, something moving, as his first address.

He remained speechless before finally saying, " It's a pleasure meeting all of you. I have to say the level of security in the building is impressive."

"Well, it's all for good reasons with *Him* locked away down here," Pax said as he lifted his hands and curled his fingers into air quotes just as he said *Him*.

There was a hush in the room as Trevor looked at each of them, attempting to read their reactions. At the time, he found himself thinking back to his briefing with Dresdin.

"Yes, of course, *Him*. I'd really love to meet him," Trevor said.

Marjorie stepped forward. She said, "Well, it's about time you met *Him*. After all, you're going to be spending a lot of time together."

"Well, I think I'm definitely ready," Trevor replied.

"Good, it's right this way," Sylvia said as she walked toward the exit of the room.

Marjorie smiled coyly as Trevor attempted to step past her.

"Well, Dr. Miles, in the next few minutes, your life's going to change."

Marjorie had been right. Trevor's life did change just as all their lives had changed over those last sixteen months.

-----:-----

The project evolved in stages. Naturally, the first stage focused on feasibility. They had concluded that if someone had done it before, then why couldn't Trevor and his team do it again. The question then became, how Like detectives, they had to solve a mystery.

They were reverse-engineering a lost technology, which relied upon a long line of other lost technologies. Yet, they were on the cutting edge of innovation. It was an exciting time. Trevor and his team were becoming increasingly aware of this.

One week, Pax turned to Trevor and said, "You do realize that we'll have to win the Nobel Prize several times over just to get close to succeeding."

Trevor simply smiled. If only that prize still existed, he'd thought to himself. Besides, he doubted if DIT's expectations of secrecy would allow for such a thing. Trevor took solace in the fact that even in their failures, they were still advancing knowledge of the human brain and anatomy. The success of their project depended on their constant drive to innovate.

Pax had limitless resources at his disposal to create a testable version of this technology. Sylvia, Marjorie, and Trevor would then determine the physiological impacts of Pax's contributions. Ultimately, it fell upon Trevor to ensure they developed a perfect marriage between technology and biology.

In spending so much time together, under such extreme pressure, strong bonds had formed. Sylvia and Pax had seemed to grow closer. Pax would vet his prototypes to Sylvia before anyone else. Together, they would present them to Trevor. Trevor had come to trust Marjorie and would often involve her in his decisions. Slowly, over time, a friendly feud began between Trevor and Marjorie, and Sylvia and Pax. Each side raced to bring this technology to life.

----:----

It had all come to this. All of the team's work has led to this moment, the results of this final test. As Trevor waited, he couldn't help thinking about how relieved he'd be. Just getting to this point, however, had come at a cost. Trevor's relationship with his wife Tia, already strained, had declined. He hoped that in completing the project, he could redirect his focus and rebuild his marriage. He resolved that no matter the result, he would prove his unwavering devotion to his wife.

In the Diagnostics Lab, with all eyes transfixed on the screen. Trevor could feel his heart pounding. He turned his head to glance at the clock for a moment. Then, suddenly Marjorie landed in his arms. She hugged him tightly, and he could feel the tempo of his heartbeat speed up. He felt his cheeks warming as she pressed against him. There was a chorus of cheers and applause.

"We did it! Trevor, we did it!" Marjorie said.

Trevor peeked around her hair to see the results on the screen. She was right. They had done the impossible, and nothing short of a miracle.

"Can you believe it?" Pax asked while shaking Trevor's hand. "What do we do now?" he added before Trevor could reply.

"Now, we do two things. First, we're going to crack open a couple of bottles of faux-champagne, and then we're going to call Mr. Dresdin to let him know it's TIME."

Chapter 4

Beth Lago, Tuesday, November 20, 2074

"I hate this part," Eccles whispered.

I rolled my eyes. "Eccles, how many stakeouts have you been on?"

"Officially or unofficially?"

"Okay … so not that many."

"I just hate waiting."

"Yeah, you and I both," I muttered.

I glanced at my watch, 3:14 AM. We still had another five hours to go in our nightshift sting operation headed by Narcotics Division. Parked in an unmarked car, we followed any vehicles coming out of an old storage facility that sat just inside the Scourge.

Within the Scourge, attacks on police were not only typical but expected. Eccles and I knew this all too well. Therefore, our operation required we go undercover.

Much to my annoyance, my cover consisted of playing the role of a doped-up prostitute. Eccles was to play the role of a john. We had to dress the parts, of course. Narcotics Division had entire dressing rooms dedicated to this kind of thing. My outfit included the kind of skirt that was all the rage in the Scourge these days. It was white-patent leather, unevenly cut, with one leg showing almost up to my hip and the other to about mid-thigh. The boots were white, six-inch-high heels, with light blue paint blotches on them. The top was a tight grey tube-top with a silver reflective strip winding around from top to bottom. I had to dye my light brown hair jet-black with a blonde streak on the right side to look authentic. I found the get-up ridiculous, and it made me uncomfortable. Eccles' costume was a lot less complicated—a wrinkled dress shirt, day-old stubble, and a pair of sloppy-looking dress pants. His hair required some effort. He'd spiked it into triangles with metal studs glued to the tips. Again, this was popular attire in the Scourge and essential to our ability to blend in.

"It doesn't look like we're going to get any action tonight," Eccles whispered.

"Action?"

"Yeah, there's no activity at the building at all."

"Right," I replied.

"Wait a second," Eccles said while looking in his rearview mirror.

"What is it?"

"I think I see a van coming."

Sure enough, a grey van drove past us and turned into the parking lot of the compound.

"Wait a second …."

"What is it?" Eccles asked.

"That van looks familiar. "

"Are you sure? Where from?"

I said, "A cold case from a few months back involving the disappearance of a young girl."

"Beth, I know you have been reading up on past cases. In fact, I've been meaning to talk to you about that."

"Okay."

"I'm just a bit – don't take this the wrong way."

"Eccles. Just come out and say what you mean, please."

"I know these last few months have been difficult."

"And?"

"Well, some of the guys are concerned that you might be …."

"Be what?"

"Well, a bit …."

"Obsessed?"

"I didn't want to bring it up, Beth, but not every case is related to Sara."

"That's where I recognize the van from."

"Do you see what I mean?"

"Eccles, listen to me a minute. The night Sara disappeared, Saints was working on that case, and that's where I saw the van."

"I see."

"Something about that case had stuck in my head. A week after Sara's disappearance, the father of the girl came to our precinct. He was fuming mad and demanded answers. Poor Saints, I'd never seen him more flustered," I said, shaking my head. "After Cap escorted the father out of the building, I followed, and I saw the man get into a van just like that one. I remember it clearly because it had impact damage along one side with red paint in the gashes."

Eccles said, "As though someone had crashed it into another car. I guess that would make the van unique. You just don't see damage like that, what with E-drivers and all," Eccles said.

"Exactly!"

The sound of the van door opening echoed down the street. Beside the entrance of the building, there was a dumpster. In anticipation of the sting operation, undercover Narcotics officers had placed microphones behind it. Eccles and I were wearing earpieces, which received the feeds. "What do you think?" Eccles whispered.

"I don't know, but something seems off."

"All right, everybody out!" A man's voice reverberated in our earpieces.

Eccles crouched down in the driver's seat and lifted up a pair of binoculars from his lap.

"What do you see?" I asked.

He pressed the night vision button on the side of the binoculars and then opened his eyes wide. Eccles lowered the binoculars slowly and said, "I'm … I'm not sure."

"Eccles, stop fooling around. What did you see?"

"We should call for backup."

"What? Why?"

"Let's go, everybody out!" we heard the male voice say.

Through our earpieces, we then heard the sound of several children, possibly girls, crying.

"Girls? How many, Eccles?"

"Take a look for yourself," Eccles stated while handing me the binoculars. I peered through the view holes, "Seven girls and one man," I whispered. I opened the car's glove compartment and withdrew my gun.

"What are you doing?" Eccles asked.

"I'm going in there; what do you think I'm doing?"

"You're joking. Right?"

"No, I'm not. Eccles, those are young girls. I can't sit here and do nothing."

"I say we call for back up."

"And then what?"

"We wait, Beth."

"Eccles!"

"Damn it, Beth. We don't even know how many people are in there."

"Well, there are at least seven girls."

"That's all you care about. Right?"

"Right now, yes, that's all I care about," I said. Eccles shook his head. "Are you coming with me or not?" I asked. He paused for several seconds, contemplating what to do. "Well?"

"I'll go with you but at least let me call for backup. Watchdog to Operations, over?"

"Operations, here?"

"Requesting back up ... Possible 10-80 in progress."

"Copy that."

Eccles hung up. He turned to me and said, "I still don't think we should go in there blind."

"Eccles, those girls had dog collars around their necks and chains around their wrists. Every second we waste puts their lives in further danger."

"Watchdog, over?"

"This is Watchdog. Go ahead."

"Sending two uniforms your way."

"ETA?"

"45 minutes."

"They have got to be joking." I scoffed. "I can't wait forty-five minutes."

"Yeah, I don't think I can either."

"Copy that."

Through our earpieces, we heard the sound of yelling, followed by a gunshot blast.

"Shots fired, I repeat, shots fired!" Eccles said.

I got out of the car and started sprinting toward the building. I glanced back to see Eccles following close behind me. We arrived at the heavy metal door where we had seen the man and the girls entering only minutes before.

"Now what?" Eccles whispered.

The brick building had fogged windows lining the top of the wall on either side of the door. I took slow and steady breaths, tiptoed each step as I peeked into every window. My heart jumped when I found one unlocked. Pushing the window inward while rising up on my toes, I realized the hinge at the top allowed it to swing inward by about a foot. I signalled to Eccles to crouch down, and I climbed up onto his shoulders. I pushed the window in and tapped Eccles' shoulder to get him to lift me up further. Legs shaking, I poked my head in through the window. At first, I couldn't see anything other than empty space. Using the ledge of the window, I lifted myself further. I realized that although I had accounted for my waist and hips fitting through the gap in the window, I had grossly underestimated the width of my shoulders and chest. Still in a skirt, I realized that this wasn't going to be easy. I wiggled my way through. On the other side, I clung to the ledge and landed on my feet. I stepped to the door and undid the lock.

"Well, well, what do we have here?" I froze as I recognized the voice as the one from earlier.

I didn't know what to do, so I improvised. "Oh, hey, baby," I said as I turned around. I clenched my teeth as the burly man eyed me from head to toe.

"Are you lost, or is this my lucky day?" the man asked.

I tried my best to shake away feelings of disgust. "That depends, baby. If you can help me score, then I'm all yours."

The man took one large step toward me. He grabbed me by the neck, squeezing my throat, and forcing me up on my toes.

"You're a pretty whore, aren't you?" he said while pulling me closer.

"You haven't seen anything yet. Let's have some fun. Is it just you here?"

"Yeah. Just me and --" He shrugged. "Well, I wouldn't worry about anyone else. You're way prettier than them."

"So it's just you and me, then?"

"It's just you and me."

"That's too bad."

"Why, do you like it when people watch?"

"No, I mean, it's bad for you."

"Why is that?"

"Because you're under arrest!" Eccles said as he burst through the door.

"You damn --" he yelled as he stepped back. He released his grasp, and I fell to the ground.

I yelled at him, "Where are the girls?"

He began laughing like a madman.

"I'll watch him. Go ahead," Eccles said as he pointed the barrel of his gun at the man's head.

Stepping further into the building, I realized it must have been a factory, now abandoned. From the streetlights outside, a dim glow descended from the windows. Metallic pipes extended above my head and then into the shadows. I'd seen the girls enter with my own eyes, but there was no trace of them.

"Hello? OLAPD ... Is there anyone in here?"

Only silence followed.

"Hello?"

I heard the sound of banging and screams. I ran in the direction of the sounds, but there was nothing but darkness. Looking around, I saw a six-by-six-foot metallic square on the ground. I looked closer and noticed footprints in the dust leading up to the square. Dropping to my knees, I banged on the metallic sheet.

"Hello?"

I felt the impacts of thumps from the other side. Sliding my fingers along the edges of the square, I came upon a rope. Wrapping it around my hand, I began pulling it to the side. Slowly but surely, the metallic lid slid open, and once I'd moved it enough, I scrambled to look inside.

From the dark hole, a small hand reached out. I grabbed it, and I pulled my hardest. A hand became an arm and then the top of a head.

I grabbed the arm below the elbow, and I heaved once more. I saw a face and my heart nearly stopped. I recognized her instantly. She was dusty and dirty, and her hair looked tangled in knots, but I knew her face. I'd seen her picture a hundred times. I pulled her up to me and hugged her. She was crying and coughing, but she hugged me back. We'd never met, but we held one another like a mother and child. A sense of relief came over me. I'd found Brooke Hastings. I heard the sounds of more cries from within the dark hole. One by one, I pulled girls out. Eventually, backup arrived. In all, we found fourteen girls in that underground, ten by ten-foot room. They ranged in age from six to sixteen. Sara was not among them.

-----:-----

In the ensuing days, we learned the building had served as a storage facility for illegal drugs list Lust, and it was going to begin serving as a storage facility for exploited girls. It represented but a single point on an entire network of human trafficking.

In spite of having entered the building before securing back up, Eccles and I received commendations. The van I had recognized did belong to the father of that missing girl. He died shortly after going to the precinct that day. It looked like a suicide. They found him in his house with an empty canister of prescription antidepressants. They never managed to find the man's van. Now that we'd found it, Homicide was going to reopen the investigation.

-----:-----

The rescue of those young girls marked the first high point in an otherwise depressing last few months. Although I didn't find Sara among those girls, we did uncover a surprising clue.

In the investigation into Sara's disappearance, we hadn't made much progress. We hadn't managed to identify the palm print found on the picture frame in Sara's bedroom until a Forensics team dusted the warehouse for prints. On the inside of the door, they found a positive match. It seemed likely the perp who had taken Sara had worked for or was working for this criminal organization. As for the involvement of these child traffickers—I tried not to think about it. For now, I felt a renewed hope that Sara might still be alive.

-----:-----

Returning Brooke to her mother was a bittersweet moment for me. In the weeks that followed, I could feel myself slipping back into depression. I thought I could keep it together, but eventually, Cap called me into his office and ordered me to take a week off. After leaving the precinct that afternoon, I went straight to the pub.

-----:-----

The next day, I awoke with a splitting headache. My eyes felt sore. Curled up in a ball, I'd fallen asleep while clutching one of Sara's sweaters.

By noon, I managed to build up enough energy to lift myself out of bed. I glanced at my flexphone. I'd left it rolled up on my nightstand the night before. A brightly illuminated message banner rolled around it. The light from the message reflected off an empty bottle of faux-rum.

<<Cap: Enjoy this time off. See you on Monday>>

In the bathroom, I peered at my reflection. Large rings had formed beneath each eye. I looked as pale as a white birch in the dead of winter.

The events of the last few days had left me lost and confused as if I was awake and active but not present. A familiar haze formed in front of me that clouded my every thought. While peering at my reflection, I felt some of that fog lifting. In the back of my mind, I sensed an idea forming. I reached for a glass and filled it with cold water. Lifting it up to my lips, I glanced at my reflection once more and then it happened. Like a piercing, shrilling flash, the idea hit me.

I reached under the end table in the living room and unfastened the ultraviolet bulb from its hiding spot. I replaced the light bulb in the lamp atop the table, and I opened the curtain slightly.

I sat and waited.

After thirty minutes, I began to worry. He'd never taken this long. An hour later, a message appeared on my phone.

<<Fifteen>>

Two hours later, at exactly 3:00 pm, I was sitting on a bench at the subway station's last stop. I was exhausted. I was out of breath. I paused to replay it all in my mind. I'd done all that I was supposed to do. I'd changed subway trains several times. I'd changed disguises and wigs in four different subway station bathroom stalls. I was certain no one had followed me. This was the last step.

A door behind the bench I was sitting on would be opening at any minute. I heard a creak. I peered over my left shoulder.

The door slid open.

I looked around to confirm I was alone.

I knew, however, there was no way they would've opened it otherwise.

I marched straight through.

The doorway led to a long hallway with faded burgundy-coloured brick covering the walls. The air smelled stale and musty. The end of the corridor appeared to be a dead end. As I approached, the wall pulled back—it was a door in disguise. Beyond it, I could see only darkness. I closed my eyes and stepped through. The door closed behind me.

In the dark, silent, three-by-three-foot room, I heard nothing but my heartbeat. It was speeding up. Adrenaline had carried me to this point, and now I felt cold with fear. Then, the walls of the room lit up as though made of light. My heart sank, and that's when I realized it wasn't my heart at all. The rectangular box I was standing in had actually dropped—I was in an elevator. Now, it was descending. It fell hard and fast for several minutes. Eventually, it slowed and then stopped. The door slid open.

A voice said, "You will proceed to the room at the end of the hall. There you will disrobe and change into the clothes provided. You will then sit in the chair provided and wait."

I followed the instructions precisely. I put on the tight white tank top, white pants and I sat down in the cold silver metallic chair provided. The walls in the room consisted of mirrors. I imagined they were two-way mirrors with dozens of cameras behind them, each of them fixed on me.

A moment later, he entered the room. He wore a dark suit, which must have consisted of the finest fabrics. He was clean-shaven, with light-brown hair slicked back. His charcoal eyes examined me from head to toe. He still had the same smug expression, brimming with confidence. He looked exactly as I'd remembered him, and yet he seemed somehow different. He grabbed a metallic chair from the corner of the room. With a slide and then a clunk, it dropped in front of me.

He sat down and studied my face. His expression then turned to concern.

"Hello, Beth."

"Hello, Cochrane."

He laughed and smiled. "You must be the only person who still calls me by that name. It's just Rogue now, Beth. I haven't seen you for at least ... seven years."

"It's been eight years."

"Right. I imagine you've come here seeking my help."

"I'm desperate."

"If you're coming to me for help, then yes, my dear, you've hit rock bottom."

My head dropped slightly.

"Beth, even though we play on, well, opposite sides. I wasn't pleased to hear what happened to you. If you've come to call in your one favour, then I'd gladly grant it to you."

"I thought you'd forgotten, Rogue."

"You saved my life once. I've been waiting a long time for this day—the day when I could finally return the favour. What do you want to know?"

"Who did this?"

"The kidnapping or the shooting?"

I glared at him.

He said, "Good. You suspected they were related, and I'm quite certain they are too."

"Tell me who did this, Rogue."

"I don't know, Beth."

"Fuck."

"Why do you give up so easily?"

"I don't have time for games, Rogue."

"Would you rather that I tell you lies? I can't give you information that I don't know."

"What information do you know?" I asked.

"Did the ballistics team recover any shell casings from the sight of the shooting?"

"Yes, they found dozens. The patrol car was riddled with them."

"Did they find anything unusual about them?"

"No, all standard calibre, generic and untraceable."

"Then it's just as I'd suspected," Rogue said before withdrawing an item from his pant pocket.

"What's that?"

"This, my dear, is supposed to be a myth. It's an open-jacket, detonate on impact, heat-seeking bullet."

"Why didn't we find one of those?"

"Well, probably because only one was fired and lucky for you, it missed. This is the bullet that nearly ended your life, and as far I know, it hasn't been invented yet."

"What are you saying?"

"It's simple, really. The people who wanted you dead are very powerful people. There is only one question you should be asking," Rogue said.

"Why."

"Why would someone try to have you killed? Why did it have to happen at that exact moment? Why was it not earlier? Why was it not later? Most crucially, why would someone take your daughter?"

"I don't know."

"Think, Beth. What's happened to you since they took Sara? What could someone assume would happen to you as a result of this event?"

"My life would stop."

"Exactly, your life and your work would completely stop. It's ironic, isn't it? The daughter of a woman, who investigates child disappearances, disappears. This can't be for the sake of theatrics."

"They knew I wouldn't be able to work Missing Persons anymore. Why would that matter? Wouldn't someone just step in and take my place? They must've known that investigations into Missing Persons cases would continue without me. It doesn't make sense."

"Right. Another detective would fill in for you and pick up where you left off. So why go to all the trouble? Unless you happen to possess information that no one else knows. Unless the combination of this information and investigating Missing Persons somehow poses a threat."

I couldn't hide the surprised expression on my face.

He said, "You didn't think I knew about your little task force. I'm a trafficker of information, Beth. This is why you came here, isn't it? This is why you brought yourself here to the belly of the beast."

"How could you know?"

"We were intercepting communications, highly encrypted. Do you know what these communications contained?"

"Tell me."

"We found instructions for the reprogramming of OLAPD's Policing databases."

"We were right."

"You were."

"What about the source?"

"We were never able to confirm where they had come from. There was no doubt that messages were aimed inside the OLA network. Beth, that's not all we found either."

"What else?"

"The day of Sara's disappearance, someone within the OLA network sent out a message carrying a series of numbers."

Numbers appeared on the wall.

I said, "They're coordinates."

"Coordinates to your house, Beth."

I shook my head.

Rogue continued, "You have a clue from the warehouse, don't you? It's okay. I know. A palm print, right?"

I nodded.

Rogue said, "Undoubtedly, your database searches have come up empty. Do you know why?"

"I have a feeling that you do."

Rogue dropped an E-sheet in front of me. "That is a classified file containing the identification of the owner of your print. He's a contractor of an extreme kind. His allegiance is to money and money alone. I'm afraid he's already dead."

"What?"

"There's a silver lining here. Two weeks ago, we tracked a money transfer to a bank in New Boston. This guy walked into that bank last Tuesday and walked out with over 200,000 credits."

"Who owns the account where the money came from?"

"We're not sure, but we think certain corporations are using the account to disguise certain covert operations."

"Which ones?"

"We're not sure."

"Can you find out?"

"Possibly. If I do, then …."

I said, "We'll be even."

"Good, Beth, it's been a pleasure as always. It's time for you to go, though. I shouldn't have to remind you to watch your back. Trust no one. It seems like you're not a threat to your enemies right now. Perhaps they think they've crippled you. Maybe they think they've broken your spirit. As long as they think that, then you're safe. Good-bye, Beth."

Rogue stepped closer. I felt a needle-prick on my neck.

When I opened my eyes, I was on that same bench in the Subway station. My head ached even worse than before, but the pain disappeared quickly. I was one step closer to finding Sara, and that's all that mattered.

Chapter 5

Beth Lago, Tuesday, November 27, 2074

A week had passed, and I still hadn't received word from Rogue. One night after a long shift, I decided to visit a downtown pub for a quick bite and a faux-beer. Earlier in the week, the mayor of OLA ordered the push back of the city-wide curfew to 10:00 pm. As a result, the downtown patios were bristling with people.

Walking along the sidewalk as I approached the Redtail Pub, I spotted a familiar face. It was Cap sitting on a patio, enjoying a drink. As though seeing Cap in such a relaxed setting wasn't enough, I did a double-take when realizing who sat across from him. There is only a handful of people I could recognize from behind and at a distance. The posture, the movements, and the mannerisms all screamed out at me. It was my old friend Willy Taylor. Driven by instinct, I stutter-stepped and ducked into a nearby café, then wondered why I was skittish. I suppose there are certain people that one would rather not run into accidentally. I hadn't seen him for years, and I didn't feel prepared to greet him appropriately.

On the drive home and for the rest of the evening, I found myself thinking back to the last time I'd seen him. I also wondered why he and Cap were sitting together.

-----:-----

The next day Cap called me into his office. When I entered, I noticed two men, whom I didn't recognize, leave abruptly.

"Those guys are from Internal Affairs," Cap said.

I nodded.

He said, "I have an assignment for you. I just needed special clearance before moving forward."

"I see," I said. Cap stood up and extended his open hand to one of the chairs in front of his desk.

I sat down.

Cap looked at me and then passed me as though searching for something on the horizon, and then he returned his gaze. "Beth, how are you doing?"

"Okay. I think."

"I don't want to hound you or make you feel smothered, but I will always want to make sure you're okay."

"I appreciate that."

"Beth, there is some information that only a few people have ever seen – sensitive information. I don't want to put you in an awkward spot here. I would ask someone else, but I'm afraid IA won't allow it."

"Okay …"

"I need you to put together a high-level report regarding Missing Persons – missing children." Cap cringed as he finished his sentence. The crows-feet bordering his clear eyes, flexed.

"Okay."

"Don't include any specific information regarding any open cases. Don't include any names, suspects, or investigation details. All we need is a census of sites of disappearance over time with frequencies for both."

I nodded.

"They need accurate information. A database search could produce false negatives. We need a person to do this manually."

"All right, then. How long do I have?"

"One week."

My jaw dropped. I knew there wouldn't be enough time to gather up all that information that quickly. I had a momentary flashback to the last report I'd done regarding Missing Persons case files. This, however, was different. Back then, I'd been looking for manipulation of data. This time around, I was assessing the severity of the situation. I knew what I was going to find wasn't going to be pretty.

"I'm counting on you, Beth," he said.

-----:-----

As I slogged through old cases for the next week, I wondered who would receive the report. I handed it into Cap early on the day of the deadline.

That evening, I had a meeting with Drew Jord, the private investigator I'd hired to work on Sara's disappearance at a café on Almeida. He was an interesting character, always wearing sweaters – even when the weather called for a t-shirt. This was only my second meeting with him. He seemed very thorough. He had useful connections in some of the neighbouring territories' police forces. He asked for pictures of Sara from different angles and at different distances. He had access to some exciting technology. He called it "Next-gen." His eyes would light up each time he used that term, without fail. The tech consisted of facial recognition software that was more precise than the one used by Ocular. More importantly, it could dynamically consider the subject's ageing using all sorts of complicated algorithms. He planned to search the Internet using the new images and the software. He also had a search bot that could search machine-to-machine, so even if a printer had received an image to print from a computer over the Internet, this bot could search it, find it, and track it back.

On my way to the house, I passed the Redtail pub. Stopped at a red light, I peered to the passenger side, and I couldn't believe my eyes. Cap and Willy were once again sitting on the patio. I ducked down. When the light turned green, I drove to the nearest off-street and parked. I checked my reflection in the rearview mirror and walked toward the Redtail Pub.

As I approached them, I pretended to look surprised.

"Willy? Cap? What are you guys doing here?"

Willy rose from his chair.

He'd only aged slightly and looked a bit more polished. He was wearing a neatly tailored suit. He still smiled through his light brown eyes, and his hairstyle had changed. His usually curly blondish-brown hair was now slicked backward.

"We're just having a faux beer – enjoying the fresh air," Willy replied.

Cap had risen as well. He looked more than a little surprised. At that moment, a waitress appeared with an e-bill. She handed it to Cap.

"I didn't know you two knew each other," Cap said.

"We met at the Academy," I replied.

"Okay, then. Well, I was about to go home to my lovely wife. Anna is expecting me for dinner. You're free to take my spot if you like," Cap said as he gestured to me from across the metal gate of the pub patio.

I looked over at Willy. He nodded approvingly.

I said, "I don't know. If you guys were leaving, then I could just …."

Willy said, "I was going to stick around for a while. Why don't you grab a seat? We can catch up for a bit," Willy said.

"Right," I said with a smile.

As I walked around the gate and into the patio, I saw Cap and Willy shake hands. Cap's back was to me. He looked over his shoulder. I pretended to look away, and I noticed Willy tucking a folder into his bag. The folder seemed uncannily familiar.

-----:-----

After sitting down, there was a long pause.
"You look great," Willy said with a smile.
"Thank you. You do too."
The patio lights turned on.
"Thank you. Geez, how long has it been?" Willy asked.
"Too long."
Willy lowered his head slightly. "Beth, I'm sorry about what happened with Sara."
"Thank you, Willy. I'm still hopeful. I'm not giving up. So, how long have you been in town?"
"About two months. I was thinking of calling you, but I wasn't sure if I should." Willy's eye wandered around the patio.
"Why not?"
Willy lowered his chin. "Well, I don't know. I thought maybe you were upset about me leaving without saying goodbye."
"Maybe a bit, but it was a strange time for all of us."
Then it occurred to me the reason I'd been avoiding him. I was worried he was still mad at me. At the Academy, we'd grown close. I'd considered him one of my best friends. In many ways, I'd admired Willy. He had a lot going for him. He was handsome, smart, and funny. He even had a way with the ladies. Perhaps most importantly, he had all the makings of an excellent cadet. For all his positive traits, he did have some faults. Willy had always been very confident, perhaps over-confident at times.

I remember one day, six months into our 12-month program, Willy received word that his sister had fallen ill back in New Texas. Willy's parents had feared she wouldn't live much longer. One night over a pint of faux beer, he explained that his sister had an immune disorder and that she was often sick. Despite the urgency in the emails he'd received, he decided against leaving right away. It was one month before Christmas break.

"I'll go back after midterms," he'd said.

True to his word, he went home during Christmas break, but sadly, his sister died before he could see her a final time.

He returned a broken man. In the days that followed, he became increasingly distant. When he started missing class and falling behind, I decided someone had to do something. My attempt to reach out to him, however, ended in an argument. The next day, he disappeared. At the time, I'd wondered if perhaps I'd been too harsh. I wondered if I'd handled things differently, then maybe he would have stayed.

"Beth, I'm sorry for leaving like that."

I turned my gaze back toward him. "I was worried about you."

"I know."

"I'd thought that I'd said the wrong thing."

Willy said, "No, no, you didn't do anything wrong, not at all. I just needed to get away and work things out. If anything, that talk helped bring me back to my senses."

"Then why didn't you say goodbye?"

"I have a thing about saying goodbye."

"A thing?"

"Yeah, I don't do it. I hate saying goodbye," Willy said with a smile.

"So ... Are you living back in New Texas?" I asked.

"No, actually, I moved closer to here in Francisco Bay, where I work." He withdrew a business card from his vest pocket and slid it across the table.

"William Taylor, Director of Security, DIT. Wow, Willy, sounds like a great gig."

"It is Beth, and it's an amazing company. The things they're doing are going to change the world – make it better. They're working on a project that's going to help eliminate tragedies like the one you're living through right now."

I perked up in my chair. "Do you mean disappearances? How?"

"I'm so sorry, Beth. I shouldn't have mentioned anything. Of course, you'd want to know more, but honestly, I can't elaborate. This company is so secretive, and they've been so good to me. I can't betray their trust."

I shook off my annoyance. "Okay. Well, nonetheless, I'm happy for you, Willy. It sounds like you've done well for yourself."

We spent the rest of the evening reminiscing. In the back of my mind, however, my thoughts kept drifting back to the project he'd mentioned. When it was time to part ways, we simply said, "See you later." We exchanged contact information and agreed to see each other again soon.

Chapter 6

Beth Lago, Monday, December 10, 2074

After arriving at the precinct, I found everyone huddled around a television in the center of the Pit. I'd never seen such a thing—everyone's attention focused in the same direction.

"What's up?" I asked.

I was collectively hushed.

I approached the television. As I peeked between the bodies, I could see that it was a press conference. A man was standing in front of a microphone. A background banner read, *D I Technologies.*

"We now hand it off to Dr. Lamont, director of the project and the man who made the initial discovery."

A short, bespectacled man stepped forward. Bald and slightly chubby, he blinked and squinted his dark, round eyes.

"A little over four years ago, a Dresdin Industrial Technologies recovery team entered an industrial park shown here. DIT had bought the 150-acre lot years earlier. As you can see, it was quite weather-worn and filled with buildings on the verge of collapse."

A slide appeared on a screen showing rundown stone structures.

"On August 31st, 2070, they made a discovery that will revolutionize our everyday lives and the security of our society."

There was a chuckle from the officers around me.

The light from an e-sheet glowed back onto Dr. Lamont's glasses as he read, "What we found, we've named Patient Zero. Frozen in a sealed tank, we found the body of a man with very peculiar implants in his head. Dresdin Industrial Technologies scientists spent the last few years studying these implants in the hopes of uncovering their purposes. I led the investigation, and I am very pleased to share our discoveries with you today. The collection of implants was installed in the human brain for purposes of recording real-time data and storing it on this."

He lifted his hand, and the camera zoomed in on a tiny chip he was holding between his thumb and his index finger. It couldn't have been bigger than a quarter-inch or so.

"This tiny chip has the ability to record 900,000 hours of information or, put another way, over 100 years. The unknown creator of the implants designed them to record all of Patient Zero's senses. I now hand it off to the CEO of Dresdin Industrial Technologies, Carl Dresdin, to complete the second part of our presentation."

A well-dressed impeccably groomed older man approached the microphone.

He stepped in front of a row of men. I examined their faces closely, and sure enough, I spotted Willy.

Carl Dresdin said, "As you know, security remains a grave concern. When we look back and think of all that we've been through, it becomes glaringly clear that we don't feel safe. Kidnappings and disappearances continue, and the number of unsolved cases continues to rise. Many of our sons, daughters, and grandchildren have disappeared without a trace. This will all end today with the birth of Digital Eyes.

"Digital Eyes will ensure that someone is always watching. A tremendous amount of effort has gone into making this invention safe, and we've already received government approval for human trials. To prove to you just how much I believe in this innovation, I will be allowing my son to be the first to receive these implants. Digital Eyes will ensure that if anyone dares commit a crime against the most vulnerable members of our society, there will be irrefutable evidence available to convict and execute said perpetrator. We hope that one day all parents will see this as a way of deterring criminals from harming our most innocent with impunity."

"What a load of crap!" one officer yelled.

"Kids aren't disappearing!" another said.

"Hey! Shut up!" Eccles barked as he put a hand on my shoulder.

"I'm sorry, Beth, I didn't mean anything by it," the officer said.

"It's okay," I replied as I walked away.

I spent the rest of the evening thinking about the press conference and Digital Eyes and how this connected back to Sara's disappearance and the virtu-card I'd received that night. Each of these threads was entwined with one another, but how?

If this technology was real, then it was a fantastic innovation. I decided it was time to go rogue again and conduct my own investigation into DIT and Digital Eyes.

Chapter 7

Dr. Trevor Miles. Tuesday, December 11, 2074

Trevor's jaw ached as he drove to work. He tended to grind his teeth whenever feeling stressed. He was still enraged from seeing the fraudulent DIT press conference from the night before.

When Trevor returned from work yesterday afternoon, he'd heard Dresdin's voice the instant he'd walked in the door. He'd been trying to figure out what his boss might have been doing in his house. When he stepped into the living room, he saw that Dresdin was, in fact, on the television speaking of the project that Trevor's team had slaved over for the past sixteen months. The entire press conference had been staged, but to what end? Why give other people credit for the job that his team had done?

-----:-----

Having arrived at work, Trevor descended in the elevator then entered the team's lab. Each of the team members looked visibly distraught. His first instinct was to comfort them, but the words escaped him.

He took a deep breath. "About the press conference last night, I have as many questions as you do. Does anybody want to discuss how we're going to handle this?"

There was no response from the group.

Pax was sitting in his usual chair. Normally, he would have placed his feet on the table with his arms crossed. Today, he was leaning forward with his elbows on his thighs, in a thinking man's pose. Sylvia sat at the table with her typical perfect posture, and Marjorie was leaning against the counter, sipping her faux coffee. All of them had the same wide-eyed stare.

Trevor's eyebrows furrowed at the silence and blank faces, "If you think I'm happy about this, then you're wrong. I'm just as angry as you are. We need to talk about what we're going to do."

He examined each of them. Again, there was no answer.

As Trevor looked at the stunned expressions, he couldn't help but think they appeared far more surprised than he felt. He'd always had suspicions regarding DIT's motives. The fake press conference had left him startled, but his team looked shell-shocked.

"Look guys, I have a meeting with Dresdin in a few minutes. I'll get some answers," Trevor said.

"You might want to think twice about that," Pax said, now slumped in a chair in the corner of the room.

"Why do you say that, Pax?"

"I don't know. Forget I said anything," Pax said as he tilted his head slightly to the side and then nudged it a few degrees backward, indicating to Trevor to look up and behind him. Pax was reminding them of the camera mounted in the upper corner of the room.

"What time is it anyway?" Pax asked as he peered at Trevor directly in another cryptic gesture.

Trevor quickly tried to discern what Pax was saying. The first thing he'd wanted to tell them was about the camera, which was a valid point if Trevor assumed correctly. The use of the cameras gave Dresdin an obvious advantage over them. Whatever they felt regarding this, they needed to know that Dresdin could always be listening. Regarding the reference to time, Trevor didn't understand it at first, but after a few seconds, he realized that Pax had also pointed to his shoulder when asking the time. Trevor nodded at Pax. Though the sleeves of Pax's polo shirt covered it now, Trevor and the rest of the team knew Pax had a tattoo on his right shoulder that read: "Leap only when it's time." A few months ago, Trevor had asked Pax what the tattoo meant, and he'd explained it referred to an old saying that stated, "Knowing when one should fight and when one should not is vitally important." Pax was right. They were in no position to fight, at least not yet. They first needed to know what they were dealing with. Trevor jotted on his pad, "Meeting tonight at the train station 7 PM". He flashed the message in front of Marjorie's eyes, and she gave a discreet nod. Trevor knew Marjorie would tell the others.

"Well, my meeting is in a few minutes, so I'm going to head upstairs. In the meantime, let's work on the closing report for the project. We'll regroup later on," Trevor said in a loud, clear voice.

Walking down the hall to the elevator, he knew he had to draw as much information from this meeting as possible. In a few minutes, Trevor would be stepping into the office of one of the richest, most powerful men in the world. Most stressful of all was the fact the press conference had clearly indicated that Dresdin could not be trusted. Although everything stated about the project was true, Dresdin had given someone else credit for Trevor's team's work. If Dresdin was capable of lying like this, if he was capable of preventing the world from knowing of their work, what else was he capable of? Trevor had to apply all of his training and expertise to assess Dresdin. Did he have an acceptable reason for lying, and if so, what was it?

Chapter 8

Dr. Trevor Miles

When Trevor stepped through the door, Mr. Dresdin was sitting behind his desk with a giant smile on his face.

"Trevor, please come in."

"Mr. Dresdin," Trevor said with a stiff nod.

"Well, what's wrong, Trevor? Why the long face? Aren't you happy with what's happened here? The work you've done has been an enormous success! I'm very proud."

"I am too."

"Trevor, I need you to stop frowning. This is a happy time."

Trevor said nothing.

Dresdin said, "Oh! I know why you're upset, the press conference? Is it due to the press conference?"

"Well ..."

"Dr. Miles, come over here for a moment, have a seat. You're making me nervous when you stand idly by the door."

Trevor walked over to the leather, upholstered chair. He sat down before continuing his response. "We just don't know what to think."

"You know what? You're absolutely right."

Trevor was too shocked to respond.

"Trevor, I always knew this would need explaining and I had planned to do it personally. The day we called the press conference, a dilemma occurred to me," Dresdin paused as he thought for a moment. "Let me put it this way. You must have noticed all of the security in this building. Haven't you? On your first day, it must have felt at least a little intimidating."

"Yes."

"Trevor, the reason for all of this is due to value. We keep all things of value in this company safe. Though secret at the time, your team's work was the most valuable element of this company. What do you think that says about your team? It says that we value you, and we don't want you to be subject to danger." Dresdin rose from his chair. He said, "Dresdin Industrial Technologies is constantly under attack from other companies wishing to steal what we've worked so hard building. These companies would do anything to thwart DIT and its interests. By presenting you and your team to the world, we would have been essentially presenting you as targets. Do you understand what I'm telling you?"

"I believe so."

"Good! It would be best if you didn't think that Dresdin Industrial is in any way ungrateful for the job you've done. It's the complete opposite. The world of corporate espionage is a dangerous place. You have to be wise, and that wisdom begins with it being protective of your assets. We've learned our lessons from the past."

"The past?"

"Of course ... ah, you would have no way of knowing to what I am referring, would you?"

"I'm afraid not, Sir."

"Don't call me, sir. It's Carl or Carlton, please."

"Okay, so Carlton it is."

"So getting back on topic ... Ah yes, the lessons learned. Before I hired you, I'd say about two years prior. We had an incident. It wasn't very serious. Well, let me put it this way. No one on our side was hurt in any way. The perpetrators faced justice, and ultimately, we learned a valuable lesson. Knowledge can be very powerful, but if placed in the wrong hands – it can cause a great deal of harm. We learned the hard way that the less information people have about how we do things, the better. This incident began when one of our rivals hired several ex-military personnel to break into our offices. They stole valuable files and schematics for various projects. Then there was the kidnapping."

"A kidnapping?" I asked.

"Yes. We had three top-level scientists kidnapped and held for ransom. The intruders broke into our offices and attempted to hack into our servers. Unable to get the information they wanted, the cowards decided to kidnap the scientists working on the project instead. I supposed they'd decided they weren't going to leave empty-handed." Dresdin shook his head. "Ironic, isn't it? Rarely does one hear of a top security company put under siege. We couldn't afford the negative publicity. The scandal would stink to high hell. We couldn't let that happen."

"So, what did you do?"

"Well, at first, we collaborated with law enforcement, we tried to pay the ridiculous ransom, and in the end, the cowards refused to release our people. We had no choice but to go in with brute force and extract them ourselves."

Trevor shook his head. Dresdin continued, "Protecting our assets, it's in everyone's best interest. The products of lessons learned. Once we retrieved our personnel, we committed never to face that situation again. We scrutinize the lives of every single person who walks through that door so no one can attack us from within, and we keep our operations and our movements secret, so we're safe from the outside. Surely, you understand."

"I think I do."

"Good! I should have told you, I agree, but please don't feel underappreciated because nothing could be further from the truth."

"Thank you. I appreciate you saying." Trevor stated.

"Well, I mean it. Now for the reason I scheduled this meeting. There are two reasons. The first is regarding a new project I have for your team."

"A new project?"

"It's a bit hard to describe. The project relates to Digital Eyes, and yet, it differs somewhat. Simply put, I would like you and your team to see if something would be possible."

"Okay, do you have the particulars?"

"I have all of the details in here." Dresdin handed Trevor a folder. Trevor opened it to the first page.

"Digital Eyes: Millennium Phase ... I'm intrigued."

"Once you read it, you'll see what this term indicates, and besides, it's a lot better than 'Phase Two,' Trevor," Dresdin said.

As he placed his hand on Trevor's shoulder, "Digital Eyes was a secret project: this project is going to require an even higher level of secrecy."

Trevor raised his eyebrow then tilted his head for a moment.

Dresdin said, "Read the file, and I promise you, things will become clearer."

"Okay."

Dresdin had been walking around the office as he spoke. Now he stopped and looked out the window. He said, "Dr. Miles, the work you and your team are doing is groundbreaking, not just for the scientific community, but for humanity as a whole. Imagine the power to preserve all of a person's memories. You and your team are giving the gift of permanency, the chance for existence beyond one's life. Despite the risks, it's still a wonderful gift for any loved one."

Trevor sat back as he absorbed Dresdin's passionate words. He understood what Dresdin meant precisely. For all his quirks, the man's words carried a degree of inspiration.

"As the leader of the project, I want to offer you an opportunity. I want to offer you the chance to select a loved one, and when the time is right, I will give you the chance to offer them this same gift. It will be complimentary, of course. Consider it a token of our appreciation for all of the exceptional work you have done for us."

The proposition left Trevor speechless. Oddly, despite his intimate knowledge of the D-Eyes project, he'd never really considered it as an option for him or his family.

"I suspect you'll want some time to think it over, and although you'll likely never admit it, you probably want to see how things turn out with Emil first. My offer stands indefinitely. Do you have any questions?"

"I don't think so. I'm at a loss for words, but I believe thanks are in order."

"Trevor, it's the least I can do. Thanks to you, DIT is now the most famous, and soon to be, the most powerful company in the world."

"Well, thanks again."

"No, Trevor, thank *you*. I'll let you convene your team and begin working on Millennium."

"Mr. Dresdin, " Trevor said with a nod as he rose from his chair.

"Oh, Trevor, wait, I almost forgot. I wanted to give you this." Dresdin handed Trevor a check.

Dr. Miles took it in his hands, and when he looked down and saw the amount, he could barely believe it.

"I hope you like it."

"Good day, Mr. Dresdin," Trevor said as he stepped out of the office and past Dresdin's secretary.

"Well, that was unexpected," he whispered to himself as he loosened his tie and rubbed his sweaty palms together. Although he has learned a lot in the meeting, he couldn't help but feel somewhat ambushed. As he walked down the hall, replaying the meeting in his head, he realized Dresdin had managed to diffuse the situation quite effectively. In one blow, he had distracted Trevor, provided him with a new assignment, an offer he would spend many a night mulling over, and an excessive bonus check. As he descended in the elevator back down to the lab, he had a sinking feeling in his chest. In the mirrored elevator wall reflection, he whispered, "What are you hiding from me?"

Chapter 9

Dr. Trevor Miles

Trevor spent the last few hours of the day reading the proposal Dresdin had dropped in his lap. In spite of its length, the proposal still managed to provide a great deal of vagueness. In reality, it was more like a formal request to do the impossible. Trevor not only had his doubts about the project's feasibility, but the more he read, the more he realized its writer didn't seem to have much of a clue either. To make matters worse, it didn't even seem to follow any contemporary proposal structure. It lacked methodology, and beside the word "objective," it read: "to complete the project." Even the Digital Eyes project, despite its secrecy, had a clearly stated objective, even if that objective ended up changing later on. Halfway through reading, he felt distracted by the prospect of having to present it to his already disgruntled team. He could just imagine Pax's snarky comments. The kid was fiery, no doubt about it. Pax's brilliance could bring a multitude of solutions. However, Pax's tendency to overreact worried Trevor.

Before leaving the office, Trevor gathered his thoughts in preparation for the meeting at the train station. In hopes of calming his concerns, Trevor did some follow-up research on DIT and the incident that Dresdin had mentioned. He didn't like what he found.

----:----

Trevor glanced at his watch. He realized he'd arrived early. He sat down on a bench in the main lobby—the literal intersection of traveller's comings and goings.

Trevor remarked that he still found himself intrigued by the train station's look regardless of the time away. The high ceilings, colourful stained glass windows, and brass lampposts gave the building a nostalgic feel—irrespective of its throwback appearance, the station utilized state-of-the-art technology. The newly invented, magnetically super-charged propelled trains routinely achieved speeds upwards of 750 MPH. Trevor found it interesting that the advent of new technology had made an antiquated mode of travel popular again, even chic.

-----:-----

Glancing up the winding white marble staircase, he spotted Marjorie descending slowly. She smiled in his direction. She had changed into a light blue dress and heels. As she stepped down, he noticed how she seemed to capture the attention of everyone she passed. Every man looked at her and smiled, and women stared at her blankly until she smiled at them, at which point, they would smile back.

"Hey!" Marjorie said as she planted an exaggerated kiss on his cheek.

"Hey."

"Where's everybody else?"

Marjorie turned around and looked up in time to see Pax and Sylvie descending the staircase. Following a round of cordial greetings, they headed to a pub near the station.

Sitting in a private booth, Trevor noticed a collective silence among the group. On the drive to the station, he'd been mentally preparing himself for an avalanche of questions. He hadn't prepared for the opposite. After each of them ordered their respective drink of choice, Trevor decided to start the meeting.

He leaned in towards the center of the table and into the white light from the lamp overhead. "Thanks for coming, guys. We have a lot to talk about, and I didn't feel the lab was the best place to do it. I have some news that concerns us all."

"Is it about the Dresdin meeting?" Pax asked.

"Some of it is. The meeting with Dresdin was very interesting."

"That's an ambiguous statement," Marjorie said.

Trevor raised his eyebrows, glared at her a moment as she managed a close-mouthed smile, all the while softly nudging her knee against his.

Trevor said, "It may seem like an ambiguous statement, but it's the absolute truth. I'm still deconstructing the meeting in my head, but at least I'm sure of a few things."

"Okay, what are they?" Pax asked, again quickly, pursing his lips and striking up a brow.

"Well, we have a new project."

"What kind of project?" Sylvie asked in a near whispering tone.

"Well, it's related to D-Eye, and it's easily the lengthiest proposal I've ever seen. I haven't finished reviewing all of it."

"You're going to have to give us more information than that," Pax said while locking eyes with Trevor and then shaking his head.

"I will, but the primary reason I called this meeting was to discuss yesterday's press conference and everyone's overall reactions."

Pax said, "I think I speak for everyone when I say we're pissed off! I mean, did he even try to explain?"

"Yes, actually, he did."

Sylvie leaned in closer. She perked up in her chair, and her eyes opened wide. "I want to hear this," she said.

"As it turns out, there are a couple of reasons. The first relates to the nature of our work with D-Eye. The new project will continue our current work, and it'll require even more secrecy than before. The second reason is due to a history of corporate espionage threats, which have been directed at DIT scientists working on past projects."

"What kind of threats?" Pax asked.

"Well, apparently, a few years ago, there was a kidnapping involving a group of DIT scientists."

Pax leaned back as he absorbed the news. There was a moment of silence as they all looked at one another.

Marjorie said, "So ... what happened? Were they okay in the end? Did they get them back?"

"Well, DIT retrieved their scientists, but from what I understand, it was only after failed attempts by the police. Taking matters into their own hands, DIT hired a security company to go in and rescue the hostages."

"What do you mean?" Pax asked.

"DIT hired a military-class security company to locate the hostages, subdue the kidnappers, and rescue the scientists."

"So, then, they saved the hostages," Sylvie said.

"Yes. They did," Trevor said in agreement.

"What happened to the kidnappers?" Marjorie asked.

"Well, that's where it gets a bit controversial. The thing is that DIT and the hired security company both claim that the kidnappers died during the rescue of the hostages. A gunfight that ensued, consisting of about 127 rounds fired by both sides, the kidnappers were shot and killed."

"What's controversial about that?" Sylvie asked.

"The controversy comes from the fact that the forensics from the scene don't match up with DIT's statements."

"In what way do they not match up?" Marjorie asked.

"Well, the nature of the wounds suggested execution-style killing. Each of the kidnappers had been shot more than once. The wounds had seemed carefully placed – in either the head or chest."

"They lied to the press about it then," Pax said.

"It looks that way. I did some more research, and I found some disturbing articles about this whole ordeal. Some reporters remain suspicious of the operation, claiming it was staged."

"Why would DIT do that?" Marjorie asked.

Trevor said, "I want to stress that these are just theories, so please do keep that in mind, but the writers of these articles claim they found connections linking the kidnappers back to DIT former employees of the security division of the company."

"They were former employees of DIT?" Marjorie said.

"Well, I don't know if they were or not. No one knows for sure."

"How could no one know for sure?" Pax said.

"Remember, these are just theories," Trevor said.

"Just come out and say it, Trevor!" Pax said.

Trevor had been trying to remain calm, but Pax's outbursts were testing his patience. He could feel his heart speeding up and jaw flexing.

"The article states that no one knows for sure because if they did work at DIT, they would have worked for the division of their security company that conducts ... well, clandestine operations."

"You can't be serious," Pax stated.

"I only did the research. I didn't write these articles, Pax," Trevor stated.

Pax said, "What I mean to say is, how can you tell us all of this and not expect us to worry?"

Trevor said, "What would you have me do, Pax? Would you want me to keep this information from all of you? No, that's not what's going to happen here. We're going to be alert, and we're going to be on point. If I believed we were in harm's way, then that's what I would have said. I think there's a lot of controversy surrounding DIT and Dresdin. Although some of their actions may warrant suspicions, we cannot act on suspicion alone. I tell you all of this so that we can be aware of the dangers out there. We need to tread carefully. That's all I'm saying."

"Okay, well, Trevor, believe me when I tell *you* that if anything happens to any one of us, then I'm holding you personally responsible," Pax growled while rising from the table. He glared menacingly at Trevor one last time before walking away.

"Pax!" Sylvie said.

Sylvie sat frozen. Trevor assumed she was trying to decide what to do.

She said, "I'm sorry about all that. He's been under a lot of stress lately. I suppose we all have. I better go."

"Of course," Trevor said.

Sylvie stood up and hurried off after Pax.

"So, I guess they're ..." Marjorie began saying upon seeing how quickly Sylvie had chased after Pax.

"Yeah, I think they've been dating for a while," Trevor said as he looked forward at the space where they'd been sitting.

"I guess everybody's been able to tell by now," Marjorie said.

"Right ..." Trevor said as he sighed and rubbed his right temple.

"What's wrong? You're not bothered by him, are you?"

"No, not really. I think we have bigger fish to fry at this point."

"Like Dresdin?" Marjorie asked.

"Yes."

Marjorie glanced around the bar for a moment. "You don't trust him at all, do you?"

Trevor sat pensively for a moment without responding.

"Is it because of the micro-expressions?" Marjorie said.

"What?"

"He tends to give off a lot of them," Marjorie said.

"I thought it was just my imagination, but you've seen them too?" Trevor said.

"Yeah, I've noticed them once or twice. What do you think they indicate? Did you notice any during your meeting with him?"

"I have no idea. Dresdin did say a few strange things during the meeting, but no, I didn't notice any micro-expressions. Even if I did, without knowing more about him, it would be impossible to quantify the significance of a handful of facial muscle contractions. We need more personal information about him," Trevor said.

"Well, that shouldn't be hard to find. I mean, the man is famous after all."

"He's famous, but what do we know about his childhood or his schooling?"

"Good point," Majorie said, staring at the ice cubes in her empty glass. "There's got to be a way to get more information."

"All things considered, we don't have enough of a reason to doubt him at the moment. Therefore, life goes on for now, and we'll need to begin working on the new project," Trevor said as he turned to Marjorie, accidentally locking eyes with her longer than he'd wanted.

"That's right. What's the new project about again?"

"Marjorie, we can say what we want about Dresdin, but one thing is for certain. The man has limitless ambition, and the new project, if successful, will be nothing short of revolutionary."

Chapter 10

Beth Lago. Thursday, December 27, 2074

Two more weeks passed, and still no word from Rogue. I was beginning to lose faith.

At the precinct, even amongst tweenies at the mall—everyone seemed to be buzzing about the press conference two weeks earlier. I eavesdropped a conversation or two, and it seemed every voice had determined conviction: every voice, but mine.

-----:-----

It was near the end of the day when Cap pulled Eccles and I into his office. The sun had already started setting, and warm rays descended from the window.

"Ramirez is finally tapped out. Stokes and Krijek are retiring, so Rams asked for my two best detectives. I hate to lose you, but I'm sure you're both going to do great in Homicide Division, Inspectors Lago and Eccles." Cap said while pushing forward a pair of badges he'd laid out on the desk in front of him.

I looked over at Eccles. He had a smile from ear to ear.

Cap said, "Technically, you'll still report to me, temporarily. Rams is retiring too, and Homicide will report to me until we hire a replacement. You haven't gotten rid of me yet."

I smiled. "Thank you, Cap."

"No, thank *you* and congratulations. I'm proud of you."

Word must have spread quickly because a casual celebratory drink turned into a wild party at the Redtail Pub.

We'd taken over the entire lower floor of the pub. It was all precinct cops, and the staff could barely keep up. They were rowdy. The night consisted of hearing the echo of tall tales and the chorus of laughter that tended to follow. At the far end of the glossy oak bar counter, I spotted Saints sitting by himself. He was reclining, both elbows on the table. His head hung low.

I took up the stool at this side. "Hey."

Saints turned his head slowly, his gaze taking several seconds before centring on me. "Beth? Is that you?"

"Saints, how much have you had to drink?"

"Not that much. Not that much at all."

"Saints, maybe it's time you called it a night."

"No, no, I want to celebrate here with you. I'm so happy for you."

"Thank you, Saints."

"I mean it, Beth. I'm just so happy."

I could see his eyes start to tear up. "I know, Saints. Eccles and I are going to miss you guys."

"You and Eccles, you guys are close. Aren't you?"

"Umm, yeah. We're partners, Saints. We're very close."

"Okay, okay. It's just that … can I tell you something?"

"Of course. What is it?"

"Nothing, Beth. I've had too much to drink. Forget it. Maybe I should get home." He twisted himself out of his stool, rocking to one side. I caught him before he dipped too far.

"How are you going to get home? Where's your car?"

"It's here. I'll take a cab. It's okay." He pulled his keys from his pocket.

"No, I was going to leave soon anyway. I'll give you a lift." I guided him toward the exit.

"No, no, I don't want you to leave your party. Not yet."

"It's okay. I was leaving too, Saints."

"Eccles! I'll meet you back at the house," I hollered as I pointed my chin in Saints' direction while lifting an invisible cup to my lips.

Eccles nodded.

I parked the car in front of the concrete building Saints had pointed to before passing out again. He'd fallen asleep a couple of times during the drive.

"Saints, you're home, buddy." I tapped him on the shoulder.

"What? Where are we?"

"You're home. That's your building, right?" I pointed out the passenger window.

"It is! Thank you! Okay then, Thanks again." He opened the door.

I heard a scratch and then a thump.

I got out and ran to the other side of the car, where I found Saints cheek-to-cheek with the sidewalk.

"Saints, seriously, how much did you drink?"

I peeled him off the pavement and wrapped his arm around my shoulders. Somehow, he found his legs, and we shuffled our way up the steps of the building.

Luckily, the doorman recognized Saints and let us in. We took the elevator to the forty-ninth floor and down to room 13. He managed to fumble his keys from his pocket. I helped it into the lock.

"Saints, I like you, but not enough to put you to bed," I said with a smile. "I'm going to lay you down here," I lowered Saints slowly onto a frumpy coach.

"Okay, okay, Beth. You really smell great. You know that?" Saints said, his arm still wrapped around me.

"No, I didn't know that, Saints, but thank you." I pulled away.

"And your hair is so soft." He reached for my head as he descended toward the couch.

I felt a tug on my neck. Saints asked, "What's this?" while holding my two pendants in his hand.

"One of those pendants is mine …."

"And the other?"

"Is Sara's." Saints suddenly turned red, and his eyes glinted as though on the brink of tears. "I see. I'm sorry."

"It's okay. When I find her, I'll give it back to her."

"Are you okay, Saints?"

"Yeah, I've just had a bit too much to drink. I get either angry or sad."

"I see. What is that you wanted to tell me earlier?"

"What?"

"Earlier … You were trying to tell me something earlier."

He paused for a moment. "Beth, just be careful—with who you trust."

"What?" I felt my muscles tighten.

"Be careful, Beth."

"Who should I be careful of? What do you mean, Saints?"

I looked down and noticed Saints had fallen asleep. I shook him a couple of times, but he wouldn't wake. I showed myself out, and I headed home. It was unsettling that my evening ended on that strange note.

December 27, 2074
Dresdin Industrial Technologies - Undisclosed Location
DIT Technician

"I ran the screenings on the Lago girl," The Technician said to his supervisor while standing in the lab. Behind a two-sided mirror, Sara Lago was in a bed taking a nap.

The DIT Supervisor said, "Okay, so what's the problem?"

"Well, there's no problem. It's just that her DNA results."

"Yeah, okay, and?" As he took a bite out of a faux bologna sandwich, the Supervisor said, faux mustard streamed down his hand. "For crying out loud!"

"So our system runs a check cross-referencing all data, including DNA."

"Okay, could you get to the point, please? Will she survive the procedure or not?"

"Well, it's not that. She should survive. It's just that she has a DNA match. It must be a mistake," The Technician said in a shaky voice.

The Supervisor rose from his chair with an annoyed grunt while he crudely wiped his face with a napkin. He said, "Let me see."

The Supervisor took a look at the name on the screen. He quickly reached for the phone, "Get me the boss. Yes, the Big Boss. Dresdin. Yes, I would definitely call this an emergency."

-----:-----

Beth Lago

The next week, I worked a lot of overtime. Eccles showed up unexpectedly one evening.

"Tell me. Is this a happening place on Friday nights?" Eccles asked.

"I suppose that would depend on what you're looking for. What are you doing here?" I lifted my gaze from the computer screen.

"I could ask you the same question."

"I'm just doing my thing."

"Yeah, you're right. This is your thing. Do you know what time it is?"

"No, actually."

"And you don't care. Is that it?"

"It's something like that. Geez, Eccles, when did you become such a nag?" I tossed him a smile.

Eccles smiled back. "I just want to make sure you're okay."

"I know."

"So I'm assuming you watched the second biggest DIT press conference in the last three weeks."

"Who didn't?"

"Emil Day—The world's first D-Eye baby. That's how the headlines are reading."

"Amazing, isn't it?"

"What? Amazing about the technology or about them using it on a child?" Eccles leaned on the side of my desk, arms crossed.

"Both, I guess," I said.

"You have to give Dresdin credit—he's a man of his word."

"Yeah." I shrugged and rolled my eyes.

"What is it? I've seen that look before," Eccles tilted his head to meet my gaze that had focused in the space past him.

"Nothing. I just did a little digging."

"Okay. What'd you find out?"

"Well, I've been looking into the Dresdins."

"Okay."

"As it turns out, Carl and his wife Rose had been trying to have kids for a few years. In the fall of 2070, doctors informed them that they'd never be able to have children of their own. Strangely, it's only recently that they've started trying to adopt. Three years ago, they received the news they'd been waiting for. By all accounts, they were delighted to adopt a baby boy whom they'd named Emil."

"This all sounds pretty normal to me, Beth."

"That's what I thought. Then I ran into some major trouble researching the backgrounds of Emil's parents, the Days. I found a news article that indicated they were presumed dead on account of a car crash."

"Presumed?"

"They never positively identified the bodies. I found another article, an editorial actually, where the reporter claims that she had previously interviewed the Days and they would never have willingly given Emil up for adoption."

"Why would someone have interviewed the Days?"

"It was just by chance. The reporter was doing an expose on the accessibility of drugs in the Red Zone. They just happened to be there that day for an interview."

"So they were drug addicts."

"Yeah, and look what the same reporter published a few days ago." I pointed at the headline on my screen.

"The Days: Alive! Drug abuse: Cause of the adoption," Eccles read aloud. "So what's the truth? What did end up happening to the Days, and did they give Emil up or not?"

"Apparently, Emil's parents had indeed willfully given him up largely due to their drug dependencies." I shook my head.

"I see."

"Eccles, I dug deeper searching for information on scandals or some sort of controversy, but I couldn't find any dirt on the Dresdins or the Days. Every article I found seemed to indicate that the Dresdins were nothing more than caring, loving parents." I leaned back in my chair, crossing my arms.

"Beth, you almost sound disappointed."

"I guess I am. I was so sure that something wasn't right. I just didn't know what that was."

"I guess we all get that from time to time. What was your hunch exactly?"

I looked into Eccles' pale green eyes. I thought about telling him about my suspicions. I knew in my heart that I trusted him. He was my partner, and by rights, there shouldn't be any secrets between us. As I started trying to articulate the words, I realized just how uncertain it all was. I had no proof. I wasn't even sure if I was sure of my own suspicions. It just all seemed too coincidental. There's a growing need to protect children from abduction, and a corporation appears promising to end child disappearances forever. It all seemed too convenient. The alternative, however, suggested a conspiracy too unbelievable to imagine. At the root of it all, somehow, I stumbled upon information that had put my life on the line. I still didn't even know what had set a target on my back. I'd grown to care about Eccles. I couldn't put him in danger too.

"I know what you're thinking," Eccles said, the corners of his mouth curling up.

"Eccles, you always think you know what I'm thinking."

"I want you to know something, though. I probably should have told you this a long time ago. Beth, the way you've carried yourself through everything. Well, it's amazing. The time, though, has come to a stop blaming yourself. You spend hour upon hour chasing every possible lead, every possible hunch. You examine every detail with a fine-toothed comb because you think you missed something that day. You obsess over the idea that you made a mistake somehow. Beth, you didn't miss anything. Nothing you could have done would have prevented what happened. Maybe there is something suspicious about the Dresdins and this whole D-Eye thing. Until you learn to trust your judgment again, you won't be able to see the truth."

I smiled, although my brow still furrowed.

He said, "It's late. Wouldn't you like to get some rest?"

"Alright. Let's get out of here."

"We can probably catch last call …."

"Eccles."

"Okay, home it is. I'm pretty tired, anyway."

-----:-----

In the weeks that followed, Willy began calling me. Our relationship had always been one in which we could lose track of each other for years and still be able to pick right back up where we left off. Not hearing from him was expected. Nonetheless, I found it nice to hear from him again.

We made plans to meet at the local bar, and as the date got closer, I found myself getting nervous and excited to see him. On the night in question, I dressed carefully in a dark blue dress.

"Wow! You look great, Willy!" I said as I gave him a big hug.

"You look beautiful, as always," Willy said with a downward inflection that seemed to emphasize the sincerity of the statement. He kissed me softly on the cheek. Today, Willy's body language and facial expressions reminded me of the Willy of old. He had a habit of smiling ever so often, even when speaking of serious matters. Gradually, the corners of his mouth would curl up.

"So, I saw you on TV at a press conference announcement for D-Eyes!" I declared.

"Which? Ah yes, in the background." He straightened his posture, sat up, and turned his profile to the side. "How did I look?"

"I'd say you looked very professional," I said with a downward nod for extra effect.

We both smiled. I realized at that moment that was something disarming about Willy. I was quite confident that Cap had delivered my report to him. However, within the context of the D-Eye launch, it seemed logical that DIT would request such data. Nonetheless, the secrecy seemed strange.

I said, "How is everything going over there?"

"I wish I could tell you all the things that we're doing, Beth. I think you would be so proud of our work, but ..."

"I know, I know, you can't talk about it."

"Beth," he said as he grabbed my hand from across the table. "... I can't tell anyone about our work, but I want you to know that of all the people I know, I would trust you above all others."

I could feel the blood beginning to rush to my face. I quickly pulled my hand away.

"I'm sorry, I didn't mean to ..." Willy stared at me with a confused expression.

"It's okay. You didn't do anything. It's just that I haven't ... it's been a long time since ..." I struggled as I searched for the words. Finally, I gave a smile and shook my head. "It's just complicated, I guess."

We talked for a little while longer before we both realized how late it had become. We decided to end our evening at around ten o'clock. As I reached up to kiss Willy goodbye on the cheek, I could feel something change in the energy between us. Placing his hand gently on the small of my back, Willy kissed me with a softness I hadn't felt in a man since Sam. I pulled back and looked him in the eyes, which he directed to the ground. When he raised his gaze to meet mine, I could see they had begun tearing.

-----:-----

I hadn't formally checked in on DIT and Mr. Dresdin for a few weeks. Every so often, I would come across an article about another child who was about to undergo Digital Eyes surgery. The parents of the children tended to be either rich or famous or both. I found the fact to be somewhat elitist, considering DIT continued to publicly assert that their product would soon become readily available to all. So far, the D-Eye baby count had risen to eighty-nine children, with the sharpest rise in procedures following Emil Dresdin's surgery.

From what I gathered, Emil had begun attending school and was leading a very normal life. All reports indicated that he'd adjusted well and had continued living the life of a typical, albeit privileged, child.

Chapter 11

Dr. Trevor Miles. Wednesday, February 13, 2075

In the diagnostics lab on the DIT campus, the team spent another day working on the Reverse-Looping Project. Dr. Miles had left Marjorie in charge as he'd fallen ill that day. That morning his eyelids felt heavy, and in the mirror, he spotted giant pillows beneath each eye. The point of him having stayed home had been so that he could get some much-needed rest. Unfortunately, he did everything but rest. Instead, he spent the morning responding to emails, reviewing files, and carefully organizing his inbox. By noon, he was driving to the lab.

When Trevor arrived at around 2:00 in the afternoon, Marjorie greeted him as he exited the elevator. She had a furrowed brow and a stiff lip.

"Hey, how's everything going?" Trevor asked as he sidestepped around her slowly. He gestured for her to follow him down the hall.

"That ... could be a loaded question."

"Could you elaborate, please?"

Marjorie stopped walking. Trevor stopped dead in his tracks and turned to face her. He hadn't noticed at first, but Marjorie had been carrying a clipboard behind her back. She pulled out the clipboard and placed it in front of them, and she stepped closer to him. She stood facing his side while holding the clipboard in her left hand. As Trevor reviewed it, she leaned in close while gently placing her hand on his forearm. He'd hardly noticed. She often invaded his personal space—her perfume—the smell of rose petals mixed with something sweet. Trevor looked down at the e-sheet then the waves of statistical data it held.

"Well, we have some new diagnostics reports," Marjorie said in a slightly elevated tone. She leaned even closer. She whispered, "We need to talk."

Trevor whispered back, "Is everything okay?" He then continued in a louder tone, "Okay, great, looks good so far."

Marjorie whispered, "It's about our progress. It's imperative." She pinned on a cheery smile. "Yes, we've been making great progress. Still, though, we'll need to run more tests," Marjorie said loudly.

"Okay, fine, tonight at 7:00 at the usual watering hole," Trevor whispered back before saying aloud, "Alright, thanks for running the tests. I'm going to check in with Pax and Sylvie," Trevor walked away down the hall.

He spent the remaining two hours of the day contemplating why Marjorie needed to talk. He suspected that perhaps the team had made a breakthrough but wanted to talk it over before communicating it to Dresdin.

Trevor only checked in with Sylvie and Pax briefly before heading back to his office. He had become increasingly comfortable with the small office Dresdin had afforded him after the first D-Eye project's completion. At first, he had resented the image—the manager locked away in an office. He had always felt more comfortable as a hands-on leader, preferring to be in the lab with his team where all the action took place. His perspective had begun to shift slightly over his tenure at DIT, however. Out in the lab, Marjorie seemed to follow him around constantly, trying desperately to distract him. Her efforts were successful. She did have something about her, though. A charm that was both disarming and deliberate. He couldn't deny his attraction for her. It was a strange feeling. It was a warm feeling, but it put him off balance. Sometimes, it felt a bit overwhelming, like looking at the sun—bright, beautiful, and intense. He was happy to have a place where he could escape and get some peace. Still, though, Marjorie wasn't the only one he felt like avoiding from time to time. The chip on Pax's shoulder had grown over the last few months, especially whenever Trevor was around. Despite Sylvie's calm, gentle qualities, Pax always seemed a step away from the edge. All in all, Trevor's office was his sanctuary, and the refuge it provided had become increasingly necessary.

Trevor had assumed a new commitment in the last few weeks. Today, however, his eyes felt sore as he read the files from the original D-Eye project. He had begun allotting time every week to review the files. It was an idea that had arisen from a meeting he'd had with Pax three weeks earlier. Pax had approached Trevor with an unsolvable problem, as he'd put it. The two had spent hours working it when Trevor realized the problem bore a striking resemblance to one they'd resolved during the first D-Eye project. However, to draw from the knowledge of that experience and apply it, they'd need the files. DIT had rigorous operating procedures regarding the D-Eye project. One of them stipulated that all relating materials had to be stored away in Dresdin's personal safe upon the project's completion. At the time, the team had agreed, as there had been no good reason to require access to the files once they'd completed the project. They'd complied without question, as they hadn't expected the Reverse-Looping project. When Trevor had first approached Dresdin with the notion of gaining access to the files, he hadn't seemed too amenable to it. Eventually, he let Trevor review the files under the condition that the files never leave Trevor's office. He also ordered that they remain locked away in Trevor's office safe when not in use.

-----:-----

Later that evening, after quickly eating dinner, he kissed Tia goodbye. He promised to be back no later than 11:00. Trevor arrived at the pub, where he'd planned to meet Marjorie. The pub was located on a one-way street just off the strip. There was no brightly lit sign, velvet rope, or group of partiers lining the sidewalk outside it. It was a well-kept secret. The stale, bland air of the outside disappeared quickly as Trevor opened the door to the pub. Stepping inside, he always felt smacked by the contrast between the liveliness inside and the boringness outside. The music was loud. The people were louder. The thing that attracted Trevor the most—they had the best faux-whiskey in town.

Trevor jostled through the dense crowd. Eventually, he reached a clear bit of space where his eyes instinctively focused on a pair of tanned crossed legs through a tunnel of people. As he walked, his eyes slowly rose up. He realized the legs belonged to Marjorie. The satisfaction in her smile was unmistakable.

She was sitting in a booth. She stood up to kiss him on the cheek.

"So, you wanted to discuss the progress of the project?" Trevor inquired.

"Yes. We've arrived at some preliminary conclusions regarding the feasibility of Reverse-Looping ... but ..."

"So is it possible, or isn't it?" Trevor asked before realizing that Marjorie hadn't finished speaking.

"Whether Reverse-Looping is possible or not is not the question we should be asking ourselves. What we should be asking ourselves is if we should even be working on this."

"What do you mean by that?"

"I mean, exactly what I said."

Trevor sipped his faux-whisky as he scanned the bar. Across from him, Marjorie tucked a hanging ringlet of blonde hair behind her ear while trying to read his expression. He had already felt slightly suspicious regarding her intentions in asking him to meet, but she'd said she needed to speak with him urgently.

"Is this the only reason you asked me down here?" he asked.

"Why do you ask that question, and why do you ask in such a tone?"

He glanced around the bar while trying to find the right words. "I'm just surprised ... you said it was urgent."

"Trevor, we're working with very powerful tools, and I'm just worried that perhaps we don't know for sure what our employer's true intentions are."

Trevor looked at her with an expression of lingering doubt.

"That's not all."

She leaned to the side, lowering her hand towards her black satchel. Trevor's eyes instinctively followed her movements until his gaze reached her legs. Quickly, he looked away. She'd worn a skirt to her knees, but whether she intended it or not, the skirt had managed to inch up her thigh. He didn't want to see her long legs, and he didn't want her to think he was looking at them either. He had made some progress in winning back his wife's affections, but he felt vulnerable to Marjorie's advances. The situation resembled one from his last few months at the Ridge, and the reminder was sobering. He felt a mixture of conflicting feelings regarding Marjorie. She was very bright, and he loved working with her from a professional standpoint. Her beauty, however, was just too much for any man to ignore, and she knew it. Even during those late nights, after working sixteen hours straight, she still managed to look beautiful. He knew that he had to be careful around her. After all, she'd communicated her intentions quite directly around the time they had completed the D-Eye project. They had come to this same bar, and after several drinks, shots, and cheerful hugs, they had both become far too comfortable. They had arrived as a group. After Pax and Sylvie left, however, Marjorie and Trevor remained alone. Something happened outside the bar while they waited for a cab together. Trevor had been in the middle of telling a story from his childhood. While reminiscing, he had become distracted for a moment. When he redirected his attention toward her, she threw her arms around him, planted her lips onto his. Thankfully, he had been sober enough to pull away.

The next day, Marjorie made it clear she respected him for doing the honourable thing.

After a few moments, Marjorie finally sat back, a grey folder in her hand.

"What's that?" Trevor asked.

"This ... is the reason why we need to be careful."

She slid it across the table. Trevor hesitated before reaching for it.

"Is this what I think it is?" he asked.

"It should be very clear what it is," Marjorie responded.

"Well, it looks like a full profile file on Carl Dresdin."

Marjorie nodded.

"Marjorie?"

"Yes?"

"This folder is missing a lot of information," Trevor said.

"Yeah, I know."

"It says here that the names of the schools he attended are — undetermined."

"Yeah, I know."

"Well, that's not true. I did an investigation of my own, remember?"

"Yes, I remember."

"The investigation indicated that the reason it had been difficult finding the information was due to Dresdin's actual first name: Carlton, not Carl."

"I'm aware of all that, Trevor."

"Okay, then you must also be aware of the fact that all of the data was confirmed under the name Carlton Dresdin."

"Well, I know that there were records of a Carlton Dresdin attending three schools during the years Carl Dresdin was of elementary, prep and high school ages. The fact that those records exist is not in dispute."

"Okay ... "

"I hired an agency to check out each of those schools. I wanted more than just proof of records ..."

"Wait ... let me guess, it's in the folder, right?"

"Yes."

"I'm going to read it, but I think I already know what it's going to say," Trevor stated as he put the folder down. "Carlton, as an alias, never actually existed, did it?"

"Exactly, you've guessed right," Marjorie said, leaning in.

"Creating a phantom Carlton Dresdin couldn't have been easy."

Marjorie added, "It couldn't have been cheap either."

"Money doesn't seem to be much of an issue for the Dresdin family," Trevor stated.

Trevor rested his chin on his thumb and his index finger in a pensive pose. She said, "Why would someone do something like this?"

"Well, the truth is, some of the clues are in the mystery itself. We know that something must have happened during the years Dresdin attended school."

"Great, that only covers eighteen or nineteen years."

Trevor smiled.

She said, "Well, it's true."

"Not necessarily. You see, this isn't just a slice of years. It's an entire portion of his life. Clearly, Dresdin doesn't want us to know the man he was. He's gone to great lengths to eliminate any trace of the real Carl Dresdin. It's difficult to eliminate a person's past. The void that remains leads to suspicion. Therefore, he created a completely new version of himself to replace the old. I think we can logically deduce a few things from these actions."

Marjorie paused before responding. "The first is that the Carl Dresdin we know is a façade. Some parts are, at least. If not the entire image."

"I agree." Trevor's face lit up for a moment as he acknowledged they were both on the same wavelength.

Marjorie continued, "Secondly, we can presume he must have hired someone to complete all of this truth concealment. These types of actions don't happen by accident. Someone with very clear intentions executes them. Our search for the truth must begin by putting together a shortlist of the people who would have had the means to carry out this type of deception."

"I couldn't agree more," Trevor stated.

"There is one thing that we're forgetting, though."

"Oh?"

"The list of actual schools Dresdin would have attended is most likely short. Even while Carl was growing up, the Dresdin family was still obscenely wealthy. If all else fails, we'll have to check out each of those schools, one by one."

"You're right, but only as a last resort. No one can know about what we're doing here. We can trust no one."

"You mean to say we can trust no one except each other," Marjorie said with a soft smile.

"Indeed."

He inhaled quickly as though something had occurred to him.

"The investigator you used to get all this info, do you trust him?" Trevor asked.

"I think it's pretty much guaranteed. A man with a crush is easily predictable."

"Oh, I see."

Marjorie giggled lightly before leaning across the table and pressing her hand on his. "Don't worry. He'll never be able to take *your* place," She said before laughing.

Trevor smiled back. "What can I say, Marjorie? We still have a lot of work ahead of us, but this is a great start."

"What's with the 'we' talk?" Marjorie asked.

"Well, you're going to need help with all this or are you saying you'd rather work on it alone?"

Marjorie gave an emphatic smile. For a moment, the light from the lamp overhead seemed designed to make her glow. Trevor knew he might be getting himself into trouble, but he couldn't see any alternative.

Trevor said, "Getting back to our original conversation — is Reverse-Looping possible or not?"

"Well, that depends."

"Depends ... On what?"

"It depends on the level of sacrifice you're willing to make."

"What sacrifice? What exactly do you mean?"

"Based on the work we've done so far, it may be possible, but there's a huge catch."

Chapter 12

Beth Lago. Thursday, February 28, 2075

I arrived at the precinct one morning to find Eccles looking like a mess. It wasn't like him to show up to work unshaven, wearing wrinkled clothes. He didn't have a flair for fashion, but he tended to dress professionally. Today, his usually neatly combed light-brown hair pointed in every direction like an extreme version of bedhead. As I drew closer to greet him, I noticed he smelled funky too. He barely acknowledged my presence.

"Hey, Eccles."

He just stared back at me. He was somewhere else. There was a look in his eyes of total distraction.

I sat down at my desk.

"Hel-lo, Eccles," I said in a clear tone, hoping to pull him gently from his preoccupied brain. "Are you okay?"

"Sandy left me," he snapped.

"I'm so sorry," I said, unable to disguise my astonishment. As I looked at him, I felt compelled to ask so many questions. I resisted, deciding instead to let him do the talking.

"She's been seeing someone else … She said that I don't care about her enough, that I don't put her needs first. She even said that I spent too much time at the precinct. Can you believe that?"

I once again bit my tongue. The fact of the matter is that we routinely worked fourteen-hour days. I had no idea how Eccles carried himself as a husband except for the few hours that I'd seen them together. If time away from each other was a factor, then she may have had a point. Sam had always given me a hard time about the same thing, and I hadn't even made detective back then. Overall, despite the time spent apart, I still didn't feel it justified her infidelity.

I walked over and sat down beside him. He was slumped over in his chair. I put my hand on his shoulder. "I'm sorry," I whispered.

"I can't be there anymore. I need a place to stay for a while." He looked up at me with bloodshot eyes. He paused as though awaiting a response. Though he hadn't yet asked me for anything, I still felt a need to extend an invitation. He was my partner, after all, and really, I had plenty of room at home.

"Look, I'm sure this thing will blow over. People get confused sometimes. Why don't you stay with me while you wait for things to work themselves out?"

"Really? You don't mind?"

"Of course, not ..." In truth, I didn't mind it in the least. I cared about his well-being overall. Besides, he really did need to get out of such a negative situation.

-----:-----

Two days later, we moved some of Eccles' belongings into the spare bedroom at the house.

As time passed, I grew increasingly surprised by how comfortable it felt having Eccles around. He turned out to be a great roommate. He was helpful, cleaned up after himself. He even assisted with some unfinished projects I had going on around the house. I was getting tired of doing everything on my own. I'd never minded the thought of being alone, but after a while, it had started to weigh on me. Having Eccles around turned out to be a refreshing change. A couple of weeks had passed, and we'd settled into a nice routine. Everything seemed to be going well until one night when Willy picked me up for a dinner date.

Willy was supposed to pick me up at 9:00 pm. I had strategically planned to answer the door before Eccles in order to avoid any awkward situations, but Willy arrived fifteen minutes early. I was just finishing getting ready when I heard the doorbell from my bedroom upstairs. I planned to run down the stairs, but Eccles had already answered the door.

"Hello." I could hear Willy say. I decided to wait at the top of the stairs before descending.

"I'm Willy. Willy Taylor."

"I *know* who you are," Eccles responded in an abrupt tone.

"Right, you must be Eccles?" Willy said.

"Yes, Beth and I are partners ... at the precinct," I noted right away that Eccles felt the need to add the last bit.

"Is she around by any chance?" I could hear the nervousness in Willy's tone.

"Yeah, I'll call her down in a minute ... Now listen, I have friends who studied with you at the academy, and I've heard all about your way with women. I'm going to say this in the clearest way possible. I swear if you hurt B – "

"Hey, guys!" I interjected in an overly cheerful tone, deciding to make an entrance before things turned violent.

"Hey," they responded simultaneously without turning away from each other.

"Is anything wrong?" I asked as I grabbed my purse from the counter and glanced one last time in the mirror.

"No, not at all," Eccles responded as he moved away from the door. The tension in the room faded slightly. I assumed that Eccles felt he'd made his point. I avoided indicating any sign of knowing what was going on.

"See you later!" I said as I walked out the door.

"Have a good night," Eccles said as he walked away.

"It was a pleasure meeting you," Willy called.

"You bet," Eccles grumbled.

We left the house and climbed into Willy's car. Willy drove one of the more high-end electric cars on the market. Since laws had prohibited the use of hydrocarbons, all cars were electric. Willy looked to have made an extra effort to look stylish, even opting to wear a tie. This was our fifth "date" in total.

It wasn't until about an hour into our night, after a couple of bottles of faux-beer, that Willy asked about Eccles.

"So, your partner is a bit protective, isn't he?"

"Yeah, he can be. He's harmless, though, and his heart is in the right place."

Willy looked around as if he was selecting his next words carefully.

"Beth ... I want you to know that ... well, I care about you a lot."

"I care about you too, Willy."

"No, you don't understand ... I want ..."

I couldn't bear to see Willy so flustered. As he looked down in embarrassment, I leaned across the table.

"I know ... me too," I said as I kissed him on the cheek.

I looked into his eyes as though completely lost in time. I pulled away suddenly as my heart was pounding, and I felt dizzy.

"What's wrong?" Willy asked.

"Nothing ..." I said as I looked downward.

"It's okay, Beth ... look at me a moment ... I'm not going anywhere. I want this, and I'll wait as long as it takes," Willy said in the sincerest tone imaginable. I looked at him for a few seconds and wondered how many women he might have used these charms on before. My mind started racing. There'd been a very clear reason Willy and I'd never connected romantically. I had seen and heard too much about his conquests to trust him fully. Perhaps I was still in a vulnerable state. I decided it was time to end our evening.

"You're very sweet, and I'm glad you're willing to wait for me. I just need to take it slow for now."

"You don't trust me, do you?" he asked as if he could read my thoughts.

"I do trust you, Willy."

"Good, thank God. Of all people, I want you to know that I will never lie to you."

I got the sensation that Willy was alluding to something else at that point.

"Why are you telling me this? Of course, you wouldn't lie to me." I wondered why he needed to reinforce my belief in him.

Willy straightened out his posture and sat upright. "Just promise me one thing."

"Yes, what is it?" I responded quickly. His tone had started to scare me.

"Whatever bad thing anyone says about me, don't believe it."

"Willy, I don't under–"

"Just agree. Please," Willy said, extending his hand across the table and bowing his head and then lifting it again.

Looking into his eyes, I saw genuine concern. He looked at me, then his hands. As though his last hope lay in me reaching out for it.

"I promise," I said as I clasped his hand. In return, he tightened his grip. He exhaled a huge sigh of relief.

"Thank you, Beth."

Despite my curiosity, I elected against questioning Willy further about his ominous statements for the remainder of our time at the restaurant.

At our evening's end, while parked in front of my house, Willy gave me a soft peck on the cheek. After climbing out of the car, I looked on as Willy drove away. Standing on the porch, while gathering my thoughts, I took stock of the night. Part of me readily accepted the idea that I may never know what Willy was talking about. I wanted to let go of my inhibitions regarding our evolving relationship, but I just couldn't. Willy was keeping something from me. I just couldn't tell if it was bad or good. When I entered the house, I noticed that Eccles had already gone to bed. I found this odd, as when we'd pulled up to the house, I thought I'd seen the blinds move slightly.

Chapter 13

Dr. Trevor Miles. Thursday, February 28, 2075 (*Time frame concurrent to the previous chapter*)

After arriving home from work, Trevor quickly changed his clothes and started preparing dinner. This was his Thursday ritual—their ritual. Since the move to Francisco Bay, he hadn't missed one dinner.

He would do anything and everything possible to repair the damage caused by his unfaithfulness. Simply apologizing would never be enough. Tia reminded him of this fact constantly.

"Words are just words," she'd say.

Every Thursday, he made sure to arrive home before Tia to prepare dinner.

The quality of the dinner was a different story altogether. He checked and double-checked the recipe. He still questioned how a recipe for a faux pumpkin risotto could precisely list all the ingredients but the most important one—pumpkin. He'd already spent an hour searching for all the materials he needed. The pots, pans, measuring cups, spoons, and a series of glass bowls all lay on the counter. Cooking wasn't his strong suit. He glimpsed at the clock as he briefly considered giving up.

"Damn it," he whispered under his breath. "Now, what am I going to do?"

He glanced at the three packages of formula on the counter. All he would need to do is add water, heat them up, and then clean up any trace of his embarrassing attempt at a home-cooked meal. The formulas consisted of all the vitamins and nutrients the body needed. They received the vaccines monthly by mail. Each order contained the three formulas, one for each of the meals of the day. It also had supplements necessary for the proper absorption of the vaccine for the plague. Law mandated compliance with the formulas and the monthly vaccine.

Looking at the mess in front of him, he wondered how Tia had managed all this time.

Trevor resigned himself to the fact that he was going to make this work. He dipped a spoon into the pot for a taste.

"No flavour is better than bad flavour," he said to himself.

Opening a cupboard, he panned for the right seasoning.

Suddenly, he heard a loud thud followed by a bump. He judged the sounds were coming from the back of the house. He hustled down the long hallway towards the three bedrooms at the end of the bungalow, where he flicked on the exterior lights—peering out each window as he passed. He saw nothing suspicious. Looking out the tall window beside the door, he decided it was safe to unlock it. He turned the doorknob. He eased the door open, gently, but felt the force of a push inward.

"Tia?" he asked.

"Trevor! Thank God," she replied as she gasped for air.

"What happened?" he asked as he wrapped his arms around her. "Tia, why are you shaking?"

"I think I was being followed."

"What?"

"It was so strange."

Trevor felt his protectiveness kicking in. He took a quick look out the open door. After failing to see anything suspicious, he shut it firmly.

They sat down at the kitchen table. She was still trembling.

Wrapping her in a linen blanket, Trevor asked, "Did this person follow you all the way home?"

"No. I don't think so."

"Tia, tell me what happened from the beginning. When did you first realize you were being followed?'

Tia lifted her gaze upwards as though trying to remember.

She said, "It started when I left work. I'd taken the elevator down to the garage."

"Alone?"

"Yes."

"Tia."

"I know, Trevor, but there wasn't anyone else around. I was one of the last to leave the office."

"Okay. What happened next?"

"Well, I'd parked the car close to the elevator like you'd told me. Before stepping out of the elevator, I made sure to have my keys in hand. The car was close, but I still peered out the elevator to make sure there wasn't anyone around."

"Was there anyone around?"

"No, well, at least I didn't see anyone at that point. I stepped out. I walked to the car," Tia paused for a moment.

"What is it?"

"I didn't see anyone in the parking garage, but ... You ever just feel like someone is near you? I could feel someone's presence."

"Okay."

"Standing at the car, I looked around quickly. I saw nothing. I entered the lock code for the door. I inadvertently looked up. That's when I saw him. I saw a man's reflection in the car window."

"What did he look like? How close was he?" Trevor asked.

"I only caught a glimpse of him through the reflection in the driver-side window. I think he had blonde hair ... and a slender face, and a tall, muscular frame. He was standing under the light, making no effort to hide. He must have been in his late twenties or early thirties.

I was so rattled that I screamed and dropped the keys. I opened the car door and slipped in as quickly as I could. I turned to look back, and he was gone. It was like he'd completely disappeared."

"He disappeared."

"I know it sounds strange, Trevor, but that's how it happened."

"Okay, so what happened after that?" Trevor asked.

"I got out of there as quickly as I could. At the garage exit, I swiped my card. I peered back one last time, and there he was again. I couldn't believe it. He was standing by the emergency exit, purposely staring at me with a strange look, Trevor. Now that he stood by the doorframe, I could see him clearly. He was abnormally large, almost seven feet, and his shoulders were wide."

"I'm glad you got a good look at him. The police will need an accurate description when we go to the station tomorrow."

"The police station?"

"Of course, Tia. We're going to report this to the police and then to the security at your work. This is absolutely unacceptable!"

"Hon?"

"Yeah?"

"You're yelling."

"Well, of course, I'm yelling. I'm angry."

"Well, try to calm down, Trevor."

"All right, all right. Wait a second. You said that you were followed."

"I was. I didn't know, though. I didn't know until I was almost home. Driving up to our street, an older woman stepped out from between two parked cars. I didn't see her until the last second. I slammed on the brakes, and I heard the screech of tires behind me. Somehow, I'd managed to brake in time. I'm not sure the old lady even realized what had happened. I glanced back into the rearview mirror to see how closely the car behind me had come to slamming into me. I couldn't believe my eyes. It was the same large man from the parking garage."

"So, he did follow you all the way home. We should go to the police station right now."

"We can go tomorrow, Trevor. The important thing is that I'm all right now. I was just a bit startled, that's all."

"Tia, if anything happened to you, I don't know what I'd do."

"Nothing will."

Trevor lowered his head. He said, "Tia, I want you to know that I'm sorry about everything that happened."

"I know you are."

"You mean everything to me. I think that sometimes people get confused. All that's happened has shown me one thing— I can't live without you. Tia, there's something that I want to ask you," Trevor said.

"Before you ask me anything, I have something to tell you."

"You do?"

"After seventeen years of marriage, I refuse to believe we can't fix this— us. You've been trying, and that means a lot. Tonight, seeing your concern, it's making me want to open myself up to forgive you."

"Really?"

"I miss you. I've been missing you. As hard as you think the last few months have been for you, they've been just as hard for me. I wasn't equipped to deal with this. Imagine I'm at home one day, and suddenly a reporter shows up asking if I wanted to comment on the allegations against you. I figured it must be some kind of cruel joke. Then he shows me pictures of my husband kissing another woman. I was devastated. I'm so thankful that Sean wasn't home to see all of that."

"I know. I know. I'm so sorry. You're right Sean doesn't need to see that. I think about that very thing almost every day."

"He wasn't there that day, but he still, nonetheless, experienced the fallout. He came home so many nights covered in bruises and scrapes, all because he felt responsible for defending his father. You're still his hero. You probably always will be."

Tia's words affected him heavily.

"We still have a long way to go, but I want you to know I'm willing to fight for our marriage."

"I'm so happy to hear you say that."

"Well, I think it's time."

Trevor didn't say anything but simply hugged his wife. After a few seconds, she hugged him back.

She pulled away and said, "You said that you wanted to ask me something."

"I do."

"What's it about? Is it about work?"

"Yes, it is. It's about Digital Eyes specifically, and well, you. I think you better sit down for this."

Chapter 14

Beth Lago. Friday, March 1, 2075

When I awoke the morning after my date with Willy, I descended to the kitchen to find Eccles already dressed and eating breakfast.

"Good morning!" he said in a cheerful tone.

"Good morning."

"I made you breakfast—formula 11-1. All set and ready to be enjoyed."

"Great. Thanks."

"Did you sleep well?" I asked as I sat at the table with him.

"I slept very well, thank you," Eccles responded without making eye contact.

"Eccles."

"I better get going. I have to run a few errands before work," Eccles said as he rose from the table.

Eccles' demeanour was definitely perplexing, at first upbeat and then abrupt. I wondered if this related to my date with Willy. Was Eccles jealous? The idea didn't feel completely farfetched since we did spend a lot of time together. I didn't know how he felt about me. I remembered when we'd first met. I'd acknowledged him as attractive with a certain mysterious charm. Maybe he'd become attracted to me. Overall, there wasn't much sense thinking about it. It would never work. He was in the middle of a separation, and I liked my relationship with Willy.

-----:-----

When I arrived at the precinct, I met back up with Eccles, and we began our day as normal. Our first order of business each day had been to meet to review our progress on the cases we had pending at the time.

As we closed up our weekly roundup meeting, I glanced down at my watch and realized that we'd finished in one-third the time. I remarked to myself that it's only during moments like these that one notices a clear measurement of change. The conference room had been reserved at this time every week for MP round-up meetings. The meetings were always three hours long, today's meeting took one hour, and last week's meeting took only two hours. The signs were visible at every turn, fewer violent crimes were happening, and the numbers were dropping quickly. Just for kicks, I decided to analyze the data one afternoon. From the start, I noticed that the frequency of violent crime reports, irrespective of geographical location, was dropping. Much to my surprise, a clear line seemed drawn in the sand. From one date in the past until now, the data indicated a decline. I pulled up a calendar just for confirmation, the date that DIT announced Digital Eyes was the line at which things began changing. Since that day, violent crimes against children had dropped by eighty percent. At least on the surface, it looked as though DIT's experiment was working. I began to wonder if these positive results could somehow transfer to adults as well. By sheer coincidence, DIT announced they'd started performing successful surgeries on adults later in the day. This wasn't overly surprising, as it had always seemed to be an eminent part of their plan, however until now, no clear timeline had been set. It became apparent that starting with children had simply been a marketing ploy by DIT, a clever marketing ploy at that. They'd effectively preyed on the public's fears.

I still hadn't received word from Rogue. The violent crime rates had dropped. At the moment, I had no clear reason to suspect DIT. Nonetheless, I couldn't help shaking the feeling that something was about to happen—things were far quiet.

Chapter 15

Eddie "Saints" Santi. Monday, March 4, 2075

Saints watched the sunrise that morning. He hadn't slept a wink. The light sheet that covered them contoured Elle's body. The softness of her legs invited his caress. Her dark hair, like thick velvet ribbons, shined at each loop. He took a mental photograph. After all, this would be the last time he would wake up beside his wife.

He'd arrived at a crossroads, the guilt had been too much to bear, and he knew he'd be walking to his death. He couldn't continue living with his betrayal.

Gently kissing Elle goodbye, he wondered if she would ever know what horrible things he'd done to ensure her safety. Saints used to always say that everyone had a weakness. He didn't think he'd been speaking of himself all along.

-----:-----

In the dead-end alley, Saints made his stand.

"I'm out ... For good."

"Excuse me?" the tall blonde man asked.

"I'm not doing this anymore."

"Let me tell you how this is going to work. We tell you when it's over." The man said while lifting his index finger to his ear. He said, "Sir? Yes. I will, Sir, it looks like you'll get your wish, Saints. After this last mission, you'll get your freedom."

"What last mission?"

"You're going to drop off a package."

The blonde man withdrew a duffel bag from the trunk of the car and handed it to Saints, "Here."

"What's in the bag?"

"Just some documents."

"And why can't you use someone else for this?" The blonde man simply glared at him.

"They're OLAPD e-sheets, aren't they?"

"Go to this website at precisely 3:14 PM. An encrypted comment on the site will appear for thirty seconds. Decode it. Those will be your instructions."

"Okay. Fine," Saints said.

"You look relieved, Saints," the blonde man said while crossing his arms. He had a broad smile on his face.

Saints smiled back with a confident glint in his eyes, as he knew that he wouldn't live out the day. He said, "She will be unharmed. Elle will be safe?"

"That was the deal."

Chapter 16

Beth Lago. Tuesday, March 5, 2075

Eccles walked up to my desk. He whispered, "I need to talk to you."

"Okay."

"In private."

In Eccles' car, he turned up the music.

"Okay, so I need to tell you something," Eccles said while locking eyes with me.

I remained silent and still.

"I've been working on something that no one knows about."

"Okay."

"Beth, there's a mole in the department. Maybe even more than one. I have good news, though. I have a lead. I think I've identified the mole."

"Eccles, should you be telling me this?"

"You're joking, right? I trust you, Beth. You trust me. Don't you?"

"Of course, I do."

"Okay good, because I'm going to need your help to bring him in."

Eccles explained how he'd done it. He told me about the three-man con team that included a hacker called the Omen. It seemed that the Omen had sold a unique encryption program before getting pinched. All the more impressive was the fact that he'd embedded it with a very useful piece of code. It was a command that, if activated, would send out a message every time the encryption program activated. Not only would the message contain the decoded message, but also the last location where the user had used it. He'd asked to speak to his arresting officer—Eccles. He offered up this information in exchange for an extension on his death sentence.

"Beth, could you believe they had the nerve to use the program while in the precinct? Then it hit me. Anyone who would use this software in that location had to be playing both sides."

"What did the message say?"

"Central train station. Main lobby. Adelaide side. 5:46 PM."

-----:-----

Eccles and I discreetly filled gym bags with the equipment we'd decided we'd need for our sting from the equipment room. We grabbed bulletproof vests, rifles, and a couple of two-way radios.

At 5:15 PM, we were in the train station parking lot.

"I still think I should be the one to go in," Eccles said.

"Eccles, you're the better shot. I need you to cover me."

"Fine. I'll be right above you in the central ventilation chamber."

"All right, let's go," I said while stepping out of the car.

I took up position in the main lobby of the train station. I glanced upwards briefly. Large columns of light cascaded down from the glass ceilings onto the crowd of travellers below.

"Are you in the nest?" I whispered.

"That's an affirmative," Eccles replied.

"Time check?"

"5:37."

"Okay."

"You know, just as a side note, red hair looks pretty good on you."

"Very funny. Try to focus, Eccles."

"Alright. We'll talk about the wig later … do you see anything down there?"

"Not really. I don't see anything even remotely suspicious."

"It's 5:41, Beth."

"Copy that. Oh, my God! Do you see my twelve o'clock? He's leaning against the post."

"Son of a bitch. It's *Saints*." Eccles said.

"I'm going over there."

"No, Beth! You can't make contact. We're not even at the deadline yet."

"Fine. He's holding a dark blue bag. Are you seeing this?" I asked.

"Yeah. I guess they were going to do an exchange."

"I wonder what kind of an exchange."

"Yeah, well, it looks like we have a no-show. It's 6:00, and no one else has shown up."

"Eccles, I don't think this is going to go down. I'm moving in."

"Copy that. Take him down."

I started walking around the lobby's perimeter and then to the area behind the post where Saints was standing. I came up beside him.

"Hello, Saints."

Saints whipped his neck back in apparent shock. He asked, "Beth? What are you ...?"

"That's right, Saints. It's over. I'm bringing you in, you son of a bitch."

"Beth. Wait a second. Something's not right. How did you find me?"

"Good old detective work, Saints. How did you think?"

"Beth. Listen to me. I don't know what you think you know, but this isn't possible."

"What in the hell are you talking about?" I asked.

"This is a setup. You're here because they want you to be here. Which means you better get out of here."

"Okay, Saints. This is what's going to happen next. We're going to walk out of here together. I have a Taser pressed up against your spine. If you try to run away, I will take you down."

"Beth. I'm sorry. I didn't know what they were going to do to you. I had no part in that. I didn't know about Sara."

"Don't say her name. Don't you dare? You don't get to say her name."

"I don't know where she is, Beth. But I can tell you that," Saints said, before suddenly jolting backward. Bright red blood splattered outwards from his chest. I ducked down and withdrew my gun. All around, I heard screams of panic spreading across the crowd like the flames of a brush fire.

"Eccles, what the fuck!"

"That wasn't me."

"What?"

"That wasn't me, damn it!"

I reached down, scrounging for the bag. Suddenly, something hit me from behind, knocking me off my feet.

"Arghh ... Eccles, I'm hit."

"Fuck, Beth. I'm going down there. Can you walk?"

"Yeah, I think so."

The majority of the people had fled the lobby. I managed to crawl to the stairwell, where I found a security guard. He helped me down the stairs.

Eccles appeared at the bottom of the steps. I was about to call out to him, and then it happened.

The ground rumbled. There was a sound like a thousand trains slamming into one another. A wall of smoke and dust pushed us back. Then I saw only black.

-----:-----

I awoke hours later in the hospital. When I opened my eyes, I found Eccles slumped over in the chair beside me. I'd suffered a concussion. The bullet hadn't penetrated through the vest. I was lucky to walk away with nothing more than a bruise.

The bag Saints had been carrying contained a bomb. It made a hole that spanned the entire ten thousand square-foot lobby of the train station when it detonated. Saints was right—someone had set him up. The shockwave destroyed the lower levels as well.

In the days that followed, search teams sifting through the rubble discovered a network of hidden tunnels. They also found large chambers that had collapsed. The bodies were unrecognizable except through DNA comparison. They confirmed one of them as the criminal known as Cochrane Rogue. I realized that Saints had been right. It was a trap. My enemy had killed the mole in one move, almost killed me, and eliminated my best chance at identifying him. I was back at square one.

The only thing that kept me going was the hope that Sara might still be alive.

Chapter 17

Dr. Trevor Miles. Wednesday, March 6, 2075

In the main diagnostics lab, Dr. Miles and the rest of the team were having a heated discussion about Reverse-Looping.

"Why don't you guys get it? Look, it's just like Marjorie said. It's only possible if the patient is dead," Pax said, a clear streak of annoyance in his tone.

"How can you know for sure?" Dr. Miles asked.

"Okay, remember how this all started? Just the very nature of the way the brain and the system work together makes it impossible. The implants are designed to record, not playback."

"But, we've been able to playback during our tests?" Trevor said.

"Yes, but only after extracting the implants and using lab equipment."

Trevor had been slowly pacing around the room. He knew Pax was right. He'd come to the same conclusions. He hoped, however, that a healthy discussion might reveal an alternative solution.

Pax said, "We've done well getting this far. We needed Patient Zero from the start, though. None of this would have been possible without him. We learned. We adapted. We replicated." Pax got up from his chair. "Let's review for a moment. Before the insertion of the implants, the right and left hemispheres are communicating in precisely the way they should. One hemisphere detects the sensory input but does not alert the subject or make the subject conscious of this input."

"It holds the information back," Trevor said as he rose as well.

"Right. The other hemisphere detects the sensory input, but before making the patient conscious of the input, it passes it through the brain's cognitive filter so that the patient can understand what the input is concerning. Once this hemisphere has gauged the importance of the input, it relays it to the other hemisphere, and then magic happens."

Trevor said, "Both hemispheres release the information to the subject's consciousness at the same time."

"And, the subject is completely unaware of what's happened. They believe they're perceiving reality as it's happening, and they are ... it's just delayed by fractions of a second.

Putting it crudely—the implants rest between the two hemispheres recording the transmissions. In effect, we built on top of a preexisting neural bridge. We're seeing the implants fuse to the brain stem. Now we can't remove the implants without damaging the Subject's brain," Pax crossed his arms, "This is why we can never remove the implants from a live patient."

"We could download the data, though, right?" Marjorie asked.

Pax said, "Yes, we can, but only after the Subject is dead. The transmission between the hemispheres is constant. The implants can record data, but they can't transmit data while they're recording."

Trevor said, "Fine, Pax, the Sending Subject cannot be alive when the implants are extracted, but what about the Receiving Subject?"

"What do you mean?"

"Well, weren't you saying that both the Sending and Receiving Subjects cannot be alive during the Reverse-Looping process."

"No, no, no, what I said was that there would be extreme complications for the Receiving Subject, but I don't know if they would die or not. All I know is that something dramatic would happen to the Receiving Subject."

"I see."

"Unfortunately, we're at a crossroads," Pax said.

Sylvie had been standing off to the side in a pensive pose. Dr. Miles knew from experience that this had often been her M.O. She would appear uninvolved, then suddenly, she would drop in a solution and stun everyone.

"Maybe we're going about this the wrong way," Sylvie said as she rose from her chair. "Maybe, we need to understand why Dresdin wants this to be done."

"I think that they'll probably want the Reverse-Looping so that they could ... I don't know, preserve someone's memories after they die and then experience them," Trevor said.

Now that he actually verbalized the concept, it suddenly didn't seem as simple as it had before.

"Why?" Marjorie blurted out while standing cross-armed.

Trevor sat back for a moment, "Indeed. Why?"

Pax said, "Thank you, Marjorie, finally someone with a little common sense. The logistics make it impossible. We just don't have the technology to take the recorded transmissions from one person's mind then implant them into someone else's consciousness. The best we can do is record it. Then at a future date, when the patient passes away, we can just take that info from the disk and use it for playback. Translating it into communicable data is hard enough. Let alone transplanting it into another person's brain. That is what it is, right?"

"Wait a minute, Marjorie's right."

"We've determined that already, Trevor," Pax said.

Trevor said, "No, wait a second. Why would you want to implant one person's memories into another person's mind? Actually, we're not even talking about memories here. We're talking about consciousness itself. Why would anyone want to experience someone else's experiences? What could anyone gain from that? I can thoroughly understand the idea of recording someone's experiences and preserving them. This concept is logical enough, but why record and replay the experiences of a loved one in one's mind?"

"What if it's not intended for a loved one?" Sylvie asked.

"You think we'd go to all this trouble for a stranger's mind. Sure, that makes much more sense, Sylvie," Pax said, rolling his eyes.

"Wait, Pax, hold on a second. I think she's right. If she means what I think she means, then we wouldn't need to play back the entire feed. Only a portion, which in relation to a life, would be a very small portion," Trevor said. "We need to know the reason Dresdin wants to do this."

Trevor got up off his chair and headed for the door.

"Trevor? Where are you going?" Marjorie asked as she followed him.

"I'm going to see Mr. Dresdin," Trevor said as he exited the room.

Marjorie followed him into the hall.

"Wait, Trevor. What are you going to ask him?"

"I'm going to ask him the question I should have asked from the start."

Marjorie glanced over her shoulder and noticed that the hallway was empty. She had been hoping to get Trevor alone, if only for a few moments. She hugged his arm.

"Wait. I want to talk to you."

"Not now, Marjorie."

"Please, I just want an answer."

Trevor stopped and turned to Marjorie and saw the fragility in her expression. "Marjorie, you are, well, anyone would be happy to be with you, but I'm married and in love with my wife."

Marjorie's posture dropped. "I saw that she's on the docket," Marjorie said.

"Yes, she's going under the knife tomorrow."

Marjorie's gaze turned downwards before looking up at Trevor. "I'm happy for you, Trevor, truly."

"If things were different. Then, things would be different," Trevor said.

"But they're not different," Marjorie said before turning around and walking away.

-----:-----

Trevor's heart was beating quicker than normal. While waiting in the elevator, he carefully formulated his question. He shook his head upon recognizing the absurdity of not having asked the question earlier. There had to be a reason for wanting to know if Reverse-Looping was possible or not. Trevor hoped that he would be able to understand the 'why' behind it all within the answer to this question. In knowing the 'why,' he would learn whether they should continue or not. If they were going to open Pandora's Box, then he needed to know the reason.

Stepping into Dresdin's outer office, he noticed that his secretary was absent from her post. Past her desk, he saw Dresdin's office door open a crack. Approaching the open door, he heard Dresdin's voice and the voice of another man talking at a low volume. Just as Trevor was about to walk away, he heard a jiggle of the office doorknob. He didn't want to look as though he'd been eavesdropping, so he hustled out of the welcome room. In the hall, he turned the corner just in time to catch a glimpse of the man. He recognized him immediately. Now Trevor had a new memory to consider. Why would Dresdin be meeting with the Francisco Bay's police commissioner?

He had gone to Dresdin's office searching for answers, but he realized that he already had his answer. His suspicions regarding Dresdin hadn't diminished at all.

As he walked to the elevator, he realized that if his theories were right about Reverse-Looping and Dresdin's plans for it, Dresdin would need help from powerful people.

When he returned to his office, he went onto the Internet looking for information on the mandates and powers vested upon police commissioners.

He had two theories regarding Dresdin's plans for Reverse-Looping. Unfortunately, both were nefarious. He decided the time had come to think several moves ahead.

Chapter 18

Dr. Trevor Miles. Thursday, March 21, 2075

"Good morning," Tia said with a smile.

"Good morning!" Trevor said while sitting on a stool in the kitchen, sipping a cup of faux coffee.

"Good morning, Mom!" Sean said. His low set gaze centered on an e-sheet, which displayed a comic book strip.

"Did you sleep well?" Trevor asked.

"I think so," Sean replied without lifting his head.

Tia looked over at Trevor, and they smiled. They'd become ever more accustomed to Sean's tendencies. This teenager's affections were distant from those of the toddler he had been. He was growing up, and they didn't mind it in the least. As long as he was still a good kid, then everything else felt secondary. They had decided not to tell Sean about Tia's impending surgery later today.

As she sat down at the table, placing her cup of faux coffee down in front of her, Sean began rising from his chair. He abruptly gathered up his things, leaned over, kissed his mother on the cheek, and gave his father a nod before leaving the room.

"I love you!" Tia said loud enough for Sean to hear.

In the distance, she could barely hear the response. "Love you too, Mom!"

Trevor and Tia sat in front of each other for a few moments, still smiling. Trevor saw a radiance he hadn't seen in months. He could feel the weight lifting.

Looking at her, he noticed that in the corners of her eyes, small tears had begun sliding down her cheeks.

"I love you." She mouthed the words to him.

"I'm so sorry." Trevor mouthed the words back to her.

Trevor rose from his seat and walked over to Tia. She remained seated and lifted her head up to him as he tilted his head downwards. They kissed as if it was their very first.

-----:-----

He'd taken the day off from work. In the days leading up to his wife's operation, he had reviewed the files of each D-Eye surgery that had taken place to date. He only wished he'd had more time. Things had moved at such a quick pace following her stalking episode. Trevor hadn't believed that she'd be interested in the surgeries, but to DIT's credit, had built up such demand for the product that it became some sort of special honour. Tia, affected by experience in the garage, had leapt at the chance of a greater sense of security. Trevor had concerns, but he took comfort because he had developed the products to be safe.

As he entered the building with his wife, he could sense the new DIT facility's structure seemed to convey a very specific message. The colourful paintings, high ceilings, and smiling children's posters all appeared intended to relax and disarm. It felt awkward hearing the DIT rep explain the D-Eye surgery to his wife in preparation for her surgery.

"You will be anesthetized, so I promise you won't feel a thing. It'll be over before you know it!"

There was no mention of any of the true details of the surgery. Trevor decided to let it slide, as he also didn't want Tia panicking unnecessarily.

After the very short debrief, Tia disappeared into a room with the nurse. She was wheeled back in while lying on a hospital bed wearing only a hospital gown. Looking down at her, Trevor couldn't help but notice how beautiful Tia still managed to look, even with a makeup-free face and her hair tucked under a transparent plastic cap. As the bed rolled along, Trevor periodically switched his gaze from her to the direction they walked. Tia, perhaps feeling anxious, placed her hand on his. He turned his head, and they locked eyes for a moment. Trevor caressed her hand, and gradually he could see a calm come over her. In an instant, her expression changed to a look he knew all too well but thought had been lost the day he confessed his infidelity. He'd forgotten how that look made him feel. It was a look of complete honesty and love.

He could feel her hand tighten as they approached the doors leading to the operating room. The nurse and orderly who had been pushing the bed along paused just before the threshold to allow them to speak to one another.

"I can't go with you," Trevor told her.

"I know," Tia said in a quiet voice.

"When you come back, I'll be right here waiting for you."

She looked at Trevor with the same expression that he so cherished. She said, "I know."

The nurse and orderly took those final words as the signal indicating that it was safe to roll her away through the swinging double doors.

Trevor knew the surgery should only take about three hours. He walked back to the waiting room and sat down. Across from his seat, upon a coffee table, lay a stack of magazines. He shook his head when noticing that at the top of the pile of scattered magazines lay a copy of the magazine he had seen outside Dresdin's office the day of his interview.

-----:-----

After an hour of waiting, he felt startled by the buzzing of an incoming call on his mobile. The earplug slid into his ear from its resting position just behind it.

"Hello?"

"Trevor, thank God! I've been calling you over and over again for hours."

"Marjorie, I must've had my phone on vibrate. What's up?"

"I think you better get down here."

"I can't, I have to bring my wife home, and she hasn't come out of surgery yet."

"Well, something major is happening. Willy Taylor was down here demanding an update on 'Reverse Looping.' He looked freaked out. He refused to say anything, but something's definitely going on."

"What did you tell him about the project?"

"I told him he'd have to wait till you returned ... but ..."

"What? What is it?"

"Well, when I came in this morning, I realized that Pax was still here from the night before. I didn't ask him any questions because I just assumed that maybe he had decided to work late with Sylvie or something, but then he called me into the boardroom ... Trevor, Pax has figured it out. He's solved the entire problem. He says we can do Reverse Looping. It'll have to involve only a portion of the source's memories, but he said it can be done."

"That's amazing news."

"I know, but there's just one thing ..."

"Oh? What's that?"

"Well, he said it's possible, but then he said something peculiar. You know the way Pax talks. He makes you wonder if he'll finally turn into a machine himself, and so I really don't know how to interpret what he said."

"Well, what did he say?"

"He said Reverse Looping is possible, but he has major concerns regarding the psychological effects of the Receiving Subject."

"Pax said that?"

"I was shocked too."

There was a pause as Trevor contemplated his options.

"Trevor, I'll try to ward them off until you get here. Just try to get here as soon as possible."

"Thanks so much, Marjorie. I just can't leave Tia alone."

"I understand but try to get here as soon as possible."

"I'll do my best."

Trevor disconnected the call and turned around to see a nurse standing before him.

"Dr. Miles?"

"Yes?"

"Your wife's surgery was a success. You can see her now if you like," the nurse said.

Entering the room, he saw Tia lying in a bed beside a window facing the now setting sun.

"Hey," Trevor said as he positioned himself beside the bed. "Are you okay? How do you feel?"

"Well, I have to say that it wasn't at all the way that nurse had described it."

He laughed aloud. "I know!"

As he drove, Trevor saw that Tia had fallen asleep. He carried her into the house, tucked her in, and told her he'd be back in a couple of hours. He rushed to DIT headquarters.

From the moment he stepped through the doors, he could sense what Marjorie had been referring to. Staff members were running around with absolute panic in their eyes. Just as Trevor entered the elevator, he heard a beep from his phone indicating he'd received a new voice message.

"Message from contact Peter ... sent ... 2 minutes ago ... message is as follows: Trevor ... new information found about your pending investigation ... must meet immediately. Peter."

Trevor felt a shudder. Peter was the private investigator that he'd hired. The man he'd hoped would solve the living, breathing puzzle of Carl Dresdin.

When they'd first met regarding the case two weeks ago, Trevor remembered feeling surprised by how quickly Peter had dismissed their suspicions.

"I've looked into all of this, and I can guarantee you that there is nothing more regarding Dresdin. Your information is just not correct." Peter had told him, with conviction, during their meeting.

Trevor trusted his friend but insisted that he review everything again as a personal favour. Trevor assumed that he would get an 'I told you so' from Peter down the road. The last thing he expected was a message from his friend, asking that they meet "immediately." Peter was your run-of-the-mill, shoot from the hip kind of guy. For him to sound so panicked just didn't fit. Trevor decided to call him as soon as he found out what was going on at Dresdin Industrial.

He descended in the elevator to his floor first. When the door opened, he exited and, not seeing anyone, decided to head to the diagnostics lab, where he found Marjorie.

"Hey! What's going on?" Trevor asked.

"I don't know, Trevor. I don't know, but Dresdin came down here ordering that you go see him immediately."

"Really ...?"

"Trevor, he had a very odd look in his eye. It was like rage and sadness. I don't know what happened, but it must have been terrible."

"Okay, I'll go right up to see him now."

Marjorie grabbed his arm. "Be careful, Trevor. He was acting very strange."

"Okay," Trevor said in a resigned tone.

Trevor walked briskly back to the elevator and headed up to Dresdin's floor. As he approached the closed door, he could hear angry yelling. Reluctantly, he knocked on the door.

"Come in!" he heard Dresdin holler from inside the office.

Trevor opened the door and stepped through. He saw Dresdin standing arms-crossed facing the door. He was leaning on the front of his desk with his head bent forward. Trevor glanced around the room and recognized Willy Taylor standing among several other men, several of which he didn't know.

"Who is that?"

"It's Dr. Trevor Miles, sir." Willy Taylor said.

Dresdin lifted his head. He said, "You finally decided to show up!"

Trevor instinctively glanced at Taylor, who shook his head quickly as if to say, "Be careful what you say."

"I'm sorry, sir, I had booked the day off. I had to accompany my wife to her surgery."

"Ah, yes, that's right. I had almost forgotten about that. It went well, I hope."

"Very well, sir, thank you."

Dresdin turned around, and Trevor noticed that his eyes were teary.

"Dr. Miles, I need something from you, and I need it now," Dresdin said in an ever-increasing tone.

"Of course, sir, what is it?"

Dresdin began to approach Trevor, and with each step, he could see a growing look of disgust spreading across his face.

After a few steps, Dresdin was now standing in front of Trevor. He stood there for several seconds staring at his face. Dresdin lifted his hand upwards, and in his peripheral vision, Trevor could see Taylor take a protective step forward—it caused Trevor to flinch.

"What's wrong? Do you think I'm going to hurt you? Come on?" Dresdin dropped his hand onto Trevor's shoulder. "No, no, I wouldn't hurt *you*. No, no, I need you now more than ever. I need you to tell me one thing. I'm going to ask you if Reverse Looping is possible or not, and I only want to hear one answer. Do you know what that answer is?"

"Yes?"

"Yes, exactly, right! So Dr. Miles, is Reverse Looping ready?"

Trevor paused for a moment. While looking around the room, he noticed that every person in the room looked down at the floor to avoid eye contact with him and avoid suggesting any form of allegiance. He was truly alone. Feeling anxious, he gave the answer he figured would cause the least trouble.

"Yes. Reverse Looping is finished," Trevor said.

Dresdin, who had already turned around, started walking away and stopped upon hearing the answer. Dresdin didn't turn around but instead raised his head to the sky before exhaling.

"Good, good, I knew you were the right man for the job."

"Dr. Miles, you can leave for now, but I will need you again very soon. Expect a phone call."

"Very well, sir, thank you," Trevor said as he backed out of the room.

Once Trevor left the office and stepped out into the hallway, he exhaled in relief. Though Marjorie had been correct in her observations regarding Dresdin, he realized that he hadn't actually gathered much more info than she had. He still didn't know what had happened. He decided to go back down to the lab and find out how close Pax was to a launch and to advise him that they needed to get it done as soon as possible.

Chapter 19

Beth Lago. Thursday, March 21, 2075

After some time spent smoothing things over with Eccles, I perceived a shift in the tide, and I could sense our friendship heading in a better direction. The incident at the train station had helped build our trust in one another. For weeks afterward, as I recovered, I wasn't much help around the house. Eccles compensated and even took care of me quite a bit.

We began going out for dinner on the weekends, and during the week, we'd play board games to pass the time. Coincidentally or not, Willy had again disappeared. This marked the fourth time that Willy had done this to me. His behaviour had grown increasingly irritated. Just when I'd start thinking things were going well, he would suddenly stop calling me and stop answering my calls. To date, I had avoided bringing it up, but by now, I had grown annoyed. The next time Willy reappeared, he was going to find out how I felt. My chance would end up coming sooner than expected.

At the precinct, the following week, Eccles and I had just started packing up for the day when the Cap burst out of his office and ordered us inside.

"Have a seat, guys. We've got a major problem. I know you guys are on loan to Homicide right now, and normally I would get someone else in Missing Persons division to work on this, but this is too high profile for those guys. I need experienced people I can trust. Listen to me very carefully. I need your full attention."

Looking at us, he cleared his throat, loosened his tie, and inhaled deeply.

"I just got off the phone with lawyers from Dresdin Industrial Technologies. The little boy, they refer to as the first D-Eye baby—Emil Dresdin …."

We both leaned in closer.

"He's missing. He's disappeared."

Both our jaws dropped. We were completely shocked.

"How long has he been missing?" I asked as I looked at my watch. It was 4:45 pm.

"He was supposed to be picked up at the bus stop by his mother, Mrs. Dresdin …" Cap looked down at his notes for a moment. "At about 1:35 pm, but he wasn't on the bus when it arrived."

I turned the timer dial on my watch back to 1:35 pm. I started the timer in order to keep track of the total time missing. Emil had been officially missing for a total of three hours and ten minutes. There was a particular protocol regarding Missing Persons cases in the Territory of Old Los Angeles and several other territories with similarly high frequencies of disappearances. The protocol gave the magistrate of the territory the authority to dictate when a search could begin.

"DIT asked for our best guys, so I'm sending you. I need you to remember that this needs to be as discreet as possible. No one, I mean, no one outside this room can know what's going on."

"No Amber Alerts then?" Eccles asked.

"No! Nothing like that will be possible! We can't even put out an All-Points Bulletin. Again, let me reiterate … nothing."

"Don't we have anything from the D-Eye system that can lead us back to him?" I asked quickly.

"Maybe … check that out. This is as high profile as it gets. Not finding Emil is not an option. You know the drill, find the point of disappearance and interview the relevant witnesses. Do everything that you would normally do. Just do it faster. Get out there and find that kid!"

Eccles and I bounced up from our chairs. Cap handed me the file as I walked by his desk.

He leaned in as I passed. "Is your relationship with the Dresdin Security head, Willy Taylor, going to be an issue?"

I looked Cap dead in the eyes before responding, "No, absolutely, not."

-----:-----

Eccles and I got into the car and drove to the Dresdins' house. They lived in a mansion on a hill, thirty minutes outside the city. When we arrived, Mrs. Dresdin greeted us at the door. Even though her eyes looked swollen and her mascara had been running, she was far prettier than I expected. She had long brown hair and clear hazel, cat-like eyes. She looked to be in her mid-thirties, but I knew from reading her biography that she was actually in her mid-forties. I took a deep breath to maintain my composure. All this time later, I still remembered all too well the terrifying feelings I'd felt while hoping for Sara's safe return. I instantly knew how desperate she was feeling, and the thought of it made me hurt for her.

"Thank God, please come in."

She hugged us as we entered. She seemed down to Earth, genuine. I felt guilty for having judged her rashly.

"Please ..." she said, extending her hand towards me.

I placed my hand in hers, and she led us down a long corridor.

"We're so glad that you've come."

"Well, we're here to help in any way we can," I answered.

Mrs. Dresdin opened a pair of French doors and led us into what looked like a conference room. There were about a dozen people inside. Willy rushed over to us.

"Hi, Beth," He said.

"William." I kept my tone professional and curt, but not rude.

A distraught Mr. Dresdin approached. He looked only a fraction of the composed man I'd seen on TV in all those press conferences and news stories.

"Hello, I'm Carl Dresdin. You must be Inspectors Beth Lago and Mark Eccles. Welcome and thank you for coming. Willy will bring you up to speed."

Mr. Dresdin had already turned to walk away when I asked, "Mr. Dresdin, I just have one question for you."

"Yes, of course."

"The D-Eye implants, couldn't they lead us to Emil somehow?"

Mr. Dresdin looked downwards as his face darkened.

"I'm afraid not, the D-Eye implants record information, but the extraction of data is impossible while the subject ... while Emil is alive. The technology is meant as a deterrent and as a tool for proving guilt."

"Thank you, Mr. Dresdin," Eccles said in a subdued tone.

Mr. Dresdin walked away slowly.

Willy had been waiting patiently to lead us to a giant wall-mounted map.

"Here's the situation, every day, Emil gets dropped off at the bus stop, here." Willy pointed to a spot on the map that had already been marked in red.

"Where's the school?" Eccles asked.

"The school is here," Willy said, again, pointing at another point on the map.

"What's the distance?"

"It'd be about ten miles."

"How many children get off at that stop?" I asked.

"Two others, but neither can remember whether or not Emil was on the bus," Willy said.

"What about the bus driver?"

"Not the regular one. She was sick today. Go figure," Willy said.

"Don't they do a headcount or attendance?" I asked.

"They do, but the bus driver calls out the children's names from a list. According to the school principal, the driver says he took attendance, but he figures since he doesn't know any of the children, one of them must have said **'here'** twice."

"So he couldn't have gotten off the bus at an earlier stop?"

"No, well, it's highly unlikely. At every stop, the bus driver fills out this form."

Willy handed me a clipboard. On the page were a series of cross streets along the left side and pre-printed columns with numbers on the right.

"The numbers indicate the number of children who get off at each stop?" Eccles asked as he scribbled furiously on his pad.

"Correct," Willy responded.

"Alright, so, he makes the stop, the children disembark, he counts and then signs in the far right column?" Eccles said in confirmation.

They all seemed to match up until the very last row, where a "3" had been pre-printed, but no signature appeared in the right column.

"Emil's stop was the last one on the route?" I asked.

"Correct," Willy answered.

Eccles began examining the sheet from over my shoulder.

"These are all time-stamped, so according to this, at 1:30 pm, the bus driver realized he was short one kid," Eccles said.

"Yes, exactly right," Willy said.

"Okay, let's assume for a minute that he never makes it on the bus. Who was the last person to see him before the bus?" I asked.

"The last person to have seen him would be his teacher. Her name is Mrs. Wallace. She's right over here," Willy said.

He took a couple of steps towards the corner of the room, where a young woman sat sobbing, her head buried in her hands.

"Mrs. Wallace?" Willy murmured while placing his hand on the woman's shoulder.

"These are investigators with the police. They've come to help," Willy said to her slowly.

Raising her head, she brushed away her dark hair from her face, revealing tear-stricken cheeks.

"Yes?" she whispered.

"We just have a few questions for you. My name is Beth, and this is Eccles. We're with the OLAPD." I stated in a clear, soft voice.

She nodded while shaking our hands, sniffling between breaths.

"When was the last time you saw Emil?" I asked.

"Well, the bell had rung, and all the children had grabbed their bags. Normally, I'd walk them out to the bus stop all together, but they were extra full of energy today. Some of the children sprinted toward the main door leading outside. I tried to stop them, but they wouldn't listen. I had to rush the rest of the children outside to keep an eye on them all at once. As we all left the classroom, Emil asked to go to the bathroom."

She started trembling, and her voice began to quiver as she struggled to continue. "I should have said no, or maybe I should have told him to wait, but Emil's one of the good kids. I figured he would be safer in the school bathroom than some of the other children would be outside unsupervised. I told him to hurry and to meet us outside."

"Listen to me carefully, Mrs. Wallace. Was there anyone in the hall when this happened?" I asked.

"No, I don't think so," she replied.

"Mrs. Wallace, think carefully. Was there anyone else around?" Eccles asked.

"No, there wasn't," she said as she concentrated on the memory. "I'm sure there was no one around."

"Okay, what happened next?"

"Well, I kept an eye on the door, waiting for Emil to come out, but I never saw him," she whispered before sobbing. "I never saw him come out again," she cried, loud enough to cause everyone in the room to stop and take notice.

I stepped toward Mrs. Wallace." I know this is hard for you, but the best thing you can do right now is to help us as much as possible, okay?" I told her in as sensitive a tone as I could.

"Okay," she said, inhaling deeply and sitting up straight.

"Why didn't you notify someone, at that point, that Emil was missing?" Eccles asked.

"After I got all the kids to board the bus, I ran back inside the school. I checked the classroom and then the bathroom, but he wasn't there. I ran back outside and asked each of the bus drivers if they had taken attendance. They all said yes, so there was no cause for concern at that point. I'd assumed that Emil must have gone outside and boarded the bus while I had gone in to look for him. There are many exits to the school. I thought that maybe he'd taken one of the others."

"Why didn't you check on Emil's bus to see if he was on board?" Eccles asked.

"Because ... I didn't know which bus was Emil's, and during all the confusion, most of the buses had already departed."

Eccles and I looked at each other for a moment.

"You think this is my fault," she cried.

Her comment struck me hard, and I didn't know how to answer. Eccles ignored the comment and moved on to his next question. "Is there anything in Emil's behaviour that indicated to you that he might have been unhappy? Does he have a habit of, you know … just running off?"

"Not running off, but he does have a habit of wandering off at times. He's such a curious little boy. Last week, we visited the Museum of Natural History, and he somehow managed to wander off without anyone noticing," she said.

I held back from drawing quick or easy conclusions this early on in the investigation. However, I couldn't help but notice how often children seemed to get away from this teacher. Thoughts of Sara entered my mind. I remembered how easily children could escape one's sight. I decided to give her the benefit of the doubt, for now.

"Mrs. Wallace, you mentioned that there were exits other than the one you were keeping an eye on?" I asked.

"Yes, there is. There's a back exit, but Emil knows not to go out that door."

Eccles and I looked at each other.

The teacher's statement was not enough to dissuade us from checking out the school in person. We knew from experience that children's behaviours often proved vastly unpredictable.

I still had other suspicions and theories circling in my mind.

"I just have one last question, Mrs. Wallace. Have you ever noticed any strangers around the school, any suspicious activity of that kind?" I asked.

"Actually, there was a couple … A man and a woman." Her eyes began to widen as she continued recalling. "They were talking to Emil. It was last week, during recess, while the children were playing outside. The playground is fenced in. I watched the kids as usual from a very short distance when I noticed Emil standing by the fence through the corner of my eye. The man and the woman were on the other side. I called to Emil, and the couple quickly walked away. I had asked Emil if he knew them, and he'd said no. I asked him what they'd said, and he told me that they 'just wanted to say hi.'"

"Do you remember what they looked like? Do you think you could describe them?"

"I never forget a face."

Eccles and I decided to split up. He went to the school to set up a perimeter. We both agreed the school was our best bet for the Point of Disappearance. He dropped Mrs. Wallace and me off at the precinct so she could help with a composite sketch of the mysterious couple.

Chapter 20

Beth Lago. Thursday, March 21, 2075. 6:49 PM

Stepping out of the car, I glanced down at my watch—6:49 PM. It's been five hours and nineteen minutes since Emil disappeared. Every passing minute ticked away more heavily than the one before it. The more time that passed, the worse our odds of finding Emil became. If one added to the equation the variable of not having access to tools like APBs or Amber Alerts, the result left little room for hope.

At the precinct, Mrs. Wallace sat in the chair beside my desk, trembling as if she'd come inside from a rainstorm. I pulled a blanket out from a drawer and placed it around her shoulders. She barely looked up to take notice. As she shivered, her stare remained focused on a random spot on the floor. I placed my hand on her hand, which she'd rested upon her knee.

"Don't beat yourself up. We're doing our absolute best to find him. Blaming yourself won't help us find him. I'm going to need you to stay focused. If you think of anything at all, then I'll need to know about it."

"Okay, I'll try."

"Good."

I decided I had to help her calm down if I expected any help from her at all.

"Would you like a glass of water?"

"Sure."

I walked away only a few steps to the water dispenser, where I poured a cup for myself and one for Mrs. Wallace. I'd only been away a few seconds, and when I returned, I could see that her posture had changed completely, and she was now looking at something on my desk.

As I offered her the glass, her eyes remained fixed on my desk's surface.

"You've found them already?" she said aloud without even a glance in my direction. I wanted to answer, but I wasn't sure what she was talking about.

"Excuse me?" I asked.

"You found them already! Or maybe you're investigating them?"

"Mrs. Wallace, I'm sorry I don't understand. You're going to have to explain."

"It's the couple from the schoolyard," she pointed at a picture on my desk.

I'd recently been reading up on the Dresdins and the Days. I'd inadvertently left some of it on my desk. Looking downwards, I realized she was pointing at a picture of the Days.

I lifted the picture and raised it in front of her eyes.

"Are these the people you saw?"

"Yes."

"Are you positive?"

"As I said, I never forget a face. Who are they anyway?"

"Could you excuse me for a moment?" I walked away from the desk while also withdrawing my cell from my pocket.

"Eccles?"

"Hey. Beth, I'm afraid I don't have any updates yet. I'm still canvassing the area around the school, though. Any luck on your end?"

"Yes, actually, I think I may have identified the couple from the schoolyard. According to Ms. Wallace, it's the Days."

"What?"

"I know. I think we've finally caught a break. I'm going to pull their address and head over there right now."

"Okay, be careful. Call me if you find out anything."

"Will do ..."

I signed out another car from the precinct garage, and after dropping off Mrs. Wallace at her house, I proceeded to the Days' apartment.

Chapter 21

Beth Lago. Thursday, March 21, 2075. 7:33 PM

The Days' lived in a rundown apartment building just outside the Scourge. Not the safest part of town, but I was too focused on our latest lead to worry about it very much. I could feel my heart pounding as I walked up to the building. Pausing for a moment, I considered alerting Willy about our latest development, but I quickly noted I hadn't discovered anything concrete, at least not yet.

Arriving at the Days' apartment building, I noticed the door to the street was wide open. Walking through the lobby towards the elevators, I saw a tattered sign hanging just above its doors. It read, "Out of Order."

The Days lived on the fourth floor. As I opened the door to the stairwell, an awful smell repulsed me. Nonetheless, I climbed the stairs, trying my best to ignore the stench. When I reached their floor, the odour was overwhelming. I began suspecting the presence of a decomposing body nearby.

I withdrew my gun from its holster as I crept down the hall.

As I passed the apartment doors, I heard a range of strange sounds. Behind one door, there was loud music blaring. Behind another, I could hear a couple screaming at each other. On I went until I arrived at apartment 418.

I knocked on the door. There was no answer.

I knocked again. Again, there was no answer.

I knocked again, and the door flung open.

"What!" a man screamed.

It was Robert Day.

I flashed him my badge. "I'm Inspector Lago of the OLAPD." I peered into the musky apartment. "Where is he?"

"Where's who?"

Where's Emil?"

"I don't know ... He's probably with his parents. Why are you asking us?" Robert scowled and shook his head.

Just then, a woman approached with messy blonde hair and dark rings below her eyes. It was Jessica Day.

"What's going on here?" she barked.

"I know you've been at school. I know you've initiated contact with him. Show me where he is, and maybe the Dresdins won't press charges," I said.

"Look, I don't know. We don't know what you're talking about," Robert said.

"Fine, then you won't mind me looking around then."

"Look all you want. He's not here!" Robert snapped as he walked away from the door.

"Just stand over there for a minute, then," I said as I stepped further into the room. "Emil!? Emil?!" I called out as I looked around the apartment.

"This is ridiculous!" Robert yelled as he sat with his arms, crossed on a ratty grey couch.

I continued looking around the room. "You still haven't explained what you were doing at the school."

"I don't know what you're talking about," Robert stated.

"Why did you go to his school? Why did you talk to him? When you gave him up for adoption, didn't you promise not to seek him out?"

Robert exhaled and shook his head. He said, "Look, we just wanted to see him for a minute, that's all. We were just standing at the fence, and he was the one who approached us."

I peered into the bedroom for a moment and noticed some suitcases. "Planning on taking a trip, were you?"

Neither Robert nor Jessica said a word.

"What's this?" I asked as I lifted two tickets from the table. "Two day passes for the Museum of Natural History, time-stamped for six days ago."

Jessica's face began to turn red.

"Jessica, if you know something, then you should tell me."

"Jessica, don't say a word," Robert warned as he clenched his fist.

I looked Jessica Day in the eyes, and I could see she had been crying. I began to think the worst. What had they done to this poor boy?

"Is he really missing?" Jessica asked as tears began streaming from her clear blue eyes.

"Jessica, please, for God's sake, if you have something to say, then tell me."

"We ..." Jessica began.

"Jessica -- shut up! Don't say another word!"

"No! You shut up, Bobby! Don't you see what's happened?"

"Jessica, please?" Robert's body language suddenly changed. His glare lowered, and his eyes were filling with tears.

"I'm done listening to you, Bobby! I'm done! He's missing ... And it's our fault!" she screamed as she rose from her seat.

Robert covered his face as he started to cry.

"What ... happened?" I asked.

Jessica looked up at me. She said, "I'm sorry, we didn't mean for him to be harmed, I swear ..."

"Jessica, please? Every minute you don't tell me is just making things worse."

"We had promised never to make contact with Emil. We signed those papers when he was still in my belly, but when I saw him on television when I saw him, something changed. I decided to change my life. I decided to get better for him. Bobby and I both got clean. We then decided we wanted to see him in person."

"Okay."

"We went to his school and saw him just that one time, only. We promised each other that we would just see him once in person ... but he was ... he was so sweet. You don't know how hard it's been to see your child from a distance and not be able to speak to him or let him hear your voice. It was so hard, but I said my goodbyes to him that day. Then a miracle happened. Bobby and I were walking down the street, and we saw Emil and his classmates entering the museum, and we followed. We kept our distance but again he approached us ... then ... then ..."

She began sobbing again, and her voice started to tremble. She said, "He asked me who I was ... and it just slipped ..."

"What did you say?"

She continued sobbing.

"What did you tell him?"

"I'm sorry, I told him that he was my son ... I told him that I was his mother," she said.

I shook my head.

"Okay! That's it! No more, Jessica!" Robert declared.

"Bobby, it's over, okay, all of it, it's over! Don't you understand? My baby is out there, somewhere!"

Jessica's words caused Robert to sit back down again.

"We tell it all now ... and you better hope ... you better hope nothing happens to him," Jessica said to her husband before turning towards me again.

"The Dresdins had told us that once Emil was old enough, and as long as we were clean, they would let us spend time with him. While at the museum, we told him that we would take him out for ice cream."

"When was that going to be?"

"It was supposed to be today," she said, biting her quivering lip.

"What happened, Jessica?" I asked.

"When we got home from the museum, we realized that we had made a grave mistake."

She looked over at Robert before speaking. "We decided that seeing more of Emil would only cause him pain."

"What do you mean? What happened?" I asked.

"I'm sorry, Bobby, no more lies ... That's not true. We were going to take him with us. We were going to take him away. He was supposed to sneak away from school to meet us for ice cream, and then we were going to take him away with us. In the end, we realized …"

"You realized?"

"We realized that his life was better off without us."

"So, you told a child to run away from his school so that you could kidnap him?" I asked incredulously.

They both hung their heads while holding each other.

"You have absolutely no legal right to see him. The Dresdins adopted him. I could understand the desire to connect with him, but there are other ways of doing it …."

"Please ... you have to believe we never meant for anything to happen to Emil. We love him."

I shook my head in disbelief.

She said, "I just wanted to see my child, can't you understand that?" Jessica said as she wiped tears from her face. "You don't know what it's like to be away from your own child! You have no idea!"

I resisted responding out of anger. "Lady, I don't think you know what you've done here. A little boy is out there by himself, and it may be your fault. You better hope he's okay."

My cell phone rang. "Hello?"

"It's Eccles. Beth, I have news."

"What is it, Eccles?"

"It's Emil."

"Okay?"

"Beth, he's dead."

"What?" I blurted.

"Meet me back at the precinct," Eccles said.

My eyes began to tear as I looked over at the Days as I disconnected the call.

"What is it? Is Emil okay? What happened ... oh God, please answer me?" Jessica pleaded as she sobbed.

I shook my head slowly, thinking of the words to say, but it mattered not. Jessica Day had read my expression.

"Oh, God ... No! No! Please!"

Jessica collapsed to the floor. Everything seemed to slow down at that moment. I didn't know what to say. My sorrow shifted toward anger. I clenched my fists, inhaled deeply as I prepared to tell the Days' what I thought of their actions. As I looked down at them, however, hugging each other while weeping, I couldn't think of a worse kind of punishment.

I held my emotions inside. "I'm very sorry for your loss." I turned around, and I walked away.

As I descended the stairs, all the memories of Sam and Sara flooded my mind without warning. I felt helpless as the tears began pouring from my eyes. I cried in the stairwell for several minutes before wiping the tears away.

Justice—I was going to get it for Emil. I promised myself.

Chapter 22

Beth Lago. Thursday, March 21, 2075. 8:54 PM

As I walked the short distance from the parking garage to the precinct front entrance, I began feeling the weight of fatigue, pulling me down with each step. The last few hours had drained both my emotional and mental wells dry. A rush had elevated my senses when beginning our search for Emil. It resonated straight into the questioning of the witnesses. I felt resolute up until that point.

Things took a turn, however, at the Day's apartment. The presence of so many intense and conflicting emotions had caused me confusion. Concerning the Days, I wanted to be angry with them. Still, in a strangely unnatural way, I partly understood their actions. They missed their son and wished for his safe return. I understood parts of the situation. I understood that they'd become drug addicts, and in a logical world, the adoption of Emil likely saved him from the pains of a troubled life. I could easily understand the existence of a payoff, which had caused the Days to start taking drugs in the first place. The Days had systematically destroyed their lives, but in the wake of the destruction, they'd somehow managed to cleanse away their addiction and change their lives for the better. Now they found themselves grieving and guilt-ridden over the death of Emil. Jessica Day had told me that I didn't know her pain, and part of me wished her statement could be true. As my thoughts drifted to Sara and the still stinging pain, I realized that behind the precinct doors lay something that I could give Emil and his family that I'd longed for in my life—the truth.

I marched forward more purposefully towards precinct doors and the truth that lay behind them.

-----:-----

Eccles was already waiting outside.

"Hey, Cap converted the conference room into a War Room. They're all in there right now."

"Okay," I said as I walked by him.

"Are you okay?" Eccles asked, following me into the precinct.

"Yeah, I'm fine. I'm just want to know what happened."

"We all do. Follow me."

As we walked through the Pit, the heads of curious night-shifters popped up to watch us as we passed. I could hear whispering, too low to make out. They were probably just wondering what was happening.

When we walked into the War Room, I felt taken aback by the rumble of dozens of overlapping conversations. After a few seconds, Cap spotted us from a distance and walked over.

"We've been waiting for you," he said before turning around to make an announcement. "Okay! We can begin."

A chubby bald man shuffled up to the front of the room, where a projector had been set up along with several other metallic boxes with lights flashing out of them.

He said, "Good evening, everyone. My name is Dr. Leo Lamont, and I'm Chief Supervisor of the Digital Eyes project. I'd like to thank Captain Gordon Baines and the OLAPD for allowing us to use their facilities. As you know, we have suffered a horrific loss in the death of Emil Dresdin. Now we have entered the phase in which the Digital Eyes technology will assist us in apprehending any guilty parties. We also hope to find some indications as to the location of Emil's body. You are here as you are law enforcement authorities, DIT lawyers, and representatives of the District Attorney's office to review Emil's Data Files to determine whether a crime has been committed."

"I thought they couldn't extract this information from Emil while he was alive," I whispered to Eccles.

"I know. I'm confused too," Eccles whispered back.

"Excuse me. Is there a question?"

"Hi, Beth Lago, OLAPD. During the course of our search for Emil, we were told that D-Eye couldn't extract any data that could help. How or why is this possible now?"

Dr. Lamont looked over at Mr. Dresdin, who nodded. While sitting at the front of the room, he stood up and turned around to address the question.

"Well, because of the Emergency Protocol."

I stared at him in confusion.

He said, "The Emergency Protocol is a system that DIT integrated into every D-Eye patient. It's a biofeedback monitoring system designed to send a signal out when detecting loss of life. At 7:33 pm this evening, the D-Eye system received a signal indicating that Emil's heart had stopped. The protocol causes the system to download Emil's files only after death, as only then can the D-eye implants shift to broadcast mode."

All eyes were glued to him as he shifted his weight.

"For security reasons, this aspect of the D-Eye system has remained a secret until now. At 7:33 pm, once DIT engineers received the signal indicating loss of life, the OLAPD dispatch center received the notification. Dispatch operators contacted officials within the DA's office to advise them, who in turn contacted the Dresdins' lawyers, and those two entities collaborated to subpoena the data. At 7:40 pm, we extracted and stored the data on the condition of full disclosure before all pertinent parties."

He paused and waited for the spontaneous whispers and exclamations to cease before continuing. "The data files contain information across all of Emil's senses. However, we will only utilize his visual and audio files. The data is time-coded. It was agreed by the Dresdins' lawyers and the District Attorney's Office that only data from 1:00 pm local time till 7:33 pm local time would be permitted."

I looked over at Eccles, who looked equally in awe.

"Please dim the lights," Dr. Lamont said.

-----:-----

The room turned dark, except for a screen that illuminated white. Gradually, the screen turned darker and darker until it and the entire room filled with shadow. I looked over at Eccles as I shook my head.

I whispered, "I knew this was too good to be true."

A few bright colours lit up the screen. Each colour appeared like a spark, then a flame igniting before fading away. Then the entire screen and room lit up like the inside of a flashbulb. When our eyes adjusted and the screen dimmed to normal brightness, the sight caused a collective gasp. To our astonishment, we were peering at a classroom from a child's low-levelled perspective. I could see Dr. Lamont say something to one of the technicians sitting in front of a laptop. The images began speeding up.

"We all agree that the time Emil spent in the classroom is not relevant at this point."

I could see Mrs. Wallace at the front of the classroom. She looked considerably happier than she would look later on in the afternoon. There was a box in the corner of the screen with numbers, which were in the negative. I assumed the system counted back from Emil's time of death. Dr. Lamont said something to the technician, and the images began slowing down to a normal pace.

"We are activating the audio now," Dr. Lamont said.

The sound of a bell rang across the speakers, and the image began shaking. He must be running, I thought to myself. Sure enough, just as Mrs. Wallace had said, the children were running out of the classroom. We could hear Mrs. Wallace calling out as she exited the frame and into the hallway.

"Come along, everyone, we're going outside now!" she said as the rest of the children, including Emil began walking out of the room.

I whispered to Eccles, "This is the eeriest thing."

"It's eerie and tragic."

We watched as Emil watched the children leaving the room. The view remained motionless as the children continued walking down the hall further and further away. Next, the view turned towards the opposite, apparently empty, end of the hallway, then back at the children. This action repeated three times until Ms. Wallace appeared in the frame.

"Are you coming, Emil?" she asked.

In an echo-like, high-pitched tone, Emil said, "I ... I have to go to the bathroom."

"Right now, Emil?"

"Yes, I have to go badly," he answered.

We could see Mrs. Wallace turn to the children who were walking away and then back to Emil. Eccles and I both knew the mistake she was about to make.

"Okay ... Emil, you can go to the bathroom quickly, then come right outside, okay?"

"Okay," he said.

We watched as Emil bounced his way down to the bathroom. He opened the door and entered a typical-looking school restroom.

I glanced over at Dr. Lamont, who looked like he was about to say something, then stopped.

I turned my gaze back at the screen and saw we weren't approaching a urinal or a stall. Instead, the view had double-backed. We could see a tiny hand pulling the door open again. The view turned down the hallway in both directions.

"No!" Mrs. Dresdin whispered as she turned and buried her face in Mr. Dresdin's chest.

We watched as the view continued down the hall in the direction opposite the children and Mrs. Wallace. We watched as Emil's little shoes popped in and out of the bottom of the frame. He was walking away.

I wondered if he was heading towards the restaurant to meet the Days.

"At this point, would the DA or local law enforcement like to add anything?"

Cap looked over at me. "Beth?"

A voice called from the back of the room. It was Willy. "Beth Lago here and her partner Eccles questioned Mrs. Wallace. I was present and can confirm that Emil's data files reflect exactly the information she provided. Would you agree?" Willy asked, looking over at us.

"I agree," Eccles responded.

"I agree," I answered.

Eccles and I looked at each other. I shook my head at him. I could sense that he wanted to bring up the Days', but I motioned him not to. I figured the evidence would speak for itself. If Emil ended up at a restaurant, then I would mention it. The tension was high in the room. I decided it wasn't the right time.

"We will now speed up the feed slightly. If anyone has any objections, then please let us know. We will slow it down to a normal speed again if needed."

The images continued pouring through. Emil was walking down the street by himself. There didn't seem to be anyone around. The images continued until Emil arrived at a diner.

"Freeze the frame, please," Dr. Lamont said. "May the record reflect that Emil entered the Apple Street Diner. Please continue."

Emil sat at a booth. He began playing with sugar packets on the table.

A waitress approached, "Hey, hon, are you lost?"

"No," he responded.

"Where are your parents?" she asked.

"They're coming soon."

I looked over at the Dresdins, who were both looking at each other in puzzlement.

In the corner of the frame, we could see a man step into the diner as the waitress spoke to Emil. They walked over.

"Hey there, little buddy!" he said.

"Stop!" Dr. Lamont said before turning in Mr. Dresdin's direction. "Sir, do you know this man?"

"We've never seen him before." Mr. Dresdin responded.

"OLAPD?"

Eccles and I conferred with each other before we both shook our heads.

I wondered if we'd arrived at an appropriate time to report on the Days, although huddled in the War Room while we waited to perceive Emil's cause of death didn't seem like the right moment. It didn't seem wise to drag the Assistant District Attorney and Cap away from the playback now that we'd approached the most crucial part. Nonetheless, an unsettling feeling in my belly compelled me to do something.

I rose from my chair and left the room. I walked over to the Assignment Board, and I approached the two street patrol officers scheduled to patrol the area surrounding the Days' residence at shift change. Luckily, they were switching in a few minutes. I asked them to go to the Days' residence and advise them they'd have to come down to the precinct to sign a deposition. The two eager officers asked if it related to the case I was working on. When I advised that it did, they both offered to start their shifts early. I didn't know how the Days' would react, but I advised the officers to be careful.

"Don't let them out of your sight," I told them.

I resolved to tell ADA Sayvian and Cap everything after the playback. This was the best I could do while still not knowing Emil's cause of death. When the two officers headed off, I discreetly re-entered the conference room.

Eccles whispered to me as I sat down, "The Days?"

"They're not the perpetrators, but I assume they're the reason Emil went to the diner in the first place. Did I miss anything?"

"Not at all. Actually, the DIT guys looked pretty confused a minute ago. I think they were trying to figure out how to stop the playback and rewind."

"That's weird."

"I agree."

Sayvian said, "Okay, so we're back on track, so just to confirm, no one in the room recognizes the man on the screen, right?"

The room remained silent.

"If we have to, we can take a frame of the face and enter it into Facial Recog," I said.

"Alright, we'll get that for you, but it'll have to overlay several frames as the images look a bit grainy," Dr. Lamont said.

Cap interjected. "Dr. Lamont, let's continue with the playback for now because we still haven't yet determined COD or this person's relevance."

On the screen, the stranger addressed the waitress. "Can you get me a coffee, black, please? And for the little tyke ..."

"Ice cream ... Chocolate ice cream!" Emil said.

There was a momentary hesitation from the waitress, which I assumed to be the effect of her instincts, but the moment passed, and the waitress turned to walk away.

"How was school today?" The man asked.

In the distance, we could hear the waitress say, "One chocolate ice cream, I'll grab the coffee order."

"So, what are you doing here alone?"

"I don't know, waiting for somebody."

"Oh, okay, so what's your name?"

"Get away from him," Mrs. Dresdin shouted, causing raised eyebrows to turn her way.

"Please, dear, you need to stay calm," Mr. Dresdin said, pulling her closer to him. She buried her face into his chest.

Cap turned to Mr. Dresdin. "Maybe it would be best that you not see the rest of this ... we'll let you know what we find out."

Mr. Dresdin's eyes looked teary as he put his hand on Cap's shoulder. He pulled Cap towards him and said something in his ear.

Cap inhaled before responding, "We will, sir, I give you my word."

The Dresdins left the room. The playback continued.

"What's that?" The man asked.

"This?" Emil responded.

Emil's gaze turned downward, and we could see that he was holding a metallic plane in his hand. "It's my toy plane."

"Where did you get it? Can I see it?"

"No, no one touches my plane."

The man grimaced and glanced around the diner. The waitress walked by, carrying a bowl filled to the brim with ice cream.

"You like ice cream?"

"Yeah."

"Yeah, my puppy likes ice cream too."

"You have a puppy?"

"Yeah, at my house, do you want to see it?"

I turned to Eccles and said, "This is disgusting."

"Sure," Emil responded.

Just like that, the stranger had lured Emil away to his car. We all watched in angst, keeping track of the landmarks they passed. There was a gas station, then a school.

"Are you tracking this?" Cap said to Eccles and me.

"Absolutely, he's headed to the valley," Eccles said.

The car pulled into a driveway, and they walked up to a white house. The man walked Emil into the house.

"Where's the puppy?"

"It's down here," he said as he called Emil towards a basement stairwell.

My heart thumped in my chest. The counter at the bottom of the screen read -0:45.

Forty-five minutes left.

I didn't know how much more I could stand to watch.

A man in a suit approached the screen. I recognized him to be Michael Sayvian, the Assistant District Attorney. He said, "The rest of this data is evidence. Since there are clear signs of a crime being committed, I'll have to ask that everyone leave except for the detectives, the Captain, and DA office representatives."

The DIT technicians and Dr. Lamont left the room.

Sayvian walked over to the laptop and pressed a key. The images resumed.

Emil walked down into the dark stairwell. We could hear his breathing become jagged.

My pulse drummed in my ears and on my face. I was beginning to get dizzy, and I could feel a spell of nausea coming on. I couldn't bear to see any more of this. I walked over to the conference table and picked up the frame of our suspect. The technicians had printed it before leaving the room.

I gestured to Cap, pointing to the sheet. He nodded.

I walked out of the room and straight to the bathroom, where I splashed cold water on my face. At the mirror above the sink, I looked at my reflection. My eyes were bloodshot.

At my desk, I scanned the image from the sheet. I logged into the Facial Recognition System, and I uploaded the picture. Faces flashed on the screen as the system searched for our suspect. I felt enraged by what I'd seen. I wondered how Eccles and the others could stomach it. Then I saw the conference room door open. One by one, each person walked out with teary eyes and reddened faces.

"It's him," Eccles said. "The frame, he's our perp."

Cap walked over, patting his forehead with a handkerchief.

"Tell me he's in the system," he said as he stared at the screen.

Sayvian also walked over while staring at his mobile. I leaned toward him. I said, "I have to talk to you."

Sayvian's eyes snapped up to mine. His expression changed as though he'd just received more news.

"Beth, I know."

"But I haven't ..."

Just then, Cap's mobile went off, and he lowered his head to read the message. Cap jerked his head and looked over at me.

I said, "Cap ... Sayvian ... I have to talk to you guys about the Days. As it turns out, they were somewhat involved in Emil's disappearance and subsequent death. I sent two patrol officers to detain them."

"We know, Beth, we know. Apparently, your officers didn't arrive in time."

I asked, "They got away?"

Sayvian and Cap looked at each other, then Sayvian stepped back and began making a phone call. I looked at my desktop computer screen as the faces flashed by.

No match yet.

Cap approached me without speaking. His action made me nervous. I looked over at Eccles, and he shrugged his shoulders and widened his eyes.

"Beth, what exactly happened at the Days' residence?"

"Cap, they're the ones who lured Emil to the diner. They had planned to kidnap, him but at the last minute, they changed their minds."

"Did you tell them about Emil?"

"Well, we had reason to believe they were involved, the teacher, Mrs. Wallace, identified them as having initiated contact with Emil. There was no way to question them about Emil's whereabouts without divulging that he was missing."

"I see. Where were you when you heard of Emil's death?"

"I was at the Days'..." I covered my mouth as a sinking feeling began.

"Did you ..."

I stepped back as I realized what was happening. I said, "I didn't tell them about Emil, but I think they guessed from my reaction ... Oh no."

Cap lowered his head and stared at his shoes.

Just then, Sayvian approached, holding his mobile against his chest. "They're sending the coroner over now."

I shook my head. "How did they ...?"

"It was an overdose ... The patrol officers arrived to find the door open, and the Days were lying on the floor. Neither of them had a pulse at the time."

I leaned back on the desk.

"The EMS said they'd just died minutes earlier while you were here, so I'm sure there'll be some questions and ..."

"I didn't tell them, Cap."

"I know. I know. There's nothing you could have done."

At that exact moment, the flashing images on the screen froze on one face.

"William Stilton-James ... charges for Forcible Confinement ... Status: At Large," Eccles read aloud.

Eccles had been standing a few steps away and unaware of the news I'd just received.

He said, "There's no address here. Wait, the database file has some personal photos. Here's one of him standing in front of the house. Wait a second, I know that block, and we've just seen that house. I know exactly where this is, and guess what?"

"It's in the valley," I responded.

"Okay, go to the address. I'll find a judge to get us a warrant. Don't go in until I call you," Sayvian said to both of us.

Sayvian looked at Cap for a moment as though confirming my state.

Cap walked over to me and said, "Beth, about the Days, I don't know what you're feeling right now, but you couldn't have done anything. Your focus at the time had been on Emil as it should have been. It's tragic. Well, let's just leave it at that. We have a suspect now. I want both of you to go out there and get that son of a bitch!"

Chapter 23

Beth Lago. Thursday, March 21, 2075. 10:39 PM Local Time

With sirens blaring, Eccles and I rushed in the direction of the valley. Eccles overrode the E-System and then gunned it the entire way. The shriek of the patrol car's tires skidding filled the air, overpowering the siren blasts.

When we arrived within a mile of the address, Eccles slowed the patrol car down and shut down the siren. He parked a hundred yards from the presumed address of the suspect, William Stilton-James.

Sitting in the car waiting, I could feel my heart beating with increasing intensity. I wanted to rush the house and take Stilton-James down. Not having yet received the green light, however, we were forced to sit and wait.

I looked at Eccles and saw the same white-hot anger that burned in me. Moments like these tested a person's limits.

There was an ominous silence between us as we waited.

"Have you received anything yet?" Eccles asked after inhaling loudly.

"No, nothing," I said.

Suddenly a beep, then a message banner rolled around my wrist.

"Arrest warrant served for William Stilton-James."

"That's it, let's go!"

-----:-----

We got out of the car and hustled to the back of the vehicle. In front of the open trunk, we quickly fastened our bulletproof vests.

We encroached upon the area surrounding the house. Looking around, I noticed most of the houses on the street looked abandoned, condemned, or both. The suspect's house, once painted white, now looked a shade of brown and was covered in shadow. The lights were off inside. The streetlamp just in front of the house had burnt out. The darkness was going to make our approach considerably more dangerous.

A grey fence, riddled with holes, wrapped itself around the front yard of the house. Knee-high weeds and tall grass sprouted out of every corner of the lawn. Parts of a broken-down barbecue toppled over rusted lawn chairs, and a dirty tricycle stood in random spots like cemetery headstone reminders of a place that once was.

A rickety-looking wooden front porch extended the length of the house's front face. Gun drawn, I stepped onto it with care.

Each step seemed to land on the wooden plank that made the loudest creak. In the corner of my eye, I saw Eccles step towards the back of the house. I wondered how much more noise his heavy frame would've made had our positions been reversed. He'd probably fall clean through, blowing our cover. Almost at the door, I decided to quickly take the last few steps, not allowing my weight to linger in one spot for more than an instant. Placing my back close to the wall at the side of the door, but not fully against it, I extended my arm. I felt a droplet of sweat slide down my face—my heart thumped against my chest. I clenched my fist and banged on the door.

"Stilton-James! This is the OLAPD. Open the door! Stilton-James! Open the door!"

There was no response.

I took a few steps to the right and peered down to the side of the house. Eccles gestured to me that he hadn't seen anything on his end. I gestured back for him to cover me while I checked the door.

I slowly extended one hand toward the doorknob while holding my gun in the other. Taking a deep breath, I turned the doorknob slowly. To my surprise, the door slid open with an ominous screech. Inside, I could see only darkness and shadow.

I took out my flashlight, illuminating the area in front of me. I cautiously stepped forward. With each step, the floor creaked under my foot.

I thought back to Emil's playback, thinking of whether I'd seen a light switch or lamp's position. I held my breath. Stilton-James could easily be hiding anywhere in the obscured house, patiently waiting to place two bullets in my chest.

I turned my head, preparing to make the call for backup, when I heard a thunderous crash beneath my feet.

Still lighting the way with my flashlight, I rushed a few steps toward the basement door, which I'd seen on the playback. Unsure of its exact location, I reached for the door's handle. I clasped it in my hand. Opening the door, I hurried down the stairs. The sounds of gargling rose up from below. I quickened my descent. At the bottom of the stairs, I took a few steps before hitting my head on what felt like a light bulb. Instinctively, I raised my hand. I grasped a string and pulled on it, and light flooded the basement. It took a split second for my eyes to refocus. I spotted a figure in front of me—it was Stilton-James. He was wriggling and squirming while hanging from a noose, and his face was beet red.

He was choking.

I quickly holstered my gun and grabbed his legs. I lifted him up.

Eccles had followed me down the stairs.

He cut the rope while I held Stilton-James up. When the rope snapped, both Stilton-James and I collapsed to the floor. Quickly picking myself up, I untied the rope from around his neck. He began coughing and heaving. When I felt he'd regained his breath, I stood up.

"Look at me!" I yelled as I stood over his body.

He slowly turned his head to glare up at me. I felt a chill.

"William Stilton-James, you're under arrest for the murder of Emil Dresdin. You have the right to remain silent. Anything you say can and will be used against you in a court of law. You have a right to an attorney. If you cannot afford one, then The People will provide you one. Do you understand these rights?"

"I want to die," he responded.

"Not yet. Soon enough, though," Eccles muttered as he handcuffed him.

-----:-----

Cap ordered a search of Stilton-James's home. As it turned out, the body of Emil Dresdin was in another room in that same basement. The coroner determined the cause of death to be acute asphyxia. Later I found out from Eccles that Emil's data files had shown him beaten severely by Stilton-James. He had tied Emil up to a table by his wrists, ankles, and neck. Stilton-James left Emil alone in the basement thereafter. Emil had struggled furiously to get loose, but the rope somehow tangled around his neck and slowly tightened. The last thirty-five minutes of the disturbing playback showed Emil gradually losing the ability to breathe. Emil Dresdin took his final few gasps of air before, ultimately, dying alone.

Chapter 24

Dr. Trevor Miles. Thursday, March 21, 2075. 6:13 PM (Same day as the previous chapter)

After arriving home, Trevor rushed up the stairs to check in on Tia. She was sleeping. He then descended to the kitchen, where he found Sean sitting at the kitchen table.

"What's wrong with Mom?" Sean asked.

"Nothing, Sean, she's just tired. How are you doing?"

"Good. No complaints," Sean said with a smile.

"What are you working on?" Trevor asked as he sat down.

"Test tomorrow in History—Late 20th and early 21st centuries."

"Really? I *must* be getting old."

"Yeah, I know what you mean. It's strange since it wasn't that long ago. I guess it was a pretty important time."

"It was ..."

"You know, I wonder sometimes," Sean said while furrowing his brow.

"About?"

"Well, I wonder if people back then knew what was going to happen."

"That's a tough question. I think it's possible some did."

"Why didn't they do something? Why didn't they stop all of this stuff from happening?"

"Well, what do you think?" Trevor asked.

Sean said, "I think that on the surface, we're not much different than animals. We're willing to do whatever we need to do to survive. The difference happens whenever a man or woman has the urge to be selfless, whenever they become willing to sacrifice themselves for others, they become sort of symbols."

"Symbols of what?"

"Of what it means to be human."

"Interesting ... Animals fight to survive, but to be human is something more?

"Exactly!"

"So, how does this apply to your original question?"

"We forget our ... humanity."

"Meaning?"

"We forget that we're not animals, we're humans, we love, we care, we protect, we laugh, we cry. And one day we die, hopefully with dignity and grace."

Trevor paused for a moment and looked at his son carefully, "What class is this for again?"

"Dad."

Trevor had always thought of Sean as clever. He just hadn't expected to hear such wisdom from him.

Trevor said, "I'm just surprised by how quickly you're maturing."

"Well, I know you think that I don't listen to you, but I do."

Trevor nodded, "I know."

"I listen to everything you and Mom tell me. Actually, I wanted to tell you about something."

"Okay."

"Alright, so there's this kid at school, Cory. He's a big, strong kid. He actually roughed me up a few times in the fifth grade. We all try to stay out of his way whenever possible."

"Okay ..."

"And well, we had a territory-wide track meet last week. By the way, I run a decent 200-meter dash. Well, at the track meet, we all couldn't help but notice that there were kids who were far bigger than Cory was. Around these other bigger guys, it was clear that Cory was the one who felt intimidated. He wasn't acting so tough anymore. We all took notice. When we got back to the school, Cory went on a rampage trying to pick a fight with everybody around him."

"That's odd. Why do you figure he reacted that way?"

Sean said, "I guess he lost his power."

"Which was?"

"His strength, Dad, he'd lost his strength."

"Why? Did he suddenly become weak?"

"Dad."

"I'm serious. If you want to be understood, Son, you have to say what you mean."

"Fine, allow me to rephrase. He didn't become weak. He was the same exact person he'd been before the track meet. What changed was our perception of him."

"I see. What happened after that?"

"Well, I think he expected everyone to fear him the way they had before."

"What do you mean by 'expected'?"

"Well, he assumed that everyone would run away and cringe at the thought of fighting him."

"If they didn't react the way he'd assumed. How did they react?"

"Well, actually, they stood up to him. They each decided to take him on finally."

"Is that so? And what was the result of that?"

"Well, most of them got beat up."

"This doesn't sound like a happy ending."

"Everything ended happily, though, because, even though they lost their respective fights, they earned something far more valuable."

"What would this valuable thing be?"

"Pride and respect, they earned the right to walk with their heads held high, Dad."

"What an interesting story."

"There's more. Well, after he had fought pretty much everyone in sight, he came after me."

"What did you do, then?" Trevor asked and leaned in.

"Well, he walked up to me, and he looked at me dead in the eye. He said, 'You're next.' I looked back at him straight in his eye, and I told him the absolute truth. I said,

"Cory, we can fight if you want, but we all know what's going to happen. You're bigger and stronger than I am, so you will likely win, but I promise you that it will cost you. You may land twice as many punches as me, but I give you my word that I will make you pay'."

"Wow, he couldn't have taken that well."

"He wasn't happy, but then he asked me what I meant."

"What did you tell him?"

"I told him that whatever he did, it would only make matters worse. If the rest of the school hadn't stood up to him yet, then they would, after this. I told him that no matter how many times he knocked me down, I would get back up again. He could punch me once or five times. It didn't matter. Every time he picked a fight with me, I would give him exactly that. Even if I had to hack at his ankles every day, I guaranteed him that one way or another, he was going to go down."

"I'd say you picked an unconventional approach, to say the least."

Sean said, "Tell me about it. You wouldn't believe what he said. Well, I guess once he'd shaken off his initial shock, he realized that he still didn't know what to do."

"So he didn't say anything."

"No, he did say something alright. As he stood over me, I could feel that he was about to knock me out with a right hook, but I refused to stand down or show that I was afraid."

"What happened?" Trevor asked in anticipation.

"He made like he was going to punch me, but I held my ground. I didn't even flinch. When he saw that I wasn't afraid, he laughed, called me crazy, and walked away."

"Well done! It sounds like you won a fight without throwing a single punch."

"Isn't it great?"

"It is. What would you have done if he took you up on your promise?"

"I don't know. I guess I hadn't thought about it."

"Well, I suppose not having a backup plan forces one to make sure their first plan works."

"No, actually, I would have followed through with my promise."

"So, you'd get beat up every day?"

"I guess so. If that's what it takes then, that's what it takes."

"Interesting philosophy you have there," Trevor said.

"Well, you'd know."

Trevor asked, "I'd know. How would I know?"

"It's your philosophy, Dad."

"Okay, please explain this to me, Son."

"Dad, you said exactly that phrase to me when all that happened, you know, when we moved. Don't you remember? I asked you what was going on, and you said we had to move. I asked you why and you said it because you'd made a choice, and now we had to move away."

"I'm trying to remember, Sean, but as you know, I had a lot on my mind at the time."

"Dad, I asked you why you'd make a choice that'd cause us to move, and you said that it was because sometimes the person who does the right thing is the one who, in the end, is forced to leave. I then asked you again why and you said because you must always do what's right, and if it means you suffer, then 'that's what it takes.'"

"Sean ... I."

"Dad, you don't have to say anything because I already know what you're going to say."

"You do?"

"Yes, I know I'm young, and I still have a lot to learn, but I want you to know I always believed that you had done the right thing, and I know eventually everyone will realize it."

Trevor admired his son's wide-eyed innocence. He couldn't help but smile.

"It's getting late, Son. You're not going to be very successful in writing your exam if you're exhausted."

"Okay, I was pretty much done anyway," Sean replied while packing up his books and then stuffing them in his bag.

"Good night, Dad," Sean said just before going up the stairs.

"Good night, Son. Love you!"

Trevor heard the steady sound of footsteps. He assumed Sean had started up the stairs. Then, he perceived a pause in the steps.

Echoing from the stairwell, he heard his son say, "Love you too, Dad."

Trevor got up from the table and turned around to flick off the light switch. In the corner of his eye, Trevor saw something on the ground. He walked over to pick it up and noticed it was a piece of lined paper. He recognized Sean's writing. The paper read:

> Assignment: Write a journal entry, a narrative or a poem about a moment in which someone you admire overcame a difficult situation. You can write it in the first person or third person.
>
> Name: Sean Martin
> Type of document: Poem
> The person chosen as the focus: My dad
> Narrative type: Written in the first person as my dad

Whatever it takes
Must we do battle just for battle's sake?
All the while knowing in our hearts
There can never be an end.
What cruel means, mean men seek
When to an end, means to The End.
Perhaps one day when the chill of November morning rain
Pierces bone to cause unrelenting pain.
A day when laughter and fickle-foolish love
Are a memory, a shadow, a never-was.
When the day turns to night, and all seems lost.
When all that remains is one last breath.
I wish you to know.
I wish you to sense.
That all the weight and all the pain;
All the loss of love

**And the loved ones lost;
Will never be enough
To bury me again.
Know that as certain as the rays of dawn's first morning light;
I will never let this end.
I will never cease to fight.**

Trevor was touched to read Sean's emotionally charged words. He gently placed the tattered sheet on the table in the spot where he'd found it and smiled.

Just then, a call came through on Trevor's mobile. He assumed it was Peter calling as Trevor had forgotten to call him back.

"Hello?"

"Trevor? It's Marjorie." He could hear a distinct sadness in her voice.

"I have terrible news."

"What happened?"

"It's Dresdin. He was going crazy earlier, and now I know why."

"What happened?"

"Apparently, Emil's missing," Marjorie said bluntly.

Trevor couldn't believe his ears. Trevor suspected kidnapping. Then he wondered who would be foolish enough to kidnap the most famous D-Eye baby in the world.

"That's terrible news."

"I know."

"What should we do?" Trevor asked.

"Well, apparently, there isn't anything to do. Dresdin doesn't want us involved. Willy Taylor was down here ordering everyone around, and he convinced Pax to teach him how to use the Playback equipment."

"Willy Taylor did that?" Trevor asked.

"Yes. Poor Emil, I can't believe he's out there, and no one has the slightest idea where he might be. I really hope he's okay."

"Of course, it's absolutely terrible. He'll turn up, I'm sure of it," Trevor stated, but in the back of his mind, he felt preoccupied with something. He said, "I'm surprised by how involved Taylor's been."

"I'm not. I never trusted him, not from the very beginning," Marjorie said.

"Okay, well, thank you for letting me know. I guess we'll have just to wait to see how we can help, if at all. We'll talk tomorrow morning."

Trevor hung up the phone and turned around. Standing alone in the kitchen, he got the distinct sense that something pivotal was happening. What exactly this meant for him, his team and his family remained a mystery.

Chapter 25

Dr. Trevor Miles. Friday, March 22, 2075. 5:46 AM

Trevor woke up earlier than usual. He got dressed, and before leaving, he gently kissed Tia on the cheek. She was still in a deep sleep. He didn't want to disturb her as the doctor had ordered that she get at least one more day's rest after the surgery.

On the drive to work, he decided to call his old friend Peter.
"Hello?"
"Hi, Peter. Trevor here. I got your message."
"Trevor, how are you?"
"Good. How are *you*?"
"Good ... listen, we need to get together. There's some stuff I need to discuss with you."
"Okay, how about tonight? Did you want to tell me any of it now?"
There was a pause before Peter responded. "I'd rather not discuss it over the phone."
"Okay, fair enough. How about the Bear Hug Pub at eight?"
"That sounds fine. Trevor?"
"Yes?"
"Watch your back in the meantime, okay?"
Trevor shrugged at the comment. When he didn't hear a snicker on Peter's end, however, he responded, "Okay. I will."
Trevor didn't know what to make of his conversation with Peter. How bad could this news be?

Trevor pulled into DIT headquarters and saw Dresdin's car was already in its reserved parking spot. Late last night, when he'd received the call from Marjorie, he'd been shocked to hear of Emil's disappearance. He felt concerned, but he found solace in remembering that children often briefly disappear only to pop up later on. He remembered that Sean had given them several scares over the years. He knew that there was a very good chance that Emil could suddenly appear, and all the worry would have been for nothing.

He entered the empty foyer and walked to the elevator. As the sound of his footsteps echoed eerily around him, he thought to himself that this was likely the first time he'd ever seen this foyer empty. He descended in the elevator and decided to get off at Dresdin's floor before continuing to his own. He exited the elevator and walked down to Dresdin's office. He arrived at the partially open door. Peeking through, he saw Dresdin hunched over and leaning on his desk. He decided to knock.

"Yes? Who is it?" Dresdin asked in a low fragile voice.

"It's Trevor, sir."

"Please come in."

Trevor stepped through. Dresdin walked over to him, flung his arms around Trevor, and hugged him.

"Sir?"

"It's over, Trevor. It's over. Emil's gone. That son of bitch killed him."

"Who?"

"That son of a bitch, William Stilton-James. Who else?"

"I'm so sorry, sir."

"It's terrible, just terrible!" Dresdin cried. After a moment, he stopped crying. He said, "We caught him though, Trevor. We caught him, and he's in custody right now."

Trevor didn't know how to respond.

"Mr. Dresdin, I'm surprised to see you at work today. I would have figured that with all the stuff going on ..."

"No, no, I haven't taken a day off in years. Besides, being at work helps keep me distracted. The worst thing is I don't know how to interpret what's happened. I don't know if it was an attack on me, DIT or ... or ..." Dresdin began to sob as he struggled to continue. "A disgusting act by a senseless man."

Trevor stood by with a conciliatory expression on his face. He understood why Dresdin would be so upset. However, the sight of a normally composed Dresdin in his dark double-breasted suit breaking down was difficult to watch. Dresdin paused for several moments before continuing.

He said, "Trevor, I need a favour from you."

"Anything, sir."

"I need you to interview him."

"Do you mean Stilton-James?"

"Yes, yes, Stilton-James. Will you do it? Please? At least do it as a personal favour to me."

Trevor turned away from Dresdin as he contemplated the request. He could feel Dresdin becoming emotional. He decided to try to appeal to his logic.

"Mr. Dresdin, the police have their psychiatrists to interview suspects. Besides, I wouldn't even be allowed anywhere near him."

"Don't worry about that. I'll figure out a way. I need to know what kind of man he is. I need to know why he harmed my baby."

Trevor's instincts told him that he should respectfully decline.

As he looked at Dresdin, he noticed, for the first time, a shade of vulnerability. He looked more human at that moment than ever before. He wondered if Dresdin's iconic, virtually celebrity status might have clouded things. As he looked upon him, perceiving the distress in his eyes, Trevor couldn't help but think that he was looking at a grieving father, nothing less, and nothing more.

Trevor said, "Of course, Mr. Dresdin. I will try to help you in any way that I can."

"Thank you, thank you, thank you so much, Trevor. I'll set up the meeting. Don't worry about that part at all."

----:----

Later that morning, Pax arrived at the lab with a smug smile on his face.

"What are you smiling about?" Trevor asked.

"I'm not smiling at all. So, I suppose you must know by now what's been going on."

"Emil?"

"Oh yeah. Well, there's that too, but other things have been going on too," Pax said while dropping his head. Trevor sensed Pax's embarrassment at having sidestepped something so major.

Trevor said, "Right. Okay. Well, I heard some news from Marjorie."

"Did Marjorie tell you about Reverse-Looping?"

"You've made a breakthrough," Trevor said while sitting down on one of the stools in the lab. Pax remained standing.

"That's right. I know, without a doubt, that we can do it," Pax said sharply, rising from his chair.

"What are these concerns that you had?"

"Right, they were more like obstacles than concerns," Pax said as he sat down.

"Okay, well, what are they?"

"It's something I realized when I went back and ran tests on some of the D-Eye playbacks. You recall the initial premise for D-Eye?"

"Of course, we wanted to record experiences."

"Exactly, this is why we chose to place the implants in the right and left hemispheres."

"Right, we did that to take advantage of the message delay between the lobes. So you remember," Pax said.

"Of course I remember, Pax, it was my idea," Trevor declared.

Pax said, "Was it? Well, anyway, we can talk about that later. The implants record the information as it goes from the left and right sides of the brain and then directly into the patient's consciousness."

"Precisely ... The implants are designed to record the information as it comes through the right temporal lobe."

"The *conceptualized* version."

"Correct. Our on-site equipment then takes that information and synthesizes it into useable data. The issue we've always had is in the synthesis of this information. Reverse-Looping caused me so many issues because I had been trying to create hardware that could synthesize the information as it played back in the patient's consciousness."

Trevor finally realized where Pax was going with this.

"We already have all the playback equipment we need."

"Exactly! It's been in the receiving patient's head all along," Pax said.

"How is one person able to comprehend the experience of another person without ...?"

Trevor realized the paradox.

"Do you see?" Pax asked.

"I understand. It would be possible, but forcing the information through could be grossly damaging to the receiving patient's mental state."

Pax said, "Well, such an extreme amount of uncertainty is its own answer. We may not know what will happen when we mix two volatile chemicals except the fact that something ..."

"Explosive will happen," Trevor said, completing Pax's phrase.

"It's not just a playback, and we're inserting consciousness itself."

"Marjorie was right," Trevor said, "the answer as to whether or not it is possible is directly connected to the answer to one question."

Pax said, "What their intentions are."

"Exactly, Pax ..."

"I know, and you're welcome," Pax said with a grin.

Trevor began walking away when Pax asked a question.

"So, what do we do now?"

"Nothing, we continue as we normally would," Trevor said. He stepped closer to Pax and pretended to look down at his watch as he whispered. He said, "Continue working and get everything ready. If things go awry, then we'll have to destroy everything." Raising his eyes in Pax's direction, Trevor smiled and patted him on the back. "Good job, Pax. Dammit, good job."

-----:-----

After a few hours, Dresdin appeared in Trevor's office.

"So, how's my ace?"

"Umm ...?"

"How are you doing, Trevor?"

"I'm doing well."

"I just talked to Pax. It looks like things are moving along very well with Reverse-Looping."

Trevor searched Dresdin's face, trying to see if he could tell what Pax had told him. As always, Dresdin's facial expression was inscrutable. Trevor made peace with the fact that he'd never met a person more difficult to read than Dresdin.

Trevor said, "Yeah, he's something else. Not a bad hire, huh?"

Trevor had almost forgotten that Dresdin had hired Pax.

"You certainly know how to pick them, sir."

Initially caught off guard by Dresdin's strangely upbeat behaviour, Trevor reminded himself that grief sometimes appeared in strange and unusual ways. The death of a child often caused people to react in unforeseen ways.

"Trevor, my only consolation through all this crap is it that we caught the guy, and we're going to make him pay."

"I understand."

"That brings me to the reason for my visit. I've set up an interview for you with Stilton-James. It's going to be in thirty minutes, so you might want to get over there."

"Oh, I didn't realize it would be so soon."

We've got to strike while the iron is hot."

"I'll head over there immediately, Mr. Dresdin."

"Listen, Trevor. When you go over there, I want you to find out who William Stilton-James really is. I want to know his strengths, his weaknesses. I want to know whom, if anyone, helped him to carry out this crime. Most of all, I want you to find out if he feels even an ounce of remorse."

Trevor looked up at Dresdin for a moment to assess his expression and confirm that he had heard him right. Dresdin's steely stare showed that he was dead serious.

Trevor said, "I'll give you a full report upon my return."

Perfect," Dresdin said as the two men left Trevor's office.

-----:-----

Dresdin turned to Trevor in the hall, lifting his finger as though he'd remembered some important detail. He asked that Trevor come close before telling him. The detail that Dresdin relayed to Trevor in confidence was puzzling. He told him to arrive at the back door of the Central Precinct at exactly two o'clock.

Trevor had so many questions.

Why was it so important to Dresdin that I speak to the murderer?

Why would I have to go to the back door?

Trevor drove to the Central Precinct in Old Los Angeles. He began shifting his focus to the task of conducting the interview. The timing and the circumstances of Dresdin's request were odd, but ultimately, he did have the job qualifications. After all, he was a psychiatrist by trade, and he had specialized in treating sociopaths in the past.

He looked at his watch. He had one minute to spare. Dresdin advised he'd be at the back door of the precinct at exactly two o'clock. It seemed an odd order, but just as Dresdin had said, the door flung open right on time. Holding the door open was an abnormally large man with straw-coloured hair and a muscular build. He was dressed in casual clothes. Trevor attempted to greet him, but the man simply gave him a look and turned his gaze into the precinct.

Unhindered by the bizarre circumstances, Trevor stepped through the door and then down the hall. The fair-haired man, who had the same bold looks that Trevor tended to associate with police officers, told him to continue down the stairs at the end of the hall. Trevor proceeded down the staircase.

At the bottom of the stairs lay the holding cells. As he saw the metallic cages before him, he realized that he didn't even know what Stilton-James looked like. After walking past a whole row of empty cells, he arrived at the final one to find a man sitting on the cell's concrete floor.

"William!" Trevor snapped in hopes of triggering an honest reaction.

The man sitting on the ground jumped up at the sound of the name. The movement reminded Trevor of how a marionette would spring up in response to a jolt running through its strings. He moved quickly, but he didn't look at all in control of his movements.

"Yes?"

"William Stilton-James?"

"Yes, officer?"

Trevor heard Stilton-James's assumption. He opted against correcting him.

"Well, William, it seems we still have questions for you."

"Okay, sure, whatever you say, officer. I'll cooperate in any way I can."

Trevor said, "I hope so. Lying will only make your situation worse."

"I understand, sir."

"We'll start with some routine questions. What's your age?"

"My age?"

"Are you going to repeat every question I ask?"

"No, I'm sorry. I'm thirty-four."

"Thank you. When did you move to Old Los Angeles?"

"What do you mean, sir? I've lived here my whole life."

"William, I've already warned you against lying."

"I'm telling the truth. I've never lived anywhere else other than Old Los Angeles."

"That's very unlikely. William, have you ever moved from Old Los Angeles?"

"No, sir."

"Stilton-James, I've already advised you against lying."

"I'm not lying, sir."

"Well, you must be lying, as according to your age, you would have been in the city during the Dark Times and then TFS, so if this is true, then you must have been one of the Scarklingas who survived TFS."

Stilton-James lowered his head. Trevor waited for a minute for a response, but none was forthcoming.

"Well? Am I looking at a ghost then? Were you one of the Scarklingas who survived?"

"No, sir," Stilton-James said in a barely discernible voice.

"Excuse me?"

"No, sir."

"Well, what is it then?"

"Sir?"

"How could you have lived in Old Los Angeles during the Dark Times and TFS and not be a Scarklinga?"

"I don't know, sir."

"If you don't know, then who would?"

"I don't know, sir."

"Come on, Stilton-James, just think about it."

"I'm sorry. I don't understand."

"Stop with these games. Tell me the truth."

"I am ..."

"No, you're not! You haven't said one honest thing."

"I don't know what you're asking me, sir?"

"This is useless!" Trevor said, throwing his arms in the air.

Trevor's actions, though random in appearance, were precise and calculated. Within his vast and ever-growing repertoire of interrogatory techniques lay a prescribed plan, which he resurrected whenever he needed the absolute *truth*. Needing truthful answers seemed like an obvious psychoanalysis strategy, but the reality of the situation revealed just the opposite. The truth was more of a reflection of the patient's perspective than an actual state of reality.

The situation before him required the more conventional version of the truth, the one in which he discerned from Stilton-James's insight into what happened. He knew that with Stilton-James, this was going to be virtually impossible. Nonetheless, he felt obligated to try at the very least. Despite the technique's unquestionable manipulative nature, it had proven to Trevor its effectiveness in past cases involving known sociopaths.

He didn't know whether Stilton-James spoke the truth or not, but his strategy was to question his initial answer. He did this irrespective of the answer's apparent truthfulness. The accusations of lying would continue, until finally, the subject felt forced to tell one hinge-pin truthful statement, which they tended to believe would miraculously convince the interviewer of the truthfulness of all their previous statements.

"I'm sorry, sir."

"Are you?"

"Yes ... sir."

"Then tell the truth!"

"I am, sir."

"No, you're not!"

"Stop saying that! Stop that!" Stilton-James yelled as he covered his ears.

After a brief silence, Trevor spoke again. "Let's try again then. Let's list all the places you've lived throughout your life ..."

"I've lived in Old Los Angeles."

"Where else?"

"We didn't live anywhere else. We were in Old Los Angeles even after Mama and Papa died. Even after the green smoke."

There was a pause as Trevor considered what Stilton-James had just said. The words echoed across the hollowness of the concrete cell.

"What did you say?"

"I'm sorry, sir, it's the truth, I swear."

"No, no, hold on. What did you say?"

"We never lived anywhere else ..."

"No, William ... even after the ... what came?"

"The green smoke, sir."

"Where did you hear of this?"

"Hear of it, sir?"

"Where did you read it then?"

"I'm sorry, sir, I can't read."

Trevor observed Stilton-James's expression closely in search of signs of deception. His demeanour seemed sincere. He decided to test his suspicions. He had to know if the "green smoke" comment emanated from memory or imagination.

"How old were you when your parents died, William?"

"I can't remember when Mama died, but papa died when I was ... I guess about nine years old."

"How did he die?"

Again, Stilton-James lowered his head.

Trevor said, "William, just say it. Sometimes it feels better to talk about these things."

"It was the green smoke."

Those words resonated within Trevor. He knew that green smoke could only mean one thing. An illiterate, uneducated man like Stilton-James may have known of The Final Stand, but it was unlikely he would know a detail like the deadly gas colour. After twenty-five years, information like that only existed in written reports and affidavits, both of which he would never have had access to.

Did TFS really kill his father?

As Trevor contemplated that notion, the depth of the tragedy paralyzed him. He considered the implications of suffering years of abuse and then losing both of one's parents. Stilton-James's past easily pointed to some different explanations for a possible diagnosis. He could be suffering from a post-traumatic disorder or some social dissociative disorder. Trevor realized that he'd need more time to understand Stilton-James's condition. Therefore, the diagnosis that other mental health professionals from the defence and the prosecution were likely to assign him.

He continued his questioning with an apologetic and acknowledging statement.

He said, "I'm sorry about your parents, William. I know it's difficult to lose a loved one, especially one as close as a parent. What did you do after your father died?"

Stilton-James lowered his head.

Trevor asked, "William?"

Stilton-James lifted his head slowly before stating, "I just tried to fight the night."

"Fight the night?"

"Papa used to say you must fight the night till morning light. We were always looking for places to sleep. It seemed like even before I opened my eyes each morning, we were looking for the next safe spot. After he died, I continued searching every day, as most places were only safe once and then never again. There was so much fighting and even more hiding. Sometimes I'd found a rock or a stick, and when the night came, I did what papa taught me. I fought till morning light."

"William, were you alone the whole time?"

"No, not all the time, there were other kids like me, and we tried to help each other."

"Really?"

"Yes, there was this one kid ... what was his name?" Stilton-James said as he looked to be trying to remember. He said, "I can't remember his name."

Trevor noticed that Stilton-James's eyes had begun to glaze over. Stilton-James remained silent for several seconds, much to Trevor's confusion. After about a minute of watching as he stared off into nothingness, Trevor decided to break the silence.

"William?"

Stilton-James snapped his gaze toward Trevor. The look in his eyes sent shivers down Trevor's back. The look was one of rage.

"How could you!"

"What?"

Stilton-James said, "How could you?"

"How could I what?"

Stilton-James slowly and ominously walked up to the bars. In the quickest of movements, he slipped his hands through the bars and began clawing in Trevor's direction. Trevor pivoted backwards in anticipation. He managed to slide back quick enough to avoid Stilton-James's reach. Trevor watched in shock as the Stilton-James swung his arms in his direction, screaming at the top of his lungs.

"William?"

"Ahhh!" Stilton-James roared.

Trevor slid backwards a few more steps back, never drawing his eyes away from Stilton-James.

He climbed up the stairs and exited the same door he had used to enter. In the stairwell, he could still hear the cries.

"How could you?"

Startled and feeling completely awkward, he left the precinct through the same path he'd taken in.

-----:-----

Thinking of what to tell Dresdin upon his return to HQ, he surmised that he didn't want to have to tell him the truth. Trevor had seen his share of disturbed patients. Stilton-James's condition puzzled and frightened him.

He didn't see how it would be possible to provide a report that excluded what he'd just seen. He wondered what Stilton-James's diagnosis would be as the man suffered from a psychological condition. He resolved that he didn't have to provide any conclusions. Perhaps he could simply state the facts about Stilton-James's past, and whatever conclusions flowed from this info would be complete of Dresdin's own making. He would simply tell Dresdin that Stilton-James had allegedly suffered years of morbidly violent abuse at the hands of the Scarklingas then allegedly witnessed his father's death at the hands of TFS.

Chapter 26

Beth Lago. Friday, March 22, 2075. 2:05 PM (The same day as the previous chapter)

As more people within the investigation circle became aware of the murder, it became increasingly difficult to keep things quiet. Inevitably, there was a leak somewhere along the line, and it only took twenty-four hours for the news of Emil's murder to become public knowledge.

Emil's death seemed to trigger a massive outpouring of emotion. There were candlelight vigils. Organizers were planning protests in front of the precinct. It seemed as though Emil's death had been the final straw for many people. There were feelings of sadness, frustration, and anger. Cap added extra security at the precinct due to the threats on Stilton-James's life. The precinct became the safest place in all of Old Los Angeles for Stilton-James.

Following his arrest, officers admitted Stilton-James into an isolated wing at OLA General Hospital. Eccles and I still hadn't questioned him because of the severity of his injuries last night.

At six this morning, Sheriff McCoy ordered the transfer of Stilton-James to the precinct for questioning. From what Cap told us, McCoy had been livid that no one had questioned Stilton-James. For some unknown reason, Eccles neglected to tell me until 10:14 in the morning, nearly two hours after Stilton-James had arrived at the precinct's lower level holding cells.

-----:-----

From behind the two-way mirrored window, Eccles and I peered into interrogation room 1. Expressionless, Stilton-James stared back at us.

"What do you think?" I whispered to Eccles, who stood beside me cross-armed.

"Don't be deceived," Eccles said without taking his eyes off of Stilton-James.

"So you're thinking the same thing that I am," I whispered.

"He doesn't look like much, but believe me, this guy has another side. I saw it with my own eyes."

From the back of the narrow Obs room, Sayvian approached. He'd been speaking to Cap and now seemed ready to confer with us.

He took up position between the viewing window and us and said, "We've got a pretty rock-solid case, but we'll want to get a motive out of him. We need to know—*why*."

Sayvian turned his head in Cap's direction as he instructed us.

Cap stepped beside me, looked through the window, and said, "He's right. We just need a motive. Do whatever you need to do to get him to cough it up."

Eccles and I nodded before peering back in Stilton-James's direction.

I would usually feel calm and composed before entering into an interview. I was typically capable of tapping into the kind of dissociation necessary for logical, organized thought. This time seemed different.

This case felt more personal than the others did, and I'd seen too much not to feel affected. The anger stirred inside, making me nauseous.

Eccles leaned in toward me, "Beth?"

"Yeah, I know. You're a hothead," I said.

"I was going to say that for once, you look as angry as I usually look before going into one of these things."

"Who'd a thought, huh?" I quipped with a half-smile.

"Not me, that's for sure. I never thought I'd ever see *you* lose your cool."

"I haven't lost anything, at least not yet. Be alert in there because if I do, then he's going to need all the help he can get."

"Are you guys ready?" Cap asked from a few feet away.

"Absolutely," I replied.

Interrogation room 1 was empty but for a metallic table and three chairs. Stilton-James sat in one chair with his hands cuffed behind his back on one side of the table. He barely lifted his head as we stepped inside. I marched over to a chair opposite him and sat down while crossing my arms. Eccles remained standing with a wide stance and his hands on his hips?

Stilton-James looked to be in his forties. He sat in the chair with a downward posture like a dying plant.

His facial features were boyish, almost comical, with perfectly rounded dark brown eyes, slightly chubby cheeks, and a relaxed expression. A childlike button nose sat at the center of a disarming face. Both his clothes and physique were frumpy but not sloppy. He wore a light grey polo-type shirt tucked into tanned coloured pants hemmed about an inch too short. His hair—precisely parted along one side and neatly pulled over. At roughly one hundred eighty pounds and five foot eight, he was slightly but not grossly overweight.

After several seconds, he perked up in his chair as though he hadn't known we were there until then. He panned back and forth between Eccles and me. We glared at him. We'd used this technique to great effect in the past. The strategy was to let the anxiety brew for as long as possible. We didn't expect Stilton-James to come out and confess without first knowing what we knew. Naturally, he would start by telling us how wrong we'd been to arrest him. The guilty ones always wanted to begin convincing you as soon as possible about their innocence. Allowing the suspect to speak without asking any questions forced them to tell their full story, which would be easily broken down upon questioning if full of lies. We'd seen all kinds of liars in the past, and most of them had well-rehearsed stories. Eventually, we would ask questions to get the story's facts, irrespective of chronology. The mistakes would flow from there. First, however, we needed to hear his story.

"Well?" Stilton-James asked.

We remained silent.

"Hello, do you think it would be possible to go home soon?" he asked.

Again, we remained silent.

"Why aren't you talking? What am I doing here? Is this some sort of game?"

By now, the perpetrator usually revealed some level of guilt, but Stilton-James wasn't even willing to acknowledge the need to deny anything. I looked over him, re-examined his posture, his facial expressions. Everything in his appearance seemed designed to disarm. He looked completely inoffensive, normal, and approachable. I began to wonder if this played into his child-luring tactics. These predatory types always seemed to use the most effective strategies to slip under a child's innate defences.

From a young age, a child tended to form bonds with certain adults, primarily their main caregivers. After a time, the child would begin to trust other adults within his or her surroundings. It's always been part of a human being's built-in survival strategy. Facial expressions, tone of voice, posture all provided a means to discern danger.

"You know why you're here," I said as I opened the file and tossed pictures of Emil's battered body on the table. "That's why."

"Oh my God, what happened to him?" Stilton-James said with desperation in his eyes and shock on his face.

His reaction looked sincere, but I knew he couldn't deny knowledge of the beating he'd given Emil.

I looked over at Eccles, noticing his jaw flexing and his eyes widening. Clearly, he was beginning to get angry.

"William, listen for a moment ... Can you hear that?" I asked.

Stilton-James looked at me, terror in his eyes.

Faintly, from the other side of the closed and barred window, the sound of chanting resonated.

"Make--him--pay ... Make--him--pay!"

"They're talking about you—you know? They want you dead. Maybe we give them their wish. Maybe we give them five minutes in a room with you!" Eccles growled.

"What do you want from me?" Stilton-James pleaded.

"We want to know what happened," Eccles said, directing his eyes and his right index finger toward the pictures on the table.

"I don't know what happened to that little boy. I woke up, I was choking from a rope, and I couldn't breathe," Stilton-James pleaded.

I couldn't believe the expression on Stilton-James's face. I didn't know what angered me more. The fact that his words and expressions seemed intended to conjure emotions of sympathy or that he refused to acknowledge what he'd done.

"William!" I yelled as I leaned in towards him. "We found this boy's body in *your* basement. Did you forget that?"

He said, "I don't know ... what happened"

I looked over at Eccles before responding.

"Fine, by all means, have it your way. We gave you the chance to fess up, but ..."

He said, "I swear to you. I don't know what happened."

Just then, Cap opened the door.

"Eccles, Beth, could you step out here a moment?"

Eccles and I left the room to find Cap, Sayvian, and another man I didn't recognize.

Cap looked over at Sayvian, "What do you think?"

"I'd like a confession, but it's tough to tell if we'll get one or not."

The man, whom I didn't recognize, jumped in, "Why don't you give me a few minutes with him?"

Sayvian turned to Cap, who nodded.

Sayvian then turned to the man. "Go ahead."

The man opened the door and entered the room.

"Could someone please explain to me who this guy is?" I asked bluntly.

"That ... is a psychiatrist ..."

"What?" Eccles asked as he stared at Cap in disbelief.

Cap said, "Look, we're looking for the truth. When he gets counsel, they'll order a psych-evaluation anyway, and when they do, we're going to need a leg to stand on."

Eccles turned away in disgust, shifting his attention back to the interrogation room window.

"Hello, William."

"Hello."

"How are you feeling?"

"Uh, fine."

"Tell me about last night."

"I don't remember."

"Okay, well, why don't we start with what you do remember."

"What do you mean?"

"Why don't you think back to yesterday and tell me what you remember, anything at all."

"I was at home watching television, and then I was hanging from a rope."

"So, you don't remember what happened in between."

"No, I told you, I don't remember."

"Does that happen often?"

"Does *what* happen often?"

"Do you often wind up somewhere and not remember how you got there?"

Stilton-James lowered his head.

"William, you can tell me. How often does it happen?"

"I don't know ... every once in a while, I guess."

"William, does anyone else live with you?"

"No."

"Do you have any family?"

Stilton-James hung his head low again. "No."

"What about your parents?"

"They're dead."

"I'm sorry. When did they die?"

"Do I have to talk about this again?" Stilton-James asked while turning stiff. His eyes widened unnaturally. He raised his sleeves, which appeared covered, from shoulder to wrist, with scars.

"William? Did your parents do that to you?" The psychiatrist asked as he pointed to the scars on Stilton-James's arms.

"No. They did." Stilton-James responded in a stern, monotone voice.

"They?"

"They hurt me, and then They hurt the mother and then father. Mother died, and then there was just Father and me. The green smoke came one night and killed him and everyone else. The green smoke came and killed them all," Stilton-James responded in a hollow voice.

"What did you say? Did you say the green smoke?"

I stepped back from the window as a distant memory struck me.

I had all but erased the memory of the day TFS had gassed Old Los Angeles, but something in Stilton-James's words caused buried memories to flow back vividly. I remembered that the fear of my father leaving before I could say goodbye had kept me awake all that night, the night of The Final Stand.

My father had been away the majority of the night, but he returned to our tent before sunrise to kiss my mother goodbye. I had been pretending to be asleep when he'd knelt to kiss me on the forehead. I was too young to understand what was happening. All I knew was that I didn't want my father to go. Grabbing onto his leg tightly, I had pleaded, "Please don't go, Daddy, please don't go!"

In farewell, he kissed me on the cheek and smiled. "Don't worry, Bethy. I'll be back." I held him as tightly as I could, but it didn't matter. He was far too strong for me to hold down. I remember him telling me that he loved me before standing up and leaving for the meeting point at the foot of the mountain.

I remember the moon was so bright that Old Los Angeles seemed to glow. Minutes later, when my mother left the tent, I had made my escape. I sprinted as fast as I could in the direction my father had gone. In an instant, I realized the source of my recurring nightmare. It was about that night.

I had heard my mother screaming in the background, but I kept running until I reached a clearing, then suddenly, the thunder of a helicopter forced me to drop to the ground. The helicopter passed high before diving low over the city. Plumes of smoke fell from the helicopter as the clouds blanketed the sparsely lit city. I could see the smoke was a brilliant shade of emerald green. It wasn't until long after that I learned what had truly happened and what the 'green smoke' was. After that, I had nightmares for weeks, imagining that the green smoke had been the last thing that everyone in the city had seen. Father had entered the city with the rest of the militia, and of course, the entire city had become a graveyard. I never saw him again. That night, he developed a cough, which didn't stop for weeks. They kept him in another tent as a precaution, but at night, I could hear the sound of coughing and deep sobs. My mother said that the gas had made him sick, but when I was old enough to understand such things, I guessed that the sight of so much death had somehow damaged him. We were never fully certain as to what had caused it, but ultimately, he never recovered. I'd buried the memory since.

The Green Smoke, I had read articles about the survivors of the gassing. There was only a handful of them, mostly children, almost all of them orphaned. In the articles, the survivors had always spoken of the "green smoke" as if it was some mythological creature. They would talk about how "green smoke" had come for them. Almost all of these survivors, over time, developed a psychological disorder of some kind. Many of them killed themselves.

The psychiatrist exited the interrogation room and approached us.

"That man has suffered traumas of the highest degree."

He turned to the window peering at Stilton-James, who was staring blankly at the wall. "I'll have to examine him further, but from what I gather, he's suffered years of abuse at the hands of the Scarklingas, then he had to watch one of his parents being gassed to death. He has only seen suffering, violence, and pain, and yet he sits there unmoved. When he says he doesn't remember, he may be telling the truth. The man you see is a facade, inside there's a monster."

"Doctor, what do you ...?"

"He's a sociopath, plain and simple, man-made sociopath," the psychiatrist said as he walked away.

-----:-----

I couldn't shake the irony. Emil had been a beacon of hope, he was just a boy, but he had become a symbol of a safe and secure future. Many believed his story to be the last step in a journey that began the day TFS had taken back Los Angeles. The hatred for the Scarklingas had been so great that people willingly sacrificed an innocent few to kill all of the Scarklingas. They couldn't have ever imagined that the sins of the past would ever come back to haunt them. They believed their actions, if hidden out of sight, would somehow disappear. Stilton-James had managed to survive the trauma he'd suffered. With only a life of pain to work with, he'd reflected his impression of the world onto it. Stilton-James and Emil both had, tragically, been in the wrong place at precisely the wrong time.

"This is ridiculous!" Eccles said under his breath.

"Perhaps you're right, but we wanted the truth, and there it is," Sayvian responded.

"So, you're backing off of him?" Eccles asked.

"No, not at all. We're still going forward. His fate will be up to a court to decide," Sayvian said as he walked away.

Cap just shook his head as he retreated to his office.

Eccles and I turned to the window where Stilton-James sat like a stone statue, completely straight and lifeless.

Chapter 27

Dr. Trevor Miles. Wednesday, March 27, 2075. 11:34 AM

A few days had passed, and Trevor still hadn't heard anything from Dresdin. He wondered if he had forgotten about the Stilton-James interview. Just after lunch, however, Dresdin appeared in Trevor's office.

"Trevor, I want to hear all about the first interview, but I'm afraid we've come upon an opportune time for your second interview with him."

"Second?"

"Yeah, I want you to do a total of three."

"Okay."

"So, same as before, the back door of the precinct. It's 12:58, be at the back door at 1:30 exactly. Remember, I want to know any and every possible defence that a raging sociopath may cook up. Go now, hurry."

Trevor followed all of the same steps as the time before. Just as the first time, the blonde man opened the door for him. Again, he neither said a word nor maintained eye contact. Descending the stairs, Trevor thought back to the words Dresdin had used. He had said sociopath to describe Stilton-James. He wondered why he'd chosen that term. He continued walking past the row of holding cells, and just as before, Stilton-James was in the last cell. This time he was sitting on the floor with his legs curled up in front of him.

"William?"

"Oh! Hello!"

"You're cheerful today," Trevor remarked as he sat down in the chair in front of Stilton-James's cell.

"Today?"

"Yeah, you weren't so cheerful the last time we spoke."

"We've never spoken before, sir."

"Excuse me?"

"I think you're mistaken, sir."

Trevor studied Stilton-James's expression. He looked like he sincerely didn't recognize him.

"You're probably right. So anyway, how are you?" Trevor asked, deciding to ignore Stilton-James behaviour for the moment.

"I'm fine."

"Fine? You're not bothered by being here in this cell?"

"No, this place is clean. They bring you food, even."

"Right ... I suppose that is a good thing."

"Yeah, it's great! They don't make you work either. They don't hurt you, beat you up, or burn you."

"What did you say, William?"

"What?"

"Did you say burn?"

"Yes."

"Who burned you?"

"Them."

"Who would ... Them be?"

"Them, you know Them. You want to see the scars?"

Stilton-James had already rolled up his pant legs before Trevor could answer, revealing a sight that caused Trevor to turn away in horror. Stilton-James had burns up and down the length of his legs.

"Oh, my ... Does that hurt, William?"

Stilton-James looked downwards before answering. "Well, yes, on account of all the infections."

"When did this happen to you?"

"Oh ... This didn't happen on one day."

"It didn't?"

"No. These down here were all from the same day," Stilton-James said while pointing to areas just below his knees. "These are the oldest, so they hurt the most because as I grew, they stretched. Now, they only hurt because of the infections."

"Those are the oldest?"

"Yes, sir ..."

"And when did you get those?"

"These have been with me since the beginning. Maybe since I was about six, I think."

"What about these?" Trevor asked, pointing to scars above Stilton-James's knees.

"It's hard to remember, and I got burned so many times."

"How many times do you estimate you were burned?"

"Oh, I don't know."
"Was it about five times, you think?"
"Oh no, I'd say it was much more often than that."
"Ten times?"
"No."
"Twenty times?"
"Umm ... "
"Fifty times?"
"I don't ..."
"One hundred times?"
"No, no, not that many times," Stilton-James said with a chuckle.

Trevor sighed in relief.

"I'd say about ninety times."

"Ninety times? I see," Trevor said as he attempted to disguise his reaction. "So we've determined that someone burned you. When did they burn you, and why did they?"

"Oh, I got burned whenever I didn't do what I was supposed to do."

"What do you mean?"

"Whenever they came to hurt me at night, if I squirmed or if I tried to run, they'd pour the oil on me."

Trevor covered his mouth again in an attempt to disguise his reaction. He glanced at his watch and realized that he was nearing the time limit Dresdin had set for him.

"I have to go now, William. I'll see you again another day."

"Okay, officer, have a nice day."

Trevor left the precinct after his second interview with Stilton-James with much the same thoughts as he'd had after his first visit. Stilton-James's childhood had been unbelievably, unjustifiably, tragic.

Chapter 28

Beth Lago. Friday, March 22, 2075 (Same date as chapters 25 and 26)

At Cap's orders, Eccles and I reluctantly took an afternoon off. We had been running on fumes for the last forty-eight hours. When we got home just after one o'clock, we both hit the sack, exhausted. Around nine, Eccles knocked on my bedroom door. I had just awoken a few minutes earlier.

"Hey."

"Hey ..."

"You want to grab a Nost or something?" Eccles asked, referring to the perennial beverage of choice. The term Nost had come from the term Nostalgic. Following the Dark Times, after the ban of all plant-based food and beverages, people had started creating homemade synthetic beverages. They'd drawn from memory to mimic the alcohol-based drinks of the past. The crude first generation of these drinks received accolades more for their effect than their quality. The makers of these drinks called them Nostalgic Drinks. As time passed, the quality of the concoctions improved greatly. Eventually, the name was shortened. People now referred to them simply as Nost. The genesis of Nost, which in essence was an artificial beer, opened the door for other drinks like Faux-Whiskey and Faux Rum. The first and most popular of all the alcoholic synthetic drinks, however, was Nost.

I thought for a moment, maybe a round of Nost would do me some good. At the very least, it should help me relax. We'd been under such stress of late that even the nap I'd taken failed to shake free the tension in my head.

"Yeah, I do, actually. Do you want to leave in twenty?" I asked.

Thirty minutes later, Eccles and I were sitting at a table at the pub near the house. I remarked to myself that it was nice to get out to unwind a bit. I looked over at Eccles as we sat at a table in the crowded pub. He wasn't wearing a tie but looked more dressed up than usual in a white collared shirt and dark sports jacket. When he was still married, I remembered he would show up to work in these horrible shirts with weird designs on them. Since the separation, he'd developed a mild sense of style. Sitting across from me at our table on the patio of the pub, he looked quite charming.

"So?" he asked.

"So?"

"What do you think?"

"I don't know ... I just don't know anymore."

"Don't tell me you feel sorry for him!" Eccles said as he lifted a bottle of Nost to his lips.

"Why? You don't?"

"No, I don't at all," Eccles responded.

"Not even a little?"

Eccles said, "No, I don't. He did something horrible, and he deserves to pay for his crimes."

"I agree. He deserves punishment for his crime, out of negligence or not. He killed Emil, and he should pay for that."

"That's right," Eccles said with a nod.

"I just can't help but wonder what would have happened had his life been different."

"You think he would have been different," Eccles said.

"Maybe ... maybe not, I don't know, and, frankly, that's the point. We will never know. He's a monster, and yes, ultimately, he's responsible for his actions. But doesn't part of you feel if things had been different for Stilton-James, then maybe Emil would still be alive?"

"Beth, he killed Emil."

"I know that."

"Good, we can't forget that. We can't forgive that. We make choices in life, and we have to live by those choices," Eccles said while clenching his fist.

"It doesn't matter anyway, we'll present the case, and it'll be up to a court to decide just like Sayvian said."

"Right, and the court will decide to give him the death penalty, and we won't have to see his miserable face again," Eccles said, raising his voice.

I turned my head away.

"You don't agree," Eccles said.

"I don't know anymore, Eccles, all this killing and where has it brought us?"

"Beth, evil will always exist. We will always have bad people around, trying to do terrible things."

"Right, I agree, we can't passively allow others to destroy the world we live in, but I question the tactics we've used. Take TFS, for instance, under the presupposed guise of eliminating the bad, and we cut away a tumour, only we were reckless. In the end, we did do away with almost all the bad, but we also neglected the chance to save the ones who needed us most, like one particularly battered child, Stilton-James. He'd needed our help, but we not only neglected the imperative to act, but we made his situation worse. If he'd had at least one parent, then he might have had a chance. We denied him that chance. A cost of making our society possible, but others paid that cost. The poor souls who'd endured so much, and we abandoned them. This event should remind us of the consequences of our actions."

"Beth, we had no choice. The Scarklingas were evil, and they got what they deserved."

"What about Stilton-James's father? What did he deserve?"

"They were ... caught in the crossfire ... they were casualties of war. In dangerous times sometimes innocent lives get caught in the middle. We had no choice." Eccles said in a firm voice that seemed to inflect upwards.

"You're not so sure anymore," I replied.

"We had to do it. The Scarklingas were animals. They were savages."

"And how exactly did they get that way? We locked them up with more of their own kind, out of sight. If they weren't evil going in, they became infernal coming out. We released them, and they turned their backs on the same society that had turned their backs on them."

"They turned their backs when they became criminals," Eccles stated, raising his voice.

"I agree, but when we stopped trying to rehabilitate, we gave up on them completely. They wreaked havoc, and they brought on chaos, so we purged what little civilization we had left and started over again."

"Yes, but we killed all the Scarklingas," Eccles retorted.

"But, at what cost?" I asked.

"The cost was high, but what happened to the Scarklingas was fair. It was an eye for an eye. The Scarklingas deserved to be punished, and gassing in the night is a soft punishment compared to the harm they inflicted on others," Eccles said.

"It's the collateral damage that troubles me, the poor innocents who needed our help, but instead were purged with everyone else."

"I know. Things are far from perfect. In a perfect world, we could go back in time, subtract all the negative experiences out of Stilton-James's life, and see if he would still kill Emil, but we can't do that. If Stilton-James was so hurt as a child, why wouldn't he care for Emil instead of harming and killing him? Wouldn't that be more logical?"

"Maybe he just treated Emil the way others had treated him."

"Or maybe, he's just plain evil."

"If that's the case, then I wish Stilton-James could suffer and feel all the pain and fear that Emil felt as he died. If he were aware of his actions and killed Emil out of hate, then the only justice possible would be for him to suffer the way Emil did."

"That would truly be 'an eye for an eye,'" Eccles said.

"It would be if it were possible," I added.

The tension in my head had now grown into a headache. Unable to cope with the loud music and people at the bar, I decided to end my night early. I told Eccles I was leaving, and he offered me a ride. I opted to walk instead. We weren't far from the house.

Having said goodbye to Eccles, I stepped out of the bar and spotted a couple kissing a few feet from the exit. I didn't mind public displays of affection, though I never engaged in them myself. I carefully stepped past the couple, hoping to avoid interrupting their loving embrace. As I slid past, I casually glanced at the man, and my initial reaction was that I recognized him, but it couldn't be ... I double-backed to confirm.

"Willy?"

"Beth ... umm ... It's not what it looks like," Willy said with lipstick still imprinted on his lips.

"Oh really, what is it supposed to look like?"

Finally, I had figured out why he disappeared every few weeks. Turning around to walk away, I berated myself for having been so stupid.

"Beth! Please wait!" Willy called out.

"Don't call me, Willy, ever," I said to him in a cool, even tone.

At that moment, I felt more anger than sadness, but later I did shed a tear for Willy.

-----:-----

Frustrated and bothered by what I had just seen, I decided to spend some time alone to clear my mind. At a nearby park, I found a bench where I sat for a moment. Slowly I felt my thoughts organizing and falling into place. So much had happened over the past few days that I hadn't had enough time to process everything.

There were brick houses in the park where I sat, which flanked each of its four sides. I remarked that any parents could easily monitor their children from their respective kitchen windows, the same way I'd done with Sara back when the world still made sense. Something was comforting about the silence of the park. I enjoyed some peace for a change when I heard one of the doors to one of the flanking houses swing open. A bright light shone out from inside. The shadow of a child stood in the doorway.

"Timmy?" An adult female voice called out from inside the house.

The little boy stopped dead in his tracks as though the woman's voice had physical strength.

"What are you doing?" the female voice asked.

"I'm not doing anything, Mommy," the boy responded before shutting the door.

It reminded me of an element of Emil's disappearance, which had always bothered me.

I hastened back to the house, got into my car, and headed for the city limits.

-----:-----

Forty minutes later, I found myself in a leather chair in the Dresdin family home's sitting room. Mrs. Dresdin was wiping tears from her eyes.

"I'm sorry to have come, unexpected like this."

"It's not a problem at all. I'm happy to help," she replied while smiling sincerely.

I smiled back. I said, "Mrs. Dresdin, the reason I've come is due to a problem that's been on my mind about the case."

"What problem would that be?" Mrs. Dresdin asked as she carefully sipped her chamomile tea.

"Well, I've worked in the Missing Persons' division. Back before joining homicide, so, unfortunately, I've seen many disappearance cases involving children from beginning to end."

"I understand and bless you for the work you do."

"Thank you, Mrs. Dresdin. I want to ask you a question regarding the disappearance, however."

"Of course, please ask me anything."

I took a deep breath before plunging into my question. "Very well, do you have any idea what would cause Emil to run away, deceive his parents, and disobey his teacher?"

"Excuse me?" Mrs. Dresdin asked, snapping her head up.

A sharp din rang out as she dropped her tear-filled cup onto its saucer.

"Forgive me, Mrs. Dresdin. I'm only searching for the truth."

Mrs. Dresdin closed her eyes slowly and nodded in agreement.

"It's just that in all my years, I've rarely seen a child act that way."

Mrs. Dresdin turned red.

I said, "I'm sorry. Perhaps I should ..."

I started to rise from my chair.

Mrs. Dresdin turned wide-eyed and motionless. She barely responded to my movements. While standing, I bent down towards the coffee table to place my teacup onto its saucer.

"Detective Lago?" Her voice was hard.

"Excuse me?" Her abrupt tone caused me to freeze in my position.

"Sit down," she commanded.

"I don't think this is the right time."

"Please." Mrs. Dresdin's insisted.

What I had perceived as anger had now dissolved into despair.

She said, "There's something you should know. It's something that I've never even mentioned to my husband."

I sat back down and remained silent, inviting her to continue.

She said, "While researching the case, did you learn anything about how Emil was as a baby or toddler?"

"Well, I know that he's been a happy child for the most part, and I know that he was quite bright."

"Yes! He was very bright. Carl and I were so happy to see how well he was doing. There was, however, one small issue."

"Okay."

"He was very well mannered for the most part, but he could often be disagreeable."

"Disagreeable?"

"Well, more like disobedient. He was never mean-spirited, but he did tend to ignore my wishes."

"Mrs. Dresdin, I think most children act that way."

"Yes, exactly, we thought the same thing, but it seemed constant, and as he got older, it was gradually getting worse. At first, the deceptions were small, but then his lies became increasingly elaborate. He had such a powerful imagination. We had taken him to see a therapist, who told us that he was simply acting out of a need for attention. We were told that the more attention we gave to his deceptive behaviour, the more it would persist."

"Okay," I said while nodding.

Mrs. Dresdin's calm expression changed. Her eyes welled up.

"I shouldn't have listened. Everything in me as a mother told me that this was the wrong thing to do, but I did it anyway," she said.

Tears began to stream down her face. Earlier in the evening, she had been patting away the smallest tears with a tissue. Now, she cried freely, letting them pour down her cheeks.

"A week before Emil's disappearance, he came to me with a story about how he had met his biological parents. He came to me to tell me about it, but at the time, I didn't believe him."

I placed my hand on the top of hers. She turned my hand over, and she held it tightly.

She said, "I lost my temper with him, and I told him that his story was implausible. The last we'd heard of the Days, they were living in another territory, still wrapped up in their addiction. Of course, I hadn't known then that they were clean and sober. I was so angry and hurt by the thought that Emil would make up such a serious lie. I demanded he admit that he was lying, and he refused. His denials only angered me more." She dropped her head, and she began breathing heavily. "He told me that it was true and that he was going to ... going to ... prove it to me."

"Mrs. Dresdin ..."

"I told him to go ahead." Whispered Mrs. Dresdin tearfully as her hands trembled.

I consoled Mrs. Dresdin as best I could. I told her that Emil's fate hadn't been her fault, but as I spoke, her eyes seemed to glaze over. I left the card of a precinct counselor on her coffee table before discreetly walking myself out.

Chapter 29

Dr. Trevor Miles. Thursday, March 28, 2075

Trevor knew he'd have to tell Dresdin everything about the interviews, but he'd been hoping for the appropriate time and place to do so. Nonetheless, he felt relieved to hear that by the time he'd arrived back at DIT Headquarters, Dresdin had already gone home. After having a brief meeting with the team, Trevor ended his day at five o'clock.

He arrived home and started dinner. His cooking skills had improved a great deal of late, and he was pleased to provide something somewhat tasty for a change. About a half-hour later, Tia, Sean, and Trevor sat down together to eat supper as a family. Trevor could feel a sense of calm at the table that night.

An hour later, having finished washing the dishes, he headed out to his meeting with Peter. They met at the Bear Hug Pub. They both ordered pints of Nost, and by the time the second round had arrived, they were only beginning to discuss the true reason for their meeting.

"So?" Trevor asked incredulously.

"So, what?" Peter asked.

"You didn't believe me, and yet you called me down here for a reason," Trevor said.

Peter took a sip of his pint before responding. "Listen, Trevor, I love you like a brother, so please don't take this the wrong way."

"Okay, let's have it."

"You, my friend, are in way over your head."

"Meaning?"

"Meaning... Do you know who your boss is?"

"Peter, could you just come out and say it."

"All right then. You want it straight, so here it is. Dresdin is a ghost. Look, I've been doing these kinds of investigations for years. The stories are always the same, predictable. Only the characters ever change. A rich husband or wife wants out of their marriage, but a prenuptial agreement holds them back, so they look for alternatives. They realize their significant other's been acting strange, so they hire a professional like me. Trust me, for someone who knows where to look, it's just a matter of time. If I dig long enough, I'll eventually find the dirt. It doesn't matter who it is. I've busted doctors, lawyers, teachers, judges, and elected officials. Everybody has a secret, and everyone has traceable dirt beneath the fingernails."

"How about billionaire CEOs?" Trevor asked.

Peter looked at Trevor with a concerned expression while shaking his head ominously.

Trevor asked, "Nothing?"

"I can't find anything on him good or bad from about the age of six till after the Dark Times. For a sizeable chunk of his life, the man simply didn't exist."

"That's impossible."

"You're telling me! Someone has gone to great lengths to dismantle any trace of the man's past. Whatever he had, hidden in there, might not ever be recoverable. Someone with that much power wouldn't have a second's hesitation at eliminating anyone who tried to uncover the truth. Trevor, we go back a long time so listen to me carefully ... If I were you, I'd stay on this man's good side and try to weather the storm."

"That might not be so easy."

"Why not?"

"Well, let's just say he's been acting very strange lately."

"The death of a child will do that."

"No, there's something else going on."

"Well, matters of the mind—that's your field, not mine," Peter said.

Just then, an idea popped into Trevor's head. He wondered if Peter had looked into Dresdin's mental health history.

"Peter, did you happen to check out ..."

"Therapists, right? You want to know if I checked for contact with therapists. Already done, my friend and I didn't find a thing."

Peter's eyes widened as though he'd just realized something.

Trevor asked, "What?"

"Nothing, it's probably nothing."

"Just tell me what you're thinking."

"If he'd been a minor at the first session and if the doctor had been assigned to him due to a crime committed as a Young Offender, then the records would have been sealed."

"Okay ... I don't see how that helps me."

"Well, Trevor, if you know the right people, then there isn't any information that's out of reach."

"I see."

"You know, the best thing about this angle is that this information can't ever be destroyed."

"That sounds great. What's the information, though?"

"Trevor, are you sure you want to do this? This can be dangerous."

"Peter, whatever it is that I'm into here, it's dangerous. Turning my head away at this point doesn't save me. I'm already under threat."

"Interesting, so just to confirm your logic here, I'm telling you that continuing your search will only bring you danger, and you say you're already in danger and stopping your search will only make things worse."

"Well, yeah, that's what I'm saying. Peter, you know as well as I do that information is power."

"Trevor, maybe I didn't make myself clear. The cover-up is massive. You will not find anything, I promise you. What is the point in searching for something that doesn't exist anymore? If these people find out what you're doing, you're done. It's over."

"It's too late, Peter. I'm in too deep now. If I turn my back now, then I know people will die, and I won't let that happen, not again."

"You need to move on, my friend. You can't keep carrying that weight around with you."

"You speak as though I have a choice."

"You do have a choice. You always have a choice."

"Well, I've made mine already."

"You could never let things be, could you? Look, Trevor, for your safety, stop what you're doing. No good can come of this. Besides, looking up, Young Offenders' records is a serious crime. Think of Tia and Sean, Trevor. If you're planning to continue, then I can't help you anymore. You're going to have to do it on your own."

Annoyed and taken aback, Trevor decided to drop the subject for now. He said, "You know you're probably right. It's not my problem anyway."

"Exactly ..." Peter said agreeably while taking a gulp of his Nost and peering at Trevor carefully.

Peter's behaviour and logic conflicted.

A theory began to occur to Trevor. He debated to himself, if Peter were concerned for his safety, then the natural thing would be to prove the threat as either real or imagined. It was as though Peter wanted Trevor to be safe, and at the same time, passive. The underlying message was to lie down and do nothing—only then would you be safe. Trevor could sense that Peter's strange behaviour suggested some kind of a plan. This meeting had been fruitless and consisted solely of Peter trying to deter Trevor's investigation. To make matters worse, Trevor had seen all sorts of deception in his friend's body language and micro-expressions. If his motive were to protect, then why not use warnings instead of threats. Peter had been entirely truthful when he told Trevor that he couldn't help him anymore. He couldn't help anymore because he'd already betrayed him.

Trevor accepted the possibility that DIT had already compromised his friend and convinced him to act as a roadblock. Oddly, some of Peter's statements seemed truthful. Perhaps this talk was Peter's attempt at warning Trevor despite his betrayal.

"So, why don't we just drop this heavy topic and finish our pints in peace," Trevor said in a tone meant to convey as much passivity as possible.

"That's it!" Peter said while lifting his glass in salute.

That is it... Trevor thought. Peter clearly could no longer be trusted.

Just then, a young twenty-something with long, chestnut brown hair and piercingly bright blue eyes approached. She held an old-fashioned camera in her hand.

"Hey there, we're just taking pictures of the patrons for upcoming promotions, may I?"

"Of course!" Peter said as he slid closer to Trevor. He placed his arm around him in a brotherly pose.

He whispered in Trevor's ear as he smiled at the camera. "Look, bud, I know this stuff is bothering you. Give it some time, and in a few months, if you're still feeling unsure, then we'll review it together, okay? Whatever happens, though, I want you to come to me for this stuff. No seeking other PI's, okay?"

"I didn't know you were so sensitive," Trevor said while looking at Peter and flashing a grin toward the camera.

Peter asked, "What was the name of that PI again?"

"Oh, I don't know. I have a feeling the person who told me all that stuff was just trying to kick up dust. You know, one of those trouble makers."

"You've got to watch out for those."

Indeed... Trevor thought.

There was a click and then a flash. At that moment, Trevor expected Peter to pull away, but he kept his arm in place.

"That was great! Thanks a lot! The picture is going to be perfect, just a pair of friends having a couple of pints of Nost at the bar," the girl said in a perky tone.

"Exactly, we've known each other since we were kids. I love this guy so much I could just kiss him ..." Peter said while pulling away in laughter.

-----:-----

After leaving the bar, Trevor got into his car and received a phone call.
"Trevor?"
"Yes?"
"It's Marjorie. Where are you? I need to talk to you."
"I'm just leaving a pub. I need to talk to you too."
"Okay, meet me at the diner by my house in thirty minutes."

-----:-----

When Trevor arrived at the diner, Marjorie was already waiting outside.
"Hey, would you like to go inside?" Trevor asked.
"No, let's talk in your car. It's probably safer in there."
"Okay."
"So, have you found out anything?" Marjorie asked.
"I'm afraid not. I think my source may have been compromised."
"What do you mean?"
"He just can't be trusted," Trevor declared.
"There seems to be a lot of that going around. I did get some info from my source."
"Okay, let's hear it."
"All right, so after Dresdin's behaviour this week, I wondered if perhaps he might have, at some point in his life, seen a psychiatrist."
"You know, I had a similar idea."
"I called a friend of mine on the East Coast and asked him if he knew of any psychiatrists or psychologists with wealthy clients. He told me he'd have to get back to me. About an hour later, he called back. Apparently, there had only been three doctors on the entire East Coast who had catered to the Dresdin's level of wealth while also practicing during the years I outlined to him. I'd felt pleased with that news, but then he said that only two specialized in working with children."
"Great!"
"That's not all. One died a few years ago, but the other one is still alive."
"Okay, just one question though, why did you focus specifically on the East Coast?"

"Well, my source found another Carl Dresdin who studied there. I didn't get a chance to tell you about all the drama at work lately. My source faxed me a yearbook picture. Could you believe that this Carl Dresdin didn't have a portrait in any of the yearbooks for any of the years he attended this school? My source did find one picture where he appears in the background. I had it blown up, and I have absolutely no doubt it's the Carl Dresdin we know."

"Excellent work, Marjorie!"

"Thank you!" she replied, smiling. "Wait, there's more, so my source is going up to the East Coast to interview this psychiatrist in one week. Hopefully, we'll get some useful information from that meeting."

"He's flying over there?"

"Yeah, I told him a phone call would suffice, but he said that the psychiatrist lives in a retirement home and is a real hermit. He doesn't speak to or see anyone, ever."

"Hopefully, he can get us some answers. I have to say, Marjorie, you've done splendid work!"

"Thanks!"

There was an awkward silence in the car as they both sat pensively.

"Trevor, I've been meaning to talk to you for the past few days."

"About?"

"Well, I thought about what you said, and you're right. I was wrong to try to come between you and your wife. I just got carried away, I guess."

"It's okay, Marjorie. I meant what I said. You're an amazing girl, and you'll make some lucky guy very happy."

"The irony is that I knew that you were going to do the noble thing. This is what attracted me to you in the first place." Marjorie paused before continuing. "Although everyone blamed you for what happened at the Ridge, I've always known in my heart that you did the noble thing."

Trevor looked at Marjorie for a moment as she spoke her heartfelt words. She had placed her palm on her chest when she had said 'heart.' Memories of my time at the Ridge rushed to his head. He hadn't spoken to a single person about that time in his life. He realized that he still hadn't resolved all of his feelings.

"Thank you ..." Trevor could feel a rush of blood rise to his head. He felt faint and tired, and yet his heart was beating with unrelenting ferocity. He could sense an ever-increasing need to release something within. He didn't like the idea of letting go of his self-control, like rolling waves of emotion, of confusion, of wondering whether or not he could even attempt to contain the burden any longer. He recognized the overwhelming desire to relieve himself of the weight now, whatever the cost. He began breathing heavily as he fought off the tears.

"I'm sorry, Trevor. I didn't mean to ..."

"No, Marjorie, it's been a long time coming."

"I didn't want to make you upset."

"No, this is good. I haven't spoken about what happened for nearly two years. I can't keep all of this inside anymore."

"Then let it out," Marjorie said as she patted his back.

Trevor inhaled, and the words began pouring from his lips.

"We were five years into the project when we began to make decisions that we shouldn't have made," Trevor said, massaging his temples and clenching his jaw.

"They'd assigned me the task of trying to revive a failed drug. The drug was an antidepressant, which had received approval for trials. Shortly thereafter, and due to reported, bizarre, side effects, it was pulled from the shelves."

"Bizarre?"

"It caused heart palpitations in some patients, while others developed symptoms that weren't present previously. In some cases, the side effects were so severe they could result in death. We calculated that the side effects occurred in thirty percent of patients, and one-third of those patients would likely die as a result of the side effects."

"No wonder they ordered a recall."

"Despite the bad signs, I was still optimistic. I had become a saviour of sorts. Months earlier, I had managed to recuperate an anti-psychotic drug for them. I suppose this had caused me to react with arrogance and pride."

"But you came to your senses eventually, right?"

"I did, but my pride confused things even further. I'd entered my career at Ridgeport with an excellent reputation. By the end of my time there, I'd stand accused of unethical practices. The irony is that I'd face blame for the very things that I'd been trying to stop Ridgeport from doing."

"You were a patsy."

"Yes, that's what I was. The company was prepared to do or say anything possible to get their product out on the market. They falsified research results, and they lied about risks and side effects. The worst thing about the whole ordeal is that some of the conspirators were my colleagues. It all reached a breaking point one day while sitting at my desk, entering results into my computer. On that particular day, I did something I'd never done before, on a hunch. I checked my security access logs. What I found was clear; someone had used my computer without my authorization."

Marjorie sucked in her breath. Trevor gripped the steering wheel.

"At the time, I'd become increasingly aware of the business side of the pharmaceutical company, and I concluded that no matter the human cost, Ridgeport was determined to recuperate their investments on a specific drug called Newday. I began to suspect that they had planned to salvage their investment by making a few major sales and then recall the product before anyone discovered the side effects. It was a game of odds. They figured they'd make a few bucks, and if death resulted then, they'd still have time before anyone traced the blame back to their drug. I conducted a small investigation of my own. Through examining the log interactions on my computer, I discovered that someone was falsifying the data for the experiments we were conducting. Then there was an announcement made that Newday would be re-launched. I was shocked when I saw the email. If anything, my team and I had determined that Newday was actually more dangerous than it had seemed at the time of the recall. There were so many signs around me telling me to get as far away from this as possible. I should have resigned and reported them to the authorities, but I didn't. Instead, I arranged a meeting with the board of directors of the company. Within the conference room of their corporate headquarters, they explained that they had the utmost confidence in my abilities. This extreme confidence caused them to make the hasty announcement. I had gone into the boardroom to berate them, and instead, they gave me an assignment. They gave me thirty days to make the drug safe and manageable. They told me that if anyone could make Newday safe, it would be me."

"They said, 'Think how famous you'll become.' They had preyed on my pride, and I let them do it. I had no idea that they were preparing me as the fall guy. I foolishly took their offer, and two weeks later, they put Newday on clinical trials. The first order of trials went to the Department of Corrections. The order was for several million dollars. The Department of Corrections, known for its corruption, had no problem accepting their inmates' possible death in exchange for kickbacks from the sale. When people started dying, the public didn't want to believe it had been Ridgeport's fault. Thirteen inmates awaiting trial, not yet convicted of their crimes, ended up dying because of Newday. In terms of blame, the board of directors had already begun tightening the noose around my neck. Within my team, they'd inserted a mole that communicated back everything to the board of directors. By day twenty of the supposed thirty-day offer, a grand jury was indicting me. Before the trial began, the incriminating evidence against me had mysteriously disappeared, which had forced the prosecution to drop all the charges. Still, as you know by then, my life had been systematically destroyed."

He paused before continuing.

"Trevor, you did all you could," Marjorie said.

"They destroy me, and for what ... A profit?"

"I'm sorry. I had no idea that you had gone through so much," Marjorie said.

"No, I'm glad we had this talk. I needed this. I'm glad to thank you, Marjorie."

"I'm here, anytime you want to talk," she said and placed her hand on his and peered at him with compassion.

They said their goodbyes, and Trevor reinforced his ongoing commitment on the drive home. Whatever was going on at DIT, he would do everything in his power to prevent the mistakes of the past.

Chapter 30

Beth Lago. Friday, March 29, 2075. 8:35 AM Local Time

The day of Stilton-James's arraignment arrived amid an ever-growing wave of public interest. In the days leading up, Eccles and I met with Sayvian on three separate occasions for testimony preparation. In my meetings with him, I sensed Sayvian becoming increasingly nervous as the arraignment date drew near. I reminded myself that the attention the case was attracting could overwhelm anyone.

All minds, regardless of age, social status, or education, seemed focused on the case. Blogs, websites, radio talk shows, newspapers and television shows all seemed to flood the public's consciousness with all matters related to the case. The obsession seemed unwavering and unanimous. The publics' thirst for information on the subject seemed insatiable, but a perceptive media continually worked to fire the flames of interest. The precinct phone lines were nearly shut down because of the onslaught of phone calls from the public and interview requests from the media. The sheriff had to hire two public relations experts to come in and relieve some of the load. He'd always seemed bent on spending as little as possible, so naturally, we felt surprised by the sight of new staff.

-----:-----

A few days earlier, a formal announcement regarding the case's particulars caused the precinct conference room to fill to the brim with media personnel. We learned that the judge presiding over the case was a relatively young one, Judge David Brown. Eccles and I both found the news relieving, as we knew him well from past cases. The appointment also seemed to relax Sayvian a bit, as he described Judge Brown as "particularly hard on murderers, especially in cases involving children."

-----:-----

After squeezing through the gauntlet of reporters and flashing cameras, we entered the courthouse and then an abnormally tranquil courtroom. The judge had ordered a closed trial, and clearly, he'd made the right choice, as, despite all the chaos outside, the courtroom was refreshingly quiet. Still, if you strained your ears, you could hear the faint sound of chanting coming from outside. Eccles and I sat in the first row beside Cap. Sayvian and his assistants sat just in front of us. A few rows behind us were the Dresdins, who still managed to look dignified despite their distraught expressions.

While I was peering around the courtroom, I spotted the Stilton-James entering the courtroom. Turning to face the front, I saw Stilton-James with chains around his ankles and cuffs around his wrists shuffling towards the defence table. As Stilton-James walked by, I could hear the sound of crying. I turned around to see Mrs. Dresdin clutching her husband's arm. Mr. Dresdin's fists clenched, and his facial expression flexed. I imagined he was summoning all his strength to remain composed.

Stilton-James's defence lawyer was a woman by the name of Jane Alana. She wasn't familiar with Eccles, Cap, or me. None of us had ever heard of her.

She looked to be in her mid to late thirties and had straight blonde hair framing a youthful but serious face. She was pretty, and though she had very sharp angular features, she still managed a degree of beauty.

"What do you think?" I whispered in Eccles's direction.

"She's got nice legs ... but ..."

I slapped Eccles in the arm. "Are you serious right now? I'm asking how you think they will plea."

"I know ... I'm just joking ... Insanity, I guess," he said.

The judge entered the courtroom.

"All rise!" the bailiff ordered.

"You weren't joking, were you?"

Eccles just smiled.

"Please be seated."

I glanced over to my right. "Her legs are pretty nice," I said.

Eccles smirked.

I glanced around the courtroom, noticing all heads were facing forward except one. Willy was looking over at me with teary eyes. He began mouthing the words, "I'm so—."

I turned my head away before he could finish.

"In the case of the indictment, Murder in the 2nd degree, how does the defendant plea?"

"Not guilty, by reason of insanity."

"In the case of the indictment, Kidnapping in the 1st degree, how does the defendant plea?

"Not guilty, by reason of insanity."

Judge David Brown said, "I have reviewed the data files, and I have decided that there is sufficient evidence to proceed to trial. Would the prosecution like to add anything before I rule on bail?"

Sayvian said, "Your honour, the accused was caught with the body of the victim in his house. He is a clear threat to society. He has past convictions for kidnapping and crimes against minors. The people ask that his bail be remanded."

"Does the defence have any objections?"

"No, Your Honour, the defence is prepared to accept remand."

"Very, well, the accused is remanded into custody awaiting trial, which will begin, one week from today. Be prepared to present your cases before the court. "This court is adjourned till one week from today."

The bailiff said, "All rise."

As we stood up, I looked over at Stilton-James, who appeared as stoic and unfeeling as ever. It was difficult to tell if he was fully aware of his surroundings. Nonetheless, he seemed docile whatever his internal mental state while the bailiff escorted him out of the courtroom.

Just as Eccles and I were preparing to step out, defence counselor Ms. Alana walked up to us.

"Detectives?"

"Counselor," Eccles responded.

"I'd like to meet with you two regarding the case," she said while looking at Eccles.

"Yes, of course, whatever you need, counselor." He shot her a broad smile. I couldn't help rolling my eyes.

"Let us know," I responded.

"Thanks," she said as she smiled at Eccles before turning around and walking away.

I glared at Eccles and shook my head.

"What?" he asked, all wide-eyed and innocent.

"What-*ever you* need!" I imitated.

"Was that too much?"

"No, not at all. You might want to wipe the drool off your face, though," I said with a smirk as I walked away.

Chapter 31

Beth Lago. Wednesday, April 3, 2075. 9:47 AM Local Time

Just past the week's midpoint, I received a call from Ms. Alana asking to meet regarding the case. I didn't quite know what to make of the fact that she hadn't asked for Eccles to attend as well. Nonetheless, I felt relieved considering the way Eccles had acted around Ms. Alana in the courtroom. A meeting with the three of us would have been awkward at best.

She had asked if I could meet her at her house. On the phone, she was quite convincing, "Don't worry about it, we'll have some faux-lemonade and discuss the case. I like to keep things informal ..."

I didn't mind formal. The circumstances required that things be formal. After all, the case we were going to be discussing involved the death of a young boy. From the start, something rubbed me the wrong way about Ms. Alana. She reminded me of so many of the girls I'd met in high school. She had a look in her eyes that felt judgmental. She seemed vain and self-calculating, and although she hadn't done anything to warrant my prejudice, I nonetheless kept my guard up and steady. Ms. Alana, with her size zero dress, her one hundred and fifteen-pound frame, and her overpriced shoes, reminded me of everything from which I'd distanced myself. She had the look of a pretty blonde-ditz, but she wasn't in the least. I'd dug up her biography. She had graduated top of her class. A year after graduating, she'd joined a prestigious firm, which has been under investigation for ties to organized crime in recent years. She had also married three times by her thirty-second birthday. Two of her ex-husbands had died in freak accidents while the third was still alive but had lost half his fortune to her in the divorce. At the time that each of her ex-husbands had married Miss Alana, they'd been millionaires. As a result, she became a multi-millionaire and the proud owner of one of the biggest estates in the entire territory. For someone widowed twice and divorced once, she'd certainly acquired the distinct habit of winding up on top. I made a mental note to tread carefully when it came to dealing with Ms. Alana.

-----:-----

"More faux-lemonade?" She asked as she poured it into my glass before I could respond.

"No, thank you. Oh, okay."

"So, please continue ... You were saying that you had just turned on the light and you had seen a pair of legs dangling."

"Right, I lifted the legs up and then Eccles came in, and he cut Stilton-James down."

"Okay, so was he unconscious when you cut him down."

"No, he seemed lucid and conscious."

"Okay, at which point did you read him his rights?"

"As soon as he was cut down."

"Okay, great, thanks. I just have one more question. At what point did you find Emil Dresdin's body?"

"We didn't find him. It was our crime scene unit that found him."

"Right, and according to the report, it wasn't hidden in any way right. It wasn't covered at all?"

"Yes, that's what the report said. As I mentioned, though, I didn't see the body myself."

"Hmm, I find that a bit odd."

I said, "Hmm, why is that?"

"I just don't see why someone would commit a crime and then leave the evidence for everyone to see."

"You'll have to ask your client about that. My guess is he never saw us coming, he picked the wrong boy this time, and it cost him."

Miss Alana glared at me unsurprised, as though she'd been waiting for me to lash out. I glared back at her in an attempt to let her know that I wasn't going to be intimidated. Our standoff lasted a matter of seconds and was deliberate on both our parts.

"Okay, well, thank you very much for answering all my questions. You've been very generous with your time," she said.

"You're welcome," I replied, returning her fake smile.

"I'll walk you out then, and I'm sure you have things that you have to attend to."

"Thank you."

As we rose from our seats, I couldn't help but ask the question that had been burning in my mind. "I'm just wondering why you asked to meet with me alone and not with Eccles."

"Oh, well, it just wasn't necessary to meet with Mark anymore."

Mark?

I asked, "Because …?"

"I met with him two days ago."

I tried not to seem surprised, "Oh … yeah … right! I forgot about that! Must be all the lemonade went to my head!" I replied while laughing aloud.

"Well, it is spiked!" she quipped back and paused before laughing.

I laughed nervously as she walked me out.

-----:-----

When I arrived back at the precinct, Eccles was at his desk. When I approached, I noticed his shoulders tensing up. He kept his gaze lowered in an attempt to avoid eye contact.

He finally acknowledged my presence by saying, "Hello," but neglected to lift his head.

"So, any reason why you didn't tell me that you had already met with Ms. Alana?"

"You didn't ask," he replied, again not lifting his head from the computer screen.

I looked at him suspiciously, but I had no retort. I decided to get some faux-coffee and continue the day as normal, for now.

Chapter 32

Dr. Trevor Miles. Thursday, April 3, 2075

Things began accelerating quickly. Working as a team, we came ever closer to solving the mystery that had become Reverse-Looping. The days passed with increasing momentum. After a week, Trevor realized that everything would come to a pass at virtually the same time. The working prototype for Reverse-Looping, the beginning of the trial of William Stilton-James, Trevor's final interview with Stilton-James, and the results of Marjorie's investigation.

With the trial beginning in a matter of days, Dresdin appeared in Trevor's office demanding an update on the interviews and the Reverse-Looping project.

"I hope you have good news for me?"

"My aim has always been to do whatever's possible."

Dresdin asked, "Okay, so Stilton-James, what kind of man is he?"

Trevor chose his words carefully. "He's ... A complicated man."

"Evil?"

"I can't discern exact details, but I can say his case is not as simple as one might think."

"But, he's evil, right?"

"For what he's done, I assume he must be."

"You're not convinced."

"Well, remember, Mr. Dresdin, I am a psychiatrist."

"What do you mean by that?"

"I'm trying to be objective."

"You must have misunderstood your role in going to interview him. I wanted to know how best to defeat him at trial."

"Right, well, I went in there trying to gather as much information as possible. Some very disturbing things came to light."

"What kind of things?"

"Well, it pertained specifically to his very traumatic past."

"So, what is it? Did he have a tragic childhood, so now he's angry at the world?"

"He has suffered trauma, yes."

"You must have seen this sort of stuff before."

"I suppose I have. Some of it, at least."

"What do you mean by that?" Dresdin asked, tilting his head, furrowing his brow, and raising his tone.

"Well, to be honest, never in one single patient."

Dresdin had been sipping on some Earl Grey, and he dropped his cup down on the saucer, nearly breaking it half upon hearing the answer. His gaze turned focused, and then he took a deep breath, pursed his lips before saying, "Are you saying Stilton-James may be the most traumatized patient you've ever interviewed?" Trevor said nothing. Dresdin took another sip of his tea. "Well, I guess now we know what to expect at trial. Thank you for interviewing him, Trevor. Despite your report, I still want you to complete the final interview."

"Alright, but the trial is starting so soon, I don't know if I'll be able to squeeze in another interview before it begins."

"That doesn't matter. Your last interview with him will be during the trial."

"Oh ... how ... is--"

"Trevor, let me worry about the details."

"Okay."

Dresdin lowered his head, turned around and left Trevor's office. He didn't even say bye to Trevor as he walked out. He didn't know how to read Dresdin's reaction. He hadn't sensed any deception at all. For the first time in a long time, all his emotions were exactly as presented.

-----:-----

Pax had booked a meeting with Trevor for later that day. In the boardroom, they discussed Reverse-Looping.

"Well, it's the same situation as before. All signs indicate it can be done, but the results could be very unpredictable."

"Right."

"What should we do?"

"I'm not sure, Pax."

"I'm not sure, Pax."

Pax began to whisper.

"Do you think Dresdin would launch something if it were unsafe? Do you think that's our responsibility?"

Trevor also lowered his voice to a whisper. "Pax, honestly, I don't see how it could be anyone else's."

In a normal tone, Pax said, "Trevor. I'm sorry you're in such a difficult position."

"You are?"

"Of course, my concern has always been the team."

"I understand."

"All things being equal, we still have a dilemma on our hands. We still don't know what to do if ... You know," Pax said, alluding to the completion of the project.

"Is that an immediate concern?"

"Yeah, it is," Pax whispered before grinning.

Trevor smiled back.

"I imagine we still have ways to go before we can finish the project, right, Pax?" Trevor said in an elevated voice.

"Dr. Miles, we're months away from a working prototype," Pax said.

"Keep plugging along then," Trevor said while pointing to his watch and mouthing the words "seven o'clock. "

Trevor felt a rush of excitement from learning that the project had finally reached completion. He wondered, though, how Dresdin would use this information. He knew he had to hold it back long enough to understand Dresdin's motives. One false move could result in disaster. He gave Pax a slow nod confirming that they would meet at their usual spot at seven o'clock.

-----:-----

After dinner that evening, Trevor rested in the living room while waiting for the time when he'd have to go and meet Pax. He'd noticed Tia watching him over dinner, and while he sat in the partially lit living room, she took the opportunity to sit with him to talk.

"Hey," Tia said while sitting down.

"Hi," Trevor said.

"So, what's wrong?"

Trevor's response was automatic. He said, "Nothing."

"Trevor, this is your wife you're talking to. I know there's something wrong, so you might as well tell me what it is because I'm not going to stop asking."

Trevor sighed and shook his head. "Tia, I think I might be in trouble."

"Okay, what happened?"

"I don't think I can tell you."

"How can I help you if you don't talk to me?"

"It's complicated."

"I have time."

"I don't know what's going to happen, Tia. I feel like things are happening around me that are out of my control."

"Okay, what's the worst that can happen?"

"Do you want to know?"

"Listen, Trevor, I love you, and I trust you, but you've got to stop being afraid."

"I'm not afraid," Trevor said.

Tia stared at him oddly. She turned away and spoke under her breath. "It can't be."

"What ... can't be?"

Again, she said under her voice, "I suppose it's time."

"Tia, what's going on?"

"Trevor, I need you to listen to me very carefully," she said.

Trevor could see tears forming in the corner of her eyes.

"Okay ..."

"Trevor, I've had a lot of time to think, and I've been struggling to understand why things turned out so poorly for you, for us. A few days ago, I remembered some wise words. Ever since remembering this conversation from years before, I've accepted just how true these words have become. Now, I can look back and realize that you deserve to know what I know."

"Which is?"

"Trevor, things will go awry for you whenever you forget who you are. You, Dr. Trevor Miles, are more than any company can ever be. You are a caring, loving, and generous person. You are a father, my best friend, and the love of my life. There isn't anything that you cannot do. All you have to do is stay true to yourself. Trust your instincts. You know more than you think."

"Tia, why are you saying these things?"

"Trevor, I have a confession to make."

"Tia ..."

"No, Trevor, please let me say this because I've been carrying this guilt for too long."

"Guilt? What could you have possibly done?"

"More than you know. Let me ask you a question ... Do you know why I married you?"

"I wonder that almost every day."

Tia said, "Stop it! I'm trying to be serious here."

"I don't know because you loved me, hopefully."

"Well, yes, I do love you, but there was more to it than that. I married you because I knew that you were capable of great things."

"Tia, you don't have to ..."

"Listen! Please!"

"Okay, okay."

"Trevor, you're special. You've always been. When I married you, it was because I saw the light in you that I had wanted to be near. When you started working at the Ridge and started shining the way you did, something changed. You were shining bright beyond everyone's expectations. I became scared. I was stupid, and I'm sorry. I guess I thought that if you became too great, you wouldn't want to be with lowly old me anymore. I felt lonely. I was afraid of losing you, so I pretended to be lonely and sad. I put pressure on you, and I inadvertently alienated you."

"Tia, what are you saying?"

"I played the role of the depressed, lonely wife so that you would pay more attention to me. It backfired, though, because you became frustrated. You started pulling away in need of freedom, and I smothered you even more."

"Why would you do this?"

"I don't know, Trevor, but I imagine that people act in strange ways when they're presented with extraordinary people. I was wrong to have held you back. I should've been congratulating you and encouraging you. Instead, I made a selfish choice. I suppose the higher you went, the further away you felt from me."

"But Tia, that's ridiculous."

"I know and believe me when I tell you I didn't know what I was doing at the time. I was acting, but I wasn't thinking of what I was doing. I was acting on instinct."

"And now?"

"Now, I've finally rationalized my actions, and I'm trying to apologize to you."

"It doesn't matter anymore, Tia. It's in the past."

"Well, there's more."

"Okay ..."

Tia took a deep breath before continuing. "Now I know that my relationship with your mother wasn't the best. I know that you probably thought we hated each other, but we didn't. We both wanted the best for you, and often people differ when it comes to deciding what's best. When your mother, God rest her soul, got sick, we travelled back home to take care of her. Do you remember? "

"I remember."

"Okay, well, when we were all in her room, and she was sleeping ... The night before she died."

"Yes ...?," Trevor asked.

"You had fallen asleep on the sofa in her room, and I had fallen asleep in the chair."

"Okay ..."

"When you awoke the next day, she had already passed, but I never told you that I spoke to her after you had fallen asleep."

Trevor covered his mouth. Tia took another deep breath.

Tia said, "Halfway through the night, she had woken up. She mumbled, and I suppose the sounds woke me up too. I rose from the chair, went to her side. I asked her if she was okay, and she replied that she was fine, just a little startled by a terrible nightmare she'd had. I asked her if she wanted me to wake you, but she urged me not to. She said that she wanted to talk to me. Confused by what was happening, I told her that perhaps it would be better if I woke you, but she said she wanted to speak to me again. Trevor ... She told me a story."

Trevor's eyes focused on Tia's every movement—her posture, her hands, her eyes.

"She told me that when you were just a baby when you got very sick. She had taken you to see doctor after doctor, and no one had seemed able to figure out what was wrong. Finally, desperate and afraid, she sought the help of an older woman known for her ability to heal the sick. You know how your mother was, she was an intuitive lady, but if she didn't see it, then she didn't believe it. She felt so frightened by your illness that she figured that it couldn't hurt to try. She wrapped you up and took you to see this woman. When she arrived with you, the woman told her she had been expecting you. Your mother told me that she snickered at that comment and that the woman told her that she knew that your mother would react that way. On that night, she told your mother that you would marry a girl named Tia and that we would have a son named Sean. The woman told your mother that she would tell me, your wife, about their conversation one day on her deathbed. She told your mother that your condition would soon improve and that you had a special purpose in life. She told your mother that there would come a time when you were going to be faced with a decision." Tia wiped tears from her eyes.

Tia said, "She said that during this time, you were going to feel afraid and alone, but in the end, you would persevere. She said that we would suffer a great trauma during the dark time, but you would manage to change the world for the better through this trauma. On that fate-filled night, she told your mother that she had to tell me, your wife, that one day I was going to realize that I had betrayed you and that this would mark the time when I was supposed to, in turn, tell you this story. Most importantly, she told your mother that as long as you follow your heart, no person or force in the world would stop you from changing the world forever. So you see, you can't fail."

Trevor leaned back as he attempted to digest what his wife was saying.

Trevor said, "Tia, I don't know what to make of all of this. Honestly, I have no idea."

"Oh ... You're not going to believe me, but the woman told your mother that you would say that. She said that my role in this was pivotal, it was up to me to tell you this, and I hope I've remembered it correctly. The woman had said to tell you that her role in life was to heal and that you had that same role. She said to tell you that your purpose in life was to make healing possible. I don't know if that helps."

"I don't know, but it might."

"I can only imagine what horrible things you must think of me. I wouldn't blame you if you ended up hating me as a result. Trevor, I'm so sorry for what I've done. I've kept this secret buried inside for nearly fourteen years, never thinking that this day would come. Now that it's here, it still feels so unreal. She told me that I would betray you and that I wouldn't realize it at the time. She said that when I finally did realize it, I would feel compelled to apologize, tearfully. The apology would be the sign that the time had come to tell you all of this."

"Tia, I have so many different ideas running through my head."

"I know, Trevor, and I'm sorry, there's just one last thing. She said when this day came ..." She sniffled as the tears now began streaming down her cheeks. "Oh, Trevor, she said this talk would be my ... catharsis, and she said soon afterward you would have one too."

"Tia, there's nothing to forgive. I love you as always, and I will continue to love you, even beyond my last breath."

Trevor hugged her tightly as she sobbed. A few moments later, his cell phone alarm went off.

"I have to go, Tia," Trevor said, lifting his wife's head with his fingertips.

"I know. It's time for you to go. When you come back, I will be waiting for you, as always."

-----:-----

Trevor had trouble shaking the weight of the conversation he'd had with Tia. He assumed that she believed every word, but he had trouble understanding all of it. A colleague had once told him, even considering all the knowledge amassed regarding the human psyche—real-life would always find a way to surprise. He hadn't known precisely what his colleague meant by this statement until tonight.

-----:-----

He and Pax sat at a booth in the usual bar where they tended to meet. Pax had already ordered a few bottles of Nost and the empties sat in front of him on the table. Trevor remarked to himself that Pax looked slightly buzzed, but he tried to keep the conversation professional.

"So, you finally did it!" Trevor said.

Pax smiled as he took a sip of Nost.

"I can't believe it." Trevor declared.

"I know I'm having trouble believing it myself."

"Is there a catch anywhere?" Trevor asked.

"You always have to be the realist, don't you?"

"Yes, I suppose I do."

For a few moments, Pax glared at Trevor, put his bottle down on the table, and became serious before responding. "It's possible, but yes, there is a catch. In all of the tests I ran, there was a strange inconsistency. In every simulation, the receiving consciousness always seemed to reject the playbacks. It reminded me of when a patient receives an organ, and the receiving body rejects the organ when it recognizes it as foreign."

"Pax, isn't that the crux of our problem, though? This whole time we've been trying to introduce another's consciousness into the receiver's mind. This entire time we've known that if we inserted the experiences which had been contextualized in another's mind, then the receiver's mind would automatically recognize the experiences as foreign."

"You're absolutely right. This is the core of the issue. However, since we initially started working on the project, our central goal has since changed. When I first started trying to solve this problem, I thought we were trying to insert a lifetime of experiences into another's mind. I know you've been trying to find out what DIT and Dresdin's purpose is for Reverse-Looping. Trevor, I know I'm the only one, probably in the whole world right now, who knows about your suspicions regarding its intent. I've given it a lot of thought, and I think you're right. If we go with your theory, then we're no longer dealing with a lifetime of experience. We're only inserting a portion of time. I've only now remembered a solution that seemed silly before but now would be possible since we're only dealing with a segment of time."

"You're being vague, Pax."

Pax shook his head slightly. He said, "If we're only trying to insert a small chunk of time, then this can be done by extracting this portion of data from the sender and then only inserting that small chunk of time, say a few hours, into the receiver's consciousness."

"Okay ..."

"Trevor, when we first started the Reverse-Looping project, I asked myself when a person is most likely to accept an alternate reality."

"While under the influence of narcotics?"

Pax said, "Ha! Very funny, the timing is terrible, but you're funny. Anyway, the answer is when we're asleep, Trevor. During this time, the brain is still using the temporal lobes to project imagined senses. The brain will accept any sort of strange, abstract ideas while in the Random Eye Movement stage of sleep."

"Well, I think you're right in abandoning 'sleep' under the old assumed goal of planting a whole consciousness. Inserting an entire consciousness of another person complete with ideas, memories, traumas and impressions while asleep would cause the receiving patient to assume they weren't dreaming at all. They'd end up believing they were this person. If the playback were short, though, with only enough time for the visceral experience, then it would be entirely possible for the receiving patient to recover their initial consciousness, and upon waking, believe they'd just had a dream or a nightmare. The damage would be minimal, at the most."

Pax said, "Exactly right!"

"Well done, Pax! I'm thoroughly impressed!"

"I thought you'd be."

"I'm confused, though. You said there was a catch."

"There is."

"Okay, well, come out with it."

"Even in REM sleep, there are some dangers."

"What kind of dangers?"

"Well, we're not implanting dreams, are we?"

"That's right. Of course, not, we're ... oh!"

"Right?"

"We're not implanting dreams. We're implanting realities, experiences, sensory-filled memories."

"Right, there's no way to prevent Spawning from that memory."

Back-Spawning and Forward-Spawning were theories the two had developed when they had first contemplated Reverse-Looping. In theory, Spawning would occur when a person received a sensory input that was foreign in origin.

They surmised that upon receiving the foreign input, the brain would search instinctively within existing memories for clues on how to make sense of the input. The premise of Back Spawning depended on a simple process. The theory stipulated that upon insertion of memory into a mind, since it existed into another's mind, there wouldn't be any memories available that would allow it to make sense. Back Spawning is the process of searching for memories to make sense of sensory data.

Forward spawning represented what they theorized if the receiving patient couldn't find the data necessary to make sense of the input. Forward-Spanning was the creation of fake memories in order to understand the sensory input. Both concepts were just theoretical, but if they were right, then the consequences of creating memories could cause severe psychological damage. Especially if the memory created was a traumatic one. Trevor realized that Pax was once again correct. Yes, Reverse-Looping was possible, but it would be hugely dangerous if not done correctly or carefully.

"Of course," Trevor said.

He then remembered what his wife had said to him earlier that evening about healing.

"What? What are you thinking?"

"I don't know yet, Pax. I need to go and think about this some more. Again, great work!"

"Thanks!" Pax said.

As Trevor got up from his chair, he spotted Pax glancing at his watch.

"Do you have to be somewhere?"

"No! Why?"

Based on Pax's reaction, Trevor knew where the young scientist planned to go. Trevor decided not to hint at any knowledge of the relationship between Pax and Sylvie.

"No reason, just make sure you don't have another drink before you go. I mean, if you're going to be driving."

"Of course not ..."

-----:-----

Trevor arrived home late, and upon entering the bedroom, he realized that Tia was already fast asleep. *Too late for a goodnight kiss*, he thought to himself.

When he finally did get into bed, Tia rolled over and rested her head on his chest. A few seconds later, he, too, fell into a deep, restful sleep.

Chapter 33

Beth Lago. Monday, April 8, 2075

Since the end of the Dark Times, murder trials are no longer decided by a jury. Now, the judge presiding over the case also ruled on the verdict. Coincidentally, I found this format the most logical one for this particular trial. After all, this was such a well-known news story that finding a juror who hadn't heard of the case would be difficult, if not impossible.

-----:-----

A buzz filled through the courtroom as the attendees exchanged opinions in the final moments.

The bailiff said, "All rise."

Judge Brown entered, sat down, and prepared to open the People vs. William Stilton-James trial.

Rising from behind the prosecution table to give his opening statement, Sayvian exuded confidence with each step. He had a presence and charisma that captured your attention, causing you to look past the limits of his below-average physical stature. His dark hair, he kept short and neat. He had a slim face, strong nose, a thin brow, broad chin, and an easy smile that always started around the eyes. He seemed cool and calm. I could easily imagine him as a politician. He spoke in a loud and clear tone, and his words were sharp and straight to the point.

"This case is simple. The evidence is undeniable. This case is, however, different from any other case ever brought before the courts. The testimony of witnesses and the evidence presented will all lead to one, and only one possible conclusion— William Stilton-James lured Emil Dresdin away to his car, then to his home. There, the accused prevented Emil from escaping. The accused then viciously assaulted Emil, leaving him for dead. When all the dust settles, there will be no other conclusion possible. If there is a lingering shadow of a doubt, then there will be one final testimony presented from Emil Dresdin himself.

You will see what he saw through his eyes.

You will hear what he heard, though his ears.

Until the moment when his tiny lungs fight for those final few breaths— you will be with him.

'The People ask that you listen carefully. We ask that you step into Emil's shoes for those final moments. You have a precious task before you, a gift. Stilton-James took so much away from Emil, but you have the chance to give something back. Convict William Stilton-James of Murder in the second degree and Kidnapping in the first degree—provide Emil Dresdin with the justice he deserves. Thank you, Your Honour."

Ms. Alana stood up from her chair and stepped into the area between the prosecution and defence tables. She caressed a tuft of blonde hair away from her cheekbone, looked down for a moment, and then began her statement.

"Your Honour, the prosecution's opening statement is correct in one sense. This case is indeed different from any other you've likely ever seen or heard of. You will hear the story of a young boy who suffered a terrible thing, over and over again, throughout his entire youth. You will hear of a boy who suffered abuse from a people known for their extreme cruelty. The Scarklingas made a victim of William Stilton-James. Once a boy, they stripped him of his innocence, his humanity. Despite the sexual, mental, emotional, and physical abuse he endured—he survived. What did little William get from society in return? He got even more tragedy, more suffering. The defendant, as a young boy, watched TFS forces kill his father. Orphaned and alone, William spent the next decade hustling, scrounging, and fighting to survive.

"Once a child filled with innocence, now all that remains is a damaged man. William Stilton-James's mental state is not a healthy one. The defendant's traumatic youth has left his mind damaged beyond repair. He has no understanding of the crimes charged against him.

"Witness testimony and evidence presented will show that William Stilton-James cannot be found guilty of actions for which he had no understanding. The court cannot convict and then execute this man, not because I say so because the law states that a conviction cannot be provable when the accused is insane.

"You will find William Stilton-James Not Guilty due to his insane state of mind. Thank you, Your Honour."

Eccles and I looked at each other.

Eccles whispered, "She's not going to just roll over and die."

I said, "She has fight in her."

-----:-----

The Prosecution's first witnesses consisted of the lead crime-scene investigator and the county coroner.

By the time these first two witnesses finished testifying, the court day had all but ended. Eccles and I had expected to testify on day one, but it appeared we would have to wait until tomorrow.

-----:-----

The next morning while standing up and facing the court, the judge asked that I swear in. As instructed, I provided my name and rank. There was an eerie silence in the courtroom.

Sayvian asked the questions we had rehearsed. I paid special attention to all the basic rules of testifying. I spoke in a clear voice. I made sure to make eye contact, and I maintained a calm composure.

Upon answering Sayvian's final question, I felt that the experience had gone according to plan. I had felt optimistic about the way things had gone. My perspective changed considerably upon Ms. Alana's cross-examination.

"Inspector Lago, are you married?"

"We object, your Honour. What's the relevance?" Sayvian asked in an annoyed tone.

She said, "I'm sorry ... I didn't realize that Inspector Lago's marital circumstance was such a concern for the Prosecution."

"Overruled for now, but make your point quickly, Ms. Alana."

"Yes, I was married, but my husband passed away."

"I'm sorry, how did he die? No, wait, I have the coroner's report right here. It says severe liver damage possibly induced by extreme drinking. Was your husband an alcoholic, Ms. Lago?"

"He had a rare genetic disorder that made his liver susceptible to several types of liver diseases. We didn't find out until the autopsy. He hardly ever drank. Drinking was just one of the possible causes of the type of liver disease, but Sam's cause was genetic."

"Genetic disorder ... Is that what they're calling it these days?"

I replied, "What did you say?"

"Forget it. It doesn't matter. So you had a daughter who disappeared, correct?"

"Yes," I said. I took a deep breath, trying to steady myself for what might come next.

Sayvian had forewarned me of the eminent rattling techniques the defence might use to fluster me. She'd try anything to get me to react emotionally. She would want to show me as biased. Triggering emotion was the easiest way of doing this.

"So, you must have wanted to find Emil then. You must have had a lot of anger inside, I mean about your little girl, Sara? You had a vendetta against the world. Didn't you?"

"Objection, Your Honour! Must the Prosecution remind the court that a distinguished public servant is currently being berated?"

"Withdrawn, Your Honour ..." Ms. Alana said as she walked away. "No further questions."

I stepped off the stand slowly.

She'd succeeded.

I was sufficiently rattled, and I couldn't let it show.

I fought the tears away.

Next, it was Eccles' turn to take the stand.

Again, Sayvian's questions were very straightforward. Just like during my testimony, Eccles seemed to have done superbly, and then Ms. Alana stood up.

"Inspector Eccles, please tell the court what you saw when you entered the basement of the house belonging to the accused."

"I saw Inspector Lago holding Stilton-James's legs."

"Why was she doing that?"

"Objection, Your Honour, whatever the answer, it would be purely speculative."

"Your Honour, I'm just trying to determine the order of events here. Allow me to rephrase... Upon seeing Inspector Lago, what did you do?"

"I withdrew my knife, and I cut him down."

"And why did you do that?"

"Because he was choking, Stilton-James was choking."

"So was anyone else in the basement when you arrived other than, Stilton-James and Inspector Lago?"

"No."

Ms. Alana stepped away from her position just in front of the witness stand. She picked up an E-sheet from the table.

She said, "Your Honour." She raised the E-sheet slightly and said, "Exhibit A."

He nodded.

She said, "Inspector Eccles, please tell the court what I've just handed you."

"It's a copy of my report."

"Please slide to page sixteen, Inspector. Now, read aloud, line sixty-one."

Eccles said, "The body of Emil Dresdin was found by the crime scene unit in the basement along the South wall."

"Now, Inspector Eccles, who was in the basement when you arrived."

"We didn't know he was there at that time."

"Your Honour. Please instruct the witness to answer the question."

"Son, just answer the question."

"Emil Dresdin. Myself and Inspector Lago." Eccles answered firmly in an attempt to recover but, still, a collective hush filled in the courtroom.

"I see." Under her breath, she said, "It must be difficult getting all those facts straight."

Sayvian stood up and said, "Your Honour."

"Ms. Alana, my patience has a limit. We've already determined from the Crime Scene Investigators that they were the ones who uncovered the body. Could we please move on?" Judge Brown said.

"I'm sorry, Your Honour." She said, "What exactly was Inspector Lago doing when you entered the basement?"

"She was holding the defendant's legs up."

"I'm sorry, could you repeat that?"

"She was holding his legs up."

"How do you know she was holding his legs up?"

"I don't know what you mean."

"How do you know she wasn't pulling him down and further choking him?"

I saw Eccles sit up in his chair. His gaze earlier seemed drifty and loose, and now it seemed transfixed on Ms. Alana. His patience was about to snap. He smiled and said, "Because that's not what was happening."

"And you know this how, exactly?"

"She would never do that."

"I see," she said with a smile and a nod.

"Look, I think I know my partner, counselor. I know she'd never do that."

"That's okay, Inspector. No further questions," she said before quickly walking away.

Eccles remained on the stand staring at Ms. Alana, shaking his head. He then stood up slowly and walked back to his place beside me on the bench.

He sat down and whispered in my ear, "I don't like that woman."

"Tell me about it," I whispered back.

Next, it was Mr. Dresdin who suffered Ms. Alana's wrath. After very carefully planned questions from Sayvian, which Mr. Dresdin answered perfectly, Ms. Alana stepped up for her cross-examination.

"Mr. Dresdin, could you please repeat for the court, your name and title, please?"

"Carl Dresdin, CEO of DIT."

"How much did DIT make this year?"

"I don't know ... I'm not sure."

"According to these budget reports, you made two hundred billion dollars."

"That sounds about right."

"Does the figure eighty-seven billion dollars mean anything to you?"

"I don't know. I don't think so."

"Isn't it the amount your company has made as a result of the development of D-Eye Technology?"

"Okay, that figure could be correct, then."

"It accounts for almost half of your company's revenue."

"Yes, I suppose so."

"What do you think of financial reports indicating that Emil's death has improved sales?"

Dresdin inhaled sharply. Shocked by Ms. Alana's question, he said, "I don't know ... I haven't been concerned with that."

"Right." Ms. Alana said with a sting of sarcasm in her voice.

"My son is dead. What exactly are you insinuating?"

"I don't know. I'm not the one on the witness stand, Mr. Dresdin, CEO of DIT."

"No further questions."

"You ...!"

Ms. Alana spoke over Dresdin. She said, "No, further questions! The witness may step down."

Ms. Alana's strategy had become clear. She seemed to be focusing all her efforts on instilling reasonable doubt by discrediting every witness the prosecution called to the stand. She fit her role perfectly. She was picking at the ankles of the prosecution's case. It wasn't a bad tactic while she waited for a chance to present her case. Any chance of winning, however, would require a substantive approach. For the time being, she didn't need to convince the court of Stilton-James's non-guilt. All she needed to do was plant a small seed of reasonable doubt and then present a killer defence case.

-----:-----

After a week of testimony, Sayvian, feeling he'd presented the best case possible, declared, "The prosecution rests."

"We will adjourn for one week, at which point the defence will present its case."

Hearing the judge's announcement triggered an air of confusion until I remembered that at the trial's opening, he had ruled that he would view Emil's data files again, privately, and independent of either the prosecution's or the defence's respective cases.

With that, the first half of the trial had ended. The news reports were abuzz with speculation regarding what other tactics Ms. Alana had up her sleeve.

-----:-----

Mr. Dresdin's cross-examination had jarred my faith in DIT slightly. Apparently, I wasn't the only one. Sayvian approached both Eccles and me, asking that we find out everything there is to know about DIT and the D-eye project. He didn't specify what to focus on, "I don't want any surprises," he'd said.

-----:-----

Eccles and I spent the next few days reading dozens of articles on DIT and the D-Eye project. We visited the DIT facilities, spoke to their engineers, and we even met with Mr. and Mrs. Dresdin a couple of times.

-----:------

Sitting at his desk, Eccles abruptly asked a question, "Do you ever wonder what Patient Zero's purpose was?"

"What do you mean?"

"Do you ever wonder why he had those implants?"

I thought for a moment. I said, "No, I've never really thought about it."

Eccles said, "I mean, there must have been a reason, right?"

"I suppose so. Honestly, I think it would be impossible to find out. You remember what the engineers said. There were absolutely no documents or literature found, just the body itself."

"Yeah, it's just odd."

"I suppose so," I said.

"I wonder if DIT managed to get it right."

"What do you mean?" I asked.

"Well, DIT found Patient Zero and, based on their evaluation, created or reverse-engineered an application for the technology."

"Okay."

"Well, what if they got all wrong? What if the technology was supposed to have had some other application?"

I said, "Okay. Like what?"

"I don't know. It's just a thought, I guess."

Later that day, I found my thoughts returning to the conversation I'd had with Eccles. I couldn't help but think that maybe he was on to something. If DIT had been wrong about applying the D-Eye technology, then there would be another application already built-in. There wouldn't be any need to adapt or manipulate anything.

Sitting at my desk, buried in e-sheets, it occurred to me that I hadn't done any actual investigating at all. In fact, all the information I'd gathered had come from DIT employees or likely biased news outlets.

I concluded that, up to this point, I only knew what they wanted me to know. I decided the time had come for a different approach.

Chapter 34

Beth Lago. Friday, April 12, 2075. 9:12 AM Local Time

The next day I arrived at the DIT campus unannounced. I pulled up to the gate and explained to the security guard who I was. Moments later, I could hear him on the phone saying, "I don't know, I guess she just showed up."

I didn't necessarily dress provocatively. However, I did make a point to smile a lot and be as charming as possible.

Finally, after much sweetness and smiling, I managed to get inside the outer gates.

The DIT campus was huge, and I felt a bit overwhelmed. Once through the gate, I parked in one of the many garages on the premises. There were several impressive-looking buildings with tall glass foyers.

After several minutes, I found the Engineering building. As I walked into the lobby, I spotted one of the scientists who'd given me a tour earlier in the week.

"Albert!" I said.

"Beth. How are you? What are you doing here?"

"Just doing some follow-up research."

"Okay, well, is there anything I can help with?"

I asked him if we could talk somewhere quiet, and he quickly found us an empty conference room.

Albert, being skinny and awkward, was also tall and lean. His affinity for Hawaiian shirts was clear as he was wearing another one today. After having offered me coffee, he asked me what was on my mind. I described the conversation I'd had with Eccles the day before. He listened intently without saying a word. When I finished, he sat still in his chair and stared at me for a few seconds before leaning back. I could see his shoulder tense up. Something had changed.

"I see," he responded slowly.
"Is there something wrong, Albert?"
"No, Beth, not at all."
"Are you sure?"
"Right, well, it seems like an interesting thought, but nothing more, I'm afraid. As you can imagine, I have a lot of work, so ... I trust that you will be able to see yourself out," he said as he got up.
"Albert?"
"Good day, Beth," Albert said while looking directly into my eyes. I felt he was trying to tell me something. It was something that he couldn't just come out and say.

I sat at the table, confused by what had just happened. I looked around and noticed there was a mirror on the far wall of the conference room. I caught myself looking at my reflection while getting the feeling that someone else was peering back at me. The hairs on the back of my neck rose.

I got up and left the conference room. I flashed my visitor pass at each of the security checkpoints, and each of the guards gave a strange look as I passed.

Initially, I'd felt that Sayvian and I were just being paranoid, but now I knew that something was happening at DIT. They were hiding something.

I could understand a billion-dollar corporation wanting to keep some things secret, but the look in Albert's eyes seemed more than mere corporate obedience. He looked genuinely scared. As much as I hated to admit it, maybe the time had come to call in a favour from Willy. I hadn't spoken to him since the night of the kiss. Maybe his guilt would compel him to share some info.

-----:-----

When I drove out of the security gate, Eccles and a patrol car were waiting on the other side.

"Seriously?" I asked as I stopped the car beside Eccles' open car window.
"We got a call regarding trespassing?"
I said, "Very funny, meet me back at the precinct. We need to talk."
"Wait a second. What are you wearing?" Eccles said as I lifted my head, trying to peer into the car.
"Meet me at the precinct," I said as I rolled my eyes.

-----:-----

At my desk, I leaned in toward Sayvian.
"Something is going on over there. I'm telling you," I said in a low voice.
"Follow me," Sayvian said before getting up.
In the now vacant war room, Sayvian said, "That may be the case, but they've been very cooperative till now."
"You're the one who told me to investigate them, for God's sake," I said.

"Beth, all I'm saying is, DIT could own this city if they wanted to and probably the whole territory. I don't remember asking you to show up at their headquarters unannounced. From now on, you'll have to tread more carefully."

"Aren't you at least a little bothered by what they could be hiding?"

Sayvian stood up and faced the window of the conference room. With his back to me, he put his hands in his pockets. He turned his head back slightly.

He said, "You were asking about other applications for D-Eye technology."

"Right, I was simply alluding to the idea that perhaps there were other applications for the technology. Apparently, that was enough to get thrown out and have security called on me."

"This could indicate one of three things," Sayvian said as he continued looking out the window. He said, "One, DIT's decision-makers don't want us to ever be thinking of other possible applications for the technology. Two, they've found another use already, and they're trying to hide it. Or three, nothing's going on, and we're basing this all on mere theories."

"So, what do we do?"

"In all honesty, Beth, there isn't anything *to* do."

"What do you mean?"

"Right. For now, we'll just have to sit and wait," Sayvian said as he exhaled deeply and smiled.

-----:-----

The next Monday, the trial restarted. One by one, Ms. Alana recalled every witness the prosecution had called. She attacked each witness' credibility. It seemed as though she had dirt on everybody. Some of her allegations bordered on ridiculous, but I reminded myself that her goal was to suggest reasonable doubt, nothing more. I found myself amazed by how quickly the testimony was going. Ms. Alana had requested a speedy trial for William Stilton-James. This, of course, rarely, if ever, happened.

-----:-----

By the third day of presenting the defence's case, things seemed to be going smoothly for Ms. Alana. That is until her second to the last witness took to the stand.

"The defence would like to call Dr. Calvin Thompson to the stand."

I recognized him as the man who had interviewed Stilton-James during our first interrogation.

"Dr. Thompson, in your professional opinion, what was the result of the trauma that William Stilton-James suffered as a child?"

"William Stilton-James is what we categorically describe as a sociopath."

"Could you elaborate for the court, please?"

"Due to the damaging effect of his experiences, William Stilton-James is no longer mentally healthy. He has no functioning conscience. He has lost the ability to gauge the difference between right and wrong. He's incapable of empathy. He feels no emotion towards himself or anyone else."

"In your professional opinion, can William Stilton-James be held accountable for his actions?"

"No, absolutely not, he's unaware of what he's done, and he, therefore, cannot be judged to be responsible or accountable."

"Thank you, Dr. Thompson," Ms. Alana said as she returned to her seat. She said, "No, further questions."

"Mr. Sayvian?" the judge asked as he looked in Sayvian's direction. Sayvian stood up. "Thank you, Your Honour."

"Dr. Thompson, are you familiar with the term 'admission of guilt'?"

"Yes, I am."

"Please tell the court what this term means."

"Well, admission of guilt occurs when a person's statements or actions point toward a feeling of guilt regarding a prior action."

"Yes, that is exactly what the definition is ... Almost word for word. Based on your testimony, could Stilton-James show 'admission of guilt' as a sociopath?"

"It's possible but rare."

"I see ... In your professional opinion, could Stilton-James show the admission of guilt and also be a sociopath?"

"Sociopaths only tend to show the admission of guilt when in imminent danger of capture or retribution. They rarely show the admission of guilt on their own."

I could sense where Sayvian was going with this line of questioning. I wondered if Ms. Alana had taken notice or not. Her apparent panicked facial expression suggested that she had.

"Objection, your Honour..."

"Yes, Ms. Alana ...?

She paused before saying, "Relevance?"

"Objection ... Overruled. Next time you decide to object, Ms. Alana, I suggest you think of a valid reason."

Sayvian looked like he was about to grin but then turned serious. He continued his line of questioning.

He said, "I see. Could you please explain to the court the reason William Stilton-James hung himself after having killed Emil?"

"Objection, Your Honour. Speculation!" Ms. Alana said loudly.

"Allow me to rephrase then. In your experience, have you seen cases in which a diagnosed sociopath commits suicide or attempts to commit suicide following a morally wrong act when there is no imminent threat?"

Dr. Thompson looked over at Ms. Alana, who lowered her head.

"Dr. Thompson, please answer the question," Judge Brown ordered.

"No," he responded.

"Then, Dr. Thompson, in your professional opinion, is it possible that Stilton-James's attempted suicide indicates that he was aware that he had done something morally wrong and that he couldn't be a sociopath as you suggest?"

Silence filled the courtroom as we collectively held our breaths.

Dr. Thompson said, "Yes, it is quite possible."

"Thank you, Dr. Thompson," Sayvian said as he walked away. Whispers swept through the courtroom.

Ms. Alana glared at Dr. Thompson as he walked, passed her.

I looked over at Eccles, who was nodding.

He whispered, "That did not turn out well for her."

Judge Brown said, "Ms. Alana, do you have any more witnesses you'd like to call?"

She looked down at a sheet on the table. Eccles, Sayvian, and I all knew the only name left on that list. She was having doubts whether or not she should call Stilton-James to the stand. It was a huge risk. After Dr. Thompson's testimony, she must have been in damage control phase.

"Ms. Alana?"

"No, Your Honour, the defence rests."

"Very well then, court is adjourned while I weigh the merits of the case and review Emil's data files. Court is adjourned until further notice."

Chapter 35

Dr. Trevor Miles. Monday, April 15, 2075. 9:01 AM Local Time

The trial had been going on for several days when Dresdin asked Trevor to make his final visit to Stilton-James's cell. The closing arguments were set for later that day.

First thing in the morning, Dresdin asked that Trevor assemble his team in the boardroom.

When they all arrived, they noticed that a projector had been set up. A technician stood over the playback equipment. Dresdin was sitting at the head of the long table.

"I know how to use the equipment that I designed," Pax had said in Dresdin's direction.

"Fair enough," Dresdin said before sending the technician away.

Dresdin had planned to have the team watch Emil's playback feed. Moments before it began, he leaned in Trevor's direction and whispered. "I want *you* to watch this."

Trevor felt a chill. Throughout the playback, he could sense Dresdin's eyes on him.

After an hour, all four team members felt nauseous, traumatized, and depressed. Dresdin ordered everyone but Trevor to leave the boardroom, and it was at that point that he alerted Trevor of his impending final interview with Stilton-James later that day. He told Trevor of logistical issues that needed resolving before the interview could be set.

"Expect a visit from me," Dresdin said in an unwavering tone, a steely look in his eye.

Trevor knew of the Stilton-James transfer to a different holding cell at the beginning of the trial, eliminating the need to visit the precinct again. As he reflected upon it, he felt acutely surprised by the fact that Dresdin presumably had the connections necessary to get him into that building as well.

On the surface, Dresdin showed impressive skill in maintaining an air of composure. However, Trevor sensed it to be nothing more than a façade. Something brewed beneath the surface. He remembered Marjorie saying she would be expecting a phone call from her PI tonight, and they'd finally get confirmation about Dresdin's past.

-----:-----

Trevor arrived at the new facility where Stilton-James lay imprisoned. He stepped through the back door at 3:03 pm. Dresdin had told him that his contact would leave the back door ajar. He needed to be there at that exact time. The door had a time-triggered alarm that would go off if left open for more than two minutes and a half. Trevor knew from experience this was a longer time frame than was typically used for these systems. The door in question was, however, the service exit for the building. Since the triggering of the alarm typically initialized a lockdown, then ninety seconds was too short a period for such benign activities as taking out the trash.

He'd received directions regarding where to find Stilton-James once inside the holding facility. After having followed these instructions, he found himself in front of Stilton-James.

"Hello, William."

"Hello ... oh no! Not you again."

"Oh! So you remember me this time?"

"Do I remember you? Thanks to you, everybody in here thinks I'm crazy."

Trevor glanced around the spot he had been standing.

"Everybody? There's no one around, William."

"Not now. When the other officers come and ask me the same questions, I tell them that I already answered those questions with you."

"What do they say?"

"What do you think they say? They tell me that I'm crazy and that you don't exist."

"But I do exist ... Right?" Trevor asked in confirmation.

"Uh ... *yeah* ... I think so ... right?"

"Well, I'm sorry about that, William. I'm afraid wires get crossed sometimes. I'm sure it was an honest mistake."

"Whatever you say, mister."

"So, William, I have a question for you."

"I know. You always have questions."

Trevor smiled. He said, "I suppose you're right. I'm afraid I still have one more question for you. It's the most important question I will ask you ... William, I'd like you to tell me about the night."

"What night?" Stilton-James asked.

"I think you know what night, William."

"Oh, that night."

"Yes, exactly, that night."

"I don't really have to talk about it, do I?"

Trevor observed Stilton-James carefully, assessing his expression. He seemed sincere.

"Actually, yes, you do, William."

"Alright, then. What do you want to know?"

"Start at the beginning. Tell me about how you met the boy."

"I was sitting in the diner minding my own business when this little kid walks in. I looked around to see everyone else's reaction to seeing if they all thought the same thing as me."

"Which was?"

"That this little boy shouldn't be alone. I looked at everybody else, but no one seemed to care. I felt like I had to do something."

"So, what did you do?"

"I walked over, introduced myself and sat down. He seemed quite nice. Yes, he was a nice boy," Stilton-James said, with an oddly childlike smile.

"What happened next?"

"We talked for a while, and he seemed so ... So unhurt... I started getting scared."

"What do you mean, William? What do you mean by unhurt, and why were you scared?"

"He didn't look like he had ever been burnt before. His arms and legs looked bare. It made me scared."

"Why did this scare you?"

"Seeing little ones who were unhurt made them angry. They were always extra bad to the unhurt ones. The worst things always happened to them."

"This scared *you*."

"I was scared of him. I didn't want this to keep happening. I had to stop them."

"So, what happened next, William?"

"I saw him sitting at the booth by himself. It isn't safe for kids to be alone, so I asked him why he was alone and where his parents were. He said he was waiting for them, but they were late. I didn't know what to do, but I decided I needed to help him hide. He wasn't safe out in the open. Usually, the children hide. I couldn't understand why he wasn't hiding."

Trevor asked, "Okay, so you were at the diner, and you decided to help, then what happened?"

"I knew that if I told him the truth, he wouldn't come with me, so I thought of a way to convince him to follow. I told him I had a puppy, all kids like puppies. I brought him to the car, and then I brought him to my usual hiding spot underground," Stilton-James said.

Trevor noticed that Stilton-James's voice had changed drastically from when he'd started speaking of the night in question. It had risen in pitch, mimicking that of a young boy. Trevor observed him. His posture had changed, he seemed more fidgety, and his facial expression seemed less controlled. Trevor had seen this effect during hypnotized regressions but never during conscious questioning. Trevor had heard of this occurring, but it was rare and usually indicated some sort of psychological trauma.

"Once you brought him underground, what happened next?"

"Umm ... I brought him underground and then ..." Stilton-James said under his breath.

"Right. What happened next?"

"I think he tried to run away, so I told him it wasn't safe outside, and he couldn't leave."

"Okay ..."

"I heard a metallic clank like he had dropped something, and then ..."

"Yes."

"I'm sorry, mister, I don't remember."

Trevor wanted to huff in frustration but managed to keep his cool.

"Try to think, William. What happened next?"

"I can't. I can't remember, sir."

Trevor felt annoyed, but he didn't see the point in continuing that specific line of questioning. He decided the best thing, for now, would be to revisit that question later on.

Trevor said, "You mentioned 'they' before. Can you tell me a little about ... 'They?'"

Stilton-James squeezed his eyes shut. He said, "They are the bad people. They are the ones who hurt everyone."

"So, you didn't want the boy to be hurt, so you helped him hide in your basement," Trevor paraphrased, then asked a question. "Do you remember what happened next?"

"Not right after, no."

"Well, tell me the next thing that you remember then."

"I woke up, and the boy was on the ground. He was all bloody. I didn't know what to do. I was scared that he might try to run away, and I wanted to help him, so I tied him up. After tying him to the table, I went upstairs to get some water and some blankets, and when I returned, he was lying lifeless on the table."

Trevor had inadvertently been holding his breath.

He cleared his throat.

He said, "I see. Do you know how or why he was lying lifeless?"
"I ... I don't know."
"What did you feel or think when you saw him there?"
"I felt sad."
"Why did you feel sad?"
"Well, because I'd failed. I'd wanted to protect him, and I'd failed."
"I see. You don't remember anything else."
"No. I don't ... wait a second ..."
"... What is it?"
"I think there was something on the ground."
"What was on the ground, William?"
"I can't... remember, but there was something small on the ground, and I picked it up and—"
"Yes?"
"I guess after picking it up, I blacked out again 'cause the next thing I remember is the feeling of choking as I hung from a rope."
"I see," Trevor said as he reflected on everything that Stilton-James had said.

Trevor instinctively knew that Stilton-James's words seemed puzzling, but as he sat back and thought for a moment, he realized that they were much more than just puzzling. They proved to Trevor that Stilton-James couldn't be a sociopath. The words that Stilton-James used could not have come from a sociopath. Sociopaths had no empathy, no conscience, and no knowledge of how normal humans behaved in emotional settings.

He watched Stilton-James's facial expressions throughout, and he failed to see any deception at all. Sociopaths were master manipulators. However, his experience had taught him that a sociopath's greatest weakness lay in an inability to convey complex emotions effectively. Like a bad actor, they may recite the lines in the script's order, but subtleties like tone were often noticeably incorrect. The theory was that since they didn't feel emotions the way humans typically did, they drew solely from imitating others' emotions. To the discerning eye, even the most masterful sociopath still made mistakes in this area. Trevor concluded that either Stilton-James had to be the most effective sociopath Trevor had ever known, or Stilton-James had received a grossly erroneous diagnosis.

He wanted to confirm his suspicions.

Trevor asked, "William, why did you hang yourself?"

He knew from experience how Stilton-James's actions might look to a jury but having seen the playback. He doubted that there was a need for Stilton-James to hang himself. Stilton-James wasn't in any immediate danger of capture. A sociopath would only look to kill him or herself if the danger was present. Lacking the presence of an imminent threat, what would possibly cause Stilton-James to hang himself?

"I don't know," Stilton-James responded.

Trevor could feel himself getting angry. He knew that the D-Eye playback only presented a part of the explanation. The part that had occurred while Emil was still alive. He felt an ever-pressing need to understand what had happened afterward.

"There must be a reason. You saw him lying there lifeless, and you felt responsible."

"I was the only one there, so I must have done it."

"So why did you hang yourself?"

"I don't know."

He noticed that Stilton-James's assumed position as a mastermind was becoming increasingly doubtful. He offered William the chance to use the hanging as a means to prove that he had done it out of guilt, but he continually refused this position. To add to the confusion, Stilton-James also wasn't taking the opportunity to deceive his way out of trouble, the way a sociopath would likely do.

"Okay, William, I want you to think of the exact thing you either saw or heard or felt the moment before you did it."

"I was standing over him, the little boy was lying on the table, and he was grey. I tried to shake him, and then I felt how cold he was. And then ..."

Stilton-James paused for a moment. He tilted his head to the side and gave me the most peculiar look. I couldn't believe what I was seeing. His eyes looked to be forming tears. He looked at me as though he felt that he was remembering something hurtful and that somehow I could ease his pain.

"I ... did it ... because ... I'd done everything I could to save him, and he still died."

Trevor felt a shudder.

Stilton-James dropped to his knees as though the weight of years of pain had finally broken through the dam.

"William ... William ...?" Trevor called. He wanted to get his attention back, but it was too late. Stilton-James was sobbing uncontrollably. Trevor realized that the cries were so loud that they were bound to attract attention. Trevor didn't know what to do. He did the only thing he could. He walked away before he got emotional himself.

-----:-----

As he headed back to DIT, he felt so many conflicting emotions. He still knew two things, Stilton-James could not be a sociopath, and someone had gone to great lengths to convince everyone that he was.

Later at the lab, he was preparing to leave for the day, and he had felt overcome with relief at the realization he'd managed to avoid Dresdin for the remainder of the day.

As he walked to the car, his relief shifted to excitement as in a few hours he'd hoped, get some answers about Dresdin via a phone call from Marjorie.

After leaving work, he decided to head to the Bear Hug Pub to have a drink to help take off the edge. The day had been so stressful, and he had already decided that he didn't want to be home when he received Marjorie's call. She'd said she'd be calling around 6:00 pm.

-----:-----

Sitting at a table with a bottle of Nost in front of him, he noticed the pub was gradually beginning to fill. There also seemed to be a crowd forming around a television set behind the bar. Several different conversations were happening at that moment. However, all conversations seemed to halt when the voice of the newscaster began speaking on the television.

"It has just been announced that after six hours of deliberation, Judge Brown, who has been presiding over the Emil Dresdin murder case, will soon be making his final ruling."

Dresdin must have spent his entire day at the courthouse awaiting the verdict, Trevor thought to himself.

All eyes in the bar seemed fixed on the television. Trevor could see on the screen that judge was re-entering the courtroom. Trevor's phone rang.

Glancing down at his watch, he noticed that it wasn't 6:00 yet.

He stepped away from the television and through the crowd.

"Hello?"

"Trevor? It's Sylvie."

Trevor could hear the distress in Sylvie's voice. There was a quiver, but he couldn't judge if she was sad or scared.

"Sylvie? Is everything okay?"

He could hear sobs and the sounds of erratic breathing. She said, "I'm at the hospital. It's Pax. There was an accident."

"What? Is he okay? Are you okay?"

There was a long pause.

"Hello?"

"Yes."

Trevor could faintly hear Sylvie's voice, only a touch above a whisper.

"What happened, Sylvie?"

"Trevor ... he's gone."

"What do you mean? What are you saying?"

"I think ... I think ... he's dead."

"What! What happened?"

"I don't know. He was supposed to call me when he got home. He said he needed to talk to me, and he sounded scared. When he didn't call me, I decided to go to his house. I drove there as quickly as I could and when I arrived there were ambulances ... and fire trucks ... and then I saw what was left of the house…. There was nothing left. They're saying there was some kind of an explosion."

"Okay, what hospital are you at? I'm going to go there now."

"No, no, don't. Pax said that he was being followed, and I didn't believe him, but there are men here who look very suspicious."

"Sylvie, that's even more reason for me to go there. If you're scared, then I can help."

"No, don't worry about me. I'm a big girl. I can take care of myself. I'm probably not even being followed. Where are you? Maybe I can go to you."

"I'm at the Bear Hug Pub," Trevor replied.

"Okay, I'll head over there now," Sylvie asserted.

"Are you sure you don't want me to go down there and get you?"

"No, no, I'll come to you. I just don't want to be alone right now, that's all."

"Come down here. You absolutely shouldn't be alone right now. I'll be waiting for you."

"I'll leave right now."

"Okay, don't be afraid, Sylvie, everything is going to be alright."

"Alright," Sylvie said.

Trevor could tell by her tone that she was no longer frantic.

The instant he hung up the phone, his phone rang again. As he answered, Trevor glanced up at the screen in the pub and saw a headline that read: "Judge's verdict is only moments away."

"Hello?"

"Trevor, it's Marjorie. We've got a problem."

"I know. I have news too."

"Oh, then you know already? I don't understand how you could know so soon."

"Well, I just found out now. It's terrible news."

"Wait for a second. I don't think we're talking about the same thing here. What are you talking about?"

"Pax."

"Pax? I'm talking about my PI. He's disappeared."

"Disappeared?"

"Something terrible is happening, Trevor. I can't help but think the worst. What happened to Pax?"

"Marjorie, you better sit down for this."

"Okay, what is it?"

"There was an explosion at his house, and I'm afraid Pax didn't make it."

"Oh, my God!"

"Sylvie called me from the hospital in tears. She sounded pretty shaken up, and she wasn't clear on the details herself."

"Oh, no! Trevor, what are we going to do? All of this is happening at the same time. It can't be a coincidence. My PI has disappeared, Pax, and the verdict in the Stilton-James's case is only minutes away."

Trevor decided at that moment that he'd rather overreact than suffer the consequences of having underreacted.

"Okay, you need to go somewhere safe. Maybe somewhere out of town. Do you have a place where you can go?"

"I can go to my aunt's house."

"Okay, pack a bag and go there now. Don't call anyone. Don't trust anyone. Call me when you get to your aunt's house."

"Trevor, I'm scared."

"I know, but you have to be strong. You'll be fine, but you have to go now. I'm going to call Sylvie and get her to do the same."

"Okay, okay ... Trevor? Whatever happens, I want you to know that ..."

"Marjorie, stop. Whatever you're going to say, you can tell me after. We're just cautious. Hopefully, if we're overreacting, we can all have a chuckle about this over a couple of Nost pints. Everything is going to be okay. Okay?"

"Okay. Trevor. I'll go now."

"Good! Go and please be careful, Marjorie."

"Okay. Goodbye, Trevor."

"Goodbye, Marjorie."

Trevor looked up at the television and saw a news headline that read: 'verdict pushed back to 6:30 pm.' Looking at his watch, he realized there was still a half-hour to go. He paid his bill and prepared to leave. As he picked up his change, he turned around, and a man stepped in his way.

"Hi, Trevor."

"Willy Taylor? What are you doing here?"

"I think you better come with me. Dresdin wants to speak with you."

He pressed forcefully into Trevor's shoulder with his hand. Though he hadn't seen Taylor holding a weapon openly, he nonetheless sensed it lay hidden somewhere underneath his jacket.

All of Trevor's concerns had begun playing back before his eyes. Ever since the D-Eye project's completion and the bogus press conference, he'd been searching for reasons to quell his concerns. He realized that everything since that point had played out exactly according to his worst fears. The verdict's announcement hadn't yet occurred, but Trevor already knew what the verdict would be. He knew from the onset that if his theories were all correct, then the true sociopath was Dresdin, he was the puppet master, and he'd always been. Somehow, he'd manipulated Stilton-James's diagnosis. He'd ensured the result he wanted. He'd struggled to understand why Dresdin hadn't been more distraught after Emil's death. Sociopaths can't empathize, and when Trevor suggested to him that he might not be acting abnormally, Dresdin's facial expression was that of contempt. Trevor recalled from his deception training that contempt was the most dangerous of all micro-expressions as it denoted extreme overconfidence. This expression always appeared when the deceiver, having just lied, reacted to the satisfaction of seeing his lie succeed. Dresdin showed exactly that when Trevor questioned him about his lack of sorrow regarding Emil's death. It was subtle, but Trevor was certain that he'd seen it.

All of this led to Trevor's suspicions regarding Dresdin's evil plans for Reverse-Looping. Trevor always knew that if he was right, then sadly, there were four loose ends that needed tying; himself, Marjorie, Sylvie and of course dearly departed, Pax.

Trevor had finally arrived at his breaking point. As for all of Dresdin's masterful planning and calculation, he still lacked the vision to realize that Trevor was not going to let him get away with any of it, even if it meant his own destruction. He had one Ace card left to play.

His shoulder had initially flexed when Taylor had placed his hand upon it. Trevor relaxed his muscles, turned to Taylor, and looked him dead in the eyes.

"I'm glad you've come, William, I've been meaning to speak to you and Dresdin, so this is perfect."

"Good, now walk toward the exit."

"Sure, no problem, just one thing though, don't ever place your hands on me again."

While in the car, Trevor thought about what he wanted to say. He felt his next words to Taylor were crucial.

-----:-----

Over the next ten minutes, Trevor gave Willy Taylor his dose of the unadulterated truth, which Willy absorbed with little to no reaction. When he finished, Willy said nothing and continued staring at the road as he drove.

At this moment, Trevor realized that the route they were taking didn't lead back to DIT.

"Where are you taking me?"

Willy Taylor said nothing.

"This isn't the way to DIT headquarters."

"We're making a stop along the way," Willy Taylor replied.

Trevor looked out the window, trying to gauge the car's speed, and consequently, the chances of surviving a leap from the car. He resolved that his best chance for escape would likely come at this other stop. He turned his gaze from the window and onto Willy Taylor as he drove. As he looked upon Willy's stone-cold expression, he wondered what thoughts ran through the mind of the man driving him to his certain death.

Thirty minutes later…

-----:------

Willy Taylor opened the door for Trevor, and the two men stared at each other intensely. As they walked through the main entrance of DIT Headquarters, Trevor noticed how different the circumstances of this day seemed when compared to the first time they'd walked these halls together, back on Trevor's first day.

Trevor stepped into Dresdin's office, and the door closed behind him.

"Trevor," Dresdin said as he got up and walked around to the front of his desk.

Trevor remained silent and didn't step forward.

"What … No greeting? At least come and sit down and talk with me for a minute."

Trevor stood still.

"Why so quiet?"

"What did you do with Pax?" Trevor asked, finally turning his eyes in Dresdin's direction.

"What do you mean?" Dresdin asked.

"An accidental explosion? Do you think that anyone is going to believe that?"

"Oh, but they already have my friend. Everything is unfolding exactly as planned."

Trevor shook his head, and he could feel himself filling with rage, but he fought to remain calm. He knew it was his only chance of getting out of this situation alive.

"What of Marjorie and Sylvie?"

"So much concern for others. Where was this concern when all of these lies were floating around?"

"Lies?"

"*Yes, lies!* Perhaps you take me for a fool. Did you think I would have let my investment go astray without an ace in hand? Lust is such a predictable thing."

"Marjorie."

"Please … I'm not that obvious."

"Sylvie."

"It's the quiet ones that you always have to watch out for, isn't it?"

Trevor took a deep breath that seemed to quiver as he exhaled. An idea suddenly occurred to him.

"You know, Carl, it must have been hard all those years, running away from your past."

"Ha! Very funny."

"I can only imagine what that trauma must have done to you," Trevor said, carefully searching Dresdin's face for a reaction. Dresdin's arrogant smile suddenly evaporated.

"You're grasping at straws, my friend."

"Am I? Well, I guess we forgive our parents' trespasses easily, then."

"What did you say?"

Trevor had a fifty-fifty chance. He picked one and went for it.

Trevor said, "A mother's love is such a precious thing."

Dresdin's face turned red.

"And yet, you still loved her. Of course, you did. You were her son, and she was your mother."

"Say another word, and I'll kill you."

Trevor realized he'd struck a chord. He decided to take another shot.

"Have you learned nothing? Did killing solve your problem the first time?" Trevor asked with conviction in his voice.

"What did you say?"

"Killing … it's a trend with you, isn't it?"

Trevor felt struck by a bolt of clarity regarding Dresdin. The obsessive need for revenge directed at Stilton-James, the hatred and rage he'd seen in Dresdin's eyes, had always been about much more than what appeared on the surface.

Dresdin said, "What are you doing … how …?"

"This is why you've done all of this. You put all of the pieces together, and you figured out Reverse-Looping's true potential. Why must you persist with all the charades then, Carl? You watched every second of our interviews, didn't you? You know Stilton-James is not a sociopath! Please? I know a sociopath when I see one, and I'm looking at one right now. You know ... I didn't understand why anyone would want to misdiagnose Stilton-James. I mean, I suspected you were sick, and we're all like pawns to you, but now I've finally figured it out. A sociopath like you knew that no one would believe Stilton-James even if he spoke the truth. Sociopaths are liars, and once identified, they can never be trusted again. Regardless of how effective Stilton-James might become at telling the truth, not only would no one believe him. Once labelled as a sociopath, his behaviour would only solidify his image. They'd think to themselves... 'This sociopath is impressive. Convincing. Brilliant. See how he manages to continue lying with such effectiveness?'"

"Are you just going to recite all of my plans back to me?"

Trevor and Dresdin stared at each other for several seconds.

Trevor said, "You, Bastard. You're not going get away with this!"

"Oh, no? Watch me."

"You think you're so clever, but your plan has holes—huge ones," Trevor said.

"Is that right? By all means, enlighten me."

"There are only two people who know what will happen with Reverse-Looping, and one of them is dead."

"I already know what'll happen," Dresdin snarled.

"No, you don't. You think you know what will happen, but you have no idea. You're a sociopath, so you don't understand the complexities of human emotions. There's no way you could know what Stilton-James's true diagnosis is, but I do."

Dresdin said, "You sure seem confident."

"If you were me, then you would be too."

"Why is that, Trevor?"

"Because if you knew what I know, then you wouldn't be doing what you're doing right now ..."

"You think that I'm afraid of getting my hands dirty. Is that it? You underestimate me. You're making a huge mistake."

"Listen to me very carefully. Whatever you do to me today or any other day, I promise you. I will make you pay. I swear on everything I hold dear. You will not get away with this. If you kill me, this will not save you. Even beyond my death, I will destroy you. I promise you, one way or another, I will make you pay for what you've done. You've underestimated me, you've underestimated what I'm capable of ... that'll be your ultimate undoing. You will pay for all of this, but it won't come the way you might think." Trevor stepped forward and pointed as he spoke, lowering his head and focusing his glare into Dresdin's eyes. "You and I have unfinished business. This kind of justice won't come down from a court, you will pay your debt to me, personally, and it be won't be quick or painless."

There was a silence as the two men stared one another down.

Suddenly, Dresdin's watch alarm went off.

The two men continued staring at one another for a few seconds then, Dresdin burst out laughing.

"Trevor, I'm not going to kill you. No, I have bigger plans for you," Dresdin said as he walked away.

As he left the office, Trevor could hear Willy Taylor ask Dresdin, "What should I do with him?"

"You know what to do," Dresdin said as he walked away.

From the threshold of the office, Willy Taylor looked at Trevor. With no knowledge of what would happen next. Dr. Trevor Miles stood up, adjusted his collar, and walked towards Willy Taylor. With composure and grace, he fearlessly marched to his fate.

Chapter 36

Beth Lago. Wednesday, April 18, 2075. 10:49 AM

We all left the courthouse and returned to the precinct together. Eccles, Cap, and Sayvian all undid their ties, and we all sat around awaiting the phone call regarding the verdict.

One hour passed and then two, and still no phone call.

As we sat around waiting, a question occurred to me. "So, Judge Brown is going to be reviewing the data files, right?"

"That's the plan," Sayvian said.

"How is he going to operate the equipment?" I asked.

"The D-Eye equipment?"

"Yeah, that stuff was really sophisticated. I've seen Judge Brown in front of a computer before ... He can barely type."

"There must be a D-Eye technician who is assisting him," Eccles said.

"But, he's supposed to be sequestered."

"Well, he is a judge. He'll be mindful of influence, I hope," Sayvian said.

Three hours from the court adjourning, Sayvian's cell phone rang.

"It's time. Let's go!"

----:----

The buzz in the courtroom silenced upon Judge Brown's entrance. All eyes simultaneously turned towards him, examining his facial expressions, trying to discern the verdict. Predictably, the Judge's expression gave nothing away.

He addressed the court. "I have reviewed all of the evidence and am prepared to render a verdict. Would the defendant please rise?"

Stilton-James stood up, the rattle of his chains echoing through the courtroom. Ms. Alana stood up with him.

"William Stilton-James, regarding the charge of murder in the second degree, this court finds that you are guilty, as charged."

Cheers erupted throughout the courtroom. William Stilton-James stood expressionless.

"William Stilton-James, regarding the charge of kidnapping in the first degree, this court finds that you are guilty, as charged."

Again, cheers filled the courtroom.

"William Stilton-James, this court is very disturbed by the crimes you've committed against a defenceless child. You have caused the death of Emil Dresdin, and your crimes cannot and will not go unpunished. I have decided to allow the victim's family to step forward to address you and the court regarding your horrific crimes. Bailiff, please escort William Stilton-James to the stand."

Stilton-James stood up and walked over to the stand with the oversized bailiff following closely.

"You will be allowed to offer responses to atonement, but only after the speakers have finished."

"Mr. Sayvian, if you could please assist ..."

"Of course, Your Honour," Sayvian said as he walked over to Mr. Dresdin, who looked pale and teary-eyed.

Mrs. Dresdin was under his arm, held tightly. I felt so much sorrow for them, but there was an air of relief in my chest. At least little Emil will have justice.

A shaken Carl Dresdin stepped up to the microphone.

"Death. Death and darkness are all I see when I look at you. You will never know the feeling of pain that we're feeling right now. You will never know the hatred that I feel in my heart for you. If I were any other man, I would ... I would ... how could you do this to him? HE'S JUST A CHILD!" Mr. Dresdin yelled before breaking down in tears. "You deserve to die for what you've done, but I wish you could suffer what Emil suffered. You're not a man. You're a coward. That's why you preyed on my innocent son. He was so good. He was so kind. He trusted you, and you kill ..." Mr. Dresdin began sobbing again. He then stared at Stilton-James with vicious eyes. "Why don't you care? How can you sit there and look at me in the face and not admit what you've done? You're not human. I don't know what you are, but you're not human. I hope you pay dearly for what you've done," Mr. Dresdin said before stepping away from the microphone.

"William Stilton-James, is there anything you would like to say to the victim's family?"

William Stilton-James leaned towards the microphone and said, "No, YOUR HONOUR."

"Very well, William Stilton-James, take your position beside your attorney and remain standing."

The bailiff then escorted William Stilton-James to his spot behind the defence table.

"William Stilton-James, for the crimes for which you have been convicted, it is the order of this court that, ultimately, you be executed by lethal injection. Before your imminent execution, you will undergo another punishment. Moments ago, the Magistrate of this Territory signed into law a new type of punishment you will be the first to endure. William Stilton-James, you have shown no remorse for your actions, and as a result, this court has decided that execution will not be sufficient. You will see everything that Emil Dresdin saw as he died. You will feel everything that Emil Dresdin felt as you viciously beat him. You will know the pain that little boy felt as he lay battered and bloodied with the sting of his seventeen bone fractures. You will know the severity of your crime, for your punishment will be equally severe. Once removed from this courtroom, you will be transferred to a facility where you will undergo the surgeries Emil underwent. You will have D-Eye implants inserted into your head. Emil's data files will feed backwards into your subconscious. Perhaps that will compel some remorse on your part. Following this procedure, you will fall into state custody, awaiting execution. May God almighty have mercy on your soul. This court is adjourned."

Chapter 37

Beth Lago. Wednesday, April 18, 2075. 6:59 PM

The shock that ran through the courtroom was instantaneous and all-consuming. For many of us, myself included, there was a feeling of surrealism. None of us expected this sort of possibility, and we had no way of knowing what it all meant.

When Eccles and I left the courthouse, we were interested in seeing crowd reactions beyond the courthouse doors. From the announcement of Emil's death until the verdict, the crowd's mood had been one of anger, verging on outrage. Now, the crowd seemed content about there being an eventual death sentence ordered. I rightly assumed they were also equally confused about the second part.

Eccles and I had our questions. Minutes after the verdict, we each received messages requesting that we meet back at the precinct.

-----:-----

Cap, Sayvian, and the sheriff were standing at the front of the packed boardroom when we arrived. Huddled together, they whispered amongst themselves. Glancing around the room, I took a seat near the back, and Eccles took up a seat beside me. The atmosphere at this meeting felt different. These gatherings tended to be casual affairs filled with chatter as the officers mingled and exchanged jokes. Still, today there was no chatting or mingling of any kind, just a group of officers sitting quietly staring at the front of the conference room.

"Alright, everybody, I've asked Sayvian to come to speak to you guys and answer any questions you may have regarding the sentence from Judge Brown and so on," Cap said as he turned to Sayvian, giving him a nod as he invited him to begin.

"Okay, so I just got off the phone with the Magistrate of the Territory, and I have some more details regarding the sentence of Reverse-Looping."

An officer from the back of the room asked, "Great, can you explain what it is?"

Sayvian answered, "The law is about fifty pages long, and I've only had limited time to review it, but in essence, it is a penalty to be administered to perpetrators convicted of crimes against D-Eye patients. The convicted perpetrator, if assigned this sentence, will undergo D-Eye surgeries and will have to experience the death of their victim, fully, through their consciousness."

Another officer asked a question, "For?"

"Making them crap their pants," Eccles blurted out to a chorus of laughter. He quickly apologized when spotting Cap's glare.

"It's just a sentence that is going to be available to judges to apply in these types of cases," Sayvian continued. "The truth is it's a landmark decision, and as far as I'm concerned, it's the fairest type of sentencing possible. After seeing what Emil saw, I imagine Stilton-James will be begging for his execution."

Cap jumped into the conversation, "Guys, look, our primary concern is justice. This sentence is the closest we'll ever come to an eye for an eye. Stilton-James will suffer through the same things as Emil. He will feel every blow, every bone breaking. He will know the damage he inflicted. Let's not be casual about what's happening here. This is a new form of punishment that is radical, severe, but fair."

"Are there any other questions?" Sayvian asked.

I stood up, "Where is this going to take place, and who will observe it?"

"As far as I know, both procedures will take place at an undisclosed medical facility, one where the implants will be inserted and another to perform the actual Reverse-Looping. In terms of observers, it'll be the D-Eye officials and their medically trained personnel."

"Are there any other questions?"

The room remained silent.

"Very, well, thank you for your attention."

-----:-----

Later that night, while patrolling the streets surrounding the Scourge with Eccles, I got the sense it would be a quiet night. I couldn't help but see that the atmosphere of calm and quiet outside matched the atmosphere inside the patrol car.

Two hours into our patrol and we'd scarcely said a word to one another. All the dramatic events of late, once charged with adrenaline, had now calmed. In the aftermath, reality began to set. I had a strange feeling in my gut, which I couldn't rationalize. Strange feelings aside, there was still an air of certainty. I had wanted justice for Emil, and I had wanted Stilton-James to feel all that Emil had felt. Now that this possibility had finally arrived, though, I couldn't shake a subtle feeling of loss. I wondered if the feeling resembled my father's feeling upon entering Old Los Angeles following the gassing. I had expected to feel relief, but there was no relief in sight. I couldn't place my finger on it, but something bothered me.

Eccles asked if I was okay.

"Yeah ... I'm fine. How are you?"

"I'm fine."

"What do you think?" Eccles asked.

"I think it's a fair outcome."

"I agree. So, what's the problem?" Eccles asked.

"I don't know. I just have a weird feeling about everything,"

"I know I have the same feeling. You know, a lot has happened over a very short period."

"I think you're right. Maybe that's part of it. I mean, things moved rather quickly on this. We went from having the first D-Eye baby killed to a brand new type of sentencing in a matter of a few weeks."

"I know it is weird, but I don't think it indicates anything bad necessarily," Eccles said in response.

"I don't know. I'm feeling continually surprised by the way things have been going. I'll be watching the Reverse-Looping very closely."

"Whatever we expect the outcome to be, we'll just have to wait and see," Eccles said.

-----:-----

A few weeks passed, and Eccles and I had returned to normal. It had now been almost a year since Eccles first moved in with me, and we had scarcely noticed the swift passage of time. We had been doing everything together. In many ways, we resembled a married couple.

Willy had attempted to call me several times over the weeks since the trial, but I had avoided his phone calls. I couldn't ignore the feelings I'd had the night I'd seen Willy locking lips with another woman. The sight made me nauseous, and though I felt recovered, annoyance arose whenever my thoughts drifted to him. with Willy out of the picture, I found myself growing fonder of Eccles.

Chapter 38

Beth Lago. Wednesday, May 15, 2075. 9:13 AM

By now, the media had dubbed the procedure "Catharsis" due to the purging of emotion, fears, and repressed feelings that they'd expected would occur. On May 15, 2075, Stilton-James arrived at another undisclosed location to undergo Catharsis. The process was to occur at 1:00 pm local time.

There was once again a whirlwind of media attention in the days leading up to the Catharsis. Cap had tried his best to keep things normal at the precinct. Perhaps sensing Eccles and I would be too distracted at our desks, he ordered us to head out on patrol duty. Eccles was particularly annoyed, but I did my best to disguise my disappointment. For some reason, though, both Eccles and I couldn't shake the feeling that something was about to go wrong.

Eccles and I were three hours into our patrol of the Scourge, and the streets were once again uncharacteristically empty. Since all news networks focused on the Catharsis, we assumed most people were at home waiting to see what would happen. Even Eccles and I couldn't resist a peek at the TV screens in various department store windows as we drove by.

One o'clock came and went with no news. We paused on a bench to eat lunch. A man was sitting a few feet away from us, listening to a news broadcast on portable satellite radio.

"We are being told that the Catharsis has begun. As mentioned earlier in our broadcast, we will have to wait a few hours to find out how Stilton-James has reacted."

After eating lunch, we headed back out onto patrol. Again, the streets were empty, and there was little to report.

Just as Eccles and I were beginning to head back to the precinct, we both received messages from Cap, "Report to the precinct immediately."

-----:-----

When Eccles and I returned, there was a flood of reporters surrounding the doors.

"What the heck is going on here?" Eccles yelled.

"I haven't the slightest idea," I responded.

One reporter held out a microphone, "Would you like to comment, officer?"

"Comment on what?" Eccles snarled.

"Comment on what has happened to Stilton-James."

"No, no, comment," he responded.

As we pushed our way into the precinct, I whispered to Eccles, "Something happened to Stilton-James."

"Yeah, I know."

"Do you know what happened?"

"No, but Cap's over there, and he doesn't look too happy."

We walked over to Cap, who pointed to his office. We stepped inside and sat down.

"Can someone explain to me why we're the last to know anything around here?" Eccles blurted out.

Cap stiffened and raised an eyebrow. "What do you mean?"

"Well, reporters out there want us to comment on what's happened to Stilton-James."

"What did you tell them?"

"Nothing, we don't know, squat!" Eccles blurted.

"Good, they don't know squat either. They're just fishing for answers. They suspect that something has happened, but they don't know what. No one knows what's happened except for the magistrate, the sheriff, Sayvian's staff, the D-eye officials who were in the room at the time, and me. What I'm about to tell you cannot leave this room. You guys better sit down."

Eccles and I looked at each other before taking our chairs.

"At 3:14 this afternoon, William Stilton-James died."

"What?" I replied, jaw-dropping and shaking my head.

"How?" Eccles asked.

"That's what I need you to find out. I need you to find out how and why Stilton-James died."

"So, we don't have a cause of death?"

"Not exactly. The coroner is suspecting cardiac arrest."

"So, they scared him to death?"

"Now is not the time for jokes, Beth."

"I wasn't joking, Cap."

"I want you to question everyone who was in that room. I mean everyone. I want you to check the backgrounds of every employee involved in the procedure. There is absolutely no margin for error here."

At that moment, the sheriff entered Cap's office and glared at him.

"That'll be all, guys," Cap said to us while not taking his gaze off Sheriff McCoy.

We left the office and retreated to the boardroom, where we sat down to plan our investigation.

"We need to know the COD," Eccles declared.

"I know. It all begins and ends with the COD," I replied.

Eccles looked up at me as though a thought had just occurred to him. I knew what he was going to ask.

"Willy, right?"

"I wonder if he was in that room."

"I'll call him, and I'll pay a visit to D-Eye headquarters."

"I'll check with the coroner," Eccles stated.

Just then, Sayvian stepped into the room and looked at both of us before stating, "Are you guys ready for this? I specifically asked Cap that you be the ones to work on this case. I need you guys to give this the fairest shake possible. Set your personal feelings aside. In this case, Stilton-James is the victim if there is a case at all.

I need to know if a crime was committed or not. Let me know if you need anything."

Eccles and I took separate cars. On my way to the DIT headquarters, I tried calling Willy's cell several times, unsuccessfully.

-----:-----

Arriving at DIT headquarters, a group of unfamiliar people greeted me. They were standing just beyond the main gate. I found this bizarre as the DIT suits so rarely left the confines of the building's securely guarded interiors. I pulled up beside them. One gentleman directed me to a parking spot that had a sign that read "RESERVED." As soon as I got out of the car, the group seemed to surround me. The gentleman who had directed me to the parking spot was standing at the forefront.

"Hello, Inspector Lago. My name is Derek Ponts. I'm here representing DIT corporate." He proceeded to introduce me to two men and two women, who I surmised by their demeanour to be his assistants. He introduced them to me as "counselors." Ponts and the other members of his team were all dressed to the nines.

"Well, Mr. Ponts, I'm glad to see that DIT has decided to summon you all out here this morning, but I'm afraid I'm not here for a tour. I'm here as an investigator."

"We're only here to assist," he replied quickly while lifting both hands.

"Okay, then, I'll need to see the facility where Stilton-James died and speak to every person who was in that room when it happened," I said as I began walking towards the main building. I looked over at Ponts, who had an irritated look on his face.

Perhaps I had been a bit abrupt, but I found it more than slightly disturbing that DIT's legal team had been awaiting my arrival before I'd even had a chance to begin investigating. Ponts still hadn't responded.

"I'll need a list, Mr. Ponts."

"Judy, please?" Ponts said to one of his assistants.

A curly-haired brunette handed me a sheet. I knew this information was available. They'd already prepared each witness before my arrival. Did they need five lawyers to deliver this information to me?

I scanned the alphabetically arranged list. I found Willy's name almost immediately, and the rest of the list consisted of doctors and nurses. Each name had a title beside it with a phone number.

"Inspector Lago, DIT asked that we make it completely clear to you they are willing to cooperate with the police in every way possible."

I'll be the judge of that, I thought to myself.

"Thank you, Mr. Ponts. I'll need to visit the facility where the procedure took place," I declared.

"Very, well ... Follow me," Ponts responded after a lengthy pause.

Mr. Ponts gestured to one of his staff. A minute later, a car pulled up, and we got in. We drove for about twenty minutes before arriving at a gated property. Ponts flashed his security pass, and we drove into what looked like an empty parking garage. We took a couple of turns around the supposed garage before he led us into a long underground tunnel. We descended into the inclined tunnel for several minutes until we arrived at a platform.

The car stopped, and we all got out. As we walked up to what looked like a security desk, Ponts headed over to a couple of well-armed guards. He spoke to them for a few minutes before telling us to follow. After passing through the airport-like security checkpoint, Ponts declared, "Welcome to the DIT Advanced Testing Site. This is where the Catharsis took place. Please follow me."

An automatic glass-sliding door opened up to an average-looking hospital. Doctors and nurses were walking around going about their respective businesses, just like any other medical hospital. There was one primary difference as this hospital was underground, heavily guarded, and secret. Ponts walked up to a desk where he spoke to a woman quietly, then led us down a hallway to a hospital room. Inside, there was one bed surrounded by several machines, none of which looked like standard hospital equipment.

As I surveyed the room, Ponts walked over to me. Another man followed closely behind.

"Inspector, this is Dr. Tartin. He oversaw the procedure," Ponts explained.

A short man with neat dark hair and a serious expression on his face extended his hand towards me.

"Hello." His loud baritone-like voice startled me.

"Hello. Dr. Tartin, Inspector Beth Lago, I'm investigating the death of William Stilton-James."

"I see."

"Can you walk me through the procedure as you remember it?" I asked.

"Yes. So I entered this room around eleven o'clock this morning after the patient had already been sedated."

"Did you notice anything particular at that point?"

"No, not at all. Heart rate was stable, blood pressure was normal."

"Okay, so what happened next?"

"Well, we proceeded with the Reverse-Looping. As expected, as the playback rolled on, the patient's blood pressure rose as well as his heart rate, but both were still within the thresholds we had anticipated to be normal."

"Okay."

"We had pre-marked the time leading up to the death of the source of the playback."

"Emil Dresdin."

"Right ... At about three hours and thirteen minutes, the playback was to end, and we would then inject Stilton-James with a solution that would wake him up. However, about a minute before the end of the playback, Stilton-James's heart suddenly stopped."

"What happened, then?"

"We initiated life-saving measures, but we were unable to revive him."

"What did the life-saving measures entail?"

"We used a defibrillator, and we administered CPR, but there wasn't much use. He was already gone."

"Thank you, Dr. Tartin."

I spent the next several hours interviewing everyone on the list. Each of them provided me with almost the same description of events. Up to this point, however, I hadn't detected any reason to doubt their answers. The fact they seemed prepped for questioning indicated the need for further investigation. It did not confirm the presence of deception or obstruction.

Looking down at my list, I noticed I had questioned almost all the witnesses but two: Willy and one of the nurses. Both had gone home for the day and wouldn't be returning until tomorrow. I asked Dr. Tartin for all the raw data from the procedure, specifically printouts of the pulse monitors and EEG. I found it odd they didn't have this data on hand, but they agreed to send it all to the precinct before noon tomorrow, which seemed reasonable.

Back at the DIT headquarters, Ponts handed me his card and, with a smug grin and told me to let him know if I needed anything, anything at all.

When I returned to the precinct, Eccles was already there. We decided to meet in the boardroom as Cap and Sayvian each wanted updates.

Eccles said, "Okay, so according to the coroner, the cause of death was a heart attack."

Eccles read my mind as I started flipping through my notes. I said, "He's 37 if that ..."

"Heart attack at thirty-seven?"

"I know it's shocking, but there are precedents of people suffering traumas severe enough to cause heart attacks even while being completely healthy."

Sayvian sat back in his chair, contemplating for a moment.

"Did she say anything else?"

Eccles looked down at his notes before responding. He said, "He didn't have any recent injuries, cuts or bruises. Apart from the marks on his neck from when he hung himself and several very old burns, all in all, the coroner described him as being in relatively good health."

Cap turned to me, "How about you, Beth?"

"Well, I visited DIT, where DIT's legal army greeted me. One of the counselors handed me a list of witnesses to the Catharsis, and I spoke to all but two of them. Oh, and I was escorted to DIT's Test Facility."

"And?"

"First of all, that building must be the most fortified medical facility ever. However, when we got down to the questioning, all of the doctors and nurses present each had the same story. Stilton-James underwent the Catharsis, and exactly one minute before the death of the source feed, Emil Dresdin, suffered a major heart attack that led to cardiac arrest. Doctors initiated standard life-saving measures, but they were unable to revive him. He was declared dead at 3:14 pm."

Cap and Sayvian looked at each other. Sayvian rose from his chair and took a couple of steps away before turning back around.

"Who are the two remaining witnesses?" he asked.

"A nurse who was present at the procedure and DIT's head of security, both weren't present for questioning," I replied.

"Willy Taylor?" Cap asked.

"Yes."

"You haven't been able to speak to him?" Cap asked in a surprised tone.

"He had already gone home for the day, and he hasn't been answering my phone calls. We're not exactly on speaking terms right now," I said.

Sayvian looked over at Cap, who seemed to bear the look of annoyance on his face that we all collectively felt.

"Okay, well, we don't have very much to go on at this point. It'll be difficult to argue the point that DIT is responsible for Stilton-James's death because Catharsis is an entirely new procedure. There's no proof of intent here. They wouldn't have had any way of knowing what would happen. We'll keep the investigation open for now, but I don't see very much changing here. I need you guys to follow up with those two remaining witnesses. For now, we'll just have to wait and see where this takes us."

Just then, there was a knock at the door.

"Yes?" Cap asked.

The door opened, and one of the rookie officers peeked in, "There's a package here from DIT, sir."

I said, "It must be the data I requested, printouts of the EEG and the heart rate monitor."

"Okay, review that stuff and let us know if you find anything. We'll regroup tomorrow."

Chapter 39

Beth Lago. Thursday, May 16, 2075. 8:05 AM

Eccles scoured through the dozens of boxes of data, which DIT had sent us over the course of the day. As we examined the various e-sheets, it became clear that only some of the information would ever benefit the investigation. At first glance, it appeared that the results of the medical tests performed on Stilton-James would be the only useful information. DIT had completed several tests on him before inserting the implants, including toxicology tests, blood tests, and urine analysis.

"Looks like DIT did their best to cover their backs," I said to Eccles as we sat in the Evidentiary Analysis Room.

"They even gave Stilton-James a cardio stress test. Talk about ironic. The guy not only passed, but he passed with flying colours," Eccles responded.

"Yeah ..." I replied under my breath as a thought had suddenly occurred to me.

I was sitting at the evidence table holding two e-sheets in my hand, and something told me to look closer. In my left hand, I held an e-sheet from DIT, with signatures of the DIT doctors who had visited Stilton-James. In my right hand, I held an e-sheet from our records, which indicated all the dates, times, and signatures of medical personnel who had visited Stilton-James. Our e-sheet, like most clipboard e-sheets, accepted information via a etch pen, which would graphically record imprints whenever an etch pen pressed against its surface. The interesting thing about our e-sheet was that no one could manipulate or destroy the information it contained once time-coded. I looked at the two documents, attempting to perceive what had caught my eye. I focused closer, and then I saw it. I couldn't believe what I was seeing.

"Eccles, did you say you had copies of all the psych reports over there?"

"Yeah ... Why, what's up?"

"Well, there's this strange 'M' signature on both these e-sheets."

"Yeah ... So what's the problem? Remember, I told you earlier, one of the reports said that one of the doctors sometimes initials his name as 'M' as his medical license was registered using his middle name in error."

"Yeah, I remember Eccles. That's not what's bothering me."

"So what is it then?"

"Well, I'm not an expert, but I'm pretty sure these signatures don't match."

I handed Eccles the e-sheets, and I stood by as he lifted them up close to his eyes.

"It's tough to tell, but I think you might be right," Eccles responded without taking his eyes away from the e-sheets. "But why would the signatures not match?"

"Well, let's say, hypothetically, the information coming from the outside is the one that's tampered with ... We know already that our e-sheet can't be forged," I said.

"Wait a second. Why would DIT track visits from mental health professionals anyway?"

"Well, there must be some logic in it. I guess they started tracking the visits that their staff were making with Stilton-James after he was sentenced, but before he underwent Catharsis."

He said, "Okay, so this e-sheet is a list of visits of DIT doctors made with Stilton-James, and this other one is a logbook of visits to Stilton-James according to our records?"

"Exactly ..." I replied.

"Interesting that their list doesn't have any specific dates—it's just a list of signatures," Eccles said.

"I know it is strange. They aren't making things easy on us. I mean, I've spent the last hour lining up each of these signatures to the names of DIT staff doctors. All but one, this mysterious 'M' signature doesn't match anyone. I know that DIT has already explained this, but it sounds like a lame excuse to me. I mean, it just doesn't make sense. It just doesn't add up."

"So, what are you thinking?" Eccles asked.

"I think they may have forged their own document, but I just don't understand why."

"Well, you said it yourself. They had a ready-made excuse, right?"

"They knew we would ask about the 'M,' didn't they?" I asked rhetorically before continuing.

Eccles said, "There was obviously a visit made to Stilton-James's cell that they don't want us to know about. The person must have been a DIT employee, and maybe they're not employed there anymore, maybe they were fired or something. Later on, another one of their doctors visits Stilton-James's cell. Upon signing into the e-sheet, the person sees the 'M' signature and reports it to DIT. DIT then sends us this document with all the signatures of all the doctors that are employed with them who also visited Stilton-James, including Dr. 'M'. They don't want us to look into this 'M' person, so they include it on their sheets with this bogus story about name confusion with one of their doctors."

"That's a pretty elaborate explanation," Eccles said.

"Eccles, think about it. It's the best explanation we have. The point of matching up these signatures is to confirm information. They knew that the damage was already done and they would never be able to change our data, so they forged their data to match it."

"There's one glaring hole in your theory, though ..."

"What's that?"

"Well, if there's another person named 'M,' where are they now?"

"That's a good question ... I guess the answer lies in what DIT hopes to hide in keeping this person away from us." I paused for a moment as a thought had occurred to me. "Do you remember our first interrogation with Stilton-James, when the doctor went in to talk to him? Stilton-James said that someone had already asked him questions?"

"Yeah, you're right, but there shouldn't have been anyone else."

"No, there shouldn't have been. I would hazard to guess that this person visited Stilton-James before the date on our e-sheet, which appears to be May 15th. He or she came before this date and somehow gained access to Stilton-James without our knowledge."

"Okay, but if that were true, then why would this person sign the e-sheet in the end?"

"Well, I'm not certain, but I assume that this signature may be a message ... it's this person's way of telling us that they were here. Maybe this person was some kind of a whistleblower." I said.

"You know there's one way to prove your theory, right?"

"I need to prove the forgery," I declared.

"Exactly ... You know it might be wise to check with the prosecution and the defence to make sure there wasn't some other doctor that might have signed their name as 'M.' Eccles said.

"If they say that they don't have anyone like that and you can prove the signatures as having been made by two different people, then we may have something," I said.

We both smiled at one another.

"This isn't over yet," I said.

"Not by a long shot," Eccles responded.
"Okay, I'll check with Sayvian, and maybe you can check with Ms. Alana."
"Okay."
The speed at which Eccles jumped at the chance of seeing Ms. Alana caused me a rush of jealousy, but I quickly shook it off and regained control over my emotions.
"Sure, sounds good," I replied.

-----:-----

Sayvian's office was in a high rise, located in the most upscale part of the city. I entered, picked my visitor pass, and took the elevator to the seventy-sixth floor.
"Dr. M.," I said once we had finished greeting one another.
"Excuse me?"
"Have you ever heard of him?"
"Yeah, the name does ring a bell, come to think of it. He did some of the psych reports on Stilton-James, right?"
"Not exactly, his or her initial appears on two log sheets pertaining to Stilton-James visits. The problem is there aren't any doctors employed with DIT who sign their names as 'M.'"
"Okay ..." Sayvian responded in a confused tone.
"I'm here to confirm if any of your medical experts or consultants sign their initial as 'M.'" I had already reviewed the trial witness lists and didn't see any names with 'M' initials.
At the time, I found it a bit odd because one would think there would be some names with 'M' initials, but there weren't. I knew from experience that not every expert the prosecution employed ends up testifying. My question to Sayvian was to ensure that I'd covered all the bases.
"Okay, I can look into that for you, but I have to admit I'm a bit intrigued to know where are you going with this? I mean, I know you're clever enough to have already reviewed the witness lists before coming here."
"Yeah, you're right. I did check the witness lists, just making sure I'm double-checking everything. The reason I'm asking this of you is because of these two documents."
After a few minutes of explaining my theory to Sayvian, he sat back and thought for a moment.
"Not bad, Beth, not bad at all." I'll send these off for analysis. It's not a huge lead, but it's promising at least."
"Great, thanks!" I said as I started to leave the room.
"We should get an answer in about twenty-four hours," Sayvian hollered just as I was preparing to open the door to the hallway. "Beth, wait for a second!"

I turned around and took a couple of steps towards him. He was still looking down at the documents when he addressed me again. "You know, you might want to check the clipboard etch pen for fingerprints and enter them into the database."

I smiled. Sayvian looked up at me when he failed to hear a response.

"You did that already, didn't you?" Sayvian asked, smiling.

"Yes ..." I replied.

"Of course, you did. Sharp, Beth, very sharp. Someone had wiped it down, right?"

"Unfortunately. Call me if you get anything. Take care, Sayvian."

-----:------

As I headed back to the precinct, I began to wonder what Eccles had found out from Ms. Alana. When I got back, Cap told me that Eccles had gone home for the day. We usually went home at the same time, but I figured that maybe he wanted to get an early start on dinner.

-----:------

When I arrived home, Eccles greeted me with an odd expression on his face. I couldn't figure out whether it was sadness or guilt, but he seemed to be avoiding eye contact with me.

"How are you doing?" he asked, his eyes softened as his eyebrows knitted together.

My mind began racing. What had Eccles done now? Having just come from a meeting with Ms. Alana, I wondered if perhaps he'd done something he regretted.

"I'm fine. How are you?"

"Fine."

"Did you find anything out from Ms. Alana?" I asked as I walked towards the living room. Eccles followed.

"Yeah, you could say that," he said.

His response seemed cryptic. Perhaps things were worse than I had previously suspected. He might have fallen for her. I knew he would be vulnerable to her advances. Her beauty made me nervous.

"Eccles, is there something you want to tell me?"

"Yes, actually, there is."

I shook my head in frustration. "Is it about your meeting with Ms. Alana?"

"Yes."

"Okay."

Eccles and I had never clearly articulated our feelings for one another. Although I didn't know what those feelings were exactly, I nonetheless felt fondness toward him that I'd assumed he reciprocated. Things had accelerated quickly between Eccles and me, a fact I had attributed to the amount of time we'd spent together. I felt our fondness for one another lacked the need for a clear definition. There was just a common understanding that we'd be there for one another no matter what. As I stood before him, I realized that he was no longer Eccles, a colleague from work. He was Mark Eccles, the man who was about to shatter my heart.

"Maybe you should sit down."

"Okay, sure," I responded as I sat down on the sofa, always careful to disguise my emotions. I could feel my heart hammering, and my hands grew slick with sweat.

As much as I had overestimated Eccles' feelings for me, I had also underestimated my feelings for him. After taking a deep breath, I decided that stalling wasn't going to make things any easier. If this was going to end, I would face it head-on and not run away from it.

"Eccles, you know, we've been working together for so long. You're one of my dearest friends."

"A friend?" he asked.

"Of course. And friends shouldn't feel afraid to tell each other anything."

"Okay," Eccles said, now looking more confused than before.

When I'd first arrived home, he had looked pensive and resolute as though he'd thought long and hard about the exact words he wanted to use. Now he looked barely able to orient himself.

"Okay, well, why don't you take a couple of moments and then when you're ready, you can tell me what you wanted to tell me," I said as I got up from the sofa.

"Beth, sit down," Eccles said without lifting his gaze from the ground.

I stopped dead in my tracks and glared at him. He lifted his eyes to look at me, and then in a gentle, inviting tone, he said, "Please."

"Okay," I said as I stepped back to the sofa. I sat down, crossed my arms and glared at him.

"Nothing happened between Ms. Alana and me."

"Okay."

"This is hard for me, so I'm just going to come out and say it."

"Okay."

"Ms. Alana told me that Stilton-James had information about ..."

"About?"

"About ..."

"For goodness sake, Eccles. Please just say it."

"Beth, I'm so sorry. I'm afraid there was something neither of us knew. Ms. Alana told me that Stilton-James had valuable information that they had planned to use to barter for his life after undergoing the Catharsis. It seems that Stilton-James had met a low-life a few years ago who had bragged about committing a horrible crime."

"Okay ..."

"He had kidnapped a young girl ..."

I jumped up as the stinging pain of a thousand stabbing knives shot through my body.

"About age six. Beth, he kidnapped her from an area around here, and it happened around 2074. I think there's a strong possibility the girl in question was Sara."

The room started to spin. I began to feel dizzy. I suddenly realized why Eccles had asked me to sit down.

"Is that everything, Eccles?"

"He could have been lying, Beth. These guys get desperate and---"

"What else did he say?" I whispered.

"I'm sorry, Beth. I'm so sorry. He said that the man had kept her locked away."

"Alive?"

"Beth, we don't know if he was telling the truth or not ..."

"Eccles! What are you saying, exactly?"

Eccles exhaled again. "He had locked her away up to at least a few years ago."

"Eccles." I pleaded with tearful eyes. "Was she alive?"

I had longed for so long to hear just one word. Eccles looked at my face before stating, "Yes ... alive."

"Beth, he didn't tell Ms. Alana everything. He didn't tell her the name of the person or the location of her imprisonment. I'm so sorry."

I fell into Eccles' arms, crying uncontrollably. I felt a small comfort at knowing that she may still be alive, but I felt an overwhelming sadness at the thought of what my baby had suffered through and that my only hope of getting her back may have died with Stilton-James. I spent the next few hours trying desperately to stop crying, but I couldn't.

Chapter 40

Beth Lago. Friday, May 17, 2075. 6:59 AM

I woke the next morning in Eccles' arms. He was still sleeping when I slipped out of bed. One glance in the mirror was all that I needed to see the effect of a tear-filled night. I took a shower, had breakfast, and decided to leave for work earlier than usual. I didn't know how I would handle what had just happened with Eccles, but I figured it was better to leave. I wanted to deal with it, but just not now. Before falling asleep, Eccles had told me the whole story about his conversation with Ms. Alana. It seemed that Stilton-James hadn't shared much information with her either. He had met a man about a year ago claiming to have imprisoned a girl in his basement. This mystery person claimed to have snatched up the girl when she'd been approximately six years old, and the description matched that of Sara.

I found it difficult to accept that had things turned out differently, then Stilton-James would still be alive, and we would have been planning how best to reignite our search for Sara. Instead, Stilton-James, along with any remaining hope of finding Sara, lay in a morgue, never again to see the light of day. I knew there was little proof to support the story and that even if it were true—the chances of finding the girl in question were low. There were far too many children disappearing at that time. Still, despite the sadness, I'd felt last night, I now felt anger and determined focus. I wanted to know what had happened to Stilton-James. I felt more driven than ever to uncover the truth.

-----:-----

We kept a billboard on the wall in the precinct's Evidentiary Analysis Room, where we would post all of our notes, pictures, and other case references. As I stood there looking at the information in its entirety, I got the tingling feeling that amidst the forest of data, there was a particular tree I'd missed. I'd felt this sensation before. Often the overlooked detail had seemed insignificant at the time. However, when placed into context with the rest of the evidence, even the smallest detail can become pivotal.

My intense concentration was interrupted by a knock at the door.

"Yes?"

"Inspector Lago, there's a woman here to see you."

As I made my way back to my desk, I pondered the identity of the woman who'd be waiting for me. Could it be Ms. Alana? For her sake, I hoped we'd never cross paths again, and something told me that it wouldn't be pretty. I understood the importance of client-lawyer privilege, but the fact remained that she chose to sit on information that could have been valuable to me, to Sara, or the girl's family.

As I approached, I could see a blonde woman sitting in the chair beside my desk. The hair colour matched Ms. Alana's, but there was something different. Perhaps the length of hair didn't match. Arriving at my desk, I examined the woman's face. She had dark rings under her bloodshot eyes. There was something vaguely familiar about her.

"Hello."

"Hi, my name is Inez."

"Hi Inez, I'm Inspector Beth Lago."

"Please ... I need your help. We need your help!"

"What's the problem?"

"Well, he's gone. He's missing!"

"Who's missing?"

"Willy! Willy's gone!"

"Willy Taylor?" I asked. Suddenly, it hit me. I finally remembered where I had seen the woman's face. She was the woman I had seen kissing Willy outside the bar that night.

"Look, I'm not looking to cause any trouble, and I just need to know if he's with you. I just need to know if you've seen him at all," Inez said.

"Me? Why would I have seen him?"

"What do you mean?" she asked, sounding equally confused.

"I'm sorry ... Why do you think he'd be with me?" I asked while extending my palms forward in a "stop" gesture.

"Well, because he never stops talking about you. Beth this and Beth that, it never ends with him."

I stood cross-armed as I struggled to understand her logic.

"I want to understand this correctly. You think that Willy has been with me because he talks about me a lot?"

"You don't know ... Do you? Oh my God, you have no idea," she said, her eyes widening.

"I have no idea about what exactly?"

"Right, are you going to tell me you didn't know he was in love with you?" Her question caused me to step back and sit down.

She said, "Great, I lose out to a girl who didn't even know it."

"So, you're saying Willy was in---"

"---Love with you, right."

"But that night, you guys were--"

"---I kissed him, and he didn't kiss me back. After you stormed off, he left me at the bar. The silly thing is, he had invited me to the bar to tell me that we couldn't be friends anymore. He said he was in love with someone, and since we had dated in the past, he felt the relationship would be inappropriate."

"I see," I said, clasping my hands on my lap so she wouldn't see them shaking.

"That whole ordeal at the restaurant really messed him up, he needed a shoulder to cry on, and I did my best to help him get back on his feet, as a friend."

"Okay, so what's happened now?"

"I've been calling him, over and over again, but he just hasn't been answering. I began to worry, so I visited his apartment, and when I got there, I noticed that the door had been jammed open, his apartment was a mess, and he was gone."

Eccles, having arrived at work, walked up to his desk.

"What's going on?" he asked.

I turned to him and said, "Willy's missing."

Eccles and I advised Cap and Sayvian about Willy's disappearance. Based on the events surrounding the case and the fact that the nurse who had witnessed Stilton-James's death had also gone missing, we easily bypassed the usual twenty-four hours required before declaring a person officially missing.

-----:-----

We headed to Willy's building, search warrant in hand. Just before leaving the precinct, Cap advised us that he'd already assigned Vasco and Andrews to the case of the missing nurse. He asked that we communicate any findings back to them. I had trouble remembering who the pair was before Eccles reminded me that we knew them as the odd couple. Vasco was the shorter than average cop, and Andrews was the hulking blond man, who unofficially held the title as the biggest officer in the entire precinct.

When Eccles and I arrived at Willy's apartment building, a very pale, tall security guard greeted us at the door. We asked him if he'd seen Willy Taylor yesterday. He responded in quick spurts.

"He came in last night and then left a couple of hours after."

"Did you see if he was with anyone?" I asked.

"No, I think he was by himself."

"Did you see how he was dressed?"

"No, not really, he must have been dressed pretty normal 'else I would have noticed."

"Thanks, Mr. Gilbert," Eccles said as he read the guard's nametag.

"Jerold Gilbert, happy to help," he said to us as we walked away.

We took the elevator to the 12th floor. Eccles and I hadn't spoken yet about the night before. As we stood, watching the floor numbers above the elevator door, I felt the growing need to say something, anything. Not knowing where or how to start, I took a deep breath. Suddenly, a bell rang, and the doors slid open to our floor.

Eccles and I stepped out, and we headed down to apartment 1201. I withdrew the key card the guard had given me. I began to insert it into the lock when I noticed someone had drilled into the socket. I placed my hand on the doorknob, preparing to open it. I looked at Eccles quickly, and we both withdrew our guns. I gave him a nod.

"Okay, Willy, it's the police. We're coming in," Eccles said as he put his hand on the door.

He motioned to me to confirm that I was ready. I nodded, and we pushed the door open, each of us pointing our guns inwards. He pointed his to the right of the apartment, and I pointed mine to the left.

"Willy? Are you here?" I asked as we continued to check each room in the apartment.

Willy's apartment looked ransacked, and someone had toppled the shelves and had tossed the drawers' contents onto the floor. Either Willy or someone else had been searching for something.

"Clear?" Eccles asked.

"Clear."

We holstered our guns.

"What do you think?" Eccles asked.

"I don't know. The guard did say he saw him leave. Maybe they trashed his apartment after he left?" I responded.

"I wish we could see exactly how he looked when he left, and maybe he was under duress," Eccles said.

Standing by a window in the living room, I looked outside, and an idea occurred to me.

"There are a bunch of banks along the street beside the building, right?" I asked.

"Yes, I think so," Eccles answered.

"Do you think they may have some surveillance cameras facing the streets?"

"It's worth a try."

I said, "Okay, let's get a crime scene unit over here, then we'll head over to these banks, and we'll see if we can figure out where Willy went."

Eccles glanced down at his phone. "I just got a message from Tech Services. They searched for the satellite tracking system from the E-ssistant in Willy's car."

"Okay."

"Apparently, someone manually disconnected it."

-----:-----

The nearest bank was the Bank of Commercial Interests. The building had a marble and alabaster main entrance. While I scouted for the security cameras with the best view of the street, Eccles went to speak to the bank's head of security.

After a few minutes, he returned with the tall man in a navy blue suit. After a cordial introduction, he led us through a door beside the main tellers, then down a long hallway. We entered a room with computer screens covering each of the walls.

"Barry? These are inspectors from the OLAPD. They're looking for video feeds from yesterday," he said. The younger man, dressed in jeans and a t-shirt, simply nodded. I assumed he was the audio-visual technician.

"Time?" Barry asked without taking his gaze away from the computer screens.

I said, "We don't have an exact time, but we have a description. We don't think he entered the bank. His apartment building is just next door, and we're hoping one of your security cameras, facing the street, might have caught an image of him passing by."

He glared at me for a moment.

Eccles said, "We realize it's a long shot. Could you please just humour us?"

The technician looked past us, I assume, in an attempt to confirm that his boss had indeed left the room.

He said, "Actually, I'll do you one better. Take the discs for yesterday for all our peripheral cameras with you. You can scan through them and bring them back when you're done."

"You're allowed to do that?"

"Well, not exactly, but I'm the only one around here who knows how to run any of this equipment. They wouldn't even know if it went missing, trust me."

He handed Eccles a stack of discs, and we discreetly exited the bank.

-----:-----

Back at the precinct, we carefully sifted through the hours of tape. The discs contained a video from cameras located either just outside the bank or had been pointing outwards to the street from the interior. Even limiting the footage to times when Willy would have been gone from work, we still had dozens of hours to watch.

"Are you okay?" Eccles asked abruptly as we stared at the screen in the audio/visual room of the precinct.

I paused for a moment before responding, "Yeah, I'm fine."

"Okay, good."

I sighed before responding. "I'm just trying to make peace with it all. I can only take each step as it comes. For all I know, it was all built on lies. These perps are, all the same, they'll all say whatever they need to, to save their own necks."

"That's true."

"Have you heard anything from Vasco and Andrews regarding the nurse?"

He said, "Last I heard, they were having about as much success as us. No leads ... no witnesses ... no trace. She left work the day of the Catharsis, she had been on her way home, and that's where the trail dead-ends. The woman just disappeared. There was a phone call to her mother, which was never answered, and then, nothing."

Finally, after several hours, Eccles turned to me. I'd seen that expression before. It was a look of defeat.

"Beth, I'm sorry to say this, but I think this may be worse than we'd expected."

Eventually, we arrived at an unavoidable conclusion. We determined that not a single image of Willy appeared on any of the discs, although one of the cameras pointed down to a patch of sidewalk just beside the entrance to Willy's building.

-----:-----

Once we'd made copies of the tapes, we returned the originals to the bank. We chased down a couple of other leads, but eventually, our search for Willy hit a dead end.

Our search for Willy ended two weeks after it had begun. Vasco and Andrews didn't fare any better in the search for the missing nurse. The crime scene investigators didn't find any unaccounted-for fingerprints at Willy's apartment. The final blow came when the handwriting analysis regarding the E-sheets was determined to be 'inconclusive.'

Sayvian had no choice but to shut down the investigation. The days that followed were dark as I slowly surrendered any lingering hope of ever finding my friend.

"There is no peace without truth!"
-Patheous

Chapter 41

Beth Lago. Friday, August 27, 2077. 9:01 AM

Ultimately, the courts cleared DIT and all its subsidiaries of any wrongdoing in William Stilton-James's death. In the years that followed, Catharsis became the standard sentence in all crimes perpetrated against D-Eye patients.

One year passed, and then two. In the aftermath, Eccles and I moved on with our lives. Nearly two and a half years after the closing of the case, our relationship rose to the next level when Eccles proposed to me. The wedding was simple: only a handful of close friends attended. Some people say that Cap got teary-eyed during the ceremony, but I didn't see it myself, and apparently, no pictures exist to confirm it.

Although things had seemed partly resolved, Willy's disappearance still bothered me immensely, as well as the disappearance of the DIT nurse. I was content with my life, but I still felt haunted by so many unanswered questions. After so many years, I still had nightmares in which Sara would appear to me. The past, it seemed, maintained a firm grip. It became increasingly clear that some feelings weren't ever going to fade away, for I still had overwhelming suspicions regarding DIT, in general, and of course, I still missed my friend Willy.

-----:-----

Things had begun settling toward normalcy, except for one strange, inexplicable thing. I'd started receiving blank plastic postcards, every few months, from different parts of the world. The cards never had a return address, and there was never any writing them. I had the postcards sent off for fingerprint analysis on a hunch, but the IDs recovered all ended up being postal employees.

Although the logical part of me knew that they were likely meaningless, I, nonetheless, held onto the hope that these postcards somehow linked to Willy. Part of me imagined that this was his way of letting me know that he was alive and okay.

I made a point to keep each of them. I stored them in a small box, which I placed at the back of my closet.

At first, the postcards had arrived every couple of months, then the frequency jumped to monthly, then every two weeks. The postcards seemed to annoy Eccles. I think deep down, he thought as I did, that these cards did come from Willy. As a result, we had several arguments about it. It was a point of friction, and he was reaching his breaking point. Finally, after months of pressure, he made me agree to get rid of them.

-----:-----

One afternoon against the backdrop of a rust-coloured sunset, while in the backyard of the house where we'd once lived as partners then as husband and wife, it finally came to a pass.

True to his word and in dramatic fashion, Eccles made a giant bonfire into which he'd said we would throw them in together. I told him that if this were to happen, then I would do it alone.

The day before, when I'd finally agreed, it had been because of the words he'd used.

He'd said, "You need to learn to let go. Only by saying good-bye to the past could we step forward into the future."

Now, standing in front of the raging fire, it suddenly became overwhelmingly real.

As I stepped toward the flames, I desperately searched my mind for some logical reason I could use to justify not throwing them in. Something had convinced Eccles that these postcards led back to Willy, and I had no way to prove otherwise. He felt threatened, and I didn't want to continue having the same fight. I wanted my marriage to be healthy and happy, but something told me to stop.

I could feel the tears building inside. I looked back.

Eccles sensed my hesitation. He mouthed the words, "You promised."

I stood frozen before the flames.

I knew what I had to do, I knew what I had promised to do, but I couldn't help feeling a swell of sadness over the whole thing. As I stepped closer, I could feel small tears begin to form in the corner of my eyes.

Brilliant sparks rose up to the darkening sky. I peered back at Eccles as I stood before the fire. His expression looked as determined as ever. I couldn't believe how difficult this was.

I took a deep breath. I extended my hand holding the stack of postcards. I could feel the hot wind blow against me as I leaned forward. As I prepared to release them, I looked down at the stack one last time. As my surroundings grew ever darker and as the light of the fire flickered upon the postcards, I noticed something. I quickly wiped the tears from my eyes, and I looked closer. I couldn't believe what I was seeing. As I held the three-inch stack, looking at it from the side, I could see something. I held the stack out of line, so I tapped it against the front part of my thigh to line them up.

It wasn't my imagination, and there was something written on the cards.

I remembered that each card had bizarre dots on the edge that I'd never understood. Now that I had them all stacked up and looked at them from the side, I could see that the dots formed some pattern. It was difficult to tell in the darkness, but they seemed to form numbers. Some of the numbers were hard to make out, so I took them with me back to the house.

Before entering, I stepped past Eccles as he shook his head. I sat the postcards on the table. I arranged them according to the postmark date instead of the date received. I looked again, and my jaw dropped. This was not by chance. This was a message. Grabbing a piece of paper, I jotted down the numbers 9-3-5-1-1-7-6 BC.

I explained the situation to Eccles, who was annoyed at first but became more and more intrigued as I continued explaining.

I asked, "What do you think this could mean?"

"I don't know ... Maybe safe deposit box numbers?" He said.

"Yes, they must be numbers to a safe deposit box!" I said.

"But what bank?"

"B-C ... Bank of Commercial Investment?"

"Wait a second, if these postcards are from ..." Eccles said.

"Willy? I think they might be, Eccles."

Eccles said, "Okay, fine ... let's say they are from Willy. Well, we checked out all the discs from that day, and there was no sign of him going anywhere near that bank, and I don't remember the Forensic Accounting Department mentioning he ever had an account at that bank."

I said, "Maybe, he set it up under an alias or a business? Besides, we only reviewed the cameras facing the street. We never reviewed the discs from the cameras inside the bank."

Eccles stood pensively for several seconds.

He said, "Okay, let me call Sayvian and ask him to get us a search warrant."

I turned and looked at Eccles for a minute. I said, "No, actually, I think it would be better to keep this between you and me. Willy didn't want anyone knowing about this."

"Okay ... but ..."

"Please, just trust me on this," I said. I kissed him and then stepped away.

"Where are you going?" He asked.

"I'm going to the Bank of Commercial Interest, where else? Are you coming?"

"Yeah, I just need to change and put out the bonfire. Can I meet you there?"

"Sure."

I got into the car and began driving towards the bank. My heart was thumping at the thought of finally, after so long, getting a break in the case. I did not doubt in my mind that the messages were from Willy. I just wondered why he'd felt the need to send me such an encrypted message.

I arrived at the bank to see it was closing in a few minutes. Realizing I didn't have enough time to wait for Eccles, I went into the bank alone. I didn't think it was possible, but the foyer entrance looked even more regal than before. I walked up to the service desk and told the receptionist that I had come to get access to safe deposit box number 9-3-5-1-1-7-6. She smiled cordially and then walked away with the sheet she had used to jot down the number. She walked over to another man with whom she whispered and then pointed in my direction. The man walked over.

"Hello, miss. Are you sure that the box number is correct?"

"I'm positive," I responded.

"Very well, please follow me."

We proceeded through a door, then down a hall to an elevator, which he had to use a key to operate. We descended a few stories, and then the door opened, revealing a security desk and a walk-through metal detector. I panicked for a moment before remembering that I hadn't brought my gun with me. I'd left in such a hurry, and I'd completely forgotten.

"Miss, I trust you know what to do from here," the man said, gesturing for me to step forward.

"Yes, of course," I said, desperately disguising my ignorance.

I stepped through the metal detector and handed a guard my purse. On the other side, a few steps forward was a door and a small computer against the wall. I truly did not know what to do next. I turned slightly to see the guards watching me attentively. I placed my hand on the flat surface of the interface, and it lit up.

"Please enter your name," the words on the screen read.

My name ... Should I put Willy's name? I didn't know what to do. I thought for a moment. Willy sent me the message, so he must have wanted me to have access to it. What would he have put down as a name to enter?

I smiled as it suddenly occurred to me.

B-E-T-H T-A-Y-L-O-R

"Accepted."

Willy. Such a joker.

The door in front of me opened, and a voice from the computer said: "Please proceed."

I stepped through the door and towards a giant wall of glass. On the other side were thousands of little boxes with numbers on them. In front of the glass window, there was another computer.

"Damn it!" I whispered to myself.

Again, I placed my hand on the screen, and it lit up.

"Please enter the box number."

Oh, okay, that's not so bad.

I entered the box number then another message popped up on the screen.

"Please enter password."

I shook my head in disbelief. What was I going to do now? I thought for several minutes, trying to guess what Willy would have put as the password this time.

"Please enter password," the computer repeated itself.

I know ... I know ...

It had to be something that Willy knew I would never forget, something that would always be on my mind. I realized what it was. I hesitatingly extended my hand towards the touch screen and entered, "S-A-R-A."

I paused before pressing the "Enter" button. I imagined that an incorrect response would get me thrown out of here and then, likely jail.

I closed my eyes. I took a deep breath and then pressed, "Enter."

"Thank you, accepted."

The sound of a machine moving and gears grinding together began. After about a minute, a tiny door opened, and a box slid out.

The voice of the computer said, "You have one hundred and twenty minutes to review the contents of your box. For privacy, please proceed to our soundproof viewing room."

A door opened to a bright room with a steel table. In the corner of the room lay another door that led to a small, private bathroom.

"For your protection, please note the door will lock behind you and can only be opened from the inside. Once you have completed your session, please replace the box in the metal slot along the wall. Thank you."

Holding the box in my hand, I set it down on the metallic table. I placed it gently, but it still made a thud when it touched the table.

I slowly opened the lid. Inside, there were two things: an envelope and a videotape. Within the envelope, there was a letter. It read as follows:

Dear Beth,

If you're reading this letter, then you have ultimately discovered the box. I never doubted you for a minute, though I imagine you needed almost three years before the pattern on the postcards became readable.

You're my oldest friend, and I have always trusted you above all others. Please take the tape within the box and watch it. It contains evidence that I think you might find interesting. Yes, Beth, what you're seeing is real. That is a videotape inside the box. I know you have a videotape player still. You can't throw anything away. This is just my letter to you. The important stuff is on the tape, which I imagine only you will be able to watch. The information on that tape will change everything. Guard it with your life.

I'm a packrat myself, it might be a bit grainy, but you'll recognize the images from my old camcorder.

Beth, be careful, trust no one. I hope we'll see each other again.

Love always,
Willy."

I smiled, then grabbed the tape and the letter, and I placed them in my purse. I slid the box back into the drawer. Walking out of the bank's secure area was considerably easier than the way in. When I finally got outside, I took a deep breath. I couldn't imagine what information was so secret to cause Willy to have to run away. Why now, after so many years, why did he have to wait so long?

Outside the bank, I looked around for Eccles' car, but I didn't see it. I got into my car and began driving back home.

-----:-----

When I arrived, I unlocked the front door and stepped inside. The first thing I saw was the figure of a man. It didn't immediately strike me that it was Eccles as the man's build was too slender. It was so bright outside and so dark inside that it took my eyes a few seconds to focus. When they finally did, I could see who the man was.

"... Sayvian?"
"Hello, Beth."
"What are *you* doing here?"
"I'm just catching up on old times. You know how it is."
"But where's--"

"—Eccles, he's just resting right now. You see, he called me, concerned ... he said he thought you were headed on a wild goose chase. I think he was probably just jealous ... Anyway, that doesn't matter. He's not important right now."

"What do you want?" I asked.

Sayvian slipped his hand into the breast pocket of his suit. He said, "I just want to know why you can never just let things go."

He withdrew a gun from his pocket.

"Sayvian, what the fuck---"

"Shut up! Do you have any idea how much money you're going to cost me? DIT is the biggest corporation in the world. They could own entire territories. Did you think anyone was going to let you throw all of that away on account of your little self-righteous crusade?"

"Sayvian, listen to me, it's Beth. You know me. We're friends, for God's sake."

"Nice try, Beth. I like that insertion of a little name familiarity. I'm not crazy, Beth. I'm just a little bit more aware of the world than you."

"How exactly do you think you're going to get away with this?"

"Simple, they call it a murder-suicide, happens all the time. Husband goes crazy and kills his wife then himself."

Sayvian walked over to me. "put this on!" he ordered fiercely as he pointed the gun at me while tossing a plastic slip tie in my direction.

"I need help," I said.

"Use your teeth," he snarled back at me.

"Get down on your knees!"

"Please, Sayvian!"

"Shut and get down!" He stepped closer and looked down at me.

"If you could only see the way you look right now. It's a shame you're so annoying. You had a lot of things going for you, a pretty face and that body. I'm going to miss you, Beth," he said as he cocked the gun.

I looked over at the table. Sayvian followed my gaze. I'd left my purse on the table by the door.

"That's right. I almost forgot—the videotape."

As he stepped away, I looked around for Eccles. Peeking around the couch and towards the kitchen entrance, I could see a pool of blood.

Oh, God!

"Is this a videotape? Wow, I haven't seen one of these in years. Cute... Too bad no one's ever going to see it."

Sayvian walked back towards me. I could feel the cold metal of the muzzle against my temple.

"Any final words, Inspector Lago?"

"Where's my husband?"

269

"Where's your husband? I think you should be a bit more concerned with yourself right now."

He pressed the muzzle against my head more forcefully.

"Wait! I just want to know one thing."

"Curious ... till the end. Okay, one final question."

"How did you know? How did you know about everything?"

"You know, you never were that great a detective because you never listened to the answers people gave you. Your loving husband called me when you made your little discovery."

"Right."

"Now, you remember?"

"Right, he called you, but I guess you missed a little detail," I said as I turned my gaze up at him.

"Beth, what detail was that?"

"You weren't the only one he called!" Cap said as he pressed his gun against Sayvian's head. "It's over, son. Drop the gun."

Sayvian paused for a moment.

"Okay, have it your way," Cap said as he swung the handle of his gun down on Sayvian's head, instantly knocking him out. Sayvian crumpled to the ground.

"Cap! Thank God."

"Are you okay? Let me get you untied."

"The tape?"

"It's over there on the ground," Cap responded.

I looked up at him as I remained seated on the ground. Cap knelt in front of me. I extended my arms and hugged him.

"Okay, okay, it's okay. I think there's something you need to do," Cap said as he began getting up.

I ran over to Eccles, who had been lying in the kitchen. I lifted his head and placed it on my lap. He'd lost a lot of blood. He had what looked like a stab wound in his left ribs. He was sweaty and must've lost passed out from the loss of blood. I rested his head on the ground and ran to grab a towel. Placing in on his wound, I applied pressure, and tears trickled down my nose. He put his hand over mine. Slowly, he lifted his eyelids, turning his gaze up at me.

"Beth."

"Don't try to talk. It's okay."

"I'm so sorry," Eccles said as he peered up at me.

"There's no need to apologize. None of us knew about Sayvian."

"Did you find what you were looking for?"

"Almost ... There's a tape."

"Okay, well, are you going to watch it, then?"

"It can wait," I responded.

"Beth, I'm not going anywhere and frankly, after everything we've all been through, I think we really ought to know what's on that tape."

By then, Cap had walked over to us. "It's okay. I'll stay with him."

I looked back at Eccles, who smiled and nodded, "Hurry up before I change my mind, goddammit."

I placed Eccles' head gently on the ground and stood up.

Videotape in hand, I headed to the basement, where I began scrounging furiously for my old videotape player. I tossed several boxes around until finally, I found it. There was an old TV in the basement, which I connected to the player. I turned them both on. After a pause, the screen lit up.

"Thank goodness," I whispered to myself.

I inserted the tape into the machine and crossed my fingers.

I pressed the "play" button.

There was a long buzzing, then a metallic clink before an image appeared on the TV.

Chapter 42

Beth Lago. Friday, August 27, 2077. 6:01 PM

A man with dark, messy hair sat down in front of the camera. The glare on his forehead suggested he was sweating. His dark eyes had a gloss to them as though hiding a measure of pain. In these first few seconds, he had yet to look directly into the camera. His gaze, instead, focused on the area just above where I imagined someone held the camera.

"Just tell them what you told me," a voice said.

I recognized it right away. It was Willy.

"My name is Dr. Trevor Miles. I'm a neuropsychiatrist employed with DIT. Um ... where do I begin? My work with DIT had been secret. However, recent developments prevent me from being able to continue to remain silent. I have reason to believe that my life is in danger. This recording may be the only way of ensuring that my message gets out—even beyond my death.

"My team oversaw the creation and development of D-Eyes and then Reverse-Looping. I also interviewed William Stilton-James on three separate occasions. Over the past few weeks, I have made some, umm, discoveries regarding the effects of Reverse-Looping."

Dr. Miles seemed to take a breath before continuing.

"Okay, so Reverse-Looping as a procedure was only communicated to us based on feasibility. We were never told of the ultimate goal."

He shook his head, and his eyelids closed. When his eyes opened again, they turned back their gaze back to the camera. This time they were glazed over.

"I now suspect, on the eve of the verdict in the case of the People v. William Stilton-James, that Reverse-Looping will become a new form of criminal punishment.

"I believe William Stilton-James will be the first patient to experience this sentence. He will suffer the full extent of a person's pain and death. The experience will kill him. Carl Dresdin, the CEO of DIT, knows this. In fact, it's part of his plan. DIT will make Stilton-James's death look like an accident, but it will be intentional. Maybe that's what Stilton-James deserves, but that isn't for DIT to decide. The reason why Stilton-James will die—the certainty of it—is based on the way the technology works and the way it interacts with the subject's brain. He dropped his head again. "The only people who could prove DIT's complicity are the members of my team, myself included. There are four of us in total."

His voice began to quiver.

"None of whom, I fear, will be alive much longer. Today, Dr. Pax Sills died in a freak explosion, which I suspect was anything but an accident. He was murdered. The other two are on the run—their survival will depend on their ability to remain hidden. As I make this recording with a new ally, I know that the worst is still yet to come."

Dr. Miles looked up and behind the camera and smiled only slightly as he said the word "ally."

He then said, "Regarding the death of one of my team members, Dr. Pax Sills, I believe he was murdered, and I believe his death was made to look like an accident. He was the first to die because he is the only person who knows Reverse-Looping, the way I do. They killed him to intimidate the rest of us. The goal that DIT has for Reverse-Looping is to make the patient suffer the death of the person they killed in order to compel a Catharsis, in other words, a purging of emotion. It is clear to me now DIT has managed to discover what Pax and I had already predicted but had kept secret— until now. The truth is that Stilton-James will die during his Catharsis. This is the only possible outcome. With his death, a new capital punishment will be born. DIT and Dresdin's over-zealousness, however, will be their downfall. They think they know what will happen during that Catharsis, but they're in for a big surprise.

"There is something about Reverse-Looping that neither DIT nor Carl Dresdin knows or understands. This lack of knowledge will be their demise. It all has had to do with Stilton-James's diagnosis, which DIT has managed to corrupt. The world believes he's a sociopath. DIT didn't know the truth, and if I'm right, his Catharsis should reveal more than they ever could have bargained. The outcome of his Catharsis is completely dependent on his diagnosis, which DIT has foolishly ignored.

"In my career, I have treated several sociopaths. I've been in rooms alone with people that would have made anyone's skin crawl. Classical sociopaths have the distinction of being unable to empathize with other humans around them. Following the three interviews I had with Stilton-James, I determined that he could not be a classical sociopath for several reasons. The most obvious one being—he felt empathy. Why did my diagnosis differ? Why did so many miss the obvious? The key lies in the fact that when I interviewed him, I didn't know his diagnosis. Following our first interview, I presumed anything but a sociopath. When I discovered his 'official' diagnosis, I could hardly believe it. Stilton-James's misdiagnosis served two purposes. One was to facilitate his conviction. No one would believe Stilton-James's words if these same people believed, first, that he was a sociopath. DIT and Dresdin think that this Catharsis will prove to the world the value of their technology. They've underestimated the intricacies of the human psyche. They will perform the Catharsis, and they'll get a rude awakening. I suspect that they haven't killed me yet because they think I'm going to tell them what they've missed. They think I will trade this information in exchange for my life, but I never will. I'm sorry for not having stopped this sooner. This fight isn't over. They think they're going to get away with this, but they won't ... not in the end.

"I would now like to send a message to my family."

He lowered his head before continuing.

"To my wife, I want you to know that I love you very, very, much. To my son Sean, Dad loves you, and I always will ... I can't say anymore ... I just ... "

Just then, the screen went to static. I sat in the dark basement, completely silent. I couldn't believe what I had just heard. Upstairs, I could hear the sound of commotion. I imagined that paramedics were taking Eccles away.

I reached for the "stop" button when suddenly ... The empty chair reappeared on the screen.

After a couple of seconds, Willy walked into the frame.

"Beth, I hope the information on this video has been helpful so far. I have another surprise for you."

As Willy stepped to the side, a pale-skinned woman entered the frame. She looked to be in her mid-forties. Her dark hair gathered up into a ponytail.

She said, "What do I do?"

"Just tell them who you are and what you saw."

The woman, whom I had never seen before, sat upright. She held her angular chin high. She had large almond-shaped brown eyes bordered by tiny crow's feet and bright red lipstick.

"My name is Bertie Keets."

She had a soft voice with a touch of an accent—Midwest perhaps.

"I'm a nurse currently employed with DIT. Well, at least I was. After the filming of this video, I assume I'll be a former employee of DIT.

"Earlier today, May 15th, I witnessed the Catharsis and subsequent death of William Stilton-James. The fact that I was present is not the reason I'm making this video deposition. The reason I'm doing this is that I'm the only one willing to admit the truth about the goings-on in that room.

"Let me begin by saying that from the start, my experience regarding William Stilton-James as well, let's say—different. I was his primary care nurse, so I knew him as something other than a mere monster. He spoke to me, and I got to know him a bit. Getting to know him as a human being and seeing what happened to him, well, I just can't keep my mouth shut about something like that. I mean, people need to know the truth."

I smiled at the matter-of-factness in her tone.

"This was a new procedure, and no one contests this fact. We did, however, have some expectations in terms of how things would play out. The first half of the Catharsis went as expected. We'd placed him under the influence of anesthetic. He'd fallen into the appropriate sedated state. His blood pressure had been normal, and his heart rate had been completely stable. When the DIT technicians started the Catharsis, William's FMRI scans immediately lit up. His EEG showed high Alpha brain wave activity, but up until that point, all activity was as expected. Everything seemed to be going well, but as we approached the Time Horizon, the moment in the playback in which Emil's heartbeat had stopped, Stilton-James's blood pressure rose to dangerous levels. We'd had a monitor set up indicating a countdown to the Time Horizon, and it seemed that with every second that ticked by, his blood pressure climbed higher and higher. I looked at the doctor's faces, the ones who were in charge of deciding when we'd have to abort the procedure, but it was like staring at a bunch of wax statues. The thresholds we'd set in advance to abort the operation passed, and no one seemed to care. Although I'd felt there were clear signs of indifference, I don't think anyone expected to see what ended up happening next. Despite an ever-rising series of warnings from the heart rate and blood pressure machines, Stilton-James suffered a massive heart attack. Whether out of total shock or lack of concern, none of the doctors reacted. I was the first to begin picking up any sort of a fuss. I started calling out to them to act, to bring out the crash cart, to do something, anything, damn it, 'He's dying!' I screamed. Finally, after several seconds the doctors began performing life-saving measures. After two jolts from the defibrillator, I was left convinced that we'd never be able to revive him, but eventually, there was a faint pulse, which gradually grew stronger. It was at that point that something remarkable happened. After having suffered a heart attack and while still under anesthetic, Stilton-James sat up on the bed as though nothing had happened. Stilton-James looked around at all of us with tear-filled eyes. He began to speak in a child-like voice. He said the following, "Come on, it's not safe here. They're going to hurt you. No, it's okay, look at my arms and my legs ... I'm not one of them. I can help you. Take my hand. I'll bring you someplace safe." Then there was a pause for about thirty seconds until he continued. 'Hello, this is one of my friends. He can help you. He always helps us. We're a team, I find them, and he takes them down into the safe place. You can trust him. Go ahead ... I'm so lucky to have a friend like him. Wait a second, that boy's toy helicopter. I forgot to give it back to him.' Up to that point, the expression on his face had been one of serenity, but then it changed to absolute shock. 'What ... did you do? What did you do to him?' Suddenly, Stilton-James collapsed back down again, and he suffered another heart attack. We were never able to revive him again. He died with an abhorrent expression on his face. I don't know what he saw in this strange memory or dream, but it was enough to scare him, literally to death."

"At that moment, we began to question everything. I'm a nurse, I'm not a psychiatrist, but I know enough to know that sociopaths do not act that way, ever. I believe that I witnessed a Catharsis in its truest form. I witnessed the Catharsis of William Stilton-James. The doctors in the room quickly began making remarks about how manipulative sociopaths could be. Still, it wasn't until I accidentally saw the FMRI scanned images taken before and after the procedure that I became convinced that he hadn't been lying at all. The Catharsis had worked to cure him, but it had also opened a box that we should have been more cautious in the opening. Like everyone else, I followed the trial, and I know that he claimed to be unable to remember what had happened that night. He had been telling the truth because the trauma had been so severe his mind had blocked it out. After Stilton-James's death, we had a meeting. They forced us to sign documents, ensuring our silence.

"I never refused to go with their story, but I never agreed to either. I never returned to work or home, for that matter. I have given my life up completely in the hope that the Good Lord will forgive me for having assisted in the disgusting act."

Willy appeared back on the screen.

"Beth, I know you're probably a little shocked by everything you've heard up until now. I know you'll need some time to sort it all out, but I do have another bit of valuable information for you. I opened that safe-deposit box and left this tape in there. I will never return to that bank. There is another safe deposit box at another bank, which I need you to recover. The bank is called the Bank of Economic Progress, and the box number is the inverse of the first one."

He paused for a moment.

"Beth, I don't know if we'll ever see each other again. I hope that I'll survive this whole fiasco. I guess I won't be getting a letter of recommendation from DIT.

"Beth, be careful. Trust no one, and well, the rest I assume you must know by now."

I know, Willy.

"Goodbye, for now, Beth."

Static again filled the screen, and the recording stopped.

I rose from the dusty sofa and withdrew the videotape from the machine. Two undisturbed hours had passed since I had first descended into the basement. After climbing the stairs, I opened the door and found that the house had fallen completely silent. I imagined the paramedics had taken Eccles to the hospital. I decided that I'd visit him, but not before visiting the precinct first. I knew Eccles well enough to know that he would ask about the case before anything else.

------:-----

I headed for the precinct with the videotape stowed away in my purse. Thinking about it for a moment, I realized that my purse might be the first unsafe place the tape had ever been. During the drive-over, ideas and strategies circled in my mind. There were so many things still left to do.

I knew I had to be careful with my next few steps. I decided that I wanted to get more information regarding Dr. Miles and Birdie Keats. Tracking down their loved ones might be a good next step. I had a vague idea as to the time of the tape's recording. The first part had been before the Catharsis and the second, after.

Nonetheless, I needed to know if they were still alive. As I walked through the Pit, I was careful not to draw any attention to myself. It was practically empty anyway.

I searched for the doctor's name in our databases. I typed it in carefully ... Dr. Trevor Miles ... I took two casual looks in each direction to make sure no eyes were peeking over my shoulders as I returned my gaze to my monitor. What I saw shocked me.

"convicted of murder and sentenced to death by Catharsis March 14th, 2077."

This had happened only a few months ago. Oh no.

Who was the victim? I wondered.

Dr. Miles's conviction had been for killing his wife, which I didn't accept that, not by a long shot. I continued reading about the case. At first, I found it confusing that I didn't recognize a single thing about it until I took note of the crime and trial location. It had happened in an adjacent territory, Francisco Bay. I continued reading the case file and determined that there had been no witnesses and that the doctor's wife's death had been one of the first cases involving an adult D-Eye victim. The trial had taken nine weeks, which for a D-Eye case was a veritable eternity. It seems that the judge in the case had trouble accepting the D-Eye files, as there were large chunks of missing data. The more I read, the more I became convinced DIT had somehow framed the poor doctor. Still, I had to keep a level head. I wasn't going to be of much use as an investigator unless I could find some proof. I rolled up my sleeves and began digging deeper into the case files.

-----:-----

Gradually I began piecing together the final few hours of Mrs. Miles' life. At the time, she had worked as a researcher for an e-newspaper. She had been working late that night. The Miles' drove separate cars. She worked across town, and he worked close to home, so he tended to get home before her. The crime had occurred on a Thursday night. Their son Sean had been conveniently away at karate class. She left work that night saying her goodbyes to her colleagues at about seven-thirty. There were sworn depositions from two workers at her office confirming this.

Her drive home, later agreed upon by both the defence and prosecution, normally took about forty-five minutes, depending on traffic. There hadn't been any witnesses or sightings of her on the way home or in her neighbourhood. Investigators found her car in the garage. The crime scene team had combed through the car and hadn't found anything unusual. Her son had arrived back from karate class at eighty thirty. The boy had then entered the house to find his mother lying lifeless on the hardwood floor.

The cause of death had been determined to be acute asphyxia due to strangulation. She had lacerations and bruising on her throat and neck. An electrical cord was still wrapped around her throat. Her body had been found lying face down in the hallway between the bedroom and the kitchen, with her head facing the bedroom. Other injuries present had been determined as ante mortem. A bruise and laceration on the back of her neck indicated impact with a blunt object. The location and nature of this blunt object remained a mystery. Police officers found and awoke Dr. Trevor Miles, who appeared to have been unconscious. He had been bleeding from a cut on his forehead. The gash had been bleeding severely by the time emergency services arrived. Investigators also found a hole on the wall, which had bloodstains in and around it. The DNA from the bloodstains was determined to have come from a single donor—Dr. Trevor Miles. The Prosecution's position on the hole had been that it had occurred during the struggle and had caused him to stagger to the bedroom, where he eventually passed out. The defence's position had been that it represented undeniable proof that Dr. Trevor Miles had indeed been assaulted and then framed for the murder. The scenario they played out was that the doctor returned home before his wife and had walked towards the bedroom. The defence claimed that someone had already entered the house, and as Dr. Miles walked down the hall, this person attacked him from behind and then slammed his head into the wall, knocking him out. The unknown intruder had then dragged him to the bedroom.

When Mrs. Miles had returned from work, she entered the kitchen before peering down the hall to see her husband's body lying in the bedroom. The defence theorized that she had rushed down the hall, at which point, the intruder grabbed her from behind. The intruder had been ready with a power cord he had ripped from a clock in the bedroom. He proceeded to hit her on the head with some sort of blunt tool, causing her to fall face down. He then wrapped the cord around her neck and strangled her.

Reviewing the evidence as an investigator, I immediately detected issues with the prosecution's description of events. The first was regarding the placement of the body. It seemed unlikely that the doctor would strangle his wife then go to the bedroom and pass out. I reviewed the files, but I couldn't find any explanation presented by the prosecution regarding why Dr. Miles had gone to the bedroom, even as a theory.

The other thing that seemed unsettling was that the blunt object used to hit Mrs. Miles remained missing. I'm sure both the defence and the prosecution had likely hoped to find that piece of evidence, as it would have proved vital to either case.

As it turned out, the D-Eye playback, which one would have assumed to be decisive for one side or the other, turned out to be questionable at best. Not only had there not been any clear image of Dr. Miles doing the deed, but there had also been big gaps of missing time. When pondering how a judge could convict someone on such light evidence, I immediately thought of Sayvian. If Sayvian's loyalty could be bought, then why not the loyalty of a judge or two? Why couldn't this be possible?

A picture began to emerge. DIT could have assigned one of their for-hire goons to break into Dr. Miles' house. This person could have knocked out Dr. Miles and then waited for Mrs. Miles to arrive to strangle her. He would then escape without a trace. The police would arrest the doctor. DIT would find a way to corrupt the data from Mrs. Miles' data files. They find a way to assign a judge from their payroll. He convicts Dr. Miles and orders him to undergo Catharsis. As a result, the doctor dies, and DIT figures they've managed to get away with the perfect setup and then cover-up.

-----:-----

After several hours at the precinct, I packed up my things and headed over to Downtown General to check on my husband. When I arrived, Cap was in Eccles' room, watching over him. I knew Cap wouldn't have trusted anyone else to do the job.

"How is he?"

"Well, he took a nasty knock on the head. The doctor said he'd suffered a concussion. He needs to be woken up every hour or so, and they're keeping him here overnight for observation."

"Cap, I just wanted to---."

"No need, Beth, I'm just glad I arrived when I did."

"What about Sayvian?"

"He's currently at the precinct in lock-up. Did you find what you were looking for?"

"Yes, I think so."

"Good."

I paused and looked at him for a moment. I expected him to ask more follow-up questions, but he didn't. He was sitting in a chair by the window, and he had the look of a relaxed man.

"You're not going to ask me anything about it?"

"No, I don't think so, Beth. Today showed me, well, it made me realize how much I will appreciate seeing my wife again when I get home. I think the time has come for me to say goodbye. I've spoken to the commissioner already, and I'm beginning my retirement tomorrow morning."

I didn't know what to say. I was happy that he was retiring and finally taking a rest after so many years of service, but I was also sad. We'd worked side by side for so long.

"I should go," he said as he rose from his chair.

"Cap, I'm so happy for you. Congratulations and good luck," I said as I extended my hand towards him.

He looked at my hand, grabbed it, and pulled me in for a big bear hug.

He said, "I'll still be around. You won't be able to get rid of this mug that easily. Meg and I will have you and Eccles over for dinner soon. Take care of yourself, kid. Don't let him boss you around, okay? I'm proud of you, Beth. I've always known you were something special. I guess I didn't know how special until now. Your father would be so proud. Get some rest. They'll fill you in at the precinct about the new set up tomorrow. So long, kid!"

Cap gave me a warm smile as he walked out of the room.

I turned my attention to Eccles, who was still sleeping, bandages wrapped around his head. I held his hand tightly and whispered in his ear, "I know what you're thinking, and I'm right there."

Chapter 43

Beth Lago. Saturday, August 28, 2077

The next morning, I awoke with a backache from the chair I'd slept in. Overnight, I had wrapped the straps of my purse tightly around my arms, and now while looking down, I noticed swollen marks on my arms.

Eccles was still sleeping when I bent down to kiss him. Upon receiving the go-ahead, I signed him out of the hospital to take him home.

He was still very dizzy and sleepy as I walked him to the car. Upon resting in the seat, he fell asleep again. When we arrived home, I helped him straight to bed. I locked him in the bedroom, sealed the windows, locked the house doors, and set the alarm. I figured he would be safe inside for about half an hour or so. I got into the car and headed to the second bank Willy had alerted me of on the tape, The Bank of Economic Progress.

When I arrived at the bank, I entered cautiously, looking at the entire layout and scrutinizing each face. There were only a handful of people there, as the doors had opened only a few minutes earlier. I told the woman at the Services Desk that I had come for a safe deposit box. I provided her with the number, and just like at the other bank, a man approached and asked to confirm the box number before escorting me down a long hallway. The security protocols were the same, and the passwords worked as before.

Once I entered the viewing room, I opened the box, and this time there were three things inside: one videotape just as before and two sealed envelopes marked 1 and 2.

Before climbing into the car, I loaded the items into my bag and left quickly. I scanned up and down the street. It seemed eerily quiet. I felt surprised by how smoothly everything had gone until I thought about it and realized that it hadn't been easy at all.

The code Willy had left had come unbelievably close to destruction and becoming lost forever. The clues Willy had left were so subtle and delivered over such a long stretch of time that he might have expected the possibility of it remaining a secret indefinitely. Surely, DIT must have believed they were home free, especially after having ruined poor Dr. Miles and his wife. I wondered what kind of life their son, Sean, had led.

When I arrived home, I disarmed the alarm and made a beeline to the bedroom, where I found my husband resting just as I'd left him. I woke him to give him a drink of water, then let him fall back asleep. I locked him in the bedroom and once again descended into the basement to review the new videotape. I inserted it into the machine and pressed play. Just like before, there were several minutes of static before it cleared up, and a chair appeared on the screen. A figure walked up to the chair and sat in it. I could see it was Willy. He looked decidedly tired, and he'd lost a lot of weight.

"Hello, Beth, if you found the first tape and then this one, then you must already know what happened to Dr. Miles. Can you believe the power of these people? Beth, they can truly do whatever they want, but one day you're going to put an end to it all. I only hope that I'm alive to see that day."

As he approached the camera, his eyes seemed to pop out of the screen. He looked at the camera, staring for several seconds and although the video was grainy and the audio was dreadful, it still, nonetheless, felt like Willy was there in the room with me.

"I hope you're ready for this.
"You likely read Dr. Miles' entire case file, and you likely know that it was a setup. They framed the poor bastard and then sentenced him. You probably already assumed that DIT was behind all of it. Poor Dr. Miles was killed in the most ironic way possible by the process he helped create. You're likely very angry about everything you've seen. There's one more bit of information that you're probably not aware of because, well, frankly, no one knows what I'm about to tell you."

I had unconsciously moved closer and closer to the television as Willy spoke. Suddenly, I heard a loud thump. I immediately pressed "pause" and climbed the stairs to the main floor. I took a glance at the security alarm system and determined that the system was still in check. I climbed the stairs again to the bedroom and unlocked the door. Sitting up in the bed was Eccles.

"Do you have anything for a headache?"
"Babe, you're back, finally!" I replied.
"Of course, I'm back. You don't think I'd let you run the show, do you?"
"Very funny ..." I replied sarcastically. "You have two choices, you can sit here, and I can bring you some medicine for your head and maybe some soup."

"Okay, and what's the second choice?"

"You can come with me, and you can find out about all the crazy stuff that's been happening for the past forty-eight hours."

Eccles looked at me and tilted his head to the side. "Do you really have to ask?"

"Okay, okay, come with me."

I grabbed his hand and walked him down the stairs with me. I had underestimated the breadth of Eccles' injuries, as he still needed me to maintain his balance as we descended the stairs. When we got to the basement, we sat down on the couch.

"What are we watching?"

"I'll fill you in, in a minute."

"Is that Willy?"

"Yes, now be quiet, and I'll tell you everything in a few minutes."

I approached the VCR. I extended my hand and pressed rewind for a couple of seconds before pressing the "play" button.

Willy continued mid-sentence, "... What I'm about to tell you. The process of Catharsis, the process of a patient undergoing Reverse-Looping, doesn't always go as planned."

I looked over at Eccles, who looked equally confused.

"Let me explain. We all know William Stilton-James, and we all know that he killed Emil Dresdin. We know that he underwent Catharsis and ultimately died. What we didn't know at the time and what I have been able to discover from my source within DIT is that Stilton-James died because he was guilty."

"Of course, he was guilty," I said aloud before realizing what Willy meant.

"Stilton-James died during his Catharsis on account of the trauma of witnessing his crime from his victim's perspective. Therefore, in effect, Stilton-James saw and felt his very own body and face killing him in his Catharsis. It only killed him because, in Stilton-James's case, he had committed the crime. So what happens, you ask, when the person undergoing Catharsis is innocent, to begin with?"

Both Eccles and I leaned in closer.

"Well, it has happened before, except no one knows it has. You see, the person drops into a paralytic coma, very similar to death, but not completely dead. Dr. Miles knew about this. When things began to go sour with DIT, he decided to keep this little cookie to himself. He called it his insurance policy. Sadly, the doctor had not accounted for DIT's proficiency in cover-ups. Dr. Miles figured that these failed Catharsis patients would ultimately expose them.

What Dr. Miles hadn't known was that DIT, and Dresdin, had already mapped out a contingency plan? They found a way of eliminating the existence of these failed Catharsis patients. They ended up switching the bodies of the innocent with 'John Doe' coma patients from other hospitals. On a given day, 'someone,' secretly working for DIT, orders a John Doe patient's transfer to another hospital. The records get forged, and the receiving hospital gets one of these poor failed Catharsis cases, and no one's the wiser ... Heavy stuff, huh?"

I looked over at Eccles, who shook his head, gritting his teeth, squinting his eyes, and clenching his fist in anger.

"In the safe-deposit box, you should have found two envelopes with numbers 1 and 2 written on them. Envelope number 1 contains all of the John Doe patients' locations, who are failed Catharsis cases and who are, of course, innocent. The other contains a letter written by Dr. Miles addressed to his son. Before you go to the media and the district attorney's office, I'd like you to find Dr. Miles' son, Sean, and bring him to the location where his father still lies and then hand him letter number two. Based on his reaction, you'll know what to do next. Again, good luck and please be careful."

The tape abruptly ended.

I looked over at Eccles before asking, "Are you ready, Eccles? It's time to make things right again."

Eccles and I looked up Dr. Miles's son's address. It seemed the boy had gone to live with his grandparents following his mother's death. Sean Miles had turned eighteen only a few months ago. He attended a high school near his grandparent's home. On the way, I explained everything that I'd uncovered regarding Dr. Miles and his conviction for allegedly killing Mrs. Miles.

-----:-----

He was walking up the driveway when the young teen spotted our patrol car. He was lanky and had the kind of awkward shuffling walk of a boy growing into a man's body. He furrowed his brow and stared us down as we pulled into the driveway.

We stepped out of the patrol car. He looked over at Eccles menacingly as his backpack, hanging by the strap over one shoulder, slid down to his hand.

"Can I help you?" the blonde-haired boy questioned, scowling.

"Hi, Sean, I'm Inspector Mark Eccles, and this is Inspector Beth Lago. Could we have a word with you?"

He glared at us for several minutes before responding.

"What do you want?"

"We just want to have a word with you," Eccles said.

He shook his head as though in disbelief and said, "Do you have any idea how sick I am of seeing cops? Can't you people just leave us alone?"

"No, actually, Sean, we can't. You see, you're in danger, and we have to take you into custody," Eccles said as he stepped toward Sean. I looked over at Eccles in confusion.

"Danger from whom?" Sean asked.

"Please, Sean, we don't have much time."

"I have to tell my grandparents."

"That's fine. You can call them from the road," Eccles said as he opened the back door of the patrol car.

Sean got in, and we began driving.

I glared at Eccles as we drove.

He whispered, "Did you have a better idea? At least it worked. What hospital are we going to?"

"Downtown Mercy," I whispered back.

We drove west as we headed toward the hospital.

"Where are we going?" Sean asked.

"You're a bit high strung, son. No need to get angry. We're just trying to help you."

"I'm not angry, I'm not high strung, and don't ever call me son. I have no father."

Eccles looked at me for a moment.

I said, "Sean, we're taking you somewhere where you'll be safe. We're almost there."

Sean didn't respond, but I could see the tension in his shoulders drop. I wondered if the hostility he had shown Eccles was due to his belief that his father had murdered his mother. Judging by how quickly he had calmed down, I thought that maybe he still had deep-seated loyalties towards his mother. In a situation with a female and male authority figure, he sided with the female.

"Why do you say that you have no father?" Eccles asked as he peered at Sean through the rearview mirror.

Sean didn't answer.

"Well?" Eccles asked.

"You guys should know. Don't you know about all the murders that happened? You must know about how my dad killed my mom."

"Sean, we know about what happened, and we didn't mean to bring it up," I said. "Were you and your mother close?"

"She ... She was my best friend." He paused for several seconds as he peered out the window. "We were all so happy. Then it all ... My friends used to come over to our house for dinner and sleepovers, and they'd go on and on about how perfect my family was. It shows how much they knew, huh?"

"What did *you* think back then?" I asked.

"I was just a regular kid. I was grossed out when they hugged or kissed, but sometimes it didn't bother me that much, and then it all changed."

"Well, looks like we've arrived."

"What are we doing at the hospital? What's going on?" Sean asked.

Eccles and I stepped out of the vehicle. Sean followed. A few steps from the car door, he turned and stared us down. I decided to take a proactive approach.

"Sean, listen to me. I know this all seems a little weird, and believe me, I get it, but I promise you, we wouldn't put you in harm's way. Inside that hospital, there is something that you need to see."

"Why? Why me?"

"I'm sorry, Sean, I can't tell you that."

"Why not?"

"Well, because there are some truths that you can't be told. Some truths you have to see with your own eyes."

"This is crazy," Sean said as he put his hands out in front of his body as if pushing away the situation away.

"Sean, what happened to your family was horrible, but you must have questions about it. You must have wondered how everything could have fallen apart so quickly."

"So … I'm *not* in danger. You lied to me." Sean snarled.

I looked into Sean's eyes. I could see there was a wall that he must've put up a long time ago. His gestures were aggressive, and his tone severe, but in those eyes, I saw a boy—a frightened boy.

I stepped toward Sean, and I softened my tone, "Well, in a way, Sean, you've been in danger all along, even before that horrible night so many years ago."

He began to take a few steps backwards, and I could feel we were losing him. I didn't want to force him into the hospital, as I wanted to leave the choice up to him.

"Sean, I had a daughter once. She'd be nine years old. She disappeared three years ago. Believe me, when I tell you, we searched everywhere for her, but she was never found. I loved her with all my heart …" I withdrew the two lockets from under my shirt. "The same way, I'm sure your parents loved you. I never found out what happened to my little girl. She just vanished one night without a trace. There's not a day that goes by that I don't think of her and wonder if she's still alive. I will have to live with those questions for the rest of my life. I wish I could know what happened. I'd just like to know. Perhaps that way, I wouldn't have so many nightmares, and I'd be able to sleep at night. Sadly, I never had that chance, but you do. Through those doors are some of the answers you've been searching for. I know you're confused, and you don't understand what's happening. But what happened with your parents—this must have confused you even more. Sean, you don't have to be confused anymore. The truth is through those doors. All you need to do is walk through them."

Sean had been looking downward and then to the different people's faces as they walked past us. He into my eyes, he said, "What was her name?"

"Her name?"

"Your little girl, what was her name?"

"Sara."

"Sara—I like that name."

He looked at me for several seconds, then at the stairs leading to the hospital entrance.

He took a deep breath. He said, "Okay, let's go."

All three of us walked up the stairs and into the hospital. We took the stairwell to the second floor, and we walked down a long hallway to room 22B.

At the threshold of the hospital room, I turned to Sean and said, "I want you to take a deep breath, Sean, because this won't be easy, but it's the truth, and the truth can, well, never be wrong."

Sean inhaled deeply. "Okay."

He took a step into the room. At first, I didn't notice any discernible reaction. Eccles and I followed him inside. The room had only one hospital bed, and within it, a man lay surrounded by all sorts of machines. At first, Sean looked at the man with an uninterested expression on his face. He then paused as his expression turned more serious. Cautiously, he took a few steps closer, peering at the man's face.

"Dad?" he asked.

"I don't understand, Dad, is that you? I don't understand. What is this?" Sean asked as he looked at both of us, trying to read our expressions. Eccles was standing guard at the entrance of the room.

"I think this will explain it all, Sean," I said as I handed him the envelope with the number two written on it.

Sean's hands were shaking as he opened the envelope and read the letter:

My Dear Son,

I know you must have so many questions. I promise I will try to answer them all. In a few hours, I will undergo a procedure referred to as Catharsis. I know that people have told you that I killed your mother. Nothing could be further from the truth. I loved your mother dearly, and she loved me.

In terms of what happened to our family, I'm afraid I'm partly to blame. I've been working for some very bad people. I'm sneaking this letter out of prison with the help of a former colleague so that you could one day know the truth. When I write you this letter, some things haven't occurred yet, but will have occurred by the time you read it. I've predicted the outcome of these things. If my predictions are correct, then you should be standing over my body. I have machines around me, keeping me alive. I am likely in a coma.

You see, Son, I didn't kill your mother. I would never have hurt her in any way. They framed me for murder in order to keep me quiet. I wanted to use Catharsis to help people, and they wanted to use Catharsis to kill people. The more they use Catharsis for killing, the more money they will make. They want a foolproof way of killing people and not receive punishment for it. Sadly, in the end, this was all about power and money.

There is a secret regarding Catharsis my employers didn't know. They still don't know, or else they wouldn't have ever thought to frame me this way. When a person undergoes Catharsis and experiences their victim's death, they will always die as a result. The mind cannot consolidate the sight of murdering one's self. There is also a massive guilt component triggered. Feeling the full extent of suffering, which one has inflicted on another soul, causes so much guilt that it will lead to imminent death.

In the case of William Stilton-James, he died, but not for the reasons DIT had intended. From what I've pieced together, he suffered a far more tragic fate.

Son, I'm going to ask two favours from you. The first is that you tell the world of what happened to Stilton-James and me. For you to be able to relay my message, then I will have to explain the nature of the truth.

Catharsis, as a sentence done properly, should only have one possible outcome: death.

This will be the case when the person undergoing the sentence is guilty. The process was supposed to be perfect. No innocent person should ever have to undergo Catharsis. DIT didn't realize that Catharsis could overturn convictions because if a patient were innocent, then the Catharsis would NOT result in death.

Sean, I was accused of killing your mother, I was tried and convicted, and I then underwent Catharsis. The fact that you're standing over my motionless body should indicate to you one thing: I was innocent. I didn't kill your mother. I love her and always will love her with all my heart.

For Stilton-James, well, his situation was far more complex. He suffered a psychotic episode. Despite having grown up in OLA, suffering horrible abuses and witnessing his father's murder, he still had goodness in him. At some point, an event caused his mind irreparable damage. After having interviewed Stilton-James, it's my opinion that he developed a dissociative disorder as a child, resulting in the creation of a second personality.

I have thought long and hard about how best to explain this ...

I want you to imagine a boy growing up in OLA during the Dark Times. The Scarklingas imprison the boy and the boy's father. These vicious people abuse them for years on end until one day something happens that changes both their lives. One night, plumes of gas descend from the sky. You remember this day from your history class as the day TFS took back Los Angeles. The boy remembers it as the day he watched his father die. The boy spends the next few months and years living alone and fighting to survive. Despite all the death and pain, this boy has lived through. He chooses to do something positive. This boy meets another boy of the same age, and together the two commit to helping all the other orphaned children they run into. They build a refuge underground where they hide the children and shelter them. The boy and his new friend make an arrangement. The young Stilton-James is to find the children, and he then leads them to other boy who then leads them to the underground shelter. Things work well for a time until one day, something unexpected occurs.

Sean, that boy was William Stilton-James. He was the boy that had committed to finding the orphaned children. He was the boy who would lead them underground. When William Stilton-James, as an adult, found Emil, he regressed to the young Stilton-James. The one who'd helped children and sheltered them. This is why Stilton-James, as an adult, led Emil down to his basement the day of Emil's death.

When Stilton-James was a young boy, I mentioned that something unexpected had occurred. The event caused Stilton-James's psychological state. After having led the children to his friend, you see, the young Stilton-James never entered the shelter again. He had never known the fate of the children once they'd crossed that threshold. One day, he found out. One rescued boy carried around a metallic toy helicopter. When the young Stilton-James found him in the streets, the boy gave Stilton-James his toy helicopter before the hand-off. Stilton-James felt so moved by this gift that he returned to the shelter for the first and last time. When Stilton-James crossed the threshold and saw what the other boy had been doing to the children, he suffered the trauma that caused his condition. Only Stilton-James will ever know what he saw, but I can only imagine how gruesome it must have been. Upon seeing it, his brain buried the memory deep in his subconscious, never to rise again until the day of Emil's death.

Emil was carrying a metallic toy helicopter in a tragic twist of fate on the night of his death. Stilton-James remarks on the object on Emil's D-Eye playback. When Stilton-James and Emil were in Stilton-James's basement, there was a struggle that caused Stilton-James to fall back and hit his head on the concrete floor. Stilton-James lost consciousness for a moment, and when he opened his eyes again, he saw the toy helicopter on the ground. There is something about Emil's D-Eye playback, which I had never understood. After having fallen on the floor, Stilton-James proceeded to beat Emil severely. On the playback, Stilton-James is saying, "how could you ... how could you ...?"

No one has ever been able to discern the word that Stilton-James had said after that. Sometimes things aren't clear until the proper context is applied. I did some investigating before your mother's death. I came across a news story about a man executed long before Stilton-James and Emil ever met. The man had tried to avoid the death sentence by leading a group of investigators to an underground shelter. In this shelter, police found hundreds of remains. Most of them were children. The man's name was Marcus Sloan. Sean, after hearing the man's name, I'm certain that on Emil's D-Eye playback, Stilton-James was screaming." How could you, Sloan? How could you?"

On the night of Emil's death, Stilton-James hit his head, saw the toy helicopter and regressed to the most traumatic memory he had. His mind travelled back to the day he saw what Marcus Sloan had done to the children, and he unleashed on Emil all the rage and fury he'd felt for Sloan that day when Stilton-James realized what he'd done. He helped Emil and placed him on a table. While not thinking logically, Stilton-James tied him up to prevent him from running away. Stilton-James then went upstairs to gather up some towels and water. When he returned, Emil was dead. The ropes Stilton-James had used to tie him up had asphyxiated him.

Sean, the reason I am telling you this is not to paint the picture of an innocent man. Does Emil deserve justice? The answer to that question is a resounding *yes*, but DIT's version of Catharsis was never about justice. Dresdin and DIT wanted to make Catharsis our new capital punishment. They wanted to make an example of Stilton-James. They wanted him to appear as evil as possible to facilitate this goal. I imagined they wanted everyone to become D-Eye patients, but they also wanted something far more valuable. They had always intended to use Catharsis as a way to kill whomever they wanted, whenever they wanted. Essentially, we gave them a license to kill. When they realized that I would stand in their way, they framed me for your mother's murder. These are evil people, but they will face justice.

Sean, today you will put an end to all of it. Attached to this letter is a key, which opens a safe deposit box. Within that box is a package I would like you to send to the biggest media outlets you can find. If you were to do this for me, you will have completed the first of the two favours I am asking of you.

The second favour will be infinitely harder. There are machines that keep me alive, and I would like you to turn them off. You see, I haven't explained everything to you yet. I am not just in a coma. The damage my mind has suffered is beyond repair. You see, the coma that results from failed Catharsis occurs because of the effect of receiving traumatic foreign memories into the subconscious. The mind cannot make sense of memory when that memory does not relate in any way. If I'd been guilty, then my mind would have accepted the memory. The mind would have accepted it as a role reversal. For someone wrongfully convicted, for someone who was likely not even present when the crime occurred, the mind tends to repeat the playback, never stopping. Each time that it plays, the mind tries to consolidate it, but it never does and never will. Around and around, it goes in an infinite loop of trauma. For me, since DIT framed me, well, the playback won't be as smooth. My loop will be crude, patched-together, creation, and the mind can't accept such incoherence. The playback that has been looping in my mind has been gradually destroying it. I'm certain that no man can take such abuse and still maintain his sanity. I'm broken, Sean, and it's time for me to return to your mother. It's time for me to go home. Please know that this isn't exactly the way I'd planned for things to work out. Nonetheless, I am glad that you finally know the truth and that you've read my words and now know that I was innocent.

You will change the world, Sean, it's your destiny, and you will avenge my death. You will take down a giant conspiracy of lies, and you will do it without ever throwing a single punch. You're the one who taught me that, Son. I love you, Sean.

Be a better man than I was, and remember that the truth has the power to change everything.

"Know that as certain as the rays of dawn's first morning light;
I will never let this end,
I will never cease to fight."
I never have, Son, and I never will.
I love you. Good-bye.

Dad

Sean stood frozen for a moment and then as though all the stress and tension that had held him up like a stone structure suddenly began to fall like a ruptured dam. He fell to the ground, along with the tears that flowed from his eyes.

I caught him, and he hugged me tightly, the way I imagined he would have hugged his mother. I hugged him the way I would have hugged Sara. The tough and rigid young man had evaporated, and all that remained was the fragile core of a boy. He sobbed as I tried to console him. Eccles placed his hand on Sean's shoulder, grasping it reassuringly.

We sat in that hospital room for several minutes as the weight of all that had happened finally crashed down upon our shoulders. I imagined the letter explained the sad story of how things had come to be, and what I didn't know until afterwards was how impossible the prospect of saving Trevor was. Amid his tearful sobbing, Sean whispered the word, "Why?" I wish I could have answered him, but how could I explain that kind of darkness, which I had trouble understanding?

After a time, Sean suddenly rose up, handed me the letter, and said, "It says that we have to end his life."

I gently pulled Sean away from me. I slipped an envelope from my pocket and gave it to him. "Sean, in this envelope, is a copy of your father's last will, and in it, he gives you the full power of attorney, active on your eighteenth birthday."

Sean looked at me with tear-filled eyes and walked to his father's side, where he rested his head upon his chest.

"I'm sorry too, Dad. I'll miss you. I do miss you. Take care of Mom. Thank you. I love you."

"Are you ready, Sean?" I asked.

"Yes," he said as he wiped tears from his eyes and reached for his father's hand.

"I'll miss you, Dad."

I cradled my arm around him, and I walked him out of the hospital room, nodding in Eccles' direction. As we walked down the hall, I turned around for a moment to see Eccles walk out of the room—seconds later, a flock of doctors and nurses rushed into that room.

Sean turned to me.

"Now, what do we do?"

"Well, now, we show the world what these people have done. Now, we make things right again. Your father was a brave man."

"I know," he replied.

Chapter 44

Beth Lago. Saturday, August 28, 2077

We dropped Sean off at his grandparent's house, and we drove back home. The next day would be an important one, and we were to visit all the hospitals in question and verify the ID's of each of the failed Catharsis patients. We sat at the table in the kitchen, and we discussed how to proceed.

"We need to build a case, a solid case, that will bring these bastards down," Eccles said with conviction in his eyes.

"Catharsis was a sham all along. We know this, but we have to help prove it. The only question is, where do we start?" I asked.

"We start with Dr. Miles. We present the case as a conspiracy to commit murder and as an obstruction of justice."

"Let's review everything for a moment, though. Dr. Trevor Miles, along with his team, determined that Catharsis could be used to help people rather than as a death sentence. DIT takes the report as a threat towards their plans to use Catharsis as state-sanctioned murder."

Eccles said, "... Right."

"Then, they frame Dr. Miles with the murder of his wife."

"... Right."

"We know he was framed, but I just realized something. Unless we can prove that DIT was involved, we'll never be able to attach the murder of Dr. Miles' wife to them. It's not enough that Dr. Miles was innocent all along. We need to find Mrs. Miles' murderer," I said.

"Okay, but that's a little easier said than done. It's not our case, and it's already been tried. I've read the case files too. There aren't many leads to follow."

"We do have one lead," I said as an epiphany hit me.

"What would that be?"
"Not what ... Who."
"Of course, Sayvian!"
"I believe he's still in county lock up at the precinct," Eccles stated.

When we arrived at the precinct, we made our way to Containment. The precinct had several holding cells on the lower level. Although it was in the precinct and everyone in the precinct at any given time had permission to be there, we still had to proceed through various security measures to get to the holding cells. When we finally arrived at the long corridor, we referred to as the 'Trench,' and we passed other prisoners on our way to Sayvian's cell. Most of the prisoners we passed didn't neglect the chance to snicker or utter some disgusting comment as we walked by. The street-smart, arrogant prisoners had a giant chip on their shoulder and weren't afraid to reveal it. Though others looked to be mere fractions of the men, they must have been on the outside. Curled up, many of them in the fetal positions, they had expressions on their faces, which seemed to emote the endless weight that impending doom must carry.

When we arrived at Sayvian's cell, we could clearly see he belonged in the second group. He had curled his bony frame up into a ball and had retreated to the farthest corner of the cell. All that remained of his tailored suit was a charcoaled shirt, pants frayed at the bottom and a dirty coat, which he was using as a blanket.

It took us several tries before he heard us calling him.
"Sayvian! Sayvian! Sayvian!"
By the third call, the huddled mass lifted its head to meet our gaze.
A raspy voice responded, "What do you want?"
"Sayvian, for God's sakes, get a hold of yourself. You've been in lockup for a few days, and you look like you've been in the hole for a month." Eccles said impatiently.
"What do you know, Eccles, have you come here to gloat? Is that what you people do? You go around and humiliate people further?" Sayvian asked sarcastically.
"I told you, Eccles, this was a complete waste of time. If he'd rather rot in here as an appetizer before his trial and execution as the main course, so be it. What do I care?" I said, tapping Eccles' arm with the backside of my hand before walking away.
"Wait!"
"Yes?"
"What do you guys want? I mean, maybe I can help you?" Sayvian asked, pleading as he stood up.
"You think you have information that could benefit us?" I asked.
Sayvian said, "I don't know, maybe."

"Maybe? Sayvian, are you not understanding what's happening here? You assaulted and threatened to kill two officers. You're going to pay for what you've done."

"Wait, that's not what I meant. I know some stuff, but I just don't know what information you need," he responded as he approached the bars.

"Okay, here's the deal. Give us the name of Mrs. Miles' killer, and we'll ask the DA to make a special exception for you, maybe even take the death penalty off the table," I stated.

Sayvian burst into laughter. He went on for several seconds before seeing our expressions.

"Are you serious?" Sayvian asked.

"I'm not laughing, are you, Inspector Lago?" Eccles said as he turned to me.

"No, there's absolutely nothing funny here to me," I replied.

Sayvian said, "Okay, listen to me. You guys have no idea what you're up against. There's no way I'm giving you that, and besides, I don't even have that information."

"Great! Suit yourself, Sayvian. I'm not the one facing imminent death." I said as I began walking away.

"Wait! Wait, I might have some information that could help you. There'll be no death penalty, right? I have your word," he said.

"That would depend on the information. Make sure it's useful information. After all, your life does depend on it."

"Okay, here it is. I don't know who killed Mrs. Miles."

Eccles said, "This isn't starting well."

"Wait, just listen for a minute. When I first got involved with DIT, I had to meet with a guy ..."

I asked, "Name?"

"I don't have a name. He had a nickname. It was like Sta ... Sto ... Stackton."

"What does he look like? I asked.

"I never saw his face. We always met in dark places like parking garages or warehouses ... Always in the dark."

"I'm waiting for the useful information, Sayvian."

"Well, this Stackton guy always had someone with him. He was this huge hulking man. He must have been at least six-foot-nine or something, just huge. I never saw his face, though."

"Okay."

"Well, when Mrs. Miles was murdered, and the case was under investigation, some of the evidence was processed at our precinct. There was one piece of evidence of particular importance."

"Which was?"

"There was a cast of a shoe print made at the scene of a size 14 boot, taken from the Miles' backyard. When I heard of the print, I assumed it was of that guy, Stackton's bodyguard."

"Sayvian? We read the case files. There was no print," I said.

"No, no, you don't understand. The judge threw the boot print cast out of court. At the trial, the judge had deemed it inadmissible, never even mentioned it in court. There was a mistake on the part of a crime scene tech. He forgot to take pictures before making the cast. The prosecution argued that there was no way of proving where the cast came from without pictures. They went back and took pictures after the fact, but it had rained by then, and the scene had become contaminated."

"That's not useful---" Eccles said.

"Thank you, Sayvian," I interjected as I motioned to Eccles that we should leave.

"Okay, great, so you gave me your word, right?" Sayvian asked.

"Yes, we did, but it all depended on whether or not the information was useful," I said.

"It is useful."

"We'll have to wait and see. You had better hope we can catch this guy, or else there's no deal. By the way, where is the cast of the print right now?"

"It should be in storage here."

I said, "Fine. We'll see what we can do with this."

"So, you'll help me then, right?"

Eccles said, "We'll have to see, Sayvian. You'll just have to wait and see."

Sayvian didn't say another word. He simply faded back into the corner of the cell and once again curled into a ball.

There was a small corridor between Containment and the security checkpoint to re-enter the precinct main level.

I asked, "So?"

"I don't know if we should go into the evidence room and sign out the cast. I don't like it. It leaves a paper trail. We don't want to show that we're working on this. They don't see us coming—that's our advantage."

I said, "Fine, and then we won't sign it out. We'll review it while still in the evidence room."

Eccles looked down while shaking his head.

"Do you have a better idea?"

"No, I guess reviewing the cast while it's still in the evidence room is our only play."

"Okay, so we'll go in there, claiming that we're following up on an old case. One of us will have to distract the archivist while the other takes pictures of the cast," I said.

We went through the checkpoint and back to the precinct main level. From there, we proceeded to the evidence room in the west wing of the precinct. When we arrived, we could see that Tom was the archivist on duty.

Tom was a nervous, jittery, average-sized guy in his mid-thirties. He was a nice enough character, always said "hello" when we passed in the halls. He did have a habit of being rather intense, though. I remember I'd ask him about his weekend, to which he would respond by saying, "It was good. Fine." If I pressed him further, then he would begin explaining, literally, almost everything he did. All the while, I'd noticed a thin film of sweat forming above his upper lip. It was a good thing that all the cops in the precinct knew him to be a nice guy because under questioning by an officer, the sheer level of nervousness he transmitted would cause anyone to doubt his claims.

"Hey, Tom, how's it going?" Eccles asked while shaking Tom's hand, vigorously and patting Tom's back with the other.

"Hi, guys! W-What's up?" Tom replied, blinking several times but still mustering a smile.

I said, "Well, Tom, Eccles and I are following up on a case, and we need to pull a couple of items."

"O-okay, I can help you with that. What are the call numbers?"

I said, "That's the thing, Tom, we're not sure, and there are a bunch of them. It'll probably be easier if we just get back there and search for them ourselves."

"Oh, you want to come back here?" Tom asked.

"Yeah, that's right. Cap wanted us to follow up on these cases for the sheriff, and you know how the sheriff can be," Eccles said.

"The sheriff ... oh yeah, he's ... he's ..."

"--A very serious man, it's true," Eccles said as he opened the door beside the kiosk window.

Eccles stepped through the door.

"Well, I guess if it's for the sheriff, then I guess it would be okay," Tom said with a nervous smile.

"Thanks, Tom. Now I do have a question for you," I said while I stood at the kiosk window.

"Okay, sure, Beth, what is it?" Tom asked enthusiastically.

"I was just wondering the other day if you ever get lonely down here. You know, you must spend long stretches of time down here with no visitors."

"Yeah, it does get a bit lonely sometimes, but I keep myself busy. I like to read up on old cases, mostly cold cases."

"Oh, really?" I asked.

"Yes, I find it keeps my mind sharp. I've always been pretty good at, you know, analyzing stuff."

"Well, that's an excellent way to spend your spare time, Tom. I can appreciate an interest like that."

"Yeah, well, I'm not at the level of you and Eccles, but I hope maybe one day I could help crack a case."

"Tom, if you work hard, it'll only improve your chances. It's not a glamorous job, though. Sometimes you get a little dirty, the hours are long, and there isn't much gratitude thrown around. Just like any job, though, there are days when you do well, and on those days, you feel like you've made a difference."

"I think I like the sound of that," Tom said with a smile.

"Good."

"Could I pick your brain for a minute?" Tom asked.

"Umm, okay," I replied.

"Well, I've been reading up on a lot of the D-Eye cases."

"You have?"

"Yes, and there are a bunch of things that bother me."

"Okay."

"Well, there's a lot of evidence missing from a lot of the cases."

"How do you mean?"

"Almost every one of the cases has a piece of information that could prove vital, but for whatever reason never gets found."

"Tom, that happens in almost every case anyway."

"Yeah, but it seems more frequent in the D-Eye cases. I'm sorry, I must be boring you."

"No, no, Tom, you're not boring me at all."

"You see, take the case of Dr. Miles."

"Dr. Miles?"

"Yeah, it was a case where this doctor, a former employee of DIT, was convicted of killing his wife. I'm not surprised you don't know about it. Not many detectives do."

"Really ...?"

"No, it was an older case, and it happened in another territory. Anyway, even though Dr. Miles was found in the house at the scene of the crime, the blunt object used to hit Mrs. Miles in the head was never recovered."

"Very interesting ... So I guess you must just read up on all the cases, I mean, to look into a case from a whole other territory. You must cover a lot of ground."

"Yeah, I guess so. It was kind of weird how it came about. Some of the evidence for that case was processed and stored here. I didn't even know about the case, but a few months ago, someone came to check out some of the stuff from that case. I looked up the case number, and I've been studying it ever since."

"Sorry, can you backtrack for a minute? Did you say someone came to check on evidence from that case?"

"Yeah ... Andrews."

"Who?"

"You know, Andrews, the big guy, seven feet tall or whatever. He's a memorable guy—huge. Every time we play his softball team and that guy steps up to the plate, forget about it. It's an instant home run."

What would Andrews be doing pulling evidence from this case?

I made a strong effort to disguise my surprise.

I said, "I see, yeah, I think I've seen him around. He is a big guy, for sure."

"So, I guess he's in homicide with you guys, right? You must know him then."

"Yeah, I do, good old Andrews."

He's not in the homicide department. He's in Missing Persons. I don't think he's ever been in homicide.

Just then, Eccles appeared at the kiosk window.

"You know, I'm going to have to come back with the call numbers. I can't find anything without the call numbers."

"That's what I keep telling everybody! Call numbers are so important," Tom said.

"We'll be back, Tom, thanks!" Eccles said in Tom's direction.

"Tom, it's been very nice speaking with you," I said as I shook his hand.

"Nice talking with you too!"

As we stepped away from the kiosk desk, Eccles whispered to me, "The cast in there is not a size a big man would wear."

"I know," I whispered back.

"How could you possibly know that?"

"It was switched, obviously," I said.

I lowered my voice even lower than a whisper, "We've got a dirty cop."

The more I thought about it, the more I realized that the existence of an inside man explained so much. Saints said he believed there was another.

-----:-----

Eccles and I left the precinct in separate cars. We had to meet somewhere we could discuss things further without the danger of anybody overhearing us. The precinct was not safe. There was a restaurant just outside the Scourge that Eccles and I had gone to for dinner one evening over a year ago. It was far from the precinct, and the booths inside were perfect for quiet conversations. Of course, it served only artificial foods but made in a diner's style from the mid-twentieth century.

I arrived first and sat down to wait for Eccles, who arrived only a few minutes later. We both ordered coffee, and the waitress left us alone for a few minutes to review the menus.

As soon as the waitress walked away, I filled Eccles in on my conversation with Tom. Glancing around the busy restaurant, I realized there was little chance of anyone hearing us. Nonetheless, I kept my voice low.

"Geez, what a coincidence," Eccles said.

"I know, tell me about it. I couldn't believe what I was hearing."

"So what do we do now?" he whispered back to me.

"Well, we have pretty good reason to believe that Andrews is dirty and likely Mrs. Miles' murderer."

"I can't believe it. Andrews? He seemed like he was one of us, one of the good guys."

"I guess we all have our secrets," I retorted, unable to provide an adequate explanation.

"We really can't trust anyone at the precinct anymore. That place has become completely tainted."

"It's just you and me at this point. What do we do now?" Eccles asked.

"Well, Andrews must think he's gotten away with everything, but what if he had doubts ..."

"He'd make sure to tie up any loose ends," Eccles responded.

"Right now, Andrews has no idea that we're on to him, but if he found out . . ." I shuddered and then straightened back up. "The trick will be in drawing him in somehow without scaring him away."

"I know what you're thinking, Beth. That look in your eyes, I've seen that look before."

"I think that we should rattle his cage a bit," I said.

The waitress returned for our orders.

"I'll have the club sandwich," Eccles said.

"What about you, darling?" There was a twang in her soft voice.

"I'll have the same."

She walked away, and we continued our conversation.

"So, you want him to panic a bit," Eccles said as he took a sip of his faux-coffee.

"People do tend to make mistakes when they panic, don't they?"

A plan had occurred to me. I spent the next several minutes working out the details with Eccles.

The tendon in Eccles' jaw twitched. "Beth, you don't need me to tell you how dangerous that plan is."

"You know as well as I do, it's our only shot. Are you saying that it's a bad plan or that it isn't going to work?"

"No, in fact, it's a brilliant plan. What scares me is how well I think it'll work." Eccles said.

I glanced down at my watch. It was just past five o'clock. At that moment, the waitress arrived with our club sandwiches.

"Two club sandwiches ..."

303

"Thank you," we replied simultaneously.

I took a bite of one of my faux-fries. I glanced up to see Eccles pensively looking out the window.

"What is it?" I asked.

"I don't know. I've just got a bad feeling about this."

"We'll be cautious. We knew what we were signing up for when we took these jobs, though, right?"

"Just be careful, okay?" Eccles pleaded.

I looked at my watch again. It was now a quarter after five.

"I'll try my best. Andrews should be finishing up for the day in a little under an hour. I say we finish our dinner quickly, and then we put our plan into action."

Eccles smirked. "You'll always be stubborn, won't you?"

"Unfortunately, there is no other way. We have no other choice."

"I know. Suppose anything were to happen to you. I don't know what I'd do." Eccles said as he turned his gaze downward.

"Nothing bad will happen, okay?" I ignored the nervousness that I felt.

We sat in our booth, eating our dinner in silence for the next several minutes until Eccles asked for the bill. Before the waitress came, Eccles said, "I love you, Beth."

"I love you, too," I replied.

Upon leaving the restaurant, we went our separate ways as we proceeded to initialize our plan.

-----:-----

Back at the precinct, I met up with the officers in the dispatch unit. I told them exactly what I needed to but didn't let them in on the plan.

In the equipment room, I strapped on a bulletproof vest. I gathered all of the other equipment I needed and looked in the mirror.

This is it, Beth. Don't be afraid. I took pendants out from under my shirt and kissed them gently. I looked into my eyes and said aloud, "You're ready."

I packed up an unmarked patrol car and headed home. On the way, I heard an announcement come across the radio:

"Attention all units, this is an APB, searching for an unknown male, approximately six feet and eight inches, straight blonde hair, muscular physique ... suspect is wanted in relation to the murder of Tia Miles. The suspect may be armed and extremely dangerous. Any sightings must report to Inspectors Lago or Eccles before apprehension. Officers ... Proceed with caution."

I smiled at the sound of the APB. We had now rattled his cage. The question was, how would he respond? If I were right, then he would respond exactly as expected.

-----:-----

I returned to the house and began setting up the equipment I had picked up. It took just over an hour to complete all the preparations.

After having set the alarm, I sat in the living room waiting. I knew I had but one shot. I had gambled using every ounce of experience I had to guess Andrews' next move. I only hoped that I had been right.

The time was 7:34, and nothing had happened yet. I was beginning to worry. The sun had already set, and darkness had surrounded the house. I couldn't help but think of how nervous Eccles had been. It wasn't like him to be so anxious about an operation, and it made me question whether we were doing the right thing. He had always been steely in the face of danger. Eccles may have had his faults, but panic in the face of a threat was not one of them.

-----:-----

It was getting late, and I had all but given up when my cell phone rang. I found it odd as I seldom received calls at this hour.

"Hello?"

"Go to the window," a deep voice ordered.

"What? Who is this?"

"Go to the window," the voice repeated.

"*Who* is this?"

"If you ever want to see your husband again, you'll go to the window."

Damn it!

I began switching off all the lights in the house, and I walked over to the window. I peeked through the blinds, but I couldn't see anything.

"What am I looking for?" I asked.

"You don't see us?"

"Us?"

"Yeah, I'm out here with a guest. Do you want to say hi ...?"

"Run, Beth! It's a trap! Run... Ugh," I heard Eccles scream before being silenced by a loud thud.

I asked, "What do you want?"

"I just want to come in, Beth, that's all."

"If you hurt him ..."

"Beth, it's a little late for that. I think you'll see that Eccles is in really bad shape. I guess that's what happens when you get in a car accident. You had me followed. I found it quite cute, and it might have worked. First, I lost him and then switched cars. I doubt he saw it coming when I rammed his patrol car at fifty miles an hour. You're awfully quiet. Are you still there, Beth?"

"Yes."

"I think you should know that your husband is bleeding profusely."

"You're not going to get away with this," I said.

"Beth ... Open the door, or I put a bullet between his eyes."

I walked over to the alarm system console. The plan had been for Eccles to follow Andrews and keep his distance. Upon Andrews' eventual arrival, Eccles would catch him in the act of attempting to kill me. Now, things had gone incredibly awry.

I had no choice now. Eccles would surely die if I didn't do something. "Okay, okay, I'll let you in."

I walked over to the door, unlocked it and in stepped Andrews. I had forgotten how big he was. He almost had to step sideways to fit through the doorframe. He held Eccles by the collar of his jacket. His body was limp and covered in blood. Andrews slammed Eccles onto the hardwood floor. I ran over to help him up when I saw Andrews' boot come towards my head. The impact of the kick caused me to fly backwards and onto the coffee table. I felt the violent weight of powerful punches thrown in my direction, hitting me in the ribs and then the gut, the temple, and then my chin. I tried to move out of the way, but I couldn't as each punch stung and then dulled my senses.

I lay dazed on the floor, I tried to lift my head, but I couldn't, I tried to move my limbs, but I couldn't. I heard the thumping sound of footsteps, at which point I managed to open my eyes slightly. As I squinted to focus, I could see Andrews lifting Eccles' head by the hair with one hand as he held a gun in the other.

"You couldn't leave well enough alone. Could you?"

"St-op. Don't. Please. It was *me*! Leave him alone. It was my fault. Please. Don't hurt him."

"You should have thought of that before," Andrews said as he pointed the gun at Eccles' head. "Say goodbye, Beth."

Suddenly, I heard a loud bang.

"NOOOOO!" I screamed.

"Don't worry. I'm coming for you, too." Andrews said as I could hear the loud sound of footsteps thumping towards me.

"No. No. No," I cried.

I knew tears were pouring from my eyes, and I could feel nothing but pain throughout my body. Eccles lay lifeless on the floor. I tried my best to crawl toward him. If it was all going to end, I wanted to be by his side.

Andrews stepped between us. "Any final words?" he asked in a mocking tone.

"Eccles! I love you! I'm sorry." I turned to look up at Andrews. I said, "You son of a bitch. I'm going to kill you! I swear!"

"Goodbye, Beth."

I heard a loud bang.

-----:-----

Everything turned white, and I found myself in a bright room with no windows or doors. I was lying in a bed with white sheets. I could feel my eyelids get heavy.

I felt the unbearable need to sleep, and I was about to succumb when I heard a voice, it was faint at first, but then it became louder. It was the voice of a little girl.

"Mommy?"

"Sara? Is that you?"

I could feel Sara's presence around me. I hadn't seen her in so many years, but I knew, without a doubt, that she was there with me.

"Where are you, Sara? Speak to me."

"Mommy, wake up!"

"I am awake, baby."

"No, you're not. Wake up."

"Sara, if I'm not awake, then waking means I'll have to leave you, and I won't do that."

"You have to go back, Mommy."

"I don't want to, baby."

"Yes, you do. You still have a job to do."

"When will I see you again?"

"Soon, Mommy ..."

-----:-----

The room turned into bright light, I opened my eyes, and as they began to focus, I could see a face in front of me.

"Willy?"

"Hi, Beth."

"Am I dead?"

"Are you dead? Ha-ha, well, let me ask you ... do you feel any pain right now?"

"Umm ... ugh ... yes."

"Then I guess the pain is the bad news. The fact that you're still alive is the good news."

"What happened to ...."

"Eccles? He's right over there," Willy said as he pointed to the bed that lay parallel to mine. Sure enough, there lay Eccles with a giant bandage wrapped around his head.

"But I saw him get shot."

"Yeah, the bullet just grazed him. Did you know he had a metal plate in his head? You must know that. Anyway, the plate saved his life, or at least his brain, for that matter. Now, I don't know if he would have survived a direct hit, but the angle and the fact his hair was already drenched in blood caused Andrews to think he was firing directly at Eccles' head."

"What about me?"

"Now, you needed a little more than luck to get you out of that one."

"You mean ... You ..."

"That's right, I saved your life," Willy said with a smile.

"But how did you know?"

"Well, I have contacts at the banks where the safe-deposit boxes were, and once I knew that the wheels were in motion, I made it my priority to make sure you were safe."

"By?"

"I've been keeping an eye on you."

"By keeping an eye, you actually mean stalking."

"No, not stalking, protecting."

"So you've been following me around for the past few weeks?"

"From a distance, it's easier to protect someone. When you go after the biggest, most powerful corporation in the world, sometimes you need a little backup. I specialize in security anyway, remember?"

"So, what happens now?" I asked.

"Well, for now, you have to rest. Once you're better, the world is going to want to know the truth. It's time to change everything, Beth."

"What about you?" I asked.

"I'm going to have to go away for a while. Even though I did the right thing in the end, I'm sure I'll get in trouble and probably get some sort of an accessory charge. When it's all said and done, I'll probably get acquitted, but you'll understand if I've lost a bit of faith in the justice system."

"Where will you go?"

"I don't know—maybe somewhere by the water. Don't worry. This isn't goodbye. I don't say goodbye. I'll come to find you soon. Tell that big lug over there that he hasn't gotten rid of me forever."

I looked down for a moment. "Thank you," I said.

"No, Beth, thank you. I was in a dark place, and I didn't think I'd ever see the light of day again. I was a bit worried that you weren't going to figure things out, but you did, and I'm thankful to you for that. You know I didn't exactly make this easy on you. I mean, a lot of things could have gone wrong. You've always been clever, Beth. I knew you'd figure it out."

"Willy, I've mis ..."

"I've missed you too ... You're the best friend I've ever had. I know you think I saved you, but the truth is ... you saved me. See you later, Beth," he said softly as he leaned down to kiss me on the cheek.

"See you later, Willy. Thank you."

Willy looked back at me for a moment before exiting the room. The sadness I may have felt at seeing him leave immediately washed away at the sight of his brilliant smile. I couldn't help but smile back, though a tear slid down my face.

-----:-----

Eccles woke up a few hours later as I sat at his side, holding his hand. The doctors had said that he had suffered another major concussion. When he opened his eyes, he smiled, then, just as quickly, he frowned.

"Hey," I whispered.

"Hey, I'm really happy to see you, but man, my head really, really hurts."

I couldn't help but laugh as I hugged him.

"I'm not joking. My head really hurts," he quipped.

"I know, but we're here, and we're alive."

"True, and that's what counts, right? We're not finished yet, though, are we?" Eccles asked.

"Almost, but not yet ..." I answered.

-----:-----

A week later, and against his doctor's orders, Eccles joined me as we visited the different hospitals confirming all the failed Catharsis patients' identities.

A week after that, we found ourselves at a press conference at the precinct.

"Come here for a second," I said.

"What?" he answered.

"Did you tie this tie yourself?"

"Umm ..."

"It doesn't matter. I'll fix it for you. There ... All better. Are you ready? Are you scared?" I asked with a reassuring smile.

"I think I'm ready, but I'm still a bit scared."

"Don't be scared. This is your day."

He turned around and walked towards the press room. Before entering, he turned to me and gave me a nod and mouthed the words, "Thank you."

"You're welcome, Sean," I whispered back.

He took another step, and the room erupted with the sound of cameras flashing and voices shouting over one another.

Cap was standing at the podium.

Eccles spotted him, looked over at me, and said, "Look at this! Typical, Cap shows up just in time to take all the credit."

"I knew he wouldn't be able to stay away," I said with a smile.

"Ladies and gentlemen, I would like to introduce Sean Miles. He has a special message for all of you," Cap said before stepping back and allowing the young man to approach the microphone.

"Good morning. First of all, I'd like to thank the OLAPD and especially Inspectors Eccles and Lago." He took a deep breath. "I spent the last several years believing my father to be a murderer. Everyone told me that he had killed my mother. Now, with the help of some friends, we now know the truth. My father said the truth has the power to change everything. I now know what he meant ..."

Eccles and I stepped away from the press conference room and into the hallway. We had never intended on facing the cameras. Eccles and I were far too shy for that. On that morning, the truth did change everything. Dozens of DIT board members and executives awoke to reporters and arrest warrants. Not surprisingly, Dresdin and his wife had disappeared without a trace—they're currently at large.

A few days after the news conference, Sean's face appeared on televisions, computer screens, e-newspapers, and e-magazines the world over. I thought it rather fitting that since this had all begun with the tragic death of a young boy, why not have it end with a brave young man at its forefront. Just like Sean, groups of widows, sons and daughters learned the tragic truth about their loved ones' fates. There were many tears and much sadness. The world seemed to grieve together, and yet there was still a sense of goodwill. During this time, I was reminded of the words that had once given me solace, "The good, the bad. We were always meant to face it together". One by one, we met with the families of the poor souls who had suffered the tragic indignity of the wrongfully convicted. Despite the darkness, however, we still found a ray of hope.

To me, it was the sight of strangers hugging and consoling each other in hospital rooms all over that showed me the true meaning of Catharsis.

-----:-----

It had now been weeks since the press conference.

Last night, I experienced a flashback of the night when I'd thought I'd died. I remembered the sound of my Sara's voice. The thought made me unbelievably sad. I decided to allow myself to succumb to the sadness one last time. I cried and cried, and then I fell into the most restful sleep imaginable. I slept well for the rest of the night, safe in my husband's arms.

When I descended to the kitchen this morning, Eccles was on the phone.

"She's right here. I'll pass her the phone," Eccles said as he motioned me to come closer.

"Beth, it's Cap. Can you come down to the precinct?"

"Sure, is everything okay?"

"Beth, I have news for you."

"Okay, what is it?"

"Beth, it's about Sara."
I felt a massive weight pulling me down.
"What?"
"Beth, we found her. We finally found her."
I stood frozen and unable to breathe. I wanted to ask a question, but I was terrified of the answer. I hoped with all my heart to finally hear those three precious words.

"Beth, are you there? She's banged up, but she's going to be okay. She's bruised, battered, and she's suffered severe trauma, but she's alive, Beth. She's alive, and she's going to need her mother. Beth, did you hear me?

Sara is alive."

The End

Part two to follow…

DARK EYES OPEN

DARK EYES OPEN

Manufactured by Amazon.ca
Bolton, ON